The Dream King's Courier
Payback

Patrice Sikora

ISBN-10: 1493614827
ISBN-13: 9781493614820

This is for Ian, who rekindled the Dream.

1

⁓

The three white-robed figures on their knees gasped and pressed their foreheads to the floor of the windowless room, as the sparkling cloud turned into a lean, bronze-skinned figure in a light blue leisure suit accented by a blue-and-gold ascot. His matching blue shoes reflected the dim light as he breathed deeply and stretched sensuously before adjusting his suit and brushing off an offending piece of dust.

A large wooden board covered with blood and gut-stained feathers occupied the space between them.

"That was good. You said there might be one, but there were two."

The trio raised their upper bodies but remained kneeling.

"Lord, did you take them both?" breathed the thirty-something, bald man in surprise.

"Yes, Adam. I took both Nathao's Rider and Courier," said Bayel, moving his hips side to side in another stretch before arching his back and then running his fingers through dark, wavy hair. "And it was significantly more satisfying than the energies released by your mass couplings and drunken celebrations. The fear is delicious, and the anger strengthens me. I am pleased with your efforts, and I want more."

"Lord Bayel, we are only too honored to serve you," said the woman. "It is wonderful, that on just our third attempt, we've been able to give you enough power to seriously hurt Nathao."

"But please be patient," interjected Adam quickly. "We're still learning how to best use our newfound resource."

"I have patience and look forward to your next effort." The God of Joy yawned. "But this wonderful excursion has made me sleepy. I will rest."

"Wait! We have new initiates waiting for you and willing to do whatever you wish," said the third person, waving his arms toward a closed door.

"Not now. I've had enough."

Without another word, Bayel dissolved into his sparkling entity and disappeared.

"Incredible! We really did it, didn't we?" squeaked the woman.

"Emily, I think we found the right combination," said Adam Bardhof quietly, his bald head shiny with sweat. "But now we have to fine-tune it and manage his expectations, so *please* be careful what you say. Don't offer more than we can deliver."

Getting to her feet, the young woman only laughed and shook her curly hair. Then she went over to help the other man get up. He groaned a little once he was standing and reached down to rub his knees.

"I really wasn't sure this would work," he admitted while bent over. "But I will never question you again, Adam."

"Ralph, you always need to have things proven before you believe," said the leader of the group, smiling. "But now that we've *all* seen that this will work, we need to find a better knife. We can't keep using a kitchen knife to sacrifice a pigeon; we need something that is worthy of this effort, something ornate, yet elegant, that will become a revered icon. And come to think of it, we should start to look beyond pigeons, too."

"Yeah, but first, maybe you ought to learn how to actually *kill* cleanly," suggested Emily, gesturing toward the splattered blood and feathers on the cutting board. "That didn't go too well. And I thought there wasn't supposed to be any blood left."

Adam shrugged and tried to ignore the flecks of red on his robe. "So, we're all learning, even Bayel. If he doesn't absorb the energy right away, I guess the blood just oozes out. I don't know. But look, we got results that were much better than we expected. As we get more experience, we'll get better."

He paused and glanced at the closed door.

"Em, why don't you go tell those new people to put their clothes back on? They can stay virgins for another night. Bayel is too tired."

2

~

"I will crush and destroy him, Veron. He has abused my patience and our rules for the last time."

The tall, trim man spun on his heel, his long, braided hair swinging sharply behind him. "He is a threat to me and to everyone else, although my esteemed peers in the Pantheon refuse to acknowledge the danger."

"Perhaps they are simply cautious," suggested the tiny man dressed in white, perched on the edge of the sofa. He was silent for a moment as he sipped from a small glass and then smacked his lips. "Nathao, you do have the best refreshments; one reason I enjoy visiting you so much."

"Veron," rumbled the King of Dreams, "do not belittle my situation with talk of 'refreshments.' Bayel has killed two of my people, including my Courier. I have been seriously damaged by that quivering, corpulent piece of effluvium. I am at risk of losing constituents and power, my dear God of Truth, and I will not sit by and let that happen."

"I will do everything possible to make sure that does not happen. I don't believe that at this point you are in danger of losing followers or status; you are, after all, ranked in the top ten of our hundreds of colleagues. However, I agree that another attack or death could be problematic. We need the faith of committed followers to feed our strength so we have the power to support their needs and answer their petitions. Of course, that in turn confirms their faith and commitment. It's the Great Circle," finished Veron in his reedy voice.

"Yes, yes," said Nathao with a careless wave of his hand. The movement sparked a subtle cascade of color down the sleeve of the gray jacket. "Sounds like a textbook sermon, but that doesn't give me the approval I want to destroy this upstart who has declared himself my rival."

"Hardly an upstart. Bayel has been popular for quite a while and seemingly content with his lot. Admittedly, this focus on you—and the violence—is new, but I can tell you the others are watching, although most are not convinced he should be eliminated. Nothing like that has been done for centuries."

"I know; I was there when Kalistos was expelled. But this ranking business and its attendant suspicions and quarrels did not start until the human academics felt the need to fill their time with something to study and quantify. I would rather we still simply understood our relationships to one another as we once did and let them flow and ebb as needed. That was when this world was a peaceful place."

"You seem to have forgotten the Troubles, Nathao...the time when we fought indiscriminately and no one was safe. I believe I remember a challenge of yours going a tad badly and having to haul your ass away to a place of refuge so you could heal."

The King of Dreams grunted. "And then I went on to wipe out that parasite who had announced his plans to feast on you next."

"We have matured along with humankind and no longer fight like animals fist against fist. Now we think and compromise. The Promethean League has done some insightful research, and their efforts to publicize behaviors and popularity have gone a long way toward less needless bloodshed," observed the God of Truth, holding out his empty glass. "I applaud their efforts."

"Because you are not subject to the daily rigors of supporting a constituency."

"On the contrary, mine is simply an alternative structure. You have the satisfaction of dealing with the masses and meeting their needs, while I influence a profession."

"Lawyers," sniffed Nathao as he walked over with the decanter from a side table. "It shouldn't surprise me that you talk of compromise."

"My people are attorneys who influence the gods they follow in their nonprofessional lives. A great many of them are among your congregants, by the way."

"Which is why I listen to your counsel. You have great influence in our realm and in the world of our human supplicants, and I congratulate you on that. Plus I consider you a friend."

"A feeling I share. And you know I do my best not to abuse my influence. But now, what do you intend to do?"

"Since I cannot yet destroy Bayel, our so-called God of Good Times who is undoubtedly hiding in his temple in Haliburum, I will rebuild and plan for the day when I have the support to do so. In the meantime I suppose I will compromise. However, I want to make sure that tactic does not make me look weak."

"Among our colleagues who count, it will not. And while Bayel has quite an establishment in the holy city, so do you," observed Veron as he accepted his refill.

"As does anyone who wishes to be a player in the Pantheon," retorted Nathao. "But all this diplomacy must wait. My first priority is to find another Courier and Rider. For the latter, there are several possibilities among those nonbelievers who have decided they need me after all, and have made a Request, but there is no one for the more important position."

"Could you promote from within? Choose someone already indebted to you?"

Nathao folded his tall frame into the big chair placed at a right angle to the sofa that supported his diminutive guest. He steepled his fingers and peered intensely at his visitor.

"No. The Courier must be different—brave enough to make what they believe is an impossible Request and in return give me the rest of their life."

"Do the Riders not do that?"

"Assuming they are not killed during their employment, there is always an end date to the service of a Rider. They simply do not know when it is until I release them. Most choose to Cross, but they do have the option to return to everyday lives. For the Courier, however, the position is forever."

"Then I wish you good luck."

3

Gwen Revmore guided the van down the rutted dirt lane to the address on the call. The property was outside of the closest small town and well off any decent street. Fields of tall dried grasses spread out on the left and right, creating a buffer between the rough road and stands of trees, mostly evergreens. It never failed to amaze her how quickly the influence of the city and suburbs disappeared once you got off the main roads. The relatively easy access to a more rustic quality of life was one reason many people lived near High Point: they could enjoy a weekend of camping or hunting, but quickly and easily return to the amenities of civilization and their jobs in the city on Monday.

Her husband, Bill, had a city job with a brokerage firm and the desk-time and stress that went with it. Gwen was grateful her work allowed her to get outside. Well, she admitted to herself, she was grateful most of the time, because being an animal control officer could mean tough working conditions and situations that just tore at your heart. There was always the chance of danger and injury, too, but at least the time behind a desk was limited and her schedule was flexible, unlike her husband's.

Thinking of Bill, she glanced at her watch. He and their son, Sam, should be on the way home from the scouts' winter camping trip. The troop had used a Council site about two hours north where there had been snow, and she hoped they weren't hitting any delays on the road.

Gwen and Bill had argued about the weekend and the wisdom of going on this particular event in light of the forecast, but Bill had been adamant. She suspected he felt guilty about choosing work over the scouts several times in the past months and missing events he had promised Sam and the troop he would help plan and run. Perhaps Sam had finally said something, or maybe the other adults had spoken up. His increasingly fanatical commitment to his job was becoming a contentious point in their marriage as well and hurting his relationships with Sam and their daughter, Becky.

Gwen wanted him to spend more time with her and the kids, but he waved aside the pleas and argued that his time in the office gave them the means to have the best of everything. Her argument that time together was vastly superior to dollars was ridiculed or ignored, making her angry and resentful. She tried to hide those feelings from the kids, but she had a feeling they knew more than they let on.

"There it is," said her partner, Frank, pointing ahead and breaking into her reverie. "Already this doesn't look good."

The small home had seen better days. The dirty white paint was peeling, some of the green shutters were missing, and the small yard was thick with an uncut lawn that looked brown and brittle in the winter chill. Traces of the latest snow flurries dusted the roof and grass. The front door was closed.

In front of the crooked picket fence that struggled to mark the front of the property, a young police officer was vomiting.

"Yellow tape and someone puking, nice."

"Yeah, well, c'mon, let's find out just how bad it is," said Gwen, suppressing her thoughts of home and husband; she reached into her pocket for a tie to pull her long, dark hair into a ponytail in preparation for work. "You got your god medal ready?"

Frank returned her grin and pulled out the chain that hung under his shirt.

"Damn right. You may not be afraid of anything, but Errin of Trian goes everywhere with me; after all, he protects those who care about animals. I can still get you one that's blessed by the Second Voice of my ward."

"Appreciate the thought, but I haven't needed it so far, my friend. You know I have no use for any of those charlatans."

Frank continued to smile tolerantly and tucked his medal back inside his shirt.

"Yet you always ask. I think that deep down inside you know you have a need for someone to pray to; you just won't admit it. But the day will come when you commit yourself. Mark my words, it will come."

"And remember your promise not to rush in anywhere without me," Frank continued, changing tack. "Sometimes you don't wait to fully assess the situation, and frankly that scares me. You lack a healthy dose of concern for possible danger."

Now it was Gwen's turn to offer a tolerant smile.

"I remember, dear senior partner; I remember."

The animal control officers stepped out of the warm van and zipped up their short blue nylon coats.

"Wait a sec," said Gwen, her breath white in the cold air. She reached back inside for a bottle of water. "I think our friend over there could use a little of this."

The slight woman walked to the patrolman who was doubled over by the fence and gently patted him on the back.

"Here, rinse out your mouth."

He twisted his head to look at her and then straightened up, a chagrined grimace on his young face.

"Thanks. Sorry. I should be better than this, but it's so bad in there."

"Nothing to be sorry about," said Gwen, her deep blue eyes sympathetic. "Take your time. Use the water."

She scanned the front of the disheveled house again and shook her head as she walked over to the small group gathered at the broken front gate. Shoving her hands into the fleece-lined pockets of her jacket, she shivered a bit.

"Well, gentlemen, what brings us out here on this clear, cold morning? You need assistance?"

"As I was telling, Frank, Gwen, it's all yours. We aren't going back in until *you* are done," said the sergeant. "You need to get rid of a big pig that's been eating something it shouldn't."

"Pig?" echoed Gwen.

"Big pig. Nasty, big pig. He's been eating his owner."

Gwen and Frank exchanged startled looks.

"Martin, you say he's been—" began the tall male ACO.

"Eating his owner," finished the grim-faced officer. "Got a call from a friend of the resident reporting he hadn't been heard from for several days. No answer to our knocks and shouts, so we forced our way in. There's what's left of a body on the floor and lots of what looked like empty liquor and beer bottles. The guy must have been on one hell of a bender.

"Whatever happened after that, the pig was busy. The guy's arms are mangled stumps, and there are chunks missing from other body areas."

"The pig—" began Frank.

"Charged us, man," interrupted one of the other officers. "And I warn you, he's fast. The bastard ran right at us, mouth wide open. We just managed to get out and slam the door."

"How many days was this guy out of touch?" asked Gwen.

The sergeant shrugged. "At least four, maybe five."

"Big pig, like this?" she continued, opening her arms and outlining a large rectangle.

"Bigger."

"A Hansen potbelly?" suggested Frank.

"Probably, and a very hungry one at that," Gwen noted as she turned to the officers again. "Why didn't you shoot him?"

"And create a PR nightmare? 'Cops shoot helpless, abandoned pig.' Oh no," said Martin emphatically. "This time you guys—the animal experts—get first crack. Then, if needed, we have ample reason to shoot."

"Whew," grunted the dark-eyed Frank as he wrinkled his nose. "I don't think a bite stick will work, and there probably isn't room for tranqs. Noose?"

"Depending on the size, I doubt that will work, but we can try. I'll bring the gun. If that thing has been eating its owner, it's gotta go anyway."

Their work boots made minor crunching sounds on the lightly frozen, brown matted grass that covered the remnants of the narrow walkway to the porch. The dirty windows flanking the front door offered no view of the inside, but the knob moved easily as Frank slowly tested a turn.

"All right, I'll go in first, and you make sure to get in right after me," said Frank, arming himself with the pole and confinement noose.

"You want to be the hero, be my guest," said Gwen. "But if it's bad, just move out of the way, and I'll shoot. This guy sounds dangerous, and he may be getting peckish as lunchtime gets close."

Frank threw her a mildly amused look and then laughed quietly.

"Just think—if that guy in there *did* drink himself to death, there might still be enough alcohol in his tissue to intoxicate the pig. We could have a nasty porcine drunk on our hands."

Frank pushed the door slowly open and gagged as the smell of decay and feces wafted out. As the scent reached Gwen, she quickly turned her head and joined her partner in sucking in a deep breath of relatively fresh air before stepping inside.

The scene was enough to make the most hardened officer flinch and vomit. The living room was littered with empty liquor bottles and chunks of what appeared to be decomposing human flesh. The debris led to the remains of a human body. Gaping holes in the torso and ragged appendages where arms had once been testified to the actions of a strong, hungry animal.

"Gads," coughed Frank. "Where *is* the beast?"

In answer, there was a deep grunt from around a corner just beyond the scene of carnage. A moment later, a huge potbelly pig ambled into view.

"I dare you to say 'nice piggy,'" murmured Gwen. "He's gotta be two hundred pounds. I don't think your little rope is going to work."

"Let me try. Remember, he was once someone's pet," said Frank, slowly moving forward with the noose ready. "Nice pork loin. Come along quietly, darling."

The black-and-white animal paused, and his whiskered chin quivered as he sniffed the air to catch their scent. The huge head turned to track the ACO as he moved slowly to the side and an angle that would make it easier to slip the noose over the massive jaw and flickering ears.

Gwen stayed where she was but slowly raised the rifle and took aim at their quarry.

Frank moved to bring the noose closer, but as he stepped forward, his foot landed on a squishy piece of what had once been the owner. He slipped a bit before catching his balance, spooking the pig. The giant beast squealed in surprise and with blistering speed launched itself at the ACO, its mouth wide open.

Without losing a beat, Gwen fired three times in quick succession, bringing down the animal. But the pig's momentum carried it into her partner, knocking him down and pinning him under its mass.

"Frank? Are you all right?" she yelled as she slapped on the gun's safety and rushed to his side to roll the dead weight of the animal off him. As she dropped to her knees to get better leverage, she also slipped on what must have been a piece of the owner, and her left hand went down hard on something sharp.

She gasped but ignored the pain as she continued to push with her good hand.

"Gods...hurt, Gwen," rasped Frank. "Ribs. I think something's broken."

"So much for your god, Errin," breathed Gwen as she bent lower and used her shoulder to push.

"Maybe not pretty, but I'm alive," whispered her partner. "Could have been worse. Glad you're good with a gun."

The shots had brought the police to the front door. When they saw that their four-legged adversary was no longer an issue, they rushed in and helped roll the pig off Frank. Once the animal was moved, Gwen backed away to let the officers handle the first aid.

"You're bleeding."

"Huh?"

"You're bleeding. Let me see that."

The young cop who had been throwing up when they arrived reached for her hand.

"Let's find some water and see what you've done here; could be some of that broken glass near your friend. The kitchen must be back there—come on."

※❈※

Gwen gritted her teeth against the pain as the cold water washed away enough of the blood for both of them to see the patchwork of glass in her palm.

"You're lucky you didn't hit something really important," mused the young man as he attempted to evaluate the situation.

"You have a name?"

"Paul."

"Well, Paul, let's just wrap this in a dish towel or something. It'll stop bleeding; my partner needs my help."

"Your partner will be fine, and this needs medical attention. I'll wrap it, but I'm gonna put you in that ambulance with your partner myself."

"My dear Paul," began Gwen with a grin, "I can take care of—"

She stopped short as the sergeant, Martin, entered the kitchen, his face white.

"Gwen, there's been an accident. I'll take you to the hospital. It's your husband and son."

※❈※

Her hand throbbed under the fresh bandaging and her eyes stung from all the crying, but the tears were not the result of the pain from the hand. In the emergency room, while a doctor treated her injuries, police and medical personnel had broken the news that her husband was dead and her son critically injured after an accident involving the members of the Cub Scout pack.

The group had been traveling in three vans on the way back from the camping trip Gwen had not wanted them to go on when a trucker lost control of his rig in the icy conditions and ran the first one off the road. The vehicle had careened down an incline and crashed into the woods at the bottom of the hill, killing the two adults inside, including Bill, and one of the two boys. Her son Sam was the lone survivor, but he was currently in surgery with life-threatening head and spinal injuries; the doctors had been very clear that his prognosis was not encouraging.

Her mind rushed from thought to thought as she sat erect and stiff in the tiny hospital waiting room. Her in-laws were on their way to the house to be with Becky after her mother had agreed to pick up the little girl from her friend's house, but said she could stay only a few hours because of some critical event at the temple. Gwen held her tongue at Karen's limited willingness to help but swore colorfully when the conversation was over and, not for the first time, was grateful for the support her in-laws had always offered.

Work knew she wouldn't be in, and Frank was upstairs in the same hospital with two broken ribs and a punctured lung.

Then her heart stopped as she realized she would have to make funeral arrangements.

"How the hell do you do that? And why is this happening to me?" she murmured, dropping her head into her one good hand. She was struggling not to give into the renewed tears and sense of despair when the air pressure in the tiny room changed slightly as the door sighed open.

Gwen looked up in surprise and her blue eyes went cold as she recognized the newcomer.

"What are you doing here?"

"Sam is dying."

Gwen threw her long hair back over her shoulder, struggling to reclaim her composure, and scowled at the austere, older man in the black jacket. Jaw clenched and eyes beginning to fill again with tears, she broke the contact and harshly squeezed her injured hand to force her mind to focus on the physical distress and not the emotional pain and desperation.

"You bastard," she said quietly, slowly raising her now-dry eyes. "I am very aware of the fact that I've just lost my husband and I could still lose my son. They are doing what they can.

"But what the hell do you care, *Grandpa*? You've never really filled that role for me. And as a great-grandfather, you haven't given my kids the time of day for years. Don't waste my time, old man. Get out of here."

"I have an idea that may save him."

"What? Why would you bother with any idea about us? You have never been part of our lives."

"I do care."

"Spare me, but just in case you have something I can use, you have sixty seconds," snapped Gwen sarcastically.

"King Nathao. I believe he would help if we ask."

His granddaughter snorted in derision.

"That's a load of supernatural crap. There are a lot of worthless gods pandering for our attentions, and I don't subscribe to any of them. Even my partner's favorite didn't protect him from major injuries today. They're a waste; just like my time here with you. Fifty seconds."

"I mean it," pressed Barnabas, his brown eyes flashing for a moment. "Let's ask the King of Dreams for help."

Gwen registered the look of power. "I've never even visited one of his chapels. Why the hell would he get involved?" she asked suspiciously.

Barnabas stood straighter, crossed his arms, and returned her heated glare without flinching.

"As you said, you've already lost your husband. But you were ready to get out of that relationship anyway, right? He wasn't there for you or the children. You'll get over that loss quickly. Focus on your son and take the chance to save him, because the doctors can't. Nathao could."

Sensing something different in the grandfather she thought she knew, Gwen played for time and control of the situation. She tilted her head to the side, leaned back in the chair, and crossed her own arms, schooling her expressions and carefully cradling her aching hand.

"My relationship with Bill is none of your business, and my son *is* my focus. Don't lecture me on family when you couldn't handle your own. And you've never talked before with me about any religion—why this sudden sense of conviction?"

The older man offered an exaggerated shrug and, echoing his granddaughter's earlier sarcasm, said, "Maybe no one seemed interested in listening."

From news reports, exposure to friends of various faiths, and her own limited religious upbringing, Gwen knew the Promethean League ranked Nathao as one of the most powerful of the hundreds of gods in the Pantheon, but that was about it. She shook her head and resolutely pushed away a sudden glimmer of desperate hope.

"I think it's a waste of time *and* probably a sizeable monetary donation."

"You're being much too cynical, and this is Sam's life we're talking about," countered Barnabas sharply as he continued to stand with his arms crossed, looking down at her. "Listen to me—you can't say it won't work until you've actually tried. It doesn't take that much effort, and it could mean Sam has a future. It's late, and the hospital chapels won't be crowded. We need to go now if you want your son to live."

"No, you listen to *me*," replied Gwen. "You don't scare me. You're a farce of a grandfather. I trust the medical professionals here more than your word about some make-believe god-king. There is nothing in my life experience that says otherwise."

There was silence as the pair stared at each other. Barnabas's mouth twitched as if he was holding back a comment, but Gwen kept her face cold and did not allow herself to react and jump as her grandfather did at the unexpected knock on the door.

The tall man in scrubs looked briefly from one to the other and then turned to Gwen.

"Ms. Revmore, I'm Doctor Dawson. I've been working with the surgical team caring for your son. Is this someone who is family?"

"Yes," responded the two simultaneously after a brief pause.

"That may be helpful. I'm sorry about your husband, and unfortunately the news I bring is not good."

❊❂❊

"Now will you come with me? There's still time."

Gwen struggled to focus on Barnabas, who now knelt in front of her as she sat on the chair, tears running down her face.

"They brought him back, and that gives us a window. But we need to use it now."

"He died."

"They brought him back."

"It may not last. They're still working on him, and it could happen again."

"That means we have to act *now*. Come," ordered the man, pulling her to her feet. "*Now*, Gwen."

The woman hesitated and said nothing as her grandfather pressed his case.

"Forget our problems, girl, and trust the King. He protects people who are dreaming and people who are just plain unconscious. Sam is in that state now."

"Why are you so sure about this guy?" she challenged, her voice cracking with the strain of managing emotions. "I don't want Sam to die, but I want to understand this."

"It's a leap of faith. Trust me; I've worked for Nathao for a long time, and I believe I have an inside track to get his attention."

"Worked for him? I don't understand."

"Shut up, stop the questions, and just come with me. Sam is running out of time."

"I—"

Barnabas grabbed her just below the shoulders and shook her hard. "Enough. Get your thoughts together. We're going."

The motion sent spasms of pain up her arm as her injured hand reacted to the sharp motion. She gasped and jerked away to cradle the hand as it began to ache intensely, but the pain instantly cleared the fog of sorrow and doubt clouding her mind; she knew she needed to take advantage of whatever this lifeline was that her grandfather dangled. She used her good hand to wipe her eyes and cheeks.

"Yes, yes, we're going. You said we need to get to the chapel?"

Barnabas nodded. "We've no time to waste." He reached for the door and paused. "Tell me what happened to your hand."

"Job hazard."

"What?"

"Glass shards, also known as pieces of broken glass. Had to shoot a bad pig, and it fell on my partner. I fell on the glass when I was trying to get it off him."

"Were you afraid?"

Gwen looked at him and almost sneered. "If I was, do you think I'd tell *you*? Now let's get going."

※※

The door to the hospital's chapel wing closed with a barely audible click, but the sound echoed in Gwen's bones, and she shivered. She paused to let her eyes adjust to the dimly lit, empty hallway and tentatively sniffed the air as the scent of burning candles teased her nose.

"I will never understand those people," muttered Barnabas.

"What?" Gwen turned to see him shaking his head as he looked at a plaque on the light-paneled wall. "You know it's the law. We are supposed to be reminded we have free will and don't have to follow any god if we don't want to. That's why they call it the Promethean League Bill of Rights."

"The League is silly, that's all," grumbled her grandfather.

"If they're so silly, how is it they publish that all-important Top 100 List of the most powerful gods? When that thing is released, it's like the world stands still while everyone digests the results, which, by the way, never seem to change very much. They also seem to know everything that happens among those supposedly greater beings and make them seem almost human. But speaking of silly, why are we whispering?"

Her grandfather frowned. "I still say the League is useless. The gods have their spats and issues, but we don't really need to know the facts. That List is based on so many things that don't matter, things like money, for crying out loud. Who cares how much money a movement has or how it's invested? And we're whispering because this is a place of contemplation and, hopefully, peace. Now, come."

The old man stalked down the carpeted corridor past several open doorways to the one tiny room dedicated to Nathao, King of Dreams. He motioned her inside and pointed toward the floor cushions.

"Sit down while we wait for assistance."

"We don't have time to wait," Gwen countered even as she drifted down onto the indicated seat and surveyed the simple space. Along with the several large gray floor pillows, the room held only a small wooden table against the far, pale gray wall. Just above the empty table, carved into the wall, was the feather emblem often used to symbolize the King.

"Grandpa," whispered Gwen, "I see electric candles, but I smell hot wax and sulfur."

"Fire code," he said as he pressed a large gray button on the wall near the table. "There are air fresheners in the outlets. It's the same in all the chapels here."

A quick, surreptitious scan of the room revealed the innocuous but fragrant plug-in units. Gwen just shook her head in disbelief.

At the same moment, a slight man in a gray robe entered and opened his arms wide as he saw the visitors.

"Barnabas, it's been quite a while."

"Greg, it has been a long time."

Astonished, Gwen watched as the two men shook hands.

"Gwen, this is Father Greg. He's the Guidant for this Chapel. Greg, this is my granddaughter, Gwen."

The middle-aged man wrapped his robe closer before sinking onto the pillow next to her. His brown eyes seemed kind, and there was genuine warmth in his voice.

"Gwen, it's a pleasure. Is there something I can do? Somehow I don't think this old man would bring you here on a social call."

"Gwen, close your mouth," admonished her grandfather. "Tell Greg about Sam."

Snapping her mouth shut, Gwen gave Barnabas a hard look, embarrassed and uncertain, but not wanting to show it.

"Go ahead," he urged. "If you can convince Greg that you need the King's help, the hardest part is over."

Gwen frowned as she turned to the Guidant. Her mind was racing as she tried to put together what was becoming a very arcane puzzle, but Greg's look was patient and encouraging as he sat with his hands folded in his lap. Glancing back at her grandfather, she was aware again of the change she had sensed before. There was a difference in his stance and attitude as he stood in his black jacket, arms crossed. An aura of authority and power seemed to envelop him, despite the anxious look on his face.

"Tell him, granddaughter," he said, enunciating each word clearly.

"Humph." She exhaled disparagingly before turning back to Greg to outline what had happened to her son and husband and the fact that Sam was fighting for his life and most likely losing.

"My overbearing grandfather here thinks a request to your King Nathao may be the answer," she finished.

"Your grandfather has a good idea," agreed Greg quietly as he studied her face. "What's bothering you about it?"

"Frankly, I think it's a waste. None of these deities care, not even for their most rabid faithful."

The Guidant nodded thoughtfully and closed his eyes as if thinking. Gwen glanced at her grandfather, who put a finger to his lips and shook his head ever so slightly.

A minute passed, and Greg opened his eyes again.

"Rider, I believe she has a good case; I have entered her Request with my support."

"Thank you. Because this is so time critical, I think a face-to-face meeting would be best. Since you approve, I'd like to use the Step here."

"Rather unconventional," said Greg, smiling as he rose gracefully from his cushion. "But as she is your granddaughter, I'm sure he will allow it and is probably waiting."

Gwen spun around to look up at her grandfather, more suspicious and confused than ever.

"What are you talking about? Request? What did I request? And who is 'he' who is waiting?"

"We're going to see King Nathao so we can press our case for him to save Sam," said her grandfather.

Gwen stared at him, struggling to suppress a faint sense of excitement and hope. "Nathao?"

"Who else? We want to ask him for help, so we have an audience and the chance to cut through all the red tape."

Astonished, Gwen turned to the Guidant. "What's he talking about?"

Greg looked at Barnabas and raised his eyebrows. "Have you explained the procedure?"

Barnabas cleared his throat and looked uncomfortable.

"Well, I didn't, no, not exactly. There wasn't the time or, on her part, the inclination to listen," he added defensively before extending his hand to Gwen.

"Girl, don't ask so many questions right now. We have a very special way we can help Sam. As his mother, do you want to take advantage of it or not?"

Gwen ignored the offered hand and lurched to her feet.

"You bastard. I'll do anything possible to save him. If you'd been part of our family, you'd know that. I just want to know what I'm getting Sam and myself into first!"

"That's only fair," observed Greg calmly. "After all, there will be a price, you know, assuming she has something of value."

Barnabas swept his gaze to the Guidant and snapped, "I am only too aware of that. Remember who *I* am."

Greg bowed slightly, but the cleric was smiling when he straightened and faced Barnabas again.

"And, of course, you are the only servant he has who is striving to do his best in a world that doesn't understand."

"Blast you," mumbled Barnabas, his indignation decidedly dissipated.

"You really should tell her what could happen once you Step."

Gwen was surprised at the almost wistful look Barnabas gave her.

"I hoped we could do this without more details, but it really wouldn't be fair," he finally admitted. "Greg, we'll talk in the back."

"Good decision. Just remember, he doesn't like to be kept waiting."

Gwen struggled to hold her now-soaring optimism in check as she followed her grandfather down a short hall to a plain room, empty except for two chairs upholstered in light blue chintz.

Was there really something to this King Nathao idea? And maybe, just maybe, would he help Sam? She suddenly remembered her in-laws followed the King and was almost smiling when Barnabas abruptly stopped and faced her in the center of the room.

"How old do you think I am?"

Thrown completely off guard, Gwen pushed her internal battle aside and shrugged.

"I suppose I could figure it out from Mom's age, but offhand, I've no idea."

"I'm considerably older than you think," said Barnabas with a sigh. "We don't have much time, so listen closely. Your grandmother, Constance, was my second wife, and your mother my second family. The first grew up a long, long time ago.

"In exchange for his help, the King requires you to work for him, and there is a side effect: a much slower aging process. I've already worked for him for a very long time, and if he accepts our Request, I can only hope he takes that into account when keeping me busy."

"What did he do for you way back when? And what do you think he'll want me to do?"

"Answers later. Right now we don't have the time," said her grandfather briskly. "Let's go, and let me do the talking."

"What do you do in this job?"

"Whatever is needed."

"Like what? And what did Greg mean when he said 'if she has something of value'? What do I need? I want details, Grandpa. If this can save Sam, I want it to work," pressed Gwen.

"Beginning to believe, are we? Well, details will have to wait, girl. Right now we have an appointment, and we don't keep the King waiting."

"But you think he can 'find' Sam? Whatever this 'finding' is?"

"We can only ask," said Barnabas, holding his hands, palms up, almost in supplication.

"The whole thing sounds ludicrous, but what the hell. There aren't any other choices right now, and I'll do anything to save my son."

Her grandfather moved closer and took her arm.

"We'll do our best. Now, relax and when I tell you to step, do it."

"Step? Where? And don't I close my eyes or something?" Gwen retorted, looking around and trying to hide her anxiety at not being the one in control.

"You've got a bad attitude, my dear. But," he added with a smirk of his own, "in a moment, closing your eyes might be a good idea. See this?"

He waved his free hand and next to them appeared a full-size picture of another plain room.

Gwen nodded slowly as she examined the scene.

"I've heard about this kind of stuff but never knew anyone who had seen—or done—it. I'm impressed, old man."

Barnabas ignored the cynicism. "That's where we're going. When I say 'Step,' you walk into that room. I'll be right behind you. Ready? Step."

Gwen stepped out with her right foot. As she shifted her body toward the image of the strange destination, there was a sudden chill and her stomach lurched as everything began to spin. Gasping, she squeezed her eyes shut and frantically searched for the floor with the leading foot. She found it and quickly brought her left foot over to share the blessed stability with its mate. Then she tentatively opened one eye.

The new room was larger than the one at the hospital chapel. The walls were beige with random dark brown stencils of a single feather. The low-pile chocolate brown rug gave just a bit under her feet, and the beige and brown fabric on the two upholstered chairs echoed the feather motif on the walls. There was also someone else present.

She blinked a few times as she recovered her balance and watched as her grandfather approached the stranger and bowed.

The new man was tall and trim. His dark gray hair sported streaks of lighter gray and was pulled back in a style that accentuated the sharp angles of his face. His forehead was smooth, and there was the hint of a beard shadow on his face. He wore dark pants, a light gray shirt with a high, buttoned collar, and a darker gray jacket that seemed to ripple with faint color when he moved.

Working to portray an air of confidence she really did not feel, Gwen walked carefully to her grandfather's side and planted her feet.

Barnabas motioned toward her. "My granddaughter, Gwen Revmore."

"A pleasure," replied the stranger kindly as he fixed her with his dark gray eyes. "Barnabas has told me much about you. You Stepped well."

"Gwen, this is King Nathao."

Determined to present a strong image, Gwen met Nathao's eyes and felt a wave of power surge through her body.

Barnabas caught her as she swayed.

"She's been under a lot of stress, sir," he said, bolstering his granddaughter for the moment it took her to find her equilibrium.

"No doubt," replied the King, still intently focused on Gwen. "Welcome to my realm, Ms. Revmore. Your grandfather is a loyal associate, and while I am very pleased to be able to help him with a Request, apparently this concerns you more than him. What can I do?"

Gwen found herself smiling just a little as her grandfather jumped in again, his voice suddenly sharp.

"If I may, sir—"

"No, you may not, Barnabas," interrupted the King just as sharply as he turned his gaze on his employee. "You said you wanted an audience for your granddaughter. Let her speak for herself."

Nathao looked back at Gwen, and his face softened just a little.

"Tell me your dream's desire, Gwen."

"My grandfather says you may be able to help my son."

The story of the accident and Sam's condition came out quickly, but Gwen suddenly realized she was also telling the King about her daughter, Becky, her job as an animal control officer, and the fact that her grandfather did not approve of her line of work. Embarrassed, she stopped and began to blush.

"Please forgive me for burdening you with all that," she ended lamely.

"If you had a decent job instead of being a dog catcher, you wouldn't be mortified to tell people what you do," suggested Barnabas rather primly.

"I have never been mortified; it's what I chose, and it's more than catching dogs," replied Gwen coolly, still looking at the King.

"You were on track to be a veterinarian."

"Things happen."

"Like that stupid husband?"

Gwen paused to control a spike of anger before addressing the King. "Once again, please forgive us for burdening you with trivia. That old man should be ashamed for lambasting the newly dead. Someone might just do it to him someday."

"If it is of concern to you, it is not trivial to me," replied the King evenly. "But now to the point of your visit."

"Sam," interjected Barnabas, stepping forward to stand next to Gwen.

"Sam is here," stated Nathao.

"Here?" blurted Gwen. "Where is 'here'?"

"My lands. I have been watching him."

"Yes, Grandpa mentioned something about that. Help me with this. Where are we? And...I mean, are you really a *god*?"

To her surprise, Nathao threw his head back and roared with laughter. Looking to her grandfather for help, Gwen found him just shaking his head.

"I'm sorry, my lord. Even the ignorant should be respectful."

"No, no," interrupted the King. "Gwen, for those who believe, I *am* a god, *their* god. There are many of us, some more powerful and useful than others, and our world is defined and supported by your beliefs. It is a breath of fresh air when a new mind explores our existence and questions our basics. This forces us to rethink and reevaluate our positions. Thank you. I have not had such a good laugh in ages."

"At my expense," observed Gwen with a tight smile. "I'm so happy to oblige."

"My lord," said Barnabas, edging closer to the King and stepping in front of his granddaughter, "I will pay for this. Just please have pity and explain how you know Sam is here."

Gwen's voice was icy as she slipped around her grandfather to confront the figure in gray.

"I'll go you one better. Just get Sam back whole, and I'll take an explanation later."

Barnabas tried to move in front again but silently obeyed as Nathao waved him aside. Gwen stood her ground and matched the intensity of the King's look as he stared into her eyes. She sensed a probing and spontaneously opened her mind, hiding nothing.

For a moment, Nathao was silent, then he tilted his head a bit.

"So resolute and fearless as you look at me and ask if I am a god. Sam *is* here, and I can reach him and guide him back. But be aware there is payment for every service."

"So I understand. Whatever it is, I'll pay," stated Gwen, knowing the King could sense her determination. "Anything for my son."

"No!" yelled Barnabas, jumping back to her side and then repeating his outburst more calmly. "No, my lord. *I* will pay. Gwen can't make a commitment because she doesn't have all the facts."

Gwen raised her chin defiantly as Nathao glanced briefly at her grandfather and then returned to her and his voiceless delving into her mind. She forced herself to relax and concentrate on Sam. After a moment, the King turned back to Barnabas, his gray eyes sparkling.

"This time, my faithful friend, you cannot make the payment. Your life is still mortgaged."

"But I'm the one who sought the audience," argued Barnabas, a little desperately.

"Then you were foolish, Rider. You of all people should know that you cannot take the responsibility and burden of payment for someone else's Request."

"But she doesn't completely understand," pleaded Barnabas.

"Whose fault is that?"

The shaggy-haired man was silent for a moment, and then he shrugged. "I suppose I was counting on your—"

"My what?" Nathao cut in. "My humanity? If you think you can play emotional games with me, you are very, very mistaken. But I will do this," continued the King as he turned back to Gwen, who had watched the exchange with great interest. "You may rescind your Request, and before you protest," he added quickly as Gwen opened her mouth to speak, "let me outline the bill for any services rendered. It is very straightforward: it is your life and your employment with me. And I must tell you my active payroll goes back a long, long time."

Gwen paused and narrowed her eyes.

"My grandfather hinted at that. Is this one of those 'you own my soul' things?" she asked.

Nathao shook his head. "No, that is not my intent at all. I simply have work that needs to be done. And no one owns souls anymore; it is too much of a bother."

"What about my family?"

This time the King raised his eyebrows.

"Nothing changes. Personnel takes care of benefits."

"They're not bad," interjected Barnabas. "Health coverage is extensive for you and your family, although we rarely need it. Raises are decent, but nothing to write home about. Well, they're not," he added quickly at Nathao's sharp glance.

"But I could live on it, and so could my family?"

"It is designed that way," Nathao said to her even as he continued to look at Barnabas.

Gwen paused, a faint sense of hope fueling her question. "Bill? My husband? Is there any chance to bring him back?"

"No," replied the King, returning his attention to her. "He is beyond my purview."

She paused at the matter-of-fact response and let the hope fade into acceptance. Then she crossed her arms. "All right then. Bring back Sam, and I'm in."

She hoped her firm tone hid the alarm she felt at striking a bargain she did not completely understand. But if it saved her son, she would do it.

"So be it," stated the King in a voice that suddenly held the hint of a deep echo. "Now, let me see your hand."

Confused, Gwen hesitated before complying and braced herself not to flinch as Nathao gently took hold of the bandaged hand. Warmth and then a tingling sensation spread through the tender area that had been probed and cleaned of glass at the hospital only hours before. After a few moments, the King released her.

"You may go. I will return your son in good time and then be in touch."

At her grandfather's tug, Gwen moved back toward the spot where the pair had entered the room and glanced once more at Nathao. Her new employer nodded, and she returned the gesture. Then Barnabas took her arm before waving his own to show a picture of the room at the hospital chapel.

He frowned for a moment and then ordered, "Step."

This time she closed her eyes, and when she opened them, she was back in the unremarkable room at the medical center. For a moment, neither she nor her grandfather moved, and then Barnabas put his hands on her shoulders.

"Welcome to the service of the King," he said quietly. "But you don't know what you've done."

"I've saved my son," replied Gwen as she pulled away and began to unwind the bandage that covered her hand. "What did he do?"

Barnabas said nothing as the coverings came off to reveal a hand with large areas of new, pink skin and a few lines where Gwen knew there had been deep incisions.

"He healed it," she said quietly. "He healed my hand. How did he do that? And why?"

"He wants you ready for whatever work he needs done," replied Barnabas. "As for how, well, that you'll have to ask him, but don't expect an answer. Now about Sam: yes, you have saved him, but he may hate you later...as my son hated me."

"Son? From your first marriage? Hated you? I suspect he had many reasons," said Gwen sarcastically as she continued to examine her hand. "I don't think Sam will hate me for this. And don't forget who dreamed up this cockamamie scheme in the first place."

"I never had this in mind."

"Maybe if you'd been more honest and upfront with me, we wouldn't be arguing now. But, I *have* saved Sam, and it *was* with your help. And what did he call you?" continued Gwen, thinking back. "Did he call you 'Rider'? Greg did too. What does that mean? Is it your job title? What do you think he'll want me to do? I don't have any special skills, except maybe catching dogs as some people think," she added with a sly, accusing stare at her grandfather.

Then she began giggle. "And, he really exists? That is so wild. He looks just like a very unpleasant philosophy professor I once had. Do the other gods look and talk like that? Wow."

Barnabas grunted and gave his sacrilegious granddaughter a shrewd look.

"The gods are what their believers make them, and that includes looks and mannerisms. A little research will tell you what others are like. As for Rider, yes, that is my job, and I'll explain when we have time. I have no idea what he plans for you, but you must have something he wants. And I have to admit, you handled that audience better than I expected."

"Thank you, I think," replied Gwen. "But what could I possibly have that a god needs?"

Her grandfather pursed his lips and was silent for a moment.

"Think about your strengths and talents and make a list. That might be the best way to figure out why he accepted your service."

"Why did he take you?"

"We are not discussing me."

"Because you still don't know?"

"Perhaps I know too well," countered Barnabas, raising his chin. "But now I suggest we go back upstairs to wait for Sam."

"Agreed," said Gwen quickly. "I want to be there when your King delivers."

"He's your King now too," pointed out the Rider.

"Not until he delivers," said Gwen, shaking her head as she turned for the door to the hallway.

The Guidant was nowhere to be seen, but in the dim light of the small hospital chapel, the pair found a lone petitioner sitting on one of the pillows with eyes closed and hands open and raised in prayer, or entreaty.

Barnabas paused and then quietly told Gwen to go upstairs, saying that he would stay and talk to the man.

"This is something we Riders do," he explained. "I'll see you later."

※※

Gwen stretched her fingers and played with her now-healed hand as she retraced her steps to her assigned family waiting room. A sense of fatigue hit her as she crossed the threshold, and then she stopped, shocked, as she caught her reflection in the window across the small space. The darkness of the winter evening had turned the glass into a mirror, and she grimaced at the image of a tired thirty-something woman in the blue uniform of a municipal employee. The light glinted off the gold badge clipped to her belt as she made a haphazard effort to shake out her long hair and tugged at the front of her nylon bomber jacket. Still looking at the sad figure in the window, she self-consciously wiped the top of each work-boot toe on the back of her legs to get off what she hoped was just dirt.

"Wow, I look like shit and I probably smell like I've been sleeping with the strays, but he answered; Nathao answered." She leaned closer to the window and tried to rub away the circles under her eyes. "Guess that isn't mascara," she finally admitted.

She pulled out her phone and paused before calling home again. She wasn't sure how much her mother might have told seven-year-old

Becky about her father and brother, but she was sure her in-laws would follow whatever tactic she had chosen.

As it turned out, Karen had only said there was an accident.

"She doesn't know anything beyond that," said her mother quietly, but with a frosty tinge to her voice. "I don't believe it is my place to tell her. Lois and Barry are here now, so I will be leaving. I can be here again tomorrow but only through dinner. After that I have services."

Gwen struggled to hold back a retort and kept her voice steady.

"Thanks for taking care of her as much as you have, Mom. I'm not sure when I'll be home. Sam is still in surgery, and I want to be here when they wrap up."

"Then I will hand you to Lois, and you can work out coverage. After that, leave me a message about your needs tomorrow."

Lois's voice quivered slightly as she said hello; she paused, and Gwen heard her breathe deeply.

"We are here as long as you need us," she finally whispered. "How is Sam?"

Gwen almost broke down at the promise of support and paused before she spoke.

"Things are looking better," she whispered back, blinking away tears. "I hope to know much more here shortly, and I'll call as soon as I do. If you have a moment, pray to your King Nathao."

"Oh, honey, I have been invoking him all afternoon," said Lois with a heartfelt sigh that bordered on tears. "Becky doesn't know about... about her father, does she?"

"No, my mother didn't tell her, and I don't want to do it on the phone."

"Then we will just wait until you get home," replied her mother-in-law with more strength and control in her voice. "Don't worry about Becky. We can stay all night and as long as you need us."

With the call ended, Gwen stared at the phone, grateful for her in-laws and disgusted with her mother.

"How can they be so understanding and supportive while you are such a bitch? What the hell does that second-rate goddess preach if you put her before your granddaughter? Being a widow yourself, you'd think you would have the heart to empathize, but apparently that's beyond your emotional capabilities. Screw it. I'll figure out how to deal with the situation, just like I've always done."

Gwen sighed and leaned back into the soft chair, relieved Becky was being cared for and acknowledging that tomorrow would be time enough to begin the funeral planning for her husband. She closed her eyes in an effort to slow her mind and think, but she kept seeing Nathao's face as he probed her mind and remembered feeling the pressures as he tested here and there. What did he find that he needed? What possible value could she have?

An unexpected knock at the door made her jump. She was rubbing her eyes as a woman in surgical scrubs entered.

"Ms. Revmore, I'm Arlene, from Doctor Dawson and the OR team. I have an update on your son, and it's all amazing news. Sam's heart and blood pressure have stabilized, and his brain functions are good. They've finished in the OR and moved him to Recovery. I must tell you that he is a miracle boy. There may be a medical journal piece in this."

Stunned, Gwen said nothing for a moment as the image of Nathao's face flashed through her mind once again.

"He did it. That bastard really did it," she breathed.

"Excuse me?" asked the nurse politely.

"Nothing, nothing," said Gwen, waving away her thoughts. "Tell me more. Tell me everything."

4

Gwen found it surprisingly easy to hold her feelings in check as she sat next to Becky at Bill's funeral. Admittedly, she shared tissues with her daughter throughout the service, but the overwhelming attendance by the scouting families and Bill's family gave her strength. And she acknowledged privately that most of the tears were for her children, not her deceased husband, and not even for herself. That realization began to feed a sense of guilt that her outward mourning might be less than honest, but she mentally shrugged and pushed those feelings aside.

The night before had been one-on-one for her and Becky. They had talked for a long time about Bill and what life might be like going forward as a family of three.

The little girl had asked some very direct questions about life, death, and money.

"Will you be able to afford my allowance, Mommy? I know you don't make as much as Daddy did."

"And who told you that, pumpkin?"

"Daddy. He said you were wasting your time, and you should have been more productive. What did he mean?"

"Hmmm," said Gwen, playing for time and composure. "He probably wanted to spend more time with you, and to do that, I would have had to work many, many hours like he did. I think we've been doing very well, and I will work hard to make sure it stays that way."

Becky sighed and leaned against her mother.

"I don't really care about my allowance. I want you here. When is Sam coming home?"

And Gwen had explained it was up to the doctors to decide, but Sam would need time in a special place to relearn how to walk and use his arms.

"That's rehabilitation, Mom."

"Yes, my daughter, that's rehabilitation, and that is what he needs."

The mental replay of that exchange brought a smile to her face as she refocused on the simple, nondenominational service at the funeral home. Like Gwen, Bill had felt a certain disdain for any higher being, and she felt he would not have appreciated a formal ceremony at any specific church or temple. But where her in-laws, Lois and Barry, had accepted her decision, Gwen's mother was sulking. She had repeatedly pressed the idea of what she called a "proper" service at the local shrine of the Lady of Carotrear, whom she diligently followed, but her daughter had firmly declined each time. The new widow could feel the dagger-looks from the seats immediately behind her, where Karen sat next to Bill's parents and brother. Karen's own estranged father, Gwen's newly reconciled grandfather, Barnabas, sat a few rows behind them.

Widowed more than two decades earlier when Gwen was a teenager, Karen had discovered companionship and fulfillment in religion; she sampled, accepted, and was then fully initiated into the cult of the Lady, a lesser-tier deity as ranked by the Promethean League and one that preached a fatalistic acceptance of life.

At first Gwen had not questioned her mother's calling, although she refused to go with her to any temple affairs. But as she got older, her doubt and then subtle opposition to Karen's involvement increased as she sensed a loss of joy and creativity in her mother's life. She blamed the sad changes on the Lady's strict regimen of behavior and worship. When she tried to talk about her suspicions to her mother, the fights would begin.

This was also the time when Barnabas and Karen began to quarrel, and his visits became fewer and fewer. By the time Gwen left for college, her grandfather was rarely around, and her mother, while present, was emotionally distant.

The sudden sound of music brought her back to the present and the celebrant's closing comments. When he motioned to her, Gwen stood to thank everyone for coming and invite them to a small restaurant nearby. Then she ushered her family down the aisle to the gathering space, where they lined up to accept the heartfelt wishes of friends and scouts. With the last of the crowd gone, the family returned to the sanctuary for their final moments with Bill, who was to be cremated. Gwen crouched down to hold Becky, who began to cry again. Bill's parents, Lois and Barry, clung to each other, sniffing, while their remaining son, Garry, stood staring at the closed coffin, blinking away tears.

And then Karen began to intone some chant.

Gwen turned to say something but paused when she saw Barnabas touch his daughter's arm. "Not now. You can pray to the Lady later. This is not the time."

For a moment Gwen tensed, expecting a sharp retort, but Karen stopped and looked coolly at her father.

"It will soothe Becky. I care about my grandchild."

The shaggy-haired man in the black jacket held her look as he straightened his shoulders and crossed his arms. Looking up from where she knelt next to Becky, Gwen thought a look of something close to respect crossed her mother's face, but it was fleeting and quickly replaced with the controlled everyday mask Karen had developed.

"As you wish," she murmured. "But the child cannot be shielded forever from the Lady. She and her brother are unchurched. They need someone to follow, to give them purpose and direction, and you have not stepped up to offer the King."

"Enough," replied Barnabas just as quietly. "Not here. We can discuss it again later, if you wish."

Gwen watched in rapt attention, straining to hear more, but Becky began to sob and, feeling a sharp sense of guilt, she turned back to her daughter and hugged her close.

"Is Daddy happy?" whispered the little girl as she clung to her mother. "Everyone says he's in a better place, but how can he be happy without us?"

"They believe he still knows what happens to us," said Gwen, gathering her daughter in an embrace. "Remember his love, baby; that's what he would want you to keep close to your heart."

An arm settled across her back, and her grandfather's voice echoed softly within their small huddle. "And you will see him again in time, Becky. We will all see him again in time."

Gwen glanced to her side, where Barnabas was on one knee. His presence was mildly unsettling, but she also felt an almost reassuring bond based on their new, common experience.

His eyes met hers. "In time, we are all reunited."

⁂

Lois had made it a point not to interfere with her son and daughter-in-law's life, not even when she could see the stresses tearing at the relationship. She knew when Gwen had changed career plans because of pressure from Bill to bring in immediate income, and she knew when Bill had been working too many hours and staying away from the family.

But she also felt strongly that it wasn't her place to say anything. She worked her own part-time job at the library, took care of her husband, Barry, who had retired years earlier from the insurance industry, and found comfort in her dreams and services at King Nathao's chapel. She had met Barnabas a few times but never while he was wearing his Rider's jacket, so when he showed up in it for the funeral, she was surprised. She immediately recognized what it meant.

In her quiet, efficient way, Lois began to research her relative by marriage and, with her prayers, began asking the King for answers. She was shocked by the answers she got.

⁂

Within days of the funeral, Gwen arranged to transfer Sam from the hospital to a pediatric rehabilitation facility in the city of Williamsford, not far from their home in suburban Tyler's Grove. The doctors there agreed his recovery to date was unprecedented but warned a full come-back would take time and a commitment from everyone in the family.

She began to balance her days between home and Becky, the rehab center and Sam, and work at the city's animal shelter, but every waking minute she remained on edge, expecting the King to materialize and order her to start working at "something."

Barnabas waved off her concerns about the lack of communication, saying the King worked in his own way, on his own time, and she needed to learn to let him set the pace.

Frustrated at her grandfather's laissez-faire attitude, Gwen used her meager free time to research her new employer, and the growing list of factoids about his power and influence fed her apprehension about the new position and absence of contact.

As part of her efforts, she located Nathao's chapel in town and one morning drove there, fully intent on going in, but after sitting in the parking lot for about twenty minutes, she allowed herself the excuse of not having enough time before work and left.

She also thought a great deal about her grandfather's comments and what she could possibly offer the King, but her list was always the same: blank, no extraordinary personal qualities that might have prompted Nathao's employment offer.

There was even one afternoon when, as she waited for Sam to finish a physical therapy session, Gwen took the quiet time to reluctantly reach back into her life to find something that might qualify, but still there was nothing she could identify; the effort ended only with a list of questions that she adamantly refused to ask Barnabas.

For his part, her grandfather said nothing more about the reasons why Nathao chose those he did, not even when he arrived on one of her days off to tell her the King wanted her immediately.

※❀※

Gwen walked Becky to the corner bus stop, where they waited in the morning chill with other parents and students exchanging observations about the weather before the children boarded the bus and the adults scattered to their respective sources of warmth.

She then drove the thirty minutes to the rehab center to spend time with Sam and on the way home did the grocery shopping. So, it was early afternoon when she finally flopped onto the sofa and allowed herself the luxury of a few quiet moments. She took a deep breath as her eyes slid shut, and her body and mind began to slip into a state of much-needed release. The delicious calm was shattered by the unexpected ring of the doorbell.

"Damn," she mumbled without moving.

She did not get up as it chimed again, and when it did not ring a third time, she sighed softly and began slipping back toward sleep. The prospect of a nice, peaceful nap teased her mind and body, and Gwen was beginning to savor the prospect of true downtime when her cell phone rang.

She groaned and with her eyes still closed reached to the nearby side table and groped around until she found the phone and grunted a hello.

"I know you're there, you lazy girl. Get up. We have an appointment."

"Grandpa," she said, making a major effort not to sound sharp, "for years you don't come around. Now, when I finally have a few moments to actually rest, you show up. What do you want? I gave you the key to the front door just a few days ago. Use it."

As she said that, Gwen heard the front door open and then the sound of someone walking toward the living room. She opened her eyes to see her grandfather pulling off his red scarf and black gloves.

"I didn't want to intrude," said Barnabas as he dropped the scarf and gloves on the coffee table, "but I *was* getting ready to use the key. It's cold out there. Now get up. There is no rest when your King calls."

Gwen turned her phone off, suddenly wide awake.

"You wouldn't be so cold if you wore a decent coat. That thing you have on is too damn thin. What does the King want?"

"Nathao wants *you,* and he wants you *now*. And the coat isn't the problem, it's just cold outside."

"Becky—" began Gwen as she got up off the sofa.

"Will be fine," interrupted Barnabas. "I'll deliver you and then come back here. I can pick her up or meet the bus. Which had you planned?"

"The bus—I was going to meet the bus. It stops right at the corner," said Gwen, trying to ignore the tightening in her gut and the uptick in her heartbeat. "It'll be cold too. Use one of Bill's coats. They're still in the closet, and you can pretend it once belonged to someone you liked. Hey, maybe you can bond after the fact."

Her grandfather scowled, but the faint hint of a smile snuck through.

"I know where the bus stops, so don't worry about Becky or me and the cold. Soon I'll be able to explain some things, and this will all make sense. But let's get going; you're expected."

"How do we get there?"

"That's the first thing I'll show you."

Barnabas led Gwen through the house to the basement.

"We need someplace with privacy," he said while he carefully negotiated the narrow stairs to the slightly musty lower level. "This should provide that."

"I'd say so," observed his granddaughter. "No one but Bill really used to come down here."

"I thought that might be the case. Sometimes a man just needs to get away."

"And you're accusing me of pushing him away and down here?"

"Every good marriage requires a male sanctuary."

Gwen could not help it as the corners of her lips curled in a small smile.

"And where were yours?"

"That's my secret, girl," he grunted. "Now let's get back to business."

He led her to the small storage room off Bill's workshop. "This is probably the best place to set up our Step. No one can stumble on it accidentally, and you will have some of that privacy."

From his pocket, he pulled a small pouch that yielded a chip of dark, shiny stone, a tiny hammer, a chisel, and a small container. Barnabas handed the container and stone to Gwen and then knelt down with the tools to dig a small hole in the concrete floor. He pressed the chip into the depression and covered it with white paste from the little container.

"Give it a moment to set, and then we can use it."

"What is it?" asked Gwen, squatting next to him and looking intently at the damp spot on the floor.

"A piece of the Master Stone that Nathao has at the Keep. It links all his Steps, and there are a lot of them."

Barnabas tested the new patch on the floor with his hand.

"Right. It's hard enough. Come here and put your finger on this."

When she did, Gwen felt a tingle run up her arm. She said so, and her grandfather nodded.

"You shouldn't have any trouble using this then. Now, stand on it and imagine the room where we met with Nathao. Think of it as a picture right in front of you, then wave your arm and make it appear."

Gwen thought about the plain, small room for several moments and then self-consciously waved her arm, but nothing happened. Taking a deep breath, she clenched her fists and tried again.

"Relax," offered Barnabas. "We all make the same mistake the first few times and try to force it. Just imagine the room in your mind's eye and invite it to show up."

"Relax, right," murmured his granddaughter in frustration as she moved off the chip for a moment, shook herself, and then moved back.

Taking another deep breath, Gwen tried to relax mentally and physically before searching for the faint hint of power from the tiny chip in the floor. She imagined drawing the tingling sensation up through her body to her mind and then slowly raised her arm in an arc as if painting a picture.

To her delight, her destination appeared, crisp and clear.

"Grandpa, it's there. I can reach out and touch it."

"That's exactly what you're going to do. Right now, you've 'opened the Window' as we call it, for lack of anything better. This lets you make sure you've reached the place you want to go; it also tells you the way is clear, and you won't knock someone over when you Step. If all you get is a Window that's black, it means the way is blocked.

"I doubt you'll have to do this much, but eventually it gets much easier. For those of us who do travel a lot, it gets to the point where we only have to think about our destination for a second, wave an arm, and it's there." Barnabas shrugged. "Not sure how, but it works."

Gwen listened closely as her grandfather continued.

"Once you've found the Window is clear, all you have to do is decide to Step through. At first, you'll feel the disorientation you had last time, but with practice that goes away too. There's really nothing to it." He made a shooing motion with his arms. "Go ahead. Try it alone. Step to the Keep, and then move so I can follow."

Unsuccessfully hiding an excited, nervous smile, Gwen checked the picture again to make sure the Window was still clear and Stepped through.

The cold and spinning did not startle her as much this time, but she stumbled a bit as she tried to move quickly so Barnabas could join her.

In a moment, he arrived and reached out to help her.

"Thanks, I'm fine. Just that dizziness for a second, but it was better than last time."

"Good. Like I said, you won't have to do this much, but the fact that you're handling it so well is good. Now, let's find the King."

Barnabas opened the door of the plain room, and Gwen's eyes widened at the sight of a glass wall with a twilit grassy yard beyond. She followed him into a hallway where the looming evening was held back by recessed ceiling lights and lamps mounted on the stone wall on her left. The expanse of glass on her right separated the bustling inhabitants of the building from a large landscaped quadrangle, which was landlocked within the four wings of what appeared to be a huge stone complex. There seemed to be three or four stories, but the first floor was the only one with the glass. In three of the wings, that glass was clear, and Gwen could see people moving about. The exception was the wing opposite them, where the wall appeared deeply tinted, obscuring any clear view of the interior.

Open sections in the glass wall in the middle of each wing offered access to lamp-lined brick walkways and to the center of the courtyard, where a small pool held a bubbling fountain lit from the inside.

Gwen refused to gawk like a tourist, but she drank in the bustle and muted din of people going about their business just like in any large corporate office.

Barnabas exchanged greetings and comments with several individuals but avoided conversation and made sure she kept walking. He guided her half the length of the wing to the open doorway in the glass and then outside, into what felt like a pleasant summer evening.

Without a word, the two walked the brick path that led around the fountain. As they passed, Gwen glanced into the glowing water and was mildly disappointed at the lack of any goldfish.

At the entrance to the darker wing, Barnabas waved her up the four stairs first. As she crossed the threshold, the absence of sound and lack of other human beings enveloped her like a heavy cocoon. The sense of isolation was compounded by the tinted glass that blocked even the limited twilight and forced the lamps inside to work harder to compensate.

There was a closed door down the hallway to the left, and directly in front of her rose a wide, carpeted staircase.

"Go up and knock on the first door on the left. He's waiting for you."

"Aren't you coming?" asked Gwen, suddenly apprehensive as she tore her focus away from the staircase and stared at her grandfather, who remained in the doorway.

Barnabas shook his head. "He has nothing to say to me. He wants you."

"But, Grandpa..." insisted Gwen, glancing at the stairs again.

"What is it, girl? Don't keep him waiting."

"What do I call him? What do I do?"

Barnabas glanced upward for a moment and sighed in annoyance.

"Don't embarrass me. Now, I have to leave, so just go. We don't keep the King waiting. *Go*. I'll see you at your house."

The old man spun on his heel and muttered something under his breath as he stomped away. The antics momentarily broke the tension; Gwen actually smiled as she watched him cross the threshold and move down the stairs to the walkway.

She faced the inside staircase again, but this time she was calm and fearless as she began the ascent, reminding herself she was here because the King had saved Sam.

At the top she inhaled deeply, settled her shoulders, and crossed the lamplit hall to the imposing dark-wood door. She knocked and, at the command to enter, pressed on the ornate brass lever. Although it looked massive, the door opened easily at her touch.

Across the room, Nathao sat behind a huge, dark wooden desk that was empty except for what looked like a black piece of clothing. Behind him, slightly to her right, French doors opened to a balcony, letting in warm air scented with something that reminded her of roses. To the left, the room stretched to accommodate two large, chocolate-brown, cloth-covered sofas that faced each other and sat at right angles to a dark leather chair. Several large, overstuffed brown, beige, and gray pillows were scattered on the floor next to the sofas; at the far end of the room was a fireplace, where wood appeared to be laid, waiting for a match.

The stone walls of the room were bare except for lamps that filled the space with a warm, yellow light.

The King leaned back in his chair, his elbows on the armrests and his fingers steepled in front of him. Maintaining what she hoped was a professional, calm demeanor, Gwen stood before him, her hands clasped behind her, chin lifted. She noticed Nathao's gray jacket seemed to shift color just a little as he moved.

"No problems getting here?" his deep voice rumbled.

"No, sir. My grandfather showed me."

"And you can Step on your own?"

"I did. With some practice I believe it won't be a problem."

"And you will get that. Do you have any questions before we move ahead?"

"I have many questions," admitted Gwen, momentarily eyeing the garment on the desk, "but they all depend on what you have in mind for me."

"Anxious? Afraid?"

Gwen frowned. "Curious perhaps, but I have never been afraid of anything before. Why should I start now?"

"Then take this coat, put it on, and show me just how strong you are," challenged Nathao.

Wary, but intrigued by the dare, Gwen couldn't hide a small, crooked smile as she approached the desk, picked up the jacket with a flourish, and swung it overhead before slipping her arms into the sleeves. The garment felt as if she had always worn it, like supple leather, soft and *warm.*

Startled at the warmth, Gwen momentarily thought of pulling off the garment, but strong, insistent thoughts of welcome rushed into her mind, and she hesitated. More waves of acceptance and support followed, and, after a few moments, she relaxed into a sense of comfort and security. As she did, she could have sworn someone rubbed her on the back; she looked behind, but there was no one there.

Chagrined, she turned back to face the King, startled to find him standing within a few inches of her.

"It has accepted you?"

"Well, it hasn't bitten me," replied Gwen, realizing just how tall he was.

"A smooth acceptance bodes well for a strong bond."

"Sounds like a great greeting card or fortune cookie. But what is this? It looks like my grandfather's, except for the cuffs."

"The silver stitching marks you as my Courier. This will explain it all."

Before she could move, Nathao's thumb was on her right temple and his pinky on her left.

"Sleep," he ordered.

She thought she felt his arms catch her as she collapsed into darkness and dreams.

※※

There was a lot of information to process as she drifted up from the King's Dream. Crucial facts and intriguing background information crowded her mind, vying for attention and making it difficult at first to focus.

Nathao had chosen her to be his Courier, his official voice and representative to his faithful and to his fellow gods. She would lead his Riders, who were his eyes and ears in the outside world and counselors to his congregants. They were also there to protect her, although she had to admit she wasn't sure why there should be any danger in this job. There would be a nanny for the kids because her hours would be irregular and—what the hell? Barnabas was romantically involved with the nanny? Gwen began to chuckle and rolled over only to find the edge of whatever she was lying on. She gasped at the quick, sudden drop and hit the floor.

"Oooh," she muttered as she gingerly pushed herself into a sitting position and stared at the cushion level of the sofa opposite her. Looking around for support, she leaned back against the sofa she had been occupying just moments before and tried to recover whatever dignity she could muster.

"Drink this."

Gwen reached up to accept the cordial glass of red liquid. A cautious sip disclosed what she decided was a nice, pedestrian port. She quickly downed the rest and levered herself back onto the sofa, where she stretched her neck and shoulders before settling to face the King, who was now sitting in the big leather chair.

"Nice HR technique. Answers many questions and raises more."

"It's efficient for the Courier. I do not give Dreams to the Riders. They must learn from each other."

"I feel special, but I must tell you I also feel a tad inadequate. If I understand everything, this is quite a job. Why me? You need someone who knows you, not an ignorant outsider like me."

"Facts can be learned; talent is innate. You will grow into your responsibilities, and in the meantime do not let anyone know your doubts," directed Nathao, his face grave. "The coat identifies you as a leader here, and attitude is vital. Unlike most of my colleagues, I choose my inner circle from those who have *not* been my followers. I do not want people with emotional attachments that could blind them to the truth. I want individuals who will speak up when necessary, even to me. I need staff who can think for themselves and who are aware that to live a full life and fully serve a god are not mutually exclusive.

"I chose you because you have several qualities rarely found together. You are intuitive and empathic. You possess a sense of fairness and a sense of outrage. And you are selfless to the point where fear is not something that concerns you. Most people describe that trait as courage, but they call those who demonstrate it 'fools' for risking everything for others. An intriguing combination of talents, and if you add knowledge and experience, I believe you will be a powerful Courier."

Gwen frowned slightly while the words sank in and reflexively began to stroke the sleeve of the jacket to calm the clothing's renewed voiceless badgering. It seemed to be demanding attention, talking to her with pressure and temperature. While this new connection felt like the return of an old, trusted friend, it was interfering with her efforts to focus on the King.

She met Nathao's patient gaze.

"I like most of the list," she said. "And courage sounds good. The fool part, well, I've been called worse. But I need to digress for a moment because every question I have is taking a back seat to this." She held the lapel of her jacket. "I suppose we've bonded because it won't stop begging for attention. What *is* this?"

The King's face softened just a bit.

"This is your sanity and your life. I cannot emphasize that enough. Never take it off when you are here, especially if you leave this complex. Never. I make these for my people who must go out into my realm where you are dealing with other people's dreams, other people's minds. This coat is your protection against assimilation into someone else's reality.

"In my chapels and the rest of the outside world, it is also a symbol of who you are. The faithful and the other gods will all recognize it immediately and respect it."

Nathao paused and then added, "There are other benefits, which the Riders and experience will teach you, but the Courier's coat has a special added protection because you must travel one place where no one else can go. There are times you must cross the River to deliver messages from me to the god on the Otherside. Once I introduce you, you will be the contact between us."

"Which River?"

"You cannot see it from here, but I will take you there soon enough. It appears that you never studied the Great or Little Theologies, correct?"

"No, sir. In school, I dabbled here and there, but a student of the gods I freely admit I was not. I have been doing some research these past few weeks, but it's been playing catch-up, and I don't have a handle on much of anyone's history." Gwen paused, concerned that the King would already be disappointed in her.

"There is a lot for you to learn then, and Armen will be your teacher. He is the oldest of my Riders and the expert on my colleagues."

Gwen caught herself reaching to stroke the sleeve of her jacket again and made it a point to tap the cuff in reproach. Her sense of indignation met a wave of cheerfulness, and the jacket rippled up the arm as if laughing.

The response deflated Gwen's growing annoyance and infused an infectious, powerful feeling of trust. That sense of support gave her the courage to ask, "What happened to your previous Courier?" She searched her Dream memory. "James was his name?"

"James was a valued employee. This is not the time to discuss his demise."

"Does this job end more often in death or in retirement?"

"For your position there is no retirement. You are mine until the end. And we can all die."

"How can you die? You're a god. And are you saying my end is death?"

"If people no longer believe in me, I will not exist. In effect, I will die. If you are careful, you are not going to die for a long time, longer than you ever dreamed."

"That doesn't answer the question about my end of service," observed Gwen wryly.

"There will be time to discuss it in depth after you are more familiar with me and my people."

A wave of giddy excitement suddenly flowed from the jacket and fed her growing anticipation of a new challenge. "All right, when do I start? I'd like to give my current employer at least a few days' notice."

"That can be done, but no more than a few. I need you here."

"And the nanny? I'd like to meet her first and then introduce her to Becky and Sam."

"I will have Barnabas arrange that," said the King, leaning back in his chair. "And now my Administrator, Marcia, will show you your office."

On cue, there was a knock on the door, and a seemingly middle-aged woman entered. Dressed in a long flowing dress of bright red flowers on a blue background, the newcomer sported short, thick, dark hair that stood straight out from her skull and a demeanor that did not invite questions.

Watching the woman move to the end of the sofas and bow, Gwen suddenly realized that what she had thought was a robe billowing in the breeze as the woman moved was really material simply rippling over what had to be a body of enormous girth. Wrenching her dark blue eyes back to meet Nathao's gray ones, she raised her eyebrows but received no response.

"Marcia, thank you for coming," said the King, turning to the new arrival. "This is Gwen, my new Courier. Clear everything in the system and give her James's old office. It is near your grandfather's," he added.

The Administrator coughed and sniffed. "I would suggest you reassign the Rider Barnabas," she said curtly, echoing Gwen's unspoken thoughts.

"No."

"You are aware of—"

"Enough. That is my decision."

"Of course, sir," replied the Administrator disdainfully. "Your decision, sir. This way, Courier."

❋❋❋

Gwen hustled to keep up with her guide as the human tsunami flowed out of the office into the lamplit hall and onto another set of wide, carpeted stairs that led to a third floor. Marcia set a quick pace as she climbed; when they reached the top landing, Gwen was short of breath while the Administrator appeared totally nonplussed.

The large woman paused and sniffed again as she peered at her charge.

"Welcome to the service of the King. Don't worry about being out of shape; the Riders get the best training available, and you will too.

"For whatever reason, he keeps two of his Riders and his Courier here; the rest of the Riders are over the Stables. So, while you will have some company, this floor is nearly empty. James used to jog up and down the stairs. He was not out of shape."

"Right," murmured Gwen, not pleased at being compared with her predecessor and already found wanting.

Marcia sailed along, talking and pointing to the doors they passed on their left.

"Claire's office is here. This is your grandfather's. It will be interesting to see his reaction to this development. But, then again, he has no choice. He's already worked with several Couriers and knows what to expect. It's part of his job."

"Yes, I expect he will be surprised. How many Couriers has he known? Do Riders have to spend more time here?"

Marcia offered a look of patient arrogance and yet another sniff. "I suggest you ask the King. Now, this is your office. Let's hope it meets with your satisfaction. And if it doesn't, you can discuss it with Himself."

The Administrator opened the door and stepped back to allow the new Courier to move in ahead of her.

"When you are done with your inspection, you are free to leave. I must go now."

Gwen barely heard the last comments. Immediately drawn to the window opposite the door, she rested her hands on the stone sill, leaned out through the glassless opening, and smiled. They were high in the Keep on an outside wall. The purple twilight softened the colors of the lawn and gardens sprawled between the main building and a wooded area she estimated was about three hundred yards away. Beyond the dense trees rose a distant range of hills that blocked anything beyond from view.

Directly below her, many of the chairs and tables on scattered patios were filled with people. The faint sound of voices floated to her window with the tantalizing smell of grilled food.

Gwen craned her neck to look up at a hazy, purplish sky that offered no stars and no source of light.

"Huh," she murmured, pulling herself back inside.

The office itself was small and contained a desk, a dresser, and a bed within its stone walls. Closer inspection of the desk revealed a computer touch screen set into the top.

A quick bounce and stretch on the bed and she grinned, very comfortable with her new space and the pending announcement to her grandfather.

※※

No sooner had his office door closed behind Gwen and Marcia than Nathao heard the lilting chimes that announced the arrival of his old acquaintance.

"Veron, I should have expected you."

"My dear King," said the tiny figure dressed in white and perched on the edge of the sofa. "Is she the one?"

Nathao paused and looked thoughtfully at the door.

"If things do in fact become as dire as you now suspect, she may be our best weapon."

"For a Rider, that is the ultimate task, is it not?" observed the little man in his reedy voice.

"My dear Lord of Justice, that is not my new Rider. That is my new Courier."

Veron was silent for a moment as he considered the King's statement.

"You are taking quite a chance."

"I am not wrong in choosing my people. She has the qualities we need, and an attitude to match if we are to castrate that bastard Bayel. She would be wasted as a Rider."

5

Gwen retraced her path to the Step room, pausing at the now-open door at the base of the staircase that led to Nathao's office. Inside, Marcia sat behind several computer screens, and beyond her stretched a room filled with people working at desks.

The Administrator looked up and nodded curtly before returning to her tasks.

Gwen allowed herself a wry grin and then spun and strode toward the grassy courtyard and the other wing. The surreal walk back to the Step room included greetings of "Welcome, Courier" from people she didn't know, but remembering the King's advice, she responded confidently with a smile and nod. At the Step, she followed her grandfather's instructions, immediately opened the Window to her home, and Stepped.

Upstairs, she found Barnabas reading a book and drinking a beer. The pale winter sunlight streamed through the living room windows and, coupled with the hum and drier air of the heating system, offered a sharp contrast to the warm twilight world she had just left.

Gwen put her hands behind her back as she entered the room and stood before her grandfather. Barnabas paused, and she was secretly pleased at the look that briefly crossed his face as he registered the fact that she was wearing the jacket.

"Your mother called. She'll pick up Becky at school. So, tell me how it went," he finally said from his seat on the sofa. "I see you're one of us. We will be working together."

"So the King told me, and apparently there's a nanny you already approve of?"

Barnabas's eyes twinkled for just a second.

"He did tell me I might have to make arrangements for that. Very nice. Did he assign one of us to work with you? Maybe Claire? That's how we usually start training new Riders because it takes so long to learn everything. And you probably won't be the only one doing some learning. I expect Nat will soon choose a new Courier. Did he explain that job as well?"

Gwen nodded, her face expressionless.

"Whoever shows up for that position won't be anyone you'll want to spend a lot of time with. I've worked with three of them so far, and I can tell you they're different. They start out fine, but before too long they get distant and engrossed in responsibilities they seem to feel are more important that the plebian jobs handed to us Riders. Sometimes we just have to tolerate them. Where's your office?"

"I'm next to you and Claire."

"Really," said the Rider, a little taken aback. "That's James's old office."

Gwen allowed her arms to fall to her sides as she walked to the sofa and took a seat. She leaned back, amazed as the jacket molded itself around her; she relished the moment as Barnabas quickly took in the silver stitching on the garment's wide cuffs. His face went white.

"By the gods!" he gasped. "That can't be. *You? You* are the new Courier?"

She raised her chin and offered a small nod. Her grandfather's mouth moved, but nothing came out. Gwen forced herself to wait for him to make the first comment.

Finally, he shook his head as he stumbled through his thoughts.

"This is definitely not what I had in mind. I thought he would return Sam and put you in an office."

"Not so. If I remember correctly, you thought *you* would be able to repay him, and I wouldn't be *'put'* anywhere. Well, surprise," shot back his granddaughter. "You aren't the only member of this family with skills someone values."

The older man glanced up, and for a moment, Gwen thought he would counter with his own acerbic comment. Instead, his look of confusion turned almost contrite.

"It's just such an important position I didn't think..." Barnabas's voice trailed off. Gwen held her tongue and waited as he swallowed and then tried to explain himself again.

"It's an honor to be one of Nathao's inner circle," he finally stated. "I am proud of you."

"You have never used that word with me before," said Gwen, her voice dripping with skepticism.

Barnabas paused again, obviously struggling with his next words.

"There are many things I wish I could change about the past, but this is not the time or place. We need to concentrate on building a new relationship, especially now, because our lives and those of our coworkers may depend on it. This job is so much more than anything you've ever experienced before, and to stay alive you will need every skill you've ever learned. Even then, you'll need the Riders to back you up."

Gwen remained silent, digesting what he had said and waiting for more. When he just kept looking at her, his eyes now sad, she prompted him.

"Tell me more about this job, Grandpa. You make it sound more dangerous and even dire than the King suggested. What else is this job? Tell me now so I'm not caught off guard and maybe"—she grinned wickedly—"just maybe I won't become 'distant' and have to be 'tolerated.'"

"All those comments will come back to haunt me," said a very chagrined Barnabas, sighing. "But it serves me right."

Gwen slid down the sofa, and for the first time in decades, she reached out to touch his arm. "Are they true?"

Her grandfather paused and then tentatively put his hand on top of hers.

"Everyone tackles it a little differently, but the Courier does things we Riders can't. Perhaps James and the others before him grew distant because people became afraid of them and their close ties to the King."

"You won't ever have to be afraid of me," said Gwen, surprised at her sudden feeling of concern for this man whose cold demeanor she had never understood.

Barnabas's voice took on a melancholy tone.

"There are some big differences between our jobs, and the biggest is that the King gives the Courier dreams. He will go into your mind to give you facts, instructions, whatever he needs you to know."

"He's done it already. It's not bad at all; it's kind of like immersion learning."

"Already?" Barnabas shook head slightly. "Well, the job can also be dangerous."

"And so can yours, like the Rider who was just lost."

"Somehow the Courier seems to get more of those assignments."

"We'll see." Gwen shrugged, working up the courage to ask the question that suddenly seemed to be of overwhelming importance. "Will they like me? Will the Riders at least give me a chance?"

Barnabas stood up. "I'll make sure the first information they get is positive. After that it's up to you, Granddaughter, or should I say, 'Courier.'"

Gwen blushed, rather enjoying the sound of the word, and the jacket responded with a hug.

"That seems so formal."

"Get used to it. At first it's a title; then it becomes your name."

"Are you just Rider, then?"

"In some places."

"Does it bother you?"

"Not anymore," admitted her grandfather. "After all, it is who and what I am. But there is one more thing. The kids and your mother. I advise you not to tell them the real story. Too many people are afraid of the King, and your mother—well, let's just say she will not like this at all."

"Like the son you mentioned from your first marriage? That's a story I want to hear."

"This is not the time, but I promise to tell you eventually. I do want to remind you that you will now be bouncing between worlds, and that may cause some physical changes. Everything here will remain the same, but the King's world is outside this time, and your body's aging process will slow. As I've hinted, that can be a problem with the people you love.

"Other gods have their own realms, too, but for some reason very few bring their people into them." Barnabas paused and pursed his lips. "Who knows why they do what they do.

"But, now, your mother is very clear about the King, and she is no fan. If she finds out about this, she'll blame me and then lecture you on how you've thrown away your life."

"Something I believe someone else in this room once told me."

Barnabas just grunted.

"Becky and your mother should be home soon, and I should be gone," he said somewhat gruffly, pulling Gwen up off the sofa and holding her at arm's length. "I'm off to tell the other Riders this juicy bit of information and arrange for the nanny."

As he released her, Gwen stepped back and opened her arms wide.

"And now I understand a little more about why you might not need a heavy coat outside. This jacket is special."

"It's so special that it will take me hours to just begin explaining, so we'll hold that for another time too. I need to see the Riders."

Gwen looked at him slyly.

"I do believe that you're bursting at the seams with this news."

"Am I now?" said Barnabas coyly as he picked up his own coat and swung it over his shoulder. "Next time, perhaps I can begin answering some of your other questions."

※※

Gwen reluctantly hung her new jacket in the bedroom closet before going back downstairs to pace the living room and rehearse what she planned to tell her mother and Becky. She wanted to share her excitement but knew better than to let any pride show through. Her mother always made sure she burst any of those bubbles.

When she saw the car pull into the driveway, Gwen settled her nerves, practiced a smile, and went to the front door to hurry her mother and daughter out of the cold winter day and into the warm house.

"Mom, I've got great news. I got a job offer today."

Karen looked at her daughter in surprise.

"I didn't know you were looking."

"I wasn't." Gwen laughed as she gave her daughter a kiss and helped her with her coat.

"What kind of job, Mom?"

"It's with a big company, managing their environmental efforts like the recycling we do, only bigger. Do you have a lot of homework?"

"Some. It's easy."

"Then go get a snack and tackle it, honey. I'll tell you all about this at dinner."

Becky headed toward the kitchen, and Gwen braced herself to deal with her mother, who was still in her coat.

"The job is deputy director of environmental outreach for a big philanthropic foundation, the Dream Trust." She had to admit she was rather pleased with herself for coming up with the name.

Her mother frowned. "Is there travel?"

"Some, but they'll help me find child care for the kids."

Gwen could see the relief blossom on Karen's face as she realized that she would not be expected to pick up that responsibility.

"What about health care and rehab for Sam?"

"I made sure of that, and it's covered."

"It sounds as if you want it."

"I do, but I told them I'd give them a final answer in a day or two. The job seems interesting, and there's the potential for growth. I don't think I can turn it down."

"Then don't," said her mother, already reaching for the doorknob. "I have services tonight at the shrine, so I have to run. I have Becky covered tomorrow, and we can talk about next week then."

"If this works, Mom, you won't have to worry about this problem much longer."

Karen offered a cold smile.

"As long as it fits my schedule, it's not a problem."

Gwen stared at the front door after it closed, angry but also sad at her mother's attitude.

Sifting through her childcare options, the new Courier suddenly snorted.

"Why the hell am I stressing here?" she murmured to herself. "The King said there was a nanny, so we get the nanny. I just hope she can drive."

※※

The nanny visited with Barnabas the next evening, and to Gwen's relief, not only could the daintily built Alana drive, but she was an accomplished chef and she met Becky's approval.

Getting ready for bed that night, Becky told her mother she had known Alana would be a good fit.

"And how did you know that?" Gwen said as she folded clothes.

"I dreamed it," said the little girl, sitting on her bed with her hands folded in the lap of her yellow nightgown.

Startled, Gwen glanced at her daughter's smug look.

"Dreamed it? When?"

"A few days ago. I dreamed about Sam too—where he was and what he saw."

"Where was he?"

"With the King."

"What king?"

"The King, Mom. He said you knew him."

Gwen's heart was beating fast.

"How long have you had these dreams?"

"For a while, and they're nice. I feel happy in them."

"Well, I suppose that's a good thing. Just don't forget to wake up, OK? I need you here," added her mother with a shaky smile.

"Oh, Mom, don't be silly." Becky laughed and jumped up to hug Gwen. "I have school. The King says I need to do well there."

"Does he now?" murmured her mother uneasily. "Maybe I need to talk to him about this."

That feeling was reinforced a day later when Gwen visited Sam. He was playing a video game in his room, something his therapists encouraged and that he embraced enthusiastically.

"Hey, big guy."

The boy in the wheelchair glanced toward the room door and grinned. "Give me a minute to save this, Mom."

"Looks like you're close to wiping out that civilization. Why don't you just finish up and not keep them waiting."

Sam barked a laugh and turned to the task at hand. Within minutes the fate of the Largoosians was sealed, and he put down the controller.

"You're early."

"And I brought lunch. Stir fry. You hungry?"

"Oh, yeah," he said, propelling his chair to where his mother stood.

Gwen put the bag of food in his lap and then leaned down for a hug and kiss.

"Therapist Tony says the sunroom should be empty for a while. Let's eat there, and he'll come get you when it's time for your afternoon session."

She pushed the wheelchair down several hallways to a large, bright room and chose a table right next to the windows that overlooked a pond and gardens.

"Got you beef and broccoli."

"My favorite," said Sam. "They put in sweet cookies?"

"Double," said his mother, pulling containers and individually wrapped cookies from the bag. Gwen was so busy getting her son set up with food that she missed the change in his face and the tears that began to slip down his cheeks. When she looked up, her own face dropped. "Sam, what's wrong? Did something happen?"

"Mom, I'm so sorry—"

As her son dissolved into tears, Gwen slid quickly to his side, knelt down, and gathered him in her arms, her heart hurting to see him in such pain.

"Honey, what do you have to be sorry for? You're doing everything right."

"Mom, the King says you're working for him, and I know it's because of me. I'm sorry. I asked if I could do the work instead, and he said no."

The words came out in a blurred rush and ended with a shaky sob.

Gwen wiped away her own tears and suppressed an intense feeling of outrage at the discovery that Nathao had not only spoken to Becky but also to Sam.

"The King talked to you?" she finally asked. "A lot?"

"A couple of times in my dreams," sniffed Sam. "I really like it, but I'm sorry you're stuck."

"Did he say I was stuck?" countered Gwen, holding her son at arm's length. "Because if he did, he was lying. I am not *stuck,* and I welcome the chance to help him because *he* helped *you.*"

"Why didn't he help Dad?" whispered the boy, his voice cracking as he fought back more tears.

"I asked, but he said he couldn't; it was too late," replied his mother, also in a whisper. "You're allowed to cry, you know, and you will see your dad again in time."

"That's what the King's people say."

"You're right, and since I'm one of them, I'd better start using it, don't you think?"

"Do you believe it?"

Gwen pulled Sam back into a hug. "I don't know yet, dear heart. I hope I will. And there's nothing to apologize for. It was my choice, and I have a feeling I'll like the job."

"What are you doing?"

"He didn't tell you?"

"I forgot to ask," mumbled Sam sheepishly. "I was too mad he wouldn't let me do it."

"Well, I'm not quite sure yet. I have to go to his chapels and meet his people..." began the new Courier, not sure she wanted her son to know much more, especially after her grandfather's suggestions of more dangerous situations than Nathao had let on.

"You're a Rider then," said Sam quietly before she continued. "That's important. I read up on Nathao, and that's an important job."

"Whatever you say, my man," said Gwen, sitting back on her heels and blinking away threatening tears. "But let's deal with it again at some later date. I have to experience the work first before I can comment."

"Can I meet the others?"

"Others?"

"Riders and the Courier."

"I suppose that could be done, and actually it's a good idea. As soon as I know more, I will ask about it. Now, you hungry?"

6

~

The knife had broken again, and Adam was struggling to manage his anger in front of the small crowd of initiates.

He glared at the white-and-gold walls of the room they used as their sanctuary and then spun around to single out Ralph.

"We need something that will stand up to bone," he snapped, consciously swirling his sleeveless, open-front robe for a regal effect. Underneath, his khaki pants and white shirt emphasized the preppie look he hoped to cultivate. "I don't want a piece of junk that forces me to saw through a sacrifice and then breaks."

Ralph grimaced at the two pieces of metal and the bloody mess that had been the rabbit.

"They told me it was the best."

"Well, they told you wrong. This is the second time you've brought back a substandard piece of equipment. We need something that will become a holy object, something more like a majestic sword, not a cheese knife," spat Adam, his bald head glistening with a sudden glaze of sweat.

Emily moved between the two men, letting her own robe swing as she swayed her hips a little more than simple walking necessitated.

"Stop it and let *me* go this time," said the curly-haired young woman, sniffing disdainfully. "If you want quality shopping, have a smart woman do it. Why don't you two just concentrate on the construction of our new worship space? Do something manly, gentlemen."

With that, she turned slowly and bestowed her smile on the other worshippers. There was silence as the group quickly parted to let Emily sashay out of the room, her head held high. Seeing the flurry of anxious glances, Adam knew he had to act quickly to salvage his standing.

Taking a deep breath, he raised his arms.

"Forgive me and our sister," he crooned, making himself once more the center of attention. "We have been working very hard since we first had the revelation of a stronger Bayel. And we are both disappointed that our efforts are not moving along as quickly as we would like.

"She is correct that we *should* be making more progress on the new sanctuary. Ralph and I will review where those plans are currently so we may have a positive report for her when she returns with what I am sure will be the perfect implement. When she brings us that masterpiece, it will be our duty to ensure that we use it to the glory and honor of Bayel.

"Now, as usual, I ask that you do not reveal this service or this consecrated room to those of Bayel's people who have not yet been chosen. Return to your daily responsibilities and know that we will meet again to celebrate Bayel."

There was some low-key murmuring as the small group broke up, leaving the two senior members of the movement alone.

"Sorry about the knife," said Ralph, hanging his head a bit. "I'm embarrassed. It was supposed to be good."

"Yeah." Adam exhaled as he slipped off his robe and used it to dry the sweat on his head. "Let's hope there's something out there that can do what we want."

"If there is, Emily will find it."

"Yeah," said Adam again. "That's all I need. She's becoming way too popular with the new people, and she knows it. I don't want a power struggle, but if she starts one, I'll make sure I finish it.

"Bayel needs power to take down Nathao, and we need to focus on getting him that power from these sacrifices. Perfection and fear are our tools. Every step and movement must be perfect, and our offering must be aware of its impending death.

"I don't need Emily to be a distraction at this point in time. When Bayel succeeds we will be revered as leaders and visionaries and she can do whatever she likes, but now we must *focus*."

"You really do believe he can push Nathao out of the Top Ten and move up? Why the King of Dreams, anyway?" asked Ralph.

"Don't you believe?" countered Adam, his eyes suddenly sharp and his bald head glistening. "If you don't, why are you here?"

"Oh, stop it. I'm only human, and I guess I still doubt once in a while. I'm not as strong and resolute as you."

Adam was pleased at the comment and backed off on his attack.

"Don't sell yourself short, Ralph. You are closer to the people precisely *because* you doubt, and that is important to me and Bayel. We need to know what they are thinking."

"But why shoot so high? Bayel is what, fifteen or eighteen according to the Promethean's last Deity Ranking Conference. Nathao is six."

"Nathao has a weakness in the way he chooses his closest people," said Adam with an arrogant shrug. "He thinks bringing in outsiders brings in strength. That's a ridiculous idea, and the fact that we—actually Bayel—just took out two of the King's top workers in one fell swoop proves it. The power he gained from their fear as they died was more than I dared hope. You felt it just as I did, and Bayel was satiated.

"Think, Ralph, of the power we can offer him with a planned, orchestrated human death. But we have to do it right. And when he defeats Nathao, we will share in that achievement. I promise you, Bayel will reward us."

7

Barnabas raced into the kitchen and found Gwen alone at the table, seemingly deep in thought. She was wearing her jacket with an untouched cup of coffee in front of her.

"I came as soon as I could. What's wrong?" he asked anxiously.

"The King has been giving Becky and Sam dreams."

The Rider dropped into the chair next to her and exhaled loudly in disgust as the tension in his body evaporated.

"That's all? I thought something serious had happened."

The sharp glare from his granddaughter stopped him cold.

"It *is* serious," she said, growling. "He's in their heads. That's unacceptable. They are off-limits to him."

"First of all, girl, no one is off-limits to the King. Second, *he* is in charge, so get over it. What dreams did they have?"

"Apparently there have been several."

"And? What were they about?"

"For Sam it was the fact that I'm working for him now. For Becky it was that, plus the fact that Sam had been in his lands, but is now going to be fine and that she should do well in school."

Barnabas pursed his lips and counted to ten before speaking but still could not keep the sarcasm out of his voice.

"You call me here to complain that Nat has given Becky dreams that tell her to do well in school? Do you know how many parents pray to have that happen to their kids?"

"The message isn't the point," countered Gwen, her tone harsh. "He was *in her mind,* and I will not condone that. And that goes for Sam too. He may have brought him back, but he doesn't have the right to invade my son's thoughts."

"As I said, get over it," retorted the Rider. "*You* don't tell *him* what he can and cannot do."

"In this case I do," shot back Gwen. "And I intend to see him and tell him to stop."

"That is not a good idea," said Barnabas, shaking his head.

"Those are my children and your great-grandchildren we're talking about. Do you want them involved with him? Especially while they're asleep and most vulnerable? You yourself said I shouldn't tell them much."

The old man shrugged in exasperation.

"I wouldn't have told them, but the King seems to believe it's the best course of action, and I trust him. I don't have a problem with it."

"Well, *I* do, and I'm going to tell him to stop. I'm not afraid of him."

Barnabas watched as his granddaughter's eyes got cold; his gut tightened at the thought of what would happen if she confronted Nathao.

"I'll warn you one more time, girl. This is not the way to deal with the King. But, if you are set on doing it, I'll come along to pick you up after it's over."

Gwen frowned. "I intend to do this now. And I welcome your support."

"Oh, it isn't support," Barnabas replied with a short bark of a laugh. "I meant it when I said I'll pick you up when it's over."

⋇⋇

Barnabas was not surprised to find Nathao waiting in the Keep's Step room when they arrived. The King sat in one of the upholstered chairs, and he acknowledged the Rider's slight bow before turning his attention to Gwen. Barnabas slipped to the side and crossed his arms to wait. He had little doubt about the outcome of the confrontation.

Gwen wasted no time with a bow or pleasantries as she strode toward the King.

For a moment, they simply looked at each other, and then Gwen took a deep breath and dove in.

"Stay out of Sam's mind, and stay out of Becky's mind," she demanded. "You are not permitted to speak with them."

Nathao regarded her for a moment before gently replying, "You do not tell me what I may or may not do. If I deem it best to give an individual a dream, I will do it."

"Not my children. You will leave them alone," said Gwen, matching his softness with an intensity that made Barnabas raise his eyebrows in begrudging admiration.

"I will tell you once more, Courier, *you* do not tell *me* what to do, or give me limits. *You* do not question *me* or my methods."

"Oh, but I do," retorted Gwen. "My mind is my own, and I will tell you exactly what to do, especially when it comes to my kids."

Barnabas winced and braced himself for what he expected would happen next.

❋❋

Gwen was furious as she mentally walled off any more beseeching and warnings from her jacket. She held Nathao's gaze.

"I *will* tell you what to do because my children are off-limits, and—"

As she tried to form the rest of the sentence, a chill spread from the base of her neck up through the rest of her head, literally freezing any thoughts in place. A fog slowly clouded her vision and her throat began to close, making the simple task of breathing a challenge, forcing her to gasp for air. Her legs began to crumble and as her hands met the floor, Gwen became acutely aware that the low-pile carpet gave her fingers nothing of substance to grab.

The harder she struggled, the thicker the fog became, and then she blacked out.

⁜

The headache was intense. No, it was more than intense; it was all-encompassing. Not only did her head pound, but her entire body echoed the waves of pain that intensified when she tried to move.

Gwen groaned and tentatively opened one eye just a slit, only to slam it shut when the light sent shards of pain slicing through her head and down her neck into her arms and even her legs. She held every muscle in her body immobile until the residual throbbing subsided.

A pause, a tentative deep breath, and Gwen tried again. This time she was ready for it, but the pain wasn't nearly as bad, and she was able to endure the discomfort enough to slowly turn her head. A careful glance to the right, and her nose practically brushed the well-worn striped slipcovers of what she decided was the back of the sofa in her living room. A similarly slow glance to the left confirmed that she was home and that she was not alone. A dark-skinned man in a familiar-looking black jacket sat in one of the chairs that matched the sofa. He smiled when they made eye contact.

"Welcome back. He went easy on you. Most of us are out for a lot longer."

Pushing herself up on one elbow, Gwen tentatively swung her feet to the floor and sat up. Her head merely hurt now. Her jacket offered a light burst of support and something like a psychic analgesic as she steadied herself, but she sensed a serious undercurrent of disappointment.

"Where's my grandfather?"

"He'll be back. He went to get Alana; he said she might as well move in now and not wait."

"How long have I been out?"

"Not very," replied the stranger in a deep, melodic voice.

"Well, I've got to...whoa." She grabbed the sofa's arm as she stood up and staggered.

The stranger made no effort to help her as she sank back down to the sofa, leaned her elbows on her knees, and held her head.

"So, it appears you're none the worse for wear. He said I could leave when I thought you were all right."

"That's all the bastard said? And, you, stop it," said Gwen, speaking directly to the coat as it forced a growing message of reproach into her mind. "You stay out until invited in."

"Whatever happened between you and the King is your business, but take my advice and let it pass. I can tell you from experience, you can't beat him," said the newcomer.

"And who are you to dispense such wisdom?"

"I am Rakeem, Rider to Nathao." The man paused slightly while Gwen looked up weakly to acknowledge him. "And I know from first-hand experience the consequences of provoking his wrath."

"Right, and apparently, now so do I."

"I suggest you learn from this. It gets worse each time."

"Look, Rakeem, I'm not ungrateful for your advice, but he's messing with my kids' dreams, and I won't let that happen."

"There is nothing you can do, and he will touch them only when he believes it's important."

"He has no idea what is important."

"I am told your name is Gwen, and you are our new Courier."

"Yes to the first point, and so I'm told to the second." She sighed as she leaned back and sank into the comfort of the sofa. A tentative tingle from the coat convinced her to reopen her mind; she was immediately embraced and offered extra pulses of energy that raced up her spine to her head.

"Let me tell you my story, Gwen. It may give you some perspective. I had two wonderful sons who were very close in age. They did everything together, and one day the younger got terribly sick. Nothing we did would break his fever, and when he slipped into a coma, the healer said there wasn't anything more she could do. The older boy was beside himself, blaming a hike he had insisted they take to hunt rabbits and where his brother had fallen into a stream and gotten a chill. I was afraid he would take his own life if his brother died and began praying for help.

"For days not one god answered, and I despaired I would lose both my sons. Then Nathao entered my life. I made a Request, and he met his end of the bargain by guiding my youngest back. Unknown to me, he also began giving my older son dreams.

"When I learned of that, I confronted the King and demanded he stop, much the same as you. We went on to clash several times; my head was much the worse for it." He smiled ruefully. "Then, the evening before my oldest was to marry and we were sharing some special father-son time, he told me that the only way he survived his brother's near-death was to dream. He said he found refuge in the dreams and an understanding that he was not responsible for his brother's condition. He knew I worked for the King, and he told me to thank Nathao for the gifts. That's what he called them—'gifts.' I was wrong. Nathao knew what he was doing."

"Touching," remarked Gwen, taking care not to move her head but tapping her left jacket sleeve in disapproval as the energy feed paused and a tendril of unhappiness filtered into her mind. "I still don't want him in my kids' minds. Your family, though, you said they knew you worked for Nathao? They didn't mind?"

The Rider was silent; he seemed to be weighing his response.

"Yes, they knew."

"My grandfather's family told him to go away."

"Unfortunately, that is more often the case. People are afraid of the King."

"Why doesn't he just give them a dream to change their mind?" said Gwen. She offered Rakeem a tight smile.

The Rider ignored the sarcasm. "You will have to learn to trust him."

"This isn't the way to go about earning someone's trust."

"Again, you're looking at it incorrectly. He does not have to *earn* anything. You, on the other hand, have to *learn* everything. You are not in a position of power here, and the sooner you understand the rules, the better it will be for all of us who must work with you."

Gwen thought she caught a hint of concern on Rakeem's face.

"Barnabas and Alana will be here shortly. I'll let the King know you're recovered." The Rider rose to leave.

"Rakeem." Gwen paused, feeling a little guilty at her behavior. "I appreciate your story, but I can't let him play with my kids' dreams. I won't."

"He doesn't play," replied the Rider as he looked down at her. "I will see you again very soon, and in the meantime, please think about what I said."

Gwen was pensive as she watched him head for the basement. She then carefully maneuvered her way to the kitchen to get something for her head, although the pounding had subsided considerably. Rakeem's story suggested the King's dreams could be comforting, and in her heart she knew that was something her children could certainly use right now. There was just something sinister about entering someone's mind without permission.

"But he entered mine," she mused. "And when Grandpa was put off by it, I told him it wasn't all that bad. I can't say it was comforting, but then it was work, right? I accept it for me, but I can't accept it for them? They said it was helpful."

Gwen reached for the acetaminophen and paused. "I want to protect them, is that so bad? And, you," she asked, looking down at the lapel of her jacket, "nothing to say?"

The coat was silent.

8

~

"Now *this* is a knife." Adam Bardhof marveled as he held the glittering silver blade by its equally shiny handle and waved it slowly in the air.

Emily coughed derisively.

"You make it look you're using a bubble wand. It's a knife, for gods' sake; hold it firmly and forcefully."

"I'm appreciating its beauty," said Adam, snarling. "I know how to use a knife."

"Then why is there another mess over there instead of a clean kill?" she countered, pointing to a pile of fur.

"C'mon, Em, he's improved a lot," said Ralph, very glad no one else was around to witness the squabbling. "And Bayel is getting better at taking up the energy."

"Without that knife—which *I* found for us, remember—the results tonight wouldn't have been nearly as good. I wonder, though, whether once he gets used to the power rush from a rabbit, we may have to go for something bigger."

"Even if we do, that great knife you found will be able to do the job," said Ralph, "because it's being used by a great leader."

Adam smiled his thanks while Emily pouted.

"Should we have a demonstration at the next meeting?" continued the pudgy man, looking back and forth between his friends, hoping to break the growing tension in the room. "We could celebrate the fact that the Leadership has signed off on the final phase of construction with no idea what it's really for. And, come to think of it, Adam, when is

Bayel going to shut them down? Especially Piale? He may have the title 'Spirit of Bayel' and everyone may think he's the only one Bayel talks to, but *we* know that isn't true."

"They can't just be 'shut down,'" retorted Emily, adjusting the shoulders of her robe in a short, annoyed movement. "Think it through, Ralph. We need Piale and the Leadership for a little while more. The Spirit is very popular, and there's money to be raised to wrap up this project. Once that's done, then we can pressure Bayel to make changes.

"Now, what do you think of my fashion adjustment to this drab, boring drape?"

Ralph looked sideways at Adam, who was still waving the knife while deep in thought.

"I think the edging is very nice, Em. I like the fact that it runs up and down the front as well as around the bottom. And I like the bright yellow. Adam, what do you think?"

"I think it might be time to talk to Bayel," said the bald man quietly. "You both bring up some important points."

"And my modifications to these gowns?" purred Emily, posing suggestively.

"They add an air of authority," said Adam, slipping off his own robe and tossing it at her. "Make mine green. I'll need it tomorrow. Thanks."

9

Gwen pulled into the driveway, turned off the truck, and just sat for a moment in the slowly chilling cab, appreciating the grayness of the sky, the silence, and the memories of her last day as a municipal employee. The official farewell party had been orderly and sentimental, but the true gathering, and the one she would cherish, had taken place the night before with the people she considered her true work spouses. She reached into the pocket of her dark blue wool civilian coat and pulled out the pigskin wallet from Frank.

Running her thumb slowly back and forth along the soft, light brown leather, she smiled as she remembered his toast.

"To my partner," he had said, raising his bottle of beer. "You always had my back. You were never afraid of what might be behind the door, down the alley, in the woods, or up the tree. We made a good pair, Gwen, and I'll miss you. I hope you appreciate this little token of my enduring friendship. And I'll always be there if you need backup—all you have to do is call."

A small smile skipped across her lips. "We did make a good pair, Frank. I hope there is someone in this new life who is as good a partner as you were." Her gaze shifted to the gray house and the slate walkway leading to the front door. "I have a feeling I'm going to find out real soon."

She was not terribly surprised to hear voices in the kitchen as she entered the house, but she scoffed when she found Alana pouring coffee for Barnabas.

"Grandpa, what are you doing here? And Alana, he's quite capable of getting his own coffee. Don't baby him."

"I don't mind," replied the nanny, her short, auburn hair bouncing as she shook her head. "I've babied him for as long as I've known him."

"We need to talk about those days. Stop grinning like that, Grandpa. Becky get off to school all right this morning?"

"Yes, she did," said Alana. "I'll meet her at the bus stop."

"I can do it."

Barnabas broke in. "No, you can't. We have a meeting."

Gwen frowned.

"Come, girl, you *do* have a job. A staff meeting is set to begin as soon as we get there. Go get your jacket."

"This is why I'm here," added Alana, sitting down at the table. "Go."

※※

Barnabas let Gwen create the Window and Step first: she was pleasantly surprised at how well both went. As she arrived in the stillness of the cream-and-brown Step room at the Keep, the Courier moved aside to give her grandfather space to arrive and paused to focus her skittish thoughts. She pushed aside the now-embarrassing memories of her last—disastrous—encounter with the King and forced her nervous excitement behind an expressionless face. Her coat offered a hug and warm sense of support.

Her grandfather arrived and deliberately moved ahead of her toward the door, where he paused and cleared his throat.

"I just want to say it isn't everyone he accepts, especially not as a member of his inner staff. And you look good in black," he added as he gestured awkwardly toward her coat.

"Are you trying to tell me you're all right with this?"

"I'm trying to tell you that I have faith in the King's judgment, and I will work with you to the best of my abilities, girl. Accept it as an olive branch."

Gwen paused and allowed herself a small smile.

"You're a bastard who did very little to help me when I could have used it, but, it's because of you that I still have Sam, and for that I owe you. Olive branch accepted."

Barnabas nodded curtly, his longish hair echoing the move, and waved his arm to usher her to the door and out of the quiet room.

This time, as she stepped into the controlled whirlwind of activity in the lamplit hallway, Gwen paid close attention to the people bustling past her. Many were shuttling in and out of the numerous glass doors nestled in the stone wall, and through one she glimpsed some rather animated people standing and pointing at what appeared to be a wall-size data screen.

She worked to match her grandfather's movements as he strode through the bustle and registered the number of people who greeted him and nodded at her. Gwen found herself smiling in return, drinking in the sense of purpose that flowed from every living being around her. Then her stomach tightened as her gaze jumped across the courtyard to the opaque windows that guarded their destination on the other side. Her jacket immediately responded with a ripple of support, and she surreptitiously caressed the right cuff in answer.

A shout startled her, and Gwen turned at the same time her grandfather moved to stand between her and a tall, skinny man weaving his way through the stream of people. He was also wearing a black jacket.

"Eli, well met," said Barnabas, clasping the scrawny, gray-haired man's outstretched hand. "I haven't seen you in days."

"If you'd come join us at the Stables a little more often, you could solve that problem."

"By the same token, you know where I am. But, enough—this is Gwen. Gwen, this is Eli, one of Nathao's other Riders."

Gwen nodded to the man, whose brown eyes danced as they looked her over from top to bottom.

"So this is your granddaughter, Barnabas? Well, more attractive than I expected, and thank the gods she looks intelligent."

"She is." The shaggy-haired Rider nearly growled. "More so than several others we have known."

Eli lifted an eyebrow and shifted his body around the other Rider to exclude him and create a more intimate space with Gwen. He smiled and folded his lanky body in a deep bow.

"Please allow me a formal welcome, my dear. Ignore that old man and keep an open mind. Many of us have very respectable skills and relationships to offer that could make your time here more enjoyable."

Not sure what to make of the exchange, Gwen smiled politely to cover her uncertainty and accepted his outstretched hand. Her jacket pulsed slightly.

"Thank you, Eli. You seem to have a comfortable relationship with my grandfather."

"We've been together so long all we have for each other are words of affection." The Rider cackled.

"He wouldn't know an insult if it bit him on the ass. He's heard them all," snapped Barnabas, brushing past Eli and taking Gwen's arm to steer her down the hall.

Once across the quadrangle, the trio paused just inside the entry to the darker, quieter King's wing, at the bottom of the large staircase.

"Do you want to tell her we're here?" asked Eli quietly.

"We're expected; just pop your head in."

"You do it. I'll take Gwen upstairs."

"No, she's my granddaughter. I take her upstairs. *You* tell her we're here."

"I really don't want to."

"I don't care."

"What is the issue here?" asked Gwen, just as softly.

Barnabas growled slightly as Eli answered. "When we arrive, we make it a point to let Marcia know we're going upstairs to the office, just in case there's something we need to know. Someone may already be there or, for any number of reasons, it may not be a good time to see the King."

"So, what's the problem?" asked Gwen.

"She can be short-tempered, and she talks," whispered the thin Rider. "She doesn't stop talking, and she's such a gossip. You don't want to get on her bad side."

"I can hear you very clearly, you irresponsible slackers! Get your-selves upstairs, immediately! They're all waiting," barked Marcia as she suddenly flowed out of her office and planted herself next to the trio at the base of the stairs, her large hands parked on her more-than-ample hips. Instead of flowers swirling on her dress, this time it was gold drag-ons baring their teeth and claws on a black background.

"Hello, Gwen," she added, moderating her tone a bit. "Welcome. I hope this meeting with the King is more productive than your last. Now you had better hurry; you've kept them waiting long enough."

The Riders just grumbled and started up the stairs.

Gwen hung back a moment and met the Administrator's insuffer-ably superior look with her own calm, confident face.

"Thank you for your encouragement, Marcia. It's comforting to know even a woman with your responsibilities still has time to keep up with the local gossip."

She heard the woman's sharp intake of breath as she turned and followed the men up the stairs, and it went a long way toward easing her annoyance at being dismissed in such a cavalier manner. She also noted that what happened in this place, at least so far, seemed to be far from private.

She used the time climbing the stairs to settle her nerves and assume a façade of strength that she carefully carried into the office behind the Riders. This time she clearly understood the jacket's ripple of purpose and support that ran across her back.

She took note of the several people already there, and when Eli and Barnabas offered a quick bow, she did the same.

"Good," said the King from where he sat. "Now we can start. Take your glasses, please, and sit down."

At the side table, Eli poured for all three of them and after accepting a glass, Gwen hung back as her grandfather and the other Rider took open places on one of the two large brown sofas that faced each other.

Nathao was in the big leather chair at the far end of the rectangle, with a large red-haired man sitting on an overstuffed brown floor pillow near him. As a subtle challenge, Gwen chose a brown pillow at the opposite end of the rectangle and directly faced Nathao and the big Rider.

The King made brief introductions.

"Gwen, this is Claire, Jensen, and Armen. You already know Rakeem and Barnabas and seem to have met Eli. You will all have time later to talk. Something has come up that needs immediate attention."

As the King began speaking, Gwen glanced around at the group. In the lamplit room, with their black jackets and somber demeanors, the Riders looked like members of a private club listening to an invited speaker.

On her left, Barnabas and Eli had taken seats next to Claire, a slight, serious-looking woman with thick, blond hair pulled back in a ponytail. The sofa on Gwen's right held Rakeem and Armen, a smaller man whose gray, bushy eyebrows spilled over the top of his metal-framed glasses. Jensen's intense red hair would have been enough to grab attention anywhere, but he was also so large that even sitting on the floor, his head nearly came to Nathao's shoulders.

Her eyes finished their circuit with Nathao, who was leaning back in his chair, his fingers steepled as he spoke. As she briefly caught his eye, her jacket warmed.

"—another Disturbance, and it is bigger than the one that took Alice and James."

Gwen sipped her drink and, at the mention of her predecessor, listened more closely.

"It is in the Southern Corner again and has not moved. We will investigate it shortly, but I want my brother to know."

At that, there were some murmurs and glances in Gwen's direction. She raised her eyebrows as she looked at her boss.

"You must move to take on your responsibilities right away," said the King. "That will mean a trip in a few minutes that may be tiring. Can you do it?"

Gwen shrugged. "If it has to be done, of course. Where are we going?"

"Sir—" began Barnabas, leaning forward on the sofa.

"Barnabas, I do not want to hear it. None of you can do it, and I do not want to wait."

"But, sir, it takes time."

"It does not have to," replied the King evenly.

"Where are we going and why?" pressed Gwen.

"You must learn to take messages from me to my brother."

"Understood. Where is he? What's his name?"

"He is the neighbor on the other side of the River I told you about previously. We will Step to the Boathouse and meet him there."

"Boathouse; got it. So what's the problem? And what's his name?"

"The problem," echoed Nathao, "is hard to explain because I myself have never experienced what you must do. And my brother has many names. I call him Luke. You may know him as Death. You will meet him, learn the rules for crossing the River safely, and eat a pomegranate."

Gwen pursed her lips to hide her growing concern and confusion.

"Pomegranate? As in Pluto, Persephone, and pomegranate?"

"Good, you know the story." The King nodded.

"Well, I know the *myth*, yes. Are you telling me there's some truth to it?"

"Honestly, Nat," snapped Claire. The blond Rider frowned deeply at the King and then slipped gracefully off the sofa to the pillow next to Gwen.

"To travel in the World of the Dead, you must be more than what you are now. We Riders cannot go into Luke's world without dying, but you can.

"You'll be protected by the fruit you eat. As you know from the myth, it grants you the protection to come and go in Luke's Kingdom. Basically, if your life leaves you while you're outside his realm you die, but if you are alive when you go to him, you will be able to leave alive because of the fruit."

"Eat all the seeds," added Rakeem, leaning forward. "They're the keys, your passports."

"That's right," agreed Claire. "Each seed represents one trip there and back."

"And when they're used up?"

"I'm not sure," admitted Claire, turning to look at Nathao.

"There must be some frequent flier clause, right?" Gwen made sure there was an edge to her voice as she pinned the King with a hard look. "What happens if I think I'm running low?"

Everyone in the room was now looking at Nathao, who remained expressionless.

"These particular fruits are from Luke's own garden. I would not worry about running out."

"I don't suppose you would," retorted his Courier.

The King regarded her calmly, his face expressionless.

"Little do you know, child, how I fear visiting my brother. Even I do not cross the River; only my Courier does."

Gwen pushed aside a nagging sense of doubt and suspicion as she reapplied her own outer mask of composed assurance.

"So, when do we leave?"

"Now. Riders, I will meet you at the Priory Step. Eli and Armen, see to what you will need. Gwen, you are with me."

Nathao stood, and the Riders rose with him. Gwen got to her feet and surrendered her empty glass to Eli's outstretched hand.

As their hands met, her jacket again offered a pulsing touch.

"Don't take off the jacket," warned the lanky man, glancing toward the King with a frown. "In case no one remembers to tell you, it offers you some protection."

"She knows that already, Rider," said Nathao with a look of patient displeasure. "Gwen, now."

She moved to follow as he strode past her and was startled as Rakeem's deep voice whispered near her ear, "Trust Nathao."

She turned quickly to find the dark Rider at her side. She paused and whispered back, "I'm still thinking about everything."

Shooting a quick, challenging glance at the rest of the group, Gwen nodded and marched after the King.

※❈※

As the pair threaded their way through the busy hall of the Keep to the Step room, Gwen took the opportunity to take a closer look at the King. She had to admit she rather liked what she saw.

Her employer was tall and moved with a smooth grace; his dark gray hair—streaked with lighter gray—was pulled back in a long braid that, when released, she figured would probably fall at least to his waist. In profile, she could still see the angular planes of his face.

His jacket was very similar to hers but was a rich gray, not black. As he moved, the clothing moved with him and faint cascades of color tumbled through the fabric. Despite his swinging arms, the garment made no sound.

Nathao turned to look down at her, and Gwen held his eyes. She remembered them being gray, but this time she realized they were the same shade as the jacket and seemed to shift in color as the coat did.

He raised his eyebrows. "Is everything all right?"

"I've never had the chance to really look at you," she replied. "The few times we've met have not exactly been relaxing conversations over tea. I'm curious."

"Then look and ask. You need to know me well, even better than my Riders, and some of them have been with me a very long time."

"Tell me what's ahead of us right now, what's going to happen. It's just a little quirk, but I do better when I have information to work with."

"We will go to the Boathouse, which is the only place my brother and I can be together without danger to either of us. I will leave you with him."

Gwen pursed her lips in displeasure and found comfort in the sense of reassurance she suddenly felt from her coat.

"It is necessary. He must know you, so you can travel freely in his kingdom. You may even meet his wife as I think she is with him now."

"She leaves?"

"It used to be that she spent half of your year with him and the rest with her mother."

"You're kidding. There really *is* a pomegranate connection?"

"Yes, Luke is not very original. Once he finds something that works, he tends to stay with it. Their arrangement has now matured, and she travels back and forth when she wishes."

"Why can't you be together?"

"Dreaming and death are too closely related to coexist for any length of time. One eventually destroys the other. We have no wish to find out who, in the end, is the stronger."

"But we all end up dead," countered Gwen.

"Or are you dreaming that state of being?" Nathao challenged as he reached to open the door to the Step room.

Gwen jumped ahead and opened it for him. He stopped and looked down at her.

"In either case, I have chosen you to be the only being that can safely travel between both worlds. My brother has always supported my choice, and I see no reason for him to disagree this time."

"Is he friendly?" she asked as the door closed behind them with a slight click, cutting off the busy sounds of the hallway.

"Luke? I suppose you could say he is; being siblings does not always let you see that. But come, I will show you the Window. Look at it carefully and Step. That way you will remember and be able to get there again on your own."

Gwen moved next to the King and watched their destination appear. Wooden walls, some chairs, and part of a table were within her range of vision. After a moment of study, she felt confident enough to Step through and discovered that she wasn't alone.

At the end of the table that she had not been able to see, a man sat behind a small pile of papers, reading. There were glasses and a wine bottle on the table along with a bowl of fruit.

He looked up and rose as she moved to make room for the King to follow.

"You must be Gwen."

She stared in disbelief at the young man in the light blue polo shirt and navy slacks. He approached with his hand out.

"I'm Luke. Welcome."

As they shook hands, a slight, rather pleasant shock ran through her jacket. But before she could entirely process the sensation, she heard a sound behind her and watched as her host's focus of attention immediately shifted.

"Brother! How are you?"

"Doing well, Luke. How are things here?" asked the King of Dreams, walking over and returning his hug.

"Busy, but quiet. You know what I mean."

"How is Percy?"

"She's fine and sends her best. Wants to know when she's going to get invited to a party over at your place. She says there's no excitement here; thinks her brother-in-law might help out in that respect."

"Tell her to keep dreaming," replied Nathao blandly.

Gwen was stunned that her employer seemed to have made a joke and amazed when Luke laughed as he waved toward the table.

"Sit. Share some wine with me."

"Gwen needs your time, Luke, and you know I cannot stay long."

"I know, but a few minutes shouldn't hurt," countered the brown-haired, younger figure wistfully. "This is the closest we have to neutral ground, and it's been so long since we've been together."

The King paused and then appeared to almost smile.

"You are right. We have some time. Tell me everything that has happened lately."

At the table, Luke filled the three wineglasses and placed one in front of Gwen before turning to talk with his brother, who accepted the second. She picked up the glass, leaned back in the simple, straight-back chair, and took a closer look at the single-room Boathouse.

The log walls were bare of hangings, and the furniture consisted of a sofa upholstered in a rose-colored material, a dark wood coffee table, and the table and chairs where she and the gods sat. Exposed beams ran along the low ceiling, and light from two oversized, lace-curtained windows filled the space, making it bright and inviting.

Gwen returned her attention to the table and eyed the bowl of fruit, especially the large pomegranate sitting next to the apples and peaches. A smaller clear bowl of water and floating lemon slices sat nearby, together with a neatly folded white cloth napkin.

"That's for you. Percy said it was the best in the garden."

Startled, she looked up to find the brothers watching her.

"When you are done here, step back, and Marcia will have instructions for you," said Nathao. He rose and clapped his brother on the shoulder. "I will send word later, Luke. Take care of yourself."

The King of Dreams walked back to the center of the room, where he turned and looked at Gwen.

"Listen to my brother. I will see you shortly."

He Stepped and left silence behind in the Boathouse. Gwen turned uncertainly to the youthful-looking god, who nodded toward the pewter bowl.

"Help yourself. We can talk while you eat. Nat says you know about Percy and me and the fruit."

Gwen could have sworn his brown eyes lit up as he grinned.

"Well, I've known that *story* for a long time," she said as she reached for the large red fruit and a nearby knife. "But I always thought it was just that, a *story*."

"It's been blown a little out of proportion, you know," said Luke, leaning back in his chair with an exaggerated sigh.

"So you didn't just steal Persephone and tick off her mother?"

The fruit was tart with lots of seeds that sent trickles of sticky juice between Gwen's fingers, but she quite forgot why she was eating as she listened to her host go into a speech that she decided had been crafted specifically to justify his actions of long ago.

"I loved her then, and I love her now," he concluded in a tone that suggested he was very pleased with himself and his conquest. "Her mother has even come around and realizes this is a marriage that was meant to be."

Gwen's look turned cynical as she reached for the small bowl of lemon-scented water and dipped in the corner of the white linen napkin. She used it to wipe the corners of her mouth and then attacked her stained fingers.

"You really believe your mother-in-law is all forgiving?"

There was pause, and Luke shook his head.

"No," he admitted, "but at least she's become cordial. Now, let's talk about you."

Gwen continued working on her hands with the lemon water as she listened closely to Luke outlining the procedure to reach him.

All contact was to begin in the Boathouse. She would Step here, and Dob, the Boatman, would take her across the River

"What if Dob isn't here?"

"That means he's busy ferrying someone over and will be back in a few minutes; he's never away for long. For this meeting, I sent him on an errand so we could have some time together. When he returns, we will cross, and I'll show you the stables, where you will pick up a horse. The road to my place is the only road you will see. Once you are on the horse and on the road, you do not get down. You are not to walk anywhere outside of my manor. It wouldn't be safe and"—he held up a hand as she moved to speak—"you will understand a little more once we cross the River."

Gwen paused as her jacket hugged her tightly as if to reinforce the warning.

"How far is your place?"

"Far enough that we will not go the entire way this time. Nat has that Disturbance to deal with and he wants you there with him."

"He did say I might get to meet your wife," Gwen observed, surveying her hands one last time and then looking back at her host. "I don't have any stains around my mouth, do I? I'd hate to make a lousy first impression."

The king peered at her face. "Uh, no, you look fine. But I don't think it would be wise to meet Percy today. Nat wants you back, and I can sense you aren't strong enough right now to make the entire trip. That will come with time, training, and some sleep. How much of that have you had lately, anyway?"

"Sleep?" Gwen snorted, shaking her long, dark hair until it settled behind her shoulders. "Let's just say it has not been at the top of my agenda."

"And that comes through. You must be better rested before you spend the time on the Otherside. What I *will* show you is really all you need. There is only one road, and you stay on it."

Feeling curiously calm and in control, the Courier raised an eyebrow and pressed for more information. "Just stay on it?"

"That's it. There are no intersections or turns to worry about." Death smiled.

"Any towns? People?"

"No."

"I suppose what I want to know is, what will I see?" asked Gwen, ignoring the tentatively reassuring back rub she suddenly got from her jacket.

"Nothing, at least until you approach my home."

"What does 'nothing' look like?" she persisted, letting a tone of annoyance slip into her voice. "I'd like to know what to expect."

"I can't really tell you," Luke admitted, "because I don't know. Everyone sees it differently."

Exasperated, Gwen sighed and rolled her eyes. "Why am I not surprised?"

"That's the way of it," said Luke with a shrug. "Just try to always incorporate enough sleep in your schedule and, of course, wear your coat. When Nat makes those for the Riders, he crafts them as a shield for his world, but when he makes the one for his Courier, he adds protection for my world as well."

"Then why the pomegranate seeds?"

"Because while the coat's protection is strong enough for your mind, the life force is weaker than thought, and your body needs something more."

Before Death could continue, someone pounded twice on the door to the Boathouse. Gwen turned abruptly and watched the door open slowly to admit a small, nut-brown man dressed in jeans and a blue plaid flannel shirt. His movements were almost mechanical as he slowly and deliberately pushed the door closed before facing the table. When he bowed deeply, his crew cut revealed a small, thin patch of hair on the crown of his head.

"Dob, this is Gwen, my brother's Courier. Remember her. When she comes here, she will have a message for me. You will take her across the River and bring her back when she returns to you. No payment is needed. Do you understand?"

Dob straightened, and Gwen met his solid black eyes as he stared at her for a moment. She caught a sense of sadness, or maybe it was emptiness, she wasn't sure, before he turned back to Luke and nodded once.

"Well done, Dob," said the king from where he sat at the table. "Return to the boat. We'll be there in a minute."

Without a word, the little man turned and left, closing the door quietly behind him.

Gwen looked at the king. "He has Chihuahua eyes. Big, dark, and sweet."

Luke looked perplexed for a moment and then burst out laughing.

"The little dog. I never thought to compare his eyes to anything, but I suppose a dog works as well as anything, because he is loyal and will certainly watch out for you now that he knows you belong here. Although, 'sweet' might be a stretch.

"But now, are you ready to do something that no other human or god can do, with the exception of my wife? Do you feel important?"

"Not so much on either count, but if Chihuahua Eyes is here, I think I feel at least a little reassured. Let's just consider this one more episode in a growing universe of adventures," she added with a theatrical sweep of her arm toward the door.

Luke offered what looked like a tolerant smile as he pushed back from the table, his chair scraping across the floor. He led the way to the door, opened it, and, echoing her earlier movement, gallantly waved Gwen through ahead of him.

"Ladies first."

With a sarcastic half-grin, the Courier walked out onto a porch that ran the length of the small building and gasped.

"This is beautiful," she breathed.

A riot of colors lined a red stone walkway. White and yellow chrysanthemums crowded together with marigolds, deep red roses, purple sweet pea, and multicolored zinnias flanking the path to a wooden dock. Enriching the visual excitement, the air was warm and the aroma from the flowers rich and sweet.

Next to the dock, Dob sat motionless in the middle of a simple, weather-worn wooden boat that looked as if it could seat four. There seemed to be room at the stern for someone to stand, and Gwen surmised that this person would be the one to power the boat with the pole that lay across the back.

Then there was the imposing River. The water flowed lazily past the Boathouse and garden, calm, blue-green, and sparkling as it reflected the overhead sun. But the inviting picture changed abruptly a few meters out, where a curtain of thick, gray fog cloaked everything beyond from view, including the opposite shore. There was vertical movement within the cloudy wall and degrees of gray that reflected the blue-green of the water where the two planes meshed, but otherwise the fog was stationary and did not flow with the water.

The stones crunched underfoot as Luke and Gwen walked the path to a large, ancient-looking tree stump. The king grasped the dull gray gavel that dangled from a fraying rope and banged it once on the top of the wood, creating a deep, almost metallic sound.

Dob climbed out of the boat and turned to face the one who had called him.

"That's all you need to do. Now walk to the boat, sit in the front, and let him do the work."

Dob offered his arm for assistance as Death and the Courier for the King of Dreams stepped into the boat. They settled on the sun-warmed wood, and Gwen swayed with the boat that rocked gently as it left the dock. As they floated away from land, Luke had one more instruction.

"Don't look back now, or on any other trip. Just sit here and look straight ahead; it shouldn't be long before you see the other shore."

"Why shouldn't I look back?"

"Let me just say it wouldn't be wise."

"That just piques the curiosity."

"Perhaps, but it wouldn't be wise," chided Luke, waving a finger in admonishment.

"All right, then." The Courier shrugged. "I won't look."

Now it was Luke's turn to sigh. "Oh, yes you will, if not now, then the next trip or the trip after that. They all do. Just remember, I warned you."

The boat picked up speed and a slight, pleasant breeze sprang up that Gwen noticed carried no hint of a river smell. The water rippled as the forward motion of the boat's prow cut a V-shaped wake. The smooth, gliding motion gave her the courage to lean over the side and look down into the water. It was surprisingly clear within a few inches of the surface, but beyond that there was only an opaque darkness despite the brightness of the day.

Craning her neck to look up, she squinted and found the sun sitting right above them in a deep-blue, cloudless sky. It was a warm sun, and somehow she found that warmth a reassuring promise that no matter what lay beyond the wall of cloud, this part of the River would be waiting for her when she Crossed back.

Refocusing on the boat and its progress, she was startled to find the fog wall suddenly right on top of them; she tensed and braced herself to meet it.

The boat slipped into the cloud bank, and once the grayness enveloped them, Gwen could not see beyond the prow or the wooden sides. There was a sudden silence as the few natural sounds that she had not consciously noted before disappeared and a cool, damp closeness set in, briefly making her shiver. When she did, her jacket immediately responded with a wave of warmth and that slight constriction Gwen now associated with a hug. Smiling to herself, she lightly rubbed the supple right sleeve and relaxed into the sense of comfort.

That relief was fleeting because a moment later, she lurched forward and awkwardly scrambled to grab the seat and side of the boat as her head spun.

"Wow. Vertigo," she whispered, breathing deeply to settle her stomach and her nerves as she struggled to discern up from down.

"Oh. Sorry, forgot to warn you about that," said Luke. "You get used to it; it tells you that you are almost to my side. See, ahead? That's the dock."

Still hanging onto the boat, Gwen stared intently in the direction her companion was pointing and a few moments later picked out a fog-haloed, faint light that got stronger as they got closer. The emerging outline of a dock under the light was a most welcome addition to the picture.

Dob helped them out, and Luke led the way down the wooden walkway, moving briskly through the damp grayness. Gwen matched his stride, wishing desperately that she could just *see* something as she listened to the water lapping against the support pilings beneath them and their footsteps echoing on the planks.

"Luke, does everyone experience this fog? Or, do they see what they want to see? And if that's the case, why don't I see anything? Will it clear only if I'm dead?"

The tanned and toned king nodded as he kept walking.

"All valid questions, but it wouldn't do for even you to know what death looks like before it's your time."

"But I know what *you* look like."

"I am only the embodiment, plus you have Nathao's wonderful jacket. So, for you, I am not Death yet."

"Can you see here?"

"Of course. This is my land."

"And Percy?"

"She can see everything now, because this is also her place. But, when she first came, she couldn't."

"Then does the fog mean I'm not really supposed to be here?"

"Listen, child of the world, would you want the burden of knowing all?" asked Luke, a hint of annoyance coloring his voice but not slowing his pace. "Would you want to know what Death would be for you? I can arrange it, but I don't recommend it."

Gwen thought for just a moment as wisps of the fog cloud floated past, almost caressing her face. She shook her head and said with a nonchalance she definitely did not feel, "No, I defer to you, the expert. But will not being able to see very far interfere with whatever I have to do here? And if everyone else can see here, why have these lamps?"

"You will see the road you need, and once inside the grounds of my home, visibility won't be a problem.

"As for the lights, they are for you and you alone. They are always lit just in case *you* visit. Another sign of how special you are."

At a loss for words, Gwen just grunted.

Their footsteps became dull thuds as they transitioned to solid ground; in the sudden silence, Gwen caught the faint sound of a stick breaking off to her left. She froze and cocked her head, listening closely as she shot a look in the direction of the noise. The drifting barrier of cloud refused to give up any visible sign of life, and she turned back to the path where Luke was waiting.

"It's a little unnerving," she shrugged, slightly embarrassed. "I get the feeling someone is watching me. Actually, stalking me is more like it. *Is* there something there?"

She glanced again to the side of the path and unconsciously stroked the cuff of her coat, which warmed in a new sense of support.

"There is nothing there that will hurt you," said the king, reassuring her. "But now perhaps you understand my earlier warning to not leave this path or the road. It's very easy to get lost. Come, please—we don't have a lot of time. You're too tired to stay here very long, and there are things you must learn."

Luke resumed his no-nonsense pace and in a few breaths, Gwen could see another fuzzy hint of yellow light. The promise of a destination grew into a series of lamps hanging along the eaves of a long, single-story building behind an apron of hard-packed dirt. Gwen eagerly reached for the brown stone wall of the structure, relishing its cool, hard feel and the connection with something solid. As she released a deep, grateful breath, her jacket rippled as if laughing.

She ignored the wordless comment and sniffed in the faint scent of hay and horse as a petite woman in a T-shirt, riding pants, and boots approached.

"Right on time, sir."

"Mistress Nora," responded Luke with a nod. "This is my brother's new Courier, Gwen. Would you ready two horses please, and show her how?"

"Of course," said Nora, her ruddy cheeks and auburn hair glowing in the lamplight. "This way, please, Courier."

The stable mistress's brisk tone and purposeful movements echoed those of her boss; Gwen grinned and shook her head ruefully as she was led to the very wide doorway in the middle of the long structure. Inside the sweet scent of hay filled the air, accented by a hint of horse.

"Could be a perfume for the right person," she murmured, looking at the back of her guide as they passed several spacious but empty box stalls lining one side of the barn.

They continued toward one end of the building where three equine heads hung over stall doors and dark, luminous eyes watched their approach.

Nora unlatched the last door and, after giving the large dark brown occupant a kiss on the offered forehead, moved inside, rustling the thick layer of straw as she plowed her way through to where a bridle and blanket hung on the wall. Uncertain what to do, Gwen waited at the door.

"No need to be afraid, Courier, just ask for permission to enter," instructed the stable mistress, waving her hand when she noticed that Gwen had not followed her.

"Is there a secret phrase or handshake?" asked Gwen, eyeing the large animal before her, who she estimated was at least sixteen hands tall.

"Simply smile and offer a kiss," said Luke's employee as she reached for the blanket. "They just want affection."

Gwen glanced dubiously at Nora's back and then at the horse, who seemed to be watching her closely.

"All right, a kiss seems easy. Come on over, darling, and let's get acquainted."

The mare stepped forward and lowered her head to meet her guest eye to eye. Gwen leaned over and planted a solid kiss on the warm, broad forehead.

The offering accepted, the horse snuffled, raised her head, and stepped back as Nora kept talking.

"You will always find tack ready for each horse, Courier. If I am not here, just use the equipment in the stall; there should always be head-gear and a blanket. Now, we don't use traditional saddles, this modified cover offers a better connection between you and your mount. It's also quicker and easier when it comes to tacking up."

With that, the athletic, lithe woman pulled over a rather sizeable wooden box and climbed up so she could reach the horse's back. She showed Gwen how to adjust the blanket-saddle: placing it high on the withers, sliding it back, and then adjusting the girth. The headgear slipped on easily, and to Gwen's surprise, it fit loosely and did not have a bit.

The first horse done, Nora motioned to the next stall and its occupant, which looked just as large and solid as the first animal.

"Now you do it."

Gwen kept her apprehension under wraps as she left the first stall for its neighbor. The latch on the door gave easily, and the Courier found herself looking into a pair of deep-brown eyes as the horse lowered its head to her level. There was a gentleness in the movement that made her feel a little more secure in what she was about to do.

"I suppose you want a kiss too?" Gwen murmured as she puckered up and again planted her lips on a warm, smooth-haired forehead.

With a small snort, the animal accepted the greeting and moved back, crunching the straw and releasing a burst of a dried-grass aroma.

In her job as an animal control officer, Gwen had dealt with thousands of situations involving strange animals, a good number of them potentially dangerous. But she could count on one hand the number of times she had faced a horse, and none had required her to saddle it.

She reached up and ran her hand firmly along the horse's back to establish a sense of contact and quickly checked under her assignment's back end for an important piece of information.

"Well, Big Boy, allow me to apologize in advance if I seem inexperienced at this, but that's because I am. Now, your mistress Nora makes it look easy; let's see if it is."

The animal craned his head around, and Gwen could have sworn he nodded. Shaking her head and smiling to herself, she gathered the tack from its pegs on the wall and recreated her teacher's example to the best of her ability.

"Not bad I suppose, Nora, but I'm still afraid I'll put something on ass-backward. It'd just be nice to maybe have a little glue or some tacky, sticky stuff on those blankets along with the girth straps."

The brown-haired woman and the horse she had saddled waited outside the stall. They snorted in unison at the mention of something more than the girth.

"No worries, you did well. In an emergency, you can even ride without any of these trappings. My pets are very well trained and will get you to the manor safely. When you're riding just make sure you don't dismount anywhere but in the courtyard there and, of course, here at the barn. Do you understand?"

"Yes, ma'am. I don't look back in the boat, and I don't get off the horse."

"I don't know anything about the boat, Courier," said Nora with a puzzled expression, "but please take my word on what to do on the road."

Gwen raised one hand in surrender and took the reins of the horse she had readied in the other.

"Just trying to remember the list of rules."

The stable mistress just shook her head and led the way back to the main door.

Outside Luke was lounging against the wall. He accepted the reins Nora handed him, led the horse to the mounting block near the door, and got on. Gwen led her animal to the block and followed his moves, marveling at the height of her final perch as she settled into the blanket. The warmth of the animal's body seeped through the material, warming her butt and legs. Whether to balance the temperature or in an act of jealousy, Gwen felt her jacket respond with a wave of warmth.

She smiled at the sensation and leaned over to breathe in the scent of horse and stroke the animal's neck.

"Mistress Nora, what's his name?"

The interest seemed to drastically improve Nora's impression of the Courier because she smiled broadly and nodded.

"That's Roscoe."

"Roscoe?" Gwen chuckled. "Well, Roscoe, my lad, nice to meet you."

"And I am being served by Hyacinth," said Luke.

As her rider mentioned her name, the mare turned, and Gwen returned what she was sure was a nod.

"Well, now that we are all acquainted, please show me what I'm supposed to do."

Death waved his arm toward the well-groomed dirt road. It left the stable yard and disappeared into the dense fog.

"This is the only road you will need. Stay close and don't stray."

The foursome left the lighted halo of the stable and, within minutes, Gwen found herself moving in a portable pocket of visibility. She could see about six feet in any direction; beyond that it was only the tedious, impenetrable gray. Roscoe took care of his passenger, and she matched his canter effortlessly, but after achieving that goal, the initial delight of riding quickly faded.

The warmth flowing from Roscoe and the jacket balanced out the chill of the damp cloud tendrils that slithered against her face, but unconsciously straining to see into the fog began to give her a headache. When she realized what was happening, Gwen transferred her gaze to the space between Roscoe's ears and concentrated on the horse and rider in front of them.

"What do you do to pass the time, Roscoe?" she whispered to her mount as the time stretched on. "This gets dull real fast."

One of the horse's ears flicked back at her comment, and she got a snort in reply. Then Luke was slowing down and raising his hand, signaling a stop.

Hyacinth pivoted so her rider faced his guest, and after prancing for a moment, the horse stood still, not breathing hard at all.

"This is as far as we need to go," said Luke. "I think you get the idea and continuing all the way to my home won't accomplish much more, especially since I sense you are getting tired."

"If this were a real visit, Roscoe would take me all way and...What happens then?" asked Gwen, leaning forward to scratch the horse's neck.

"Someone will be waiting for you when you arrive, and we deal with whatever situation you bring."

Gwen nodded. "Are you going on home?"

"Yes. You should return to my brother by retracing our path here. Remember the rules. I expect I will see you soon."

"My best to your wife."

Luke smiled. "She'll be pleased to know the new Courier is a woman. So now, hail and farewell."

"Hail and farewell, then," replied Gwen, swaying gently as Roscoe began to turn back toward the stables. "All right, my friend, let's go home."

Without further urging, the horse launched into a smooth canter, and Gwen matched his movement. The trip back seemed shorter than the excursion out, and as they arrived at the stable, Nora was waiting at the door, an anxious look on her face.

"I trust it went well?" she asked eagerly.

"For what it was, yes, I think it did, and Roscoe was wonderful," said Gwen, sliding off the horse for the long drop to the ground. "Thank you for your services, my dear."

The horse turned and nibbled her hair, then moved on his own toward the stable and his bed. Nora reached out and shook Gwen's hand.

"Well done, Courier. Hail and farewell."

"Until next time, Nora."

As she walked back to the boat, Gwen grimaced and sighed as she realized the ride had awakened muscles in her legs she hadn't used in a long time. Her jacket sent a hint of some feeling she couldn't quite identify, but she stroked the right cuff anyway, sure that more understanding would come with time.

"A little hurtin' won't matter, but we'd better find some way to get some horseback riding in on a regular basis. Can't show up at Luke's hobbling and unable to walk."

The jacket responded with a slight squeeze.

The return boat trip was uneventful, especially now that Gwen could anticipate the vertigo. Back on the boathouse porch, she paused and turned to drink in the picturesque plantings, the shimmering river and fog, and the dark, motionless figure who sat on the dock with his back to the land. Dob had not made one sound on the trip, not even a response to her "thank you" as he helped her out of the boat.

"Who knew this was all here?" she mused. "And now it's my playground."

10

The tiny room resonated with memories of that first attempt at a live sacrifice. He, Ralph, and Emily had been a team then, and times had been good.

Adam Bardhof forced himself to put those reflections aside and concentrate on the immediate situation. He was about to take a step that could bring him closer to his goal of power—or possibly cost him his life. Striving for a sense of inner strength and purpose, he paused and then stood up to face Bayel.

"Lord, I asked for this meeting because I have a suggestion that I believe would greatly improve our communication with your community of followers."

The well-groomed god's face remained impassive. He put his hands in the pockets of the beige safari jacket he wore over his khakis and waited silently.

Trying to ignore the knot tightening in his chest and the sweat beading on his forehead, Bardhof folded his hands and continued. "Sir, we will not be able to move our efforts forward in as timely a fashion as long as you do not have a recognized spokesman to the temple faithful."

The god said nothing for a moment, as if thinking, and then he nodded slowly.

"You are correct, but while I have decided my current Spirit would not be accepting of our new practices and have stopped communicating with him, he *has* been loyal for many years, and I do not wish to see him die before his time."

"I understand and support that humane reasoning, my lord," said Adam, opening his arms to underscore his statement. "But perhaps someone else could be chosen to take on the responsibility as your voice. Spirit Piale has not made his lack of contact with you public, so whoever you chose for this position could work closely with the Spirit, and no one else would have to know that anything has changed."

The God of Joy slowly rocked back and forth, seeming to contemplate the idea, and Adam thought he detected a slight, raw chuckle before he spoke.

"And to whom would the responsibility go, my dear servant?" he finally asked with a knowing tone in his voice.

Adam felt himself begin to blush as he realized his plan might actually be accepted, and he quickly lowered his head.

"To whomever you feel would be the best candidate," he murmured.

"Hmmm. Our Emily perhaps? A woman might be the best choice to take on a new, politically delicate role."

Adam struggled to quash a sudden rush of anger. When he felt calm enough to speak, he looked at Bayel.

"My lord, if you believe Emily would be the best candidate, then so be it."

"But you do not agree," stated the god.

"No, sir, I don't. However, that may be because I lack your wisdom and insight. I would accept your decision."

"Nicely played," said Bayel as he seemed to laugh to himself again. "You have certainly learned the ways of a politician, Adam, something our Emily has not. No, I fear our Emily is too volatile and strong-willed to be my voice. She might even change my words."

There was a tense moment of silence as Bardhof forced himself to wait.

"No," said Bayel finally. "Our Emily would not be a good choice. You, however, listen to me."

"I do my best, my lord."

"And a more visible position of power would please you?"

"It would allow me to better serve you, my lord."

"Ralph. Would he support you?"

"Ralph has been with me since the beginning of my dream to make you more powerful; he won't flinch now."

"And our Emily?" asked Bayel, raising an eyebrow.

Adam paused as he weighed the possible danger of what he was about to say.

"Emily has also been with me from the start, but she has become increasingly impatient and combative. My lord, she's become a tiresome bitch."

Bayel grinned broadly and then laughed. "I was beginning to wonder if you had the balls to stand up to her."

Relief and a newfound sense of confidence washed over Adam.

"I've tried to balance my distress at her impatience with the strength and energy she has brought to our venture, but I think she's become a liability and could sway your constituency in directions that are not in your best interests."

"And what do you suggest?" prompted the god, a coy expression on his brown face.

"My lord, we are almost ready to take the step to a human offering. I propose that when the construction is complete, we give Emily the honor of consecrating your new sanctuary with her blood."

Adam braced himself and stood tall as he watched Bayel and waited for his answer. He was not disappointed.

Bayel's grin returned, and a greedy look crept into his eyes.

"Now, that is the thinking of a leader—*my* leader—Adam. Revel in what I am about to tell you: I will choose you as my new Spirit, and I will speak only through you. However, when I decide to move on this, you will work with Piale, who has been faithful all these years. You will also arrange for my celebration with our Emily."

※※※

Adam desperately hoped he had been right when he told Bayel that Ralph would support him. In his new office, he toyed with the idea of greeting his old friend from behind his recently delivered, expansive teak desk, but at the last minute opted for the friendlier venue of the white leather sofa that occupied the far wall.

Crossing his legs and draping his arm along the back of the furniture to simulate a relaxation he did not really feel, Adam waited for the knock at the door.

"Enter."

Ralph poked his head in.

"You wanted to see me?"

"Yes. Come in, please. We need to talk. Here, come sit. Can I get you anything? A drink?"

There was an awkward moment as Ralph scanned the sumptuously appointed room and ran his hand through his short, unruly black hair. He slowly moved to the opposite end of the sofa and sank onto the cushion, obviously uncomfortable.

"I heard you got a new job, Adam. This is very nice. Congratulations."

"This *is* nice, but I wouldn't be here without you, and I want you to know that I don't forget my friends and supporters. I'm sorry I didn't get the chance to tell you myself first. Things got a little busy. Now, how about a drink?"

"Yeah, sure. Thanks."

Adam strode to a side table and reached for a decanter. With his back to Ralph, he asked matter-of-factly, "How are you and Emily getting along?"

He turned as Ralph coughed, in time to catch the embarrassed, blanched look on his friend's face.

"Emily?"

"I know you're sleeping with her. It's no problem. We were done as a couple a long time ago."

Ralph accepted the drink and stared into the glass.

"Look, uh, if you would rather I didn't see her—"

"Stop. I just told you it's no problem. I just want to know how you really feel about her because I have some information I want to share, and it concerns her future."

"You two broke up, and she's the kind of girl who needs to be with someone to feel complete. I guess I was the easiest target," mumbled Ralph.

Adam banked his inner excitement.

"Target? Easiest target? Did you *not* want to be her partner?"

The other man sat up with a new, almost aggressive, energy.

"C'mon, Adam, I don't mind being second to you—it's the way we work best—but I don't need your used girlfriends too. She came to me, and I felt sorry for her. I don't really think she's involved emotionally in this, and I know I'm not."

Bardhof covered his sense of satisfaction with a sip of his drink.

"Then enjoy it while you can get it because we are going to take this community to a new level, and I want you right beside me."

"Does Bayel agree?"

"Completely. He knows how faithful you've been and agrees that Emily is becoming something of a liability."

Ralph's dark eyes were steady over the rim of his glass, but he was silent for a moment after he swallowed.

"That word 'liability' has a sinister tone to it, Adam."

"Only if you want it to. Bayel and I see this as an opportunity to give Emily a position in his church where she will forever be revered by his followers."

"Forever?"

"Forever. But, before I explain anything more, I need to know you're with me all the way. Once we take the steps I envision, there will be no turning back." The bald man peered at the other man intently.

"I am," said Ralph, a little too forcefully. "And I have to tell you I felt stupid and, yeah, hurt when I heard about your new position from the damn receptionist."

Adam slid across the sofa to grab Ralph's hand.

"And this is one of the reasons I need you so much. I'm not good with other people. I can deal with Bayel, but I need you to be my connection to everyone else. Will you do that? Will you be my right-hand man? And, by extension, that means being Bayel's top guy, after me of course," he added quickly.

Ralph grinned and snorted.

"Of course. On all counts."

11

Marcia was waiting when the Courier Stepped to the Keep from the Boathouse. The portly woman barely gave Gwen time to catch her breath—or her balance—as she handed her what looked like a granola bar.

"Eat this," ordered the Administrator in a tone that did not invite debate. "Your body needs something until you can get a decent meal. You are to Step to the Tikett Woods and meet one of the Riders. The others are at the Disturbance. I will show you the Step. Ready?"

"Tikett Woods?"

"An area of the King's lands. Now, are you ready?" asked the large woman a little sharply.

Her attitude fueled a nascent feeling of resentment in Gwen, who allowed a hint of that aggravation to color her response.

"I've met Death and returned. I believe I am ready for anything you can hand me."

Marcia just raised her eyebrows.

"Feeling our oats already, are we? That's nice, sweetie, but you have no idea what I can hand you. Now, pay attention."

The Administrator conjured a picture with a forceful wave of her giant arm, then put her hands on her hips, and stared at Gwen.

The Courier pushed aside her feelings to focus on the scene and, when she felt she had it fixed in her mind, she turned back to Marcia and cavalierly saluted her with the hand that held the food bar. She then Stepped into a clearing surrounded by tall, mature trees in full leaf.

She headed toward a cluster of wooden benches, angry with herself, and tore open the food bar.

"Idiot, you let her get to you. Don't react to her comments and sink to her level. That's what she wants. What is her problem?"

Thoughts of Marcia roiled in her mind as she scanned the perpetual purple twilight and bit into the chewy granola bar. The tart flavor of cranberries cut through the bother, and the smooth hint of honey tugged at Gwen's attention, breaking her negative thought pattern. She took a deep breath and let the frustration slip away.

"There are more important things," she murmured.

She leaned back, savoring the rich flavors of the food bar, and surveyed the field around her, especially the random groupings of ornamental grasses that seemed to glow and sparkle in the dimness.

The thick upper canopy of tree leaves cut the already-limited light, leaving the floor of the woods in deeper shadows, but Gwen was still able to see quite well. She wondered briefly if Nat's wine had anything to do with that and received a brief, deep back rub from her jacket.

"Oh, you can do that too? Don't stop; it feels great," murmured the King's newest employee as she stretched and enjoyed the release of tension. "You really are amazing, and I'm glad you are mine."

The black material suddenly melted against her, and a new, intense sense of acceptance and oneness overwhelmed Gwen. She gasped as a tentative caress touched parts of her mind and triggered an intimacy of thought she had never before experienced. It offered the promise of never again being alone, and that unexpectedly brought tears to her eyes.

"Your name is Nan, and you are one of a kind. When I end this job, you go with me."

This time the hug from the coat was deliberate and intense, with no hints of the playfulness of earlier interactions.

The granola bar dangled from her hand, forgotten, as Gwen sank deeply into the embrace, closed her eyes, and turned inward to explore the offer of friendship and much more. She was so involved with the experience that she was unaware of Jensen's approach until he was directly in front of her, calling her name.

Startled, she quickly sat up and blinked self-consciously.

The Rider was mounted on a dappled gray horse and holding the reins of another. His face was impassive, although Gwen thought one side of his mouth turned slightly higher.

"Well met, Courier. *Is* everything well?"

"Quite well," responded Gwen, deciding to believe it was a smile and not a sneer that he offered. "Quite well, indeed."

She straightened her jacket. "We're just getting to know each other."

"Ja, that's good. Has it revealed a name?"

"Yes—"

"*Stop!*" interrupted the big man, holding up a hand. "That is enough for me to know. The name is for you only. To share is a very special event that should be determined by the coat itself. To know you are bonding so well, though, that is good. Come now, we must meet the others."

Gwen used the bench as a mounting block and settled into a simple but more conventional saddle than those used on Luke's side of the River.

She sighed as she shifted and acknowledged a few already-protesting muscles.

"Do you need help with something?" asked Jensen as he moved next to her.

"No, I'm just amazed that in this one day I end up on two different horses when I haven't ridden in years. I'm gonna hurt. I am definitely going to hurt."

Again, there was that slight curl of the lip, and then Jensen led off.

The horses' hooves made a soft pounding sound on the forest floor as they picked up speed. Alternating between a trot in the clearer areas and a walk through the denser parts of the woods, the pair cleared the trees. The horses slowed to splash through a small running stream at the base of a line of brownish hills that stretched to the right and left as far as Gwen could see. On the far side of the water, the rest of the Riders were lounging in an outcropping of rocks. A small fire burned, and, woven in with the smell of wood, Gwen could pick out something savory. She eyed the two pots over the flames intently as her stomach growled.

Everyone rose as the newcomers approached; Gwen was pleased at the look of concern she was sure she spotted on her grandfather's face.

Gwen felt Nan warm slightly as Nathao strode to the front of the group.

"Any problems?"

"No, sir, not a one," said Gwen, swinging down from the saddle, making sure she did not wince at her complaining muscles. "And here?"

"We have located the Disturbance. This way."

The King abruptly turned and strode toward the nearest hill. The Riders followed with the exception of Armen, who took the horses from her and Jensen and motioned for them to go with the group.

Gwen hurried to keep up with the King and felt a battery of communication from Nan that she only partly understood. At the crest of the hill, Jensen crouched down on her right while Barnabas appeared on her left.

A ribbon of dense white cloud floated along the bottom of the valley below them, undulating slowly around and through the sparse vegetation. An occasional blast of bright light flashed inside as if the long, filmy form contained a rotating lighthouse beacon.

Gwen also felt, as much as heard, a faint hum.

"What's going on?" she whispered to her immediate companions.

"I'm not sure," said the bigger Rider. "It seems similar to what James said he witnessed the first time, but I think it's a lot bigger now."

"I wouldn't mind going down to check it out. It seems to be inviting us in and might actually be some fun," murmured Gwen.

She shrugged off a sudden series of contractions from Nan and stretched to get a closer look, enjoying the sense of welcome she felt coming from below.

"No," hissed her grandfather, grabbing the back of her collar and dragging her back.

Her jacket and Jensen concurred.

"We don't go down until the King orders us," reprimanded the taller Rider, firmly laying his hand on her shoulder, reinforcing her grandfather's coarser approach.

Nan went limp as if in relief.

They watched in silence for a few more minutes, and then Jensen deliberately guided her back below the crest with the others as Barnabas followed. The group settled halfway down the hill, and the King spoke first.

"Jensen, you talked to James last. What do you think?"

"I think it's growing," said the blue-eyed Rider. "That is more than a puff. And, the Courier says she felt it pulling at her."

Gwen turned to him in surprise. "You didn't? It seemed to be asking us to come down and join it."

"No," replied Jensen matter-of-factly.

Gwen looked around the circle of businesslike faces, all focused on her. "Anyone feel it? And a hum?"

The only answer was a collective negative shake of heads.

"You are more sensitive," said Nathao, breaking the silence. "Alice was too. She undoubtedly felt the power, but missed the danger. So did Saber, her guide dog. Be glad you were with the Riders.

"Now," continued the King as Gwen stored away the information and ignored what felt like an *I told you so* from Nan. "It is enough that we know it is growing and trying to lure people here, because it is obvious who is responsible."

"Bayel," said Claire.

"No question," agreed Eli.

The puzzled expressions around the circle prompted a sigh of exasperation from Claire and the question, "Remember how Bayel is depicted in his shrines?"

"Of course," said Gwen, excitedly jumping into the conversation, feeling truly confident for the first time around the Riders. "He's the life force holding all joy. They show him as a sparkling cloud that descends to envelop you in rapture. It's done different ways in different temples. Some use glitter and paint, while others have latticed walls they build fires behind so the flames sparkle through the engraved image."

"How do you know all that?" Barnabas asked his granddaughter suspiciously.

"I read a lot," she replied lightly.

"There is also the prevalent use of drugs and alcohol to induce what is supposed to be a state of ecstasy and communion with other members of the congregation," added Claire with a smug grin.

Gwen frowned slightly at the female Rider before turning back to her scowling grandfather. "I have no idea what she's talking about."

"So, the appearance fits," continued the King, deftly bringing the conversation back to the issue at hand. "But not the evil and the deaths we have suffered."

"Bayel has never been associated with killing, but he may have changed," suggested Eli quietly. "Gods do that over time."

"As worshippers change, the nature of the god can change," agreed Rakeem.

Claire leaned forward. "According to the latest numbers from the Promethean League, there's been a resurgence of interest in his church, although they don't offer any reasons."

Barnabas then posed the question on everyone's mind. "Why would he bother you, Nat?"

"I do not know. I have already brought in Lord Veron, who has concurred with my original suspicion. He has agreed to talk to Bayel if our initial efforts fail."

"He's already killed two of your people," noted Eli.

"All the more reason to talk to him with the support of the Lord of Justice. That kind of behavior is very unlike Bayel."

"What if he *has* changed? What do we do then?" pressed Claire.

"First, we deal with the current situation. I do not want this Disturbance to grow any stronger and threaten visitors' dreams," said the King, rising to his feet in one graceful move and effectively ending any more discussion. "It cannot be allowed to remain."

With that, he began walking back up the hill, not bothering to hide his presence this time when he reached the top. The Riders followed and arranged themselves in a line on either side of him.

Gwen stood between Nathao and Eli and almost immediately began to sense the pull from the valley again. She tentatively stretched out her hand to better enjoy the feeling, but her jacket began to urgently pinch her and project a new sense into her mind that Gwen could only identify as whining. Annoyed, she moved to tap a sleeve in displeasure, and in that one moment when her concentration shifted, a surge of evil and pain blasted into her mind, threatening to engulf her thoughts and burn away her identity.

For several frantic seconds, she struggled to hold back the power as it battered her mental defenses again and again. Then it was gone, and she fell to her knees, gasping. As she looked up, she realized Nathao was in front of her, acting as a shield and pointing at the Disturbance with both hands.

"Be gone!" ordered the King. His deep voice shook the valley and echoed in Gwen's bones, bolstering her shaken confidence.

Her hands scraped against the coarse vegetation and small rocks of the hill, but she did not feel the minor scratches as she leaned around her employer to see into the valley. The ribbon cloud was dimmer, and ragged holes were beginning to appear. Slowly the slender entity began to shed wisps of dandruff that melted into nothing. In moments, the Disturbance was gone.

Gwen exhaled loudly as she stood and wiped dirt from her hands, still concentrating on the spot where the intruder had been.

"You were right about the evil. That was nasty," she said matter-of-factly.

"Did you doubt me?" rumbled the King, also watching the valley, his arms crossed and his face stony. "But it is well enough that you felt it because you will recognize it if it develops again.

"I trust you are also now more aware of the potential dangers we face. Until you are familiar with our political situation in the Pantheon, do not try to make friends with something that may be a delegate for another god. They do not all mean you well."

"Understood," replied Gwen as she shrugged off another *I told you so* squeeze from Nan.

She trailed the Riders as they silently navigated their way down to where Armen and the horses waited. Nathao told them to take some time to eat, then walked away.

"We like to think he needs his space," said her grandfather, coming up beside her as the tall figure crossed the stream and disappeared into the trees on the other side. "But we don't really know what he does when he goes off like that."

Claire, Eli, and Jensen talked quietly among themselves as they began opening the saddlebags propped up against one of the bigger rocks.

Gwen moved to help and join the conversation, but her grandfather and Rakeem both interceded and steered her to a nearby boulder.

"Rest. You've already accomplished a lot today," said the dark Rider. "Rest for a moment."

As she sank to the ground, the Courier suddenly realized just how tired she really was and gratefully leaned against the rock. Her jacket cushioned her back as she quietly sighed, closed her eyes, and allowed herself to relax into the calmness and peace radiating from Nan. She was somewhat annoyed when, after what seemed like a just a few minutes, someone invaded the tranquility, shaking her shoulder gently and telling her to wake up.

She struggled to pry her eyes open and squinted at the sight of Barnabas kneeling in front of her, offering a cup.

"Grandpa," she murmured.

"Drink this, girl. You've had a bit of a nap."

"Nap?"

The liquid from the cup was cool until it hit the back of her throat and sparked a coughing fit as it burned its way down to her stomach.

"Blech! What is that?"

"Something to replace some of the energy you used today. He said you were over with his brother longer than he expected. Drink again."

Gwen peered into the cup at the ubiquitous red liquid and then suspiciously eyed Barnabas.

"Drink it," ordered her grandfather quietly.

Wrinkling her nose in distaste, Gwen took another sip and, this time, when she swallowed, the burning became a pleasantly warm, invigorating sensation that made finishing the drink a pleasure.

"How long was I out?" she asked, stretching and handing the cup back to Barnabas. "And why did that happen?"

Nathao suddenly appeared next to her. He lowered himself into a squat and balanced effortlessly on his toes.

"Even with Luke's protection and the strengths I have woven into your jacket, you are not entirely immune to the effects of my brother's world. Sleep is the way your body recharges after fighting the pull of Death there. The more you cross, the stronger you will become."

"Luke did say something about needing enough rest," said Gwen, struggling not to yawn but losing that battle.

Nathao took her wrist, and a very pleasant tingling moved up from his warm, dry grasp into her chest and the rest of her body. As the King released his hold, Gwen took a deep breath and stretched once more.

"Gods, I feel fantastic."

Barnabas glowered at the King.

"You never did that for me."

"I am aware of that," replied Nathao without any expression as he stood in one easy movement. "Get Gwen some food. Once she has eaten, we will talk."

Barnabas gestured to Armen, who brought over a bowl of something hot.

Gwen took a deep breath, savoring the aroma. "That smells wonderful. Did you make it, Armen?"

The grizzled Rider nodded curtly and turned away to walk back to his fire.

Too hungry to notice the abrupt response, Gwen dug into the thick meal. She made an effort to savor every spoonful and not slurp it down, even though she was suddenly ravenous. At the same time, she took the opportunity between mouthfuls to watch the Riders interact as they cleaned up the site.

The talk was subdued with a few bursts of laughter, usually after Eli or Claire said something. Everyone was involved, suggesting no one was exempt from physical chores, and she remembered her grandfather's comment that they were all equals.

With one more equal than the others, she thought as a silent Claire came over to take her now-empty bowl. The green-eyed Rider paused for a moment before she offered her hand to help Gwen stand.

The Courier nodded her thanks and hoped she had passed whatever evaluation seemed to have been made. She wanted to know this other woman as a friend and possible ally in dealing with the testosterone-heavy band that was gathering around the still glowing cook fire.

Gwen followed Claire and settled between her and Eli. He was the first to speak.

"What's the plan, Nat? Obviously we have to stop Bayel."

"We will keep any other incidents contained and short. We cannot let that evil infect anyone's dreams, and I will not lose more staff."

"So what do you order?" asked Claire, hugging her knees to her chest.

"We watch the area closely and destroy any new Disturbance as soon as it appears. Barnabas, Claire: you will ride out from here to maintain the quadrant. Armen, Jensen: you will spell them later.

"We will also talk. Gwen, you will meet with Bayel's top priest, called the Spirit of Bayel. Determine why these encroachments are occurring. Then make sure he understands that I will not tolerate them.

"Rakeem and Eli, you will accompany her."

"You want me to tell Bayel's Spirit to keep his god out of your backyard?" asked Gwen skeptically.

Nathao regarded her calmly. "Soon you will feel very tired. While you are asleep, I will give you a Dream that will tell you what to say and do. As you already know, it is not a difficult process, and it is thorough and efficient. You will have the words to say what I wish expressed."

"Tired? I'm not tired. That drink and energy boost you gave me just a little bit ago, they did the trick. Hey, I could go another couple of hours," protested Gwen with a wave of her arm.

Nathao said nothing, and she quickly scanned the Riders for some sign of support. No one moved, and her stomach tightened at the thought she had just made a major blunder.

Then Nan offered her a pat across the back, and a hint of acceptance touched her mind. To buy a few seconds of time and rein in her embarrassment, the Courier shook out her long hair before she looked again at Nathao and tugged the jacket's lapel.

"She says you're right."

"We needed you awake for this conference. The energy is temporary. Remember, I am the King of Dreams and when I tell you to sleep, you will sleep."

As the King spoke, a sense of deep lethargy began to seep through Gwen's body. With a small, annoyed sigh, she realized she had no choice but to surrender. She leaned over toward Eli, who caught her as she slumped.

※❈※

Claire helped him ease Gwen onto a thick blue blanket spread out by Rakeem and Jensen while Barnabas hovered in the background.

Nathao knelt at his Courier's side, and after a few breaths, placed his hands on either side of her head. He closed his eyes and stayed that way a few seconds before leaning back on his heels.

"She is very tired." He paused and nodded at Rakeem. "You and Eli stay here until she wakes. Make certain she returns safely to her home. I have explained everything to her, and she will give you the instructions and details you need for the trip to Bayel's temple."

※❈※

Gwen reluctantly opened her eyes just a bit and squinted for a few moments at the purple eternal-evening sky overhead. With a small grunt, she rolled to her side and spotted Eli at the nearby fire.

"Welcome back." He grinned.

She yawned and propped herself up on an elbow.

"You're actually smiling at me."

"I'm more easily won over than some of the others. You've done well with everything thrown at you so quickly. James once confided to me that he never really liked the trips across the River. He said they sapped all his energy, even when he was prepared. Are you hungry?"

The unchanging twilight gave her no clue how long she had been sleeping, but her stomach's rumbling suggested it had been quite a while. Nan's presence lightly touched her mind and, as she got to her feet and stretched, the jacket matched her movements.

"Mmmm. Very. And I *was* tired. That thing the King did—you know, give me energy only to take it away again—there isn't a lot of that sleep-awake-sleep-awake business, is there? And where is everyone?" she asked, scanning the empty campsite.

"Following orders. Barnabas and Claire are riding a circuit around the area where Bayel has been showing up. Armen and Jensen are with the King. Rakeem is also doing a bit of scouting and should be back shortly."

The Rider brought over a big mug of juice and a granola bar just like the one Marcia had given her, gods only knew how long ago. She slowly paced the campsite as she ate, dissecting the instructions and information Nathao had left in her head. As she swallowed the last bite, she refocused on Eli, who was back at the fire.

"I'm supposed to go home and rest. Then you, Rakeem, and I get to the heart of this matter. I do remember everything he put up here," she said, tapping her forehead. "And the whole process isn't that bad."

Eli just shrugged. "I've seen it work. I've also seen it change people."

"So my grandfather hinted. How many people, and I'm assuming they were Couriers, have you seen changed? How long have you worked for Nathao?"

Eli cocked his head and ignored the first question completely. "Longer than you."

Gwen offered her most unguarded, genuine grin.

"It's just that you seem more comfortable and self-assured than most of the others. How long does that take?"

The Rider paused and before he could answer, they both heard and felt the soft pounding of hooves.

"Well, here comes Rakeem," Gwen observed with another smile, wagging a finger at her companion. "Saving you from an answer and ending an awkward situation. How do we get back to my place?"

The gangly Rider rose and gazed at her thoughtfully as Rakeem arrived.

"There's a Step not too far from here. We take that."

✖❖✖

The ride under the tall trees to the new Step was short, but Gwen had to admit she would never be able to find the nondescript spot again.

"How do you guys know where these things are?" she asked as she twisted in the saddle to survey the area with a critical eye.

"Maps and a Nathao-version compass," said Eli, holding up a small, flat, round device that had been sitting on his mount's withers, just in front of the saddle. "You don't really think we know the entire realm, do you?"

"Well," shrugged the Courier, "you *are* Nathao's Riders, and you *are* in your element, aren't you? I would assume you know your way around."

Eli shook his head with another surprising smile. "Some of that is so wrong. There are a few of us who couldn't find their way across the quad at the Keep if there weren't a path."

Gwen dismounted and flinched as her legs protested the time in the saddle.

"I hope I don't become one of those."

"The Couriers I've known have been eerily good at finding their way around these lands, given practice and time. So, for you, the omens are positive."

The gray-haired Rider tucked away the location device in a backpack that hung from his saddle, then slid easily to the ground.

Rakeem was already removing the saddle and hackamore from his horse.

"We'll store these in the chest over there," said the dark-skinned man, nodding toward a large polished wooden box under a tree. "The animals live out here around the Steps."

"Don't they need to be brushed down or something?" asked Gwen dubiously as the animals began wandering off. "The horses at Luke's are in a stable and seem to get lots of doting care."

"Well, I certainly don't know about Luke's operations," said Rakeem, clearing his throat and sounding a little defensive. "But our four-legged friends show up at the stables back at the Keep when they want attention."

The equipment disappeared into the trunk, and the Riders picked up their packs. Eli gestured for Gwen to open a Window to her home and then to Step first.

It was quiet as they moved from the basement to the first-floor kitchen, where Alana had left a nightlight on and a note on the counter. Becky had done well that evening, but the nanny suggested that Gwen see her off to school in the morning. Nan concurred with a light wave of warmth.

"OK, guys, what time tomorrow?" whispered the Courier, turning to her escort.

"We'll be here right after your daughter leaves," said Eli, also reading the note.

"I'll be ready," mumbled Gwen through a stifled yawn.

"Get to sleep," said Rakeem gently as he laid his hand on her arm. "You did a lot today, Courier."

After the men left, Gwen struggled to keep her eyes open long enough to set the alarm on her radio and then gratefully fell into bed and a deep, restorative sleep, courtesy of the King's dream.

12

~

"What happened?' demanded Bayel, manifesting in the almost-finished underground sanctuary. "He has a new one, and I almost took—" He paused. "Her. I almost took her. But Nathao interrupted."

Adam bowed low.

"My lord, we didn't plan on the Dream King's presence. This was meant to entice only the Riders, so you could drink more deeply and gain strength against your target."

"What about the new one? She reached out to me. I want her."

Ralph glanced at Bardhof, then stepped forward, his arms wide.

"We will find out about the new Rider, my lord. She must be a replacement for the one you already enjoyed. What a sweet success it would be to take the new one too. But until we know more, enjoy the strength our sacrifice has given you and know we will continue to build your power step by step."

"Hmm." Bayel absently toyed with the buttons on the cuffs of the salmon-colored silk shirt that exposed a large section of his hairless bronze chest. The shirt was tucked into tight-fitting red leather pants that outlined well-defined muscles and ended just above rope sandals on immaculately manicured feet.

"Nathao now knows I am strong enough to continue to enter his lands; I expect he will retaliate again in some soft, ineffective, political way. When he does that, it will signal to the Pantheon how weak he truly has become. We must be prepared to take whatever advantage presents itself. I want this power you have promised."

Emily moved to stand between the two men and smiled fearlessly at the well-groomed god.

"Lord Bayel, you are the focus of everything we do. We do not wish to move faster than is safe or beneficial for you."

The God of Joy smiled for the first time that visit, and Emily practically purred as she inched closer.

"To the uneducated, King Nathao may appear to have position and strength superior to yours, but we know better; soon you will be able to reveal your true nature to the masses. Those same masses will give you the power to claim your rightful place among the gods and shower you with adulation and respect. Please do not fret."

The lean, tall god pinned her with his gaze.

"Fret? I do not *fret*, lovely Emily, but I do *want*. And now I want Nathao and that woman."

"And they will be delivered," replied the woman in a placating, almost patronizing voice as she bowed.

Adam and Ralph glanced at each other over the bent figure of their colleague and then turned their attention to Bayel, who was considering the top of Emily's curly head with a calculating gaze.

13

The chilly wind at the school bus stop kept conversation to a minimum, and after the kids were gone, the adults quickly scattered. As she jogged back to her house, Gwen reviewed the King's Dream and organized her thoughts.

In the kitchen, she pulled off her gloves and grabbed a tissue as her thawing nose began to run. From their places at the large rectangular table, Alana and the newly arrived Rakeem and Eli commented on her red face.

"This jacket may keep a lot of me warm, but not everything, and it's raw out there," she retorted. "As you sit here sipping your hot coffee."

"We have a few minutes," observed Rakeem, lifting his cup in salute to Alana.

Gwen sat down and put her hands on her face to help warm it up.

"Alana, the car keys are on—"

"The counter, where they always are," interrupted the nanny. "I'll be at the bus stop for Becky. Don't worry. Everything here is under control. You go to work."

"Well, gentlemen, as the lady says, everything here is under control. Finish your coffee, and off we go."

"A moment, please. Civilized behavior requires we give this brew its proper attention," said Rakeem as he breathed in the aroma coming from his cup before promptly draining it. "Eli, you ready?"

"Not quite," said the older-looking man. "I don't relish scalding my throat. I'll never understand how you do that." He slurped the hot liquid loudly in protest and then sighed. "I suppose that will have to do. My thanks, Alana, perhaps next time I will be permitted to finish it all."

At the Basement Step, Rakeem opened a Window to the chapel in Haliburum and made sure Gwen got a good look so she could remember it.

"Right," she said after studying the view for a moment. "Now we have to find"—here she paused to sift through the information Nathao had given her—"Laciane. She's the Guidant, Mother Laciane. We have to find her."

"We deal with her quite often," said Eli. "She's very competent."

Gwen Stepped after Rakeem into a room very similar to the ones at the Keep and the hospital. Here the chairs were upholstered in pale-violet twill damask with a light blue pattern of feathers. The pale-blue walls echoed the motif with random feather stencils in white and violet.

Nan rippled and offered a sense of support and excited anticipation, which Gwen acknowledged with a slight shrug. She moved to follow Rakeem to the door but was stopped by Eli's hand on her arm.

"Let him announce our arrival this one time," said the Rider, motioning for her to stay where she was. "Laciane may not know Nat has chosen a new Courier; this way no one is surprised."

Gwen crossed her arms and narrowed her deep blue eyes. "Are you afraid I'll embarrass you?"

"First impressions last forever," countered Eli. "This is more to make sure she's not caught off-guard. Laciane is important to us, plus we like her, so we don't want her to feel, oh, ambushed, I suppose. This will only take a minute. Her office is just down the hall."

They waited in silence until Rakeem's expressionless face reappeared.

"Please come this way. the Mother is anxious to meet you, Courier."

"Pray tell, are there any last-minute special instructions the King may have forgotten to give me?" asked Gwen, still a little annoyed.

"Just be polite," said Eli, ignoring the Courier's sarcasm. "Manners are valued."

A low-level din of conversation filled the well-lit, wood-paneled hallway. People in gray pants and tunics, or in long robes, rustled past on business, moving aside to clear the way for Gwen and the Riders with a nod or a murmured greeting. The trio negotiated the brief walk to the Guidant's outer office, where the young man at the desk jumped to his feet.

"Courier, Rider; Mother Laciane says please go right in."

"Thank you, Preston," replied Eli as he ushered Gwen ahead of him into the office, not allowing her any time to talk.

Inside, Mother Laciane stood next to a large desk neatly littered with piles of books and journals. The petite woman seemed to glide toward Gwen as she offered her hand and a smile.

"Courier, welcome to the service of the King. It's a pleasure to be able to assist with whatever errand our lord has given you."

Gwen could not help but return the warm smile and firm handshake. The aura of authority around the woman was palpable, and Gwen was sure that her dark eyes missed little as they quickly assessed her. Nan seemed very excited.

"Please, sit," said Laciane, waving to the chair at the side of her desk. She moved back to her own seat behind the books and rang a bell. The acolyte they had passed outside appeared at the door.

"Preston, see that we are not interrupted."

The young man bowed calmly, but Gwen thought he seemed a little nervous.

"Yes, Mother. No interruptions."

"Thank you."

"Are they always in such awe?" asked Gwen curiously as Laciane leaned back.

The Guidant paused for a moment at the question and then nodded a bit.

"In awe? If you had decided to give your life to a particular god, and, suddenly three of his chosen servants appeared, how would you feel? I may be a veteran of these visits, but it is still a pleasant rein-forcement to actually see you and know the King we worship exists and remembers who we are. For us mere mortals, it is something to stir the embers of our faith."

"Faith, yes," echoed Gwen, wryly thinking of her own mixed feelings about Nathao and picking up on Laciane's comment that separated her from "mere mortals." She still felt quite mortal.

"And, remember, faith can weaken if it isn't nourished with the proper spiritual food. Just as a god grows weak without the faith of his or her constituency, so the constituency needs acknowledgment if it is to remain strong in its faith.

"Now, what can I do for you, Courier?" The Guidant smiled, folding her hands on her desk after the mini-sermon.

"I must talk to the head priest for Bayel, the Spirit of Bayel. Nathao, um, our lord, believes you would be the most persuasive in getting us an audience."

"Bayel?" Laciane frowned. "I can certainly do it. I've known Carmen Piale since before we took vows. I never understood why he stayed with Bayel, but then, that's faith, isn't it?"

"I suppose," agreed Gwen with a noncommittal nod. "How soon do you think we could do this?"

"Let me ring him right now," offered the Guidant. "I'm not sure of his schedule these days. I know they have undertaken a major building project, and I think Carmen has been very busy with that. But let me try. In the meantime, why don't you three wait in the chapel?"

"Give the believers a thrill." Gwen smiled, trying to seem friendly and down-to-earth.

"Give the believers food for their faith," replied Laciane, shaking a slender finger at her visitor. "As I said earlier, just as a god grows weak without our faith, so we need the gods' acknowledgment of us to remain strong."

"Sorry, forgot," said Gwen, now quite sure the Riders were unhappy with her performance. Nan's reassuring presence did nothing to help her confidence.

Her discomfort was obvious, and the Mother softened her tone.

"No, *I* am sorry, Courier. I often forget that Nathao chooses his closest staff from among those who doubt, so you are new to this. However, I guarantee that eventually you *will* believe as we do.

"Now, go help those in the chapel who could use a little one-on-one time to bolster their faith. Go show yourselves."

Gwen followed the Riders down the bustling hall to a set of double doors that led to a large, but near-empty, gathering space. Once there, her escort turned to head for several large sets of doors that she expected led to the main sanctuary, but before they took two steps, Gwen grabbed their sleeves and pulled them aside to a nearby closet.

"Help me here, guys—what are we supposed to do? Sit and be stared at in there?"

"We actually go to the chapels on a regular basis," explained Eli quietly. "We Riders are expected to talk to the faithful, counsel them, and offer support. So, what Laciane said makes sense. You won't have to do it a lot; just watch us, and if you want to try, we can back you up."

"All right, I'll watch. And instinctively I understand that these people need some positive feedback, but this faith is almost childlike in its innocence."

"Again, as the Mother said, it's a two-way relationship," countered Rakeem. "We reassure the faithful that their god remembers and values them, and *they* remain strong in their support of the King. It is *that* faith that gives Nathao the power he needs to stand up to challenges like Bayel."

"And this is not just for the King," added Eli. "Suppose Bayel's intrusions begin to interfere with normal operations in Nat's realm? What do you think would happen if everyone's dreams became nightmares?"

Gwen looked from one Rider to the other and shrugged.

The tall, scrawny man crossed his arms and raised his eyebrows. "They would lose faith and turn to another god for comfort."

In a flash, it came together for Gwen, and she pursed her lips. "If that were to happen, the King loses power, becomes vulnerable to more attacks, and eventually could be destroyed. That would not be good for us, would it?"

Eli smiled grimly. "With no constituency there is no employer, no one with whom to align ourselves. That means no protection. We would be targets and expendable."

"What god would trust us?" continued Rakeem. "And what would you do with something you couldn't trust?"

"I'd delete it," murmured Gwen.

"Exactly. In fact, my dear colleague, have you considered who among us would be in the greatest danger if anyone in the Pantheon were to make a successful move against the King?"

When Gwen said nothing, Rakeem mirrored Eli and crossed his arms while thoughtfully considering a point in the air above her head.

"Someone perceived to be *very* close to Nathao. In a one-of-a-kind position. Hmmm, could that possibly be the Courier for the King of Dreams?" he mused, still looking at nothing in particular.

Eli picked up the lesson. "Whose mind does the King enter? To whom does he give special Dreams? Who speaks for him? Marcia may run things at home, but the Courier represents him where it counts: here. We Riders are secondary."

Nan sent a brief pulse of energy, and Gwen briskly straightened the jacket and tossed her hair back while standing straighter herself.

"Then, may I strongly suggest you get the hell into that chapel, Riders, and do your job?" she ordered. "I never imagined there were politics and in-fighting in the Pantheon. I just thought everybody prayed and tithed. So what *do* we do?"

"We sit and wait. They come up to us."

"And?"

The riders both shrugged.

"Improvise," said Eli.

⁂

Nan was oozing contentment as Gwen sat quietly on one of the many pillows in the dim, gray, cavernous room, trying to blend into the back wall while the Riders moved farther out among the faithful. She watched as they walked to different parts of the chapel and sat down. As Eli had said, people slowly began to approach, and there were quiet, intent discussions that often ended with a gentle touch on the arm, shoulder, or top of a bowed head.

After watching nearly an hour's worth of the interactions, the Courier let her eyes and mind wander. Gazing around the vast open space, she wondered why all of Nathao's holdings were called chapels; to her, this met the criteria of a cathedral at least.

The vivid stained-glass windows set high in the walls glowed, giving life to scenes of rest and sleep. Gwen did not recognize them all, but from where she sat, she could pick out some of the more popular ones, including the Dreaming Child, the Sacred Pillow of Rest, and the Holy Feather, the symbol most often used to represent the King.

Most of the outside light remained trapped near the ceiling, with very little settling down to the level of the worshippers. The effect was dramatic.

Thick gray candles in sconces on the smooth gray stone walls of the spacious rectangular sanctuary supplemented the subdued natural light but left the many small nooks along the walls in shadow. There, Gwen knew, supplicants would be meditating and reaching for communion with their King.

She was so engrossed in her observations that she did not notice when someone sat next to her. Startled at the sound of a cleared throat, she turned and jumped slightly.

"I'm sorry, Rider, I didn't mean to startle you," whispered the wide-eyed young man who was sitting cross-legged with his clenched hands in his lap.

"Yes?"

"I had hoped you, well, the King...I mean, I came here not really expecting—" The youth grew red with embarrassment. "I don't know what I expected. Actually, I didn't think there'd be anything to this business at all."

Gwen remained expressionless, hiding her own fright that this boy might actually want some guidance. She tentatively reached for Nan, but there was no response.

"What are you hoping for?" she asked calmly.

"Aren't you supposed to help me with this?" he asked in frustration.

"With what? What are you looking for?"

The supplicant sighed. "I don't know. There's so much being taken from me right now, I need something to hold onto. I thought I had lost my dreams, but decided to come here one more time before—"

The teenager's head bowed, and Gwen thought for a moment that he would cry. Looking frantically toward the room for Eli or Rakeem, she saw they were both busy and of no immediate help.

Remembering what she had seen the Riders do, the new Courier took a deep, quiet breath and reached out to touch the boy's hand.

"Tell me," she said. He looked up and the pain in his brown eyes went right to her heart. "Tell me your dream's desire."

"I want a goal and meaning in my life. I can't find my purpose for being here. I want a place to belong, where I feel valued."

"Did you ever think that's asking for a lot at one time? Maybe you should break it down to something like, oh, what you want to be when you grow up?" suggested Gwen.

She maintained a concerned but composed exterior as the young petitioner ignored her comments and began a litany of his trials and tribulations.

"The bottom line," interjected the Courier when he finally paused for breath, "is that you want someone to solve all your problems for you."

The boy looked startled. "No, I need help, support."

"Look into yourself and be honest. If support and guidance are what you truly will accept, the King will help you. If you want an across-the-board solution to all your perceived issues, I'm sorry to tell you there is nothing here for you, or anywhere else for that matter. The gods do not bail you out. At least the honest ones don't."

The youth lowered his eyes and was silent for a moment.

"Thank you for showing me that insight into myself," he finally murmured.

"Now that you've started the journey, see it through. You may not like the first answers you come up with, but persevere, and the King will help you."

Gwen fought a smug smile. She was very pleased with herself for offering what she felt was sage advice and a creative analogy. She could not wait to tell the others what a fabulous job she had done and how this was not difficult at all.

That confidence vanished in a flash when the boy asked, "Would you give me the King's blessing, Rider? I feel it would strengthen me as I try to find my way."

"Blessing?" breathed the Courier.

"Yes, blessing. Or are you saying I don't deserve it? Am I not worthy?" blurted the boy as panic began to show in his face.

"Of course, of course, you deserve a blessing from the King," Gwen reassured him as she struggled to cover her own growing sense of confusion. "I'm just trying to decide which would be best for your situation."

She cast desperately about in her mind for an appropriate phrase that she had heard somewhere, but there was nothing. Nan remained silent.

Trying to appear confident, she placed her hand on the bowed head.

"Nathao, King of Dreams." She suddenly found some words she hoped would do. "Our King sees you when you're sleeping. He knows when you are awake. He knows if you've been bad, or good—"

"For goodness' sake," finished a hushed voice next to her. Taking her hand from the boy's head, a very relieved Gwen turned to find Rakeem.

"Take those thoughts, hold them close, and Nathao himself will be with you," the bemused Rider told the confused-looking youth as he raised him from the pillow. "Take a moment to meditate before leaving the chapel. It will give you strength."

The boy nodded and hurried off, clearing the way for Rakeem to claim the space on the vacant gray pillow.

"Wherever did you ever come up with that blessing?" he asked, settling down and trying not to grin.

"It just happened to be somewhere in the recesses of my mind and seemed to have all the key buzz words, you know? Hell, Rakeem, I've never blessed anyone before!"

"That's obvious, but a Santa Claus benediction? The jolly old elf is not part of our tradition. I don't know how the King will take that."

"Trust me, he's laughing himself silly," retorted Gwen, a little hurt that her creative effort with the boy was unappreciated and then annoyed when her jacket suddenly reestablished contact with a light mind touch.

She settled back with a sharp tap on Nan's cuff and let Rakeem handle the worshippers who began approaching. After a few minutes, Eli came and sat with them in companionable silence, so Gwen was able to compare his style of counseling with that of his partner. Before she had the chance to take on another case by herself, Mother Laciane's aide appeared with a request that they follow him back to the office.

As they left the sanctuary, Gwen glanced back and saw dozens of eyes watching their departure. They dipped if she caught their gaze, but she noticed they always came back for more.

Once in the Guidant's office, it was a different story. Here was an individual who knew what was real in her world.

"I've finally been able to contact Carmen Piale," she began briskly. "He had planned to take this afternoon off, but says he can stay to meet with you. Obviously, he asked me what it was about; I told him I didn't know. Can you fill me in? Is there something we should be concerned about?"

Gwen frowned as she sorted through her memory and the instructions in Nathao's Dream.

"The King didn't say anything that would preclude telling you what's going on. Actually, I think your input would be very valuable." She turned to Rakeem and Eli. "Gentlemen?"

"Do what you think is best," said Eli while Rakeem remained silent.

Accepting the leadership role, Gwen quickly outlined the situation suggesting Bayel's involvement.

"We've got to stop these intrusions. I will talk to this Spirit and try to find out what he knows and why this is happening at all. Tell me, is Piale opinionated? Is he a difficult person to get to know?"

Laciane shook her head, her dark eyes suddenly bright as she considered what she had just learned.

"No, he's very open and flexible; I find it hard to imagine him involved in any sort of intrigue. He never was much for backroom politics, and

I suspect that's why he has lasted so long with Bayel, a god known for his whims. But now, Piale is expecting you, and Bayel's temple is quite a distance from here. Do you know the city at all?"

Gwen shook her head. "I hate to admit it, but I've never been here before."

"Ah," said the Mother with a quick smile. "You will learn to love it; it is so alive. But, it is also the biggest of the holy cities and very crowded, so stay close to the Riders. If you can, please fill me in on what happens."

※※

There were three cities that were considered sacred, and the major gods all had a presence in them, but of the three, Haliburum was prime. Here even the lesser deities made sure to have some representation, small though it might be.

Its wide avenues and extensive mass transit systems moved the millions of people who came year-round on pilgrimage, as well as the masses who lived and worked in the city and its suburbs. Broad sidewalks paralleled the roadways, and the pedestrian bridges that crowned the avenue intersections were nearly as congested as the streets beneath.

As Gwen paced the sidewalk with the Riders, the first thing she really appreciated was the respite from the weather back home. There it was still bitter cold winter, but here the warm sun was coaxing out spring blooms on the plants and trees that lined the walks and filled the numerous pocket parks. Brightly colored, vocal birds flitted above, and interesting scents teased her nose as she kept up with the Riders while taking in the scenes around her.

The mountains in the distance still had snow near their peaks, and the gradation of color on their sides from white to brown to green echoed the city's architectural timeline of old to new building styles and trends.

Eli explained that zoning requirements limited buildings to a maximum of five stories. The ruling was intended to maintain an open feeling and ensure that sunlight would reach the streets. There were no restrictions on a building's footprint as long as it incorporated the required ratio of open space.

Under those guidelines, some worship sites covered an entire city block, with greenery and gardens prominently featured. At the other extreme, some sites were no bigger than a door in a wall.

"I never realized there were so many gods out there," observed Gwen as she marveled at the buildings and the cascade of uniforms worn by people dedicated to one deity or another.

"This is a place of power," said Rakeem. "If you want to be *any*one, you must be *here*. I think something like eighty percent of the people in the city work for either a religious movement or some faith-related business."

"The rest are bureaucrats who run the city itself," muttered Eli.

"Probably," agreed Rakeem with a smile.

"But you have to admit there's a certain beauty to it," insisted Gwen. "I mean the color, the people, and the excitement of being where decisions are made on so many different levels, secular and religious. I think I could like it here."

"I think you're beginning to feel the thin air and that power I was just telling you about," remarked the dark Rider. "And you will come to know this city very well."

"Thin air or not, it's beautiful," breathed the Courier, barely missing another pedestrian as she craned her neck to take in the view of another sacred site rather than watching where she was going.

"I suppose so," said Rakeem, pulling her quickly out of the way and nodding an apology to the other person. "Just remember that our employer is part of it too. And since you are wearing a coat that those in-the-know will recognize as his, please be careful where you are walking."

"Sorry," muttered Gwen, refocusing on their task and the sidewalk ahead of her. "Tell me, guys, just how much weight does Nat carry versus Bayel now? Back when I dabbled here and there, the King was powerful, but scary. Bayel was the place to have a good time, although few really believed he had any clout or, I suppose, really cared."

"Bayel is a moderate heavyweight who consistently ranks in the top twenty of the Prometheans' Top 100 list of the gods, but he's never broken into the top ten," answered Eli as they continued to weave their way along the sidewalk. "He has a huge number of followers, but usually they are young people searching for that 'something;' once they find there isn't much behind the fun that Bayel's people call worship, they leave. That means Bayel's base of power is always shifting, and *that* is a major factor in his continued lag behind bigger names like Nat.

"Our employer, on the other hand, has a well-defined protocol. A big part of being his follower is conviction. His power base is immense because those who follow him are with him for good. That means, while he may not be at the center of any pageant or have the brightest shrine in the city square—"

"He's a big hit at all the senior citizen centers and neighborhood bars, right?"

Stopped in midsentence, Eli turned to face his colleague, a sour look on his face.

"I can see how Bayel might have attracted you."

Gwen grinned, unable to contain her excitement about the city and, suddenly, her job.

"Suffice it to say that your King is respected and listened to everywhere. Don't you take your job lightly," Eli said, adding the last sentence slowly and deliberately. "Now let's pick up the pace as we have an appointment, Courier."

The three threaded their way through the river of pedestrians and before long could pick out Bayel's temple. Pastel pennants flew from every available point of the large beige temple, and a steady stream of people flowed up and down the steep, wide front stairway. The Riders and Courier paused in the park that filled the block across the avenue from the main entrance and watched the activity.

"Popular guy, isn't he?" murmured Rakeem.

"More so than I remember," admitted his partner.

They watched for a few more minutes, then Gwen shrugged to settle her jacket comfortably on her shoulders as Nan offered a reassuring pat. "Shall we go, gentlemen? Is there a side entrance for emissaries of other gods?"

"Actually, there *is* an office door around that side," said Rakeem. "Follow me."

They slipped into the crowd of people crossing the street, and, once at the temple, Rakeem led them past the ornate gates in the low iron fence that marked the front of the property to the side of the building and a plain wooden gate in a wall of trimmed boxwood hedges.

A flagstone path meandered through a well-tended garden of pastel flowers ending at another wooden door with no bell or knocker. Without a word, Rakeem moved to open the door while Eli positioned himself behind Gwen.

In the pale-peach reception room, the Riders moved to let Gwen take the lead but flanked her on either side. The woman at the light oak desk smiled as they came in.

"Yes?"

"We have an appointment," replied Gwen, politely folding her hands in front of her.

The receptionist adjusted her large tortoiseshell glasses and stared momentarily at the three in their black jackets before jumping slightly.

"Oh! King Nathao's people! Yes, the Spirit is expecting you. Yes, yes. Please follow me."

Ceiling-to-floor woven wall hangings placed between tall, narrow windows matched the beige carpet in the hallway and helped control the noise of people moving purposefully from office to office. All wore the uniform of Bayel's followers: white sleeveless robes, open in the front like long vests. A few curious individuals tossed glances their way, but Gwen caught a few other looks that seemed more threatening— "hungry" was the first word that came to mind. She kept her observations to herself but made it a point to hold eye contact a second longer than would have been polite with those maintaining the colder stares.

Their guide provided a stream of idle chitchat as they wended their way down what Gwen surmised was the side of the temple that ran perpendicular to the boulevard, and then to a turn and a hallway that would have run along the back of the building. Just beyond the corner was a door to a small anteroom. Inside, the woman clasped her hands in front of her.

"If you will wait just a moment, I'll let the Spirit know you are here."

But before she could move, the inner door opened and a slightly stooped, white-haired man walked out. He moved with a quiet grace, and his face showed few of the wrinkles of a harried or worried executive.

"Thank you, Sister; I'll take care of our guests. Courier, I am honored. It was extremely pleasant to hear from Laciane, but I admit I was surprised when she told me you wished to meet. Please come in and let me know how I can help with whatever it is you need."

Gwen allowed herself to be ushered into the next room and was underwhelmed by the physical atmosphere. It echoed the bland coloring she had seen everywhere else, and there was a lack of anything that might reflect the personality of the inhabitant. What she did find curious was that the simple, light-colored desk and chairs close to the door didn't even fill half the room. The rest was a carpeted emptiness. One of the many tinted windows was open slightly, allowing in fresh air that smelled of cut grass.

"Please sit. Can I get you something to drink?" asked the Spirit in a voice that also struck her as bland and colorless.

"No, thank you," said the Courier, taking one of the two chairs across the desk from Piale and feeling the supportive presence of the Riders standing behind her. "While we appreciate your hospitality, we are here on serious business."

Piale's brow furrowed. "I am disturbed to hear that something may be amiss. Please, tell me the nature of this business. We have always valued our relationship with the King of Dreams and would not wish to have troubles between us."

"I do hope you can help, because this could affect many, many people," said Gwen, leaning forward and peripherally aware that Nan was accommodating her every move better than ever. "There have been some disturbances in the King's domain—disturbances that have had the potential to hurt some of those passing through.

"At first they were small events, but at least one was sizeable enough to hurt members of the King's staff. The very latest may have touched the dreams of unsuspecting sleepers. This cannot continue."

"I don't understand." The Spirit frowned. "Are you suggesting Lord Bayel is somehow involved?"

"The evidence points to him."

Gwen described the entity they had witnessed but did not mention that Nathao had destroyed it. She also left out the deaths of her predecessor and the Rider, Alice and her guide dog.

The Spirit listened without interruption or expression; when Gwen finished, he remained silent for a moment as if listening to someone else. Then his face fell.

"Courier, I am embarrassed to say I have no answer for you. I am deaf when it comes to my Lord Bayel."

Not certain what he meant, Gwen waited patiently and did not respond as Piale's brown eyes closed and his shoulders sagged.

His voice weak, he whispered, "I have not been in communion with him for some time, and I don't know why there is silence. Perhaps he has chosen to retreat and allow us to find our own way. The space behind you in this office is to accommodate him when he wishes to appear, but it has been empty for longer than I care to remember."

"Has this happened before?" she asked gently, conscious of his embarrassment and pain and not sure what to do when a few tears slipped down his cheeks.

"Not to my knowledge. I can only believe my advancing age has built a barrier between us. In the meantime, I lead the people as if nothing has changed."

"Spirit, I understood your position to be a lifelong service that ended only with death."

"And so it has been...until now," said Piale as he reached inside his robe and pulled out a white handkerchief. "Excuse me," he apologized as he dabbed at the corners of his eyes. "I have not told anyone of my dilemma, and admitting it to you now is difficult.

"Your news troubles me greatly. If I have no contact with Bayel, how can we understand what he is trying to do?"

"The King has said he will ask Lord Veron to get involved," said Gwen gently. "Perhaps we can get information from Bayel that way. I don't mean to be insensitive, but is there the possibility that Bayel is speaking with someone else?"

"I would assume if that were happening, the chosen person would have come forward by now," said Piale, regaining his self-control as he concentrated on carefully folding the handkerchief before returning it to its hiding place under his robe. "I must tell you my situation has been going on for some time."

"And no one knows?"

"As I said, I have not told anyone. How could I, Courier? Consider the internal strife that would create. I may no longer have the spiritual confidence of Bayel, but I can at least continue to maintain the secular operations of his estate."

"Very wise." Gwen nodded. "But how long do you think you can keep going like this?"

"As long as I must," said the Spirit with a small, sad smile. "I took vows many years ago, and this is where my heart is. I may not understand his actions, but I must believe Bayel is acting in the best interests of all who love him. That being said, I will do whatever I can to solve this puzzle you have brought."

"And we *will* solve it, sir," said Gwen, rising from her chair and extending her hand. "Have faith. I'll be in touch."

Piale also stood and accepted her hand. As he came around the desk to see them out, Gwen impulsively hugged him.

"Be strong," she whispered.

✸✸

At the chapel, Mother Laciane had been called away, so the three left word with Preston and Stepped to the Keep, where Marcia waited.

"I have assignments for you, Riders," said the Administrator in a no-nonsense tone. "Courier, the King is expecting you."

Gwen looked at the Riders in surprise. "Really?"

"Sometimes it's like this," Rakeem assured her. "We'll catch up later."

With a shrug, a half-hearted wave, and a cool glance at Marcia, the Courier headed for the King's office.

Crossing the quadrangle in the twilight, Gwen passed the bubbling fountain and looked again into the backlit water, still expecting to find fish.

'Gotta talk to him about that,' she thought to herself.

Soft noise escaping from the Administrator's office brushed her ears as Gwen entered the otherwise quiet King's wing. Nan pulsed for a moment, and then the jacket's presence faded into the back of the Courier's mind. She took the stairs two at a time and paused to catch her breath before knocking on Nathao's door.

Inside Gwen was surprised to find her boss with a guest.

"Sorry, sir, Marcia told me to come up. I can come back later."

"No, Courier, please come in. This is someone who would like to meet you."

The King was in his big chair, and near him, on one of the sofas, sat a diminutive man dressed in what appeared to be white, raw silk. There was a Panama hat sitting next to him, and he held a cordial glass filled with a light yellow liquid.

"Lord Veron, my Courier, Gwen. Courier, this is the Lord Justiciar."

Surreptitiously reviewing what she knew of the God of Truth, Gwen walked to the floor pillow she had taken as hers and bowed slightly to the smaller figure. "Lord Veron."

"Courier, well met," exclaimed the little figure in a reedy voice. "I've looked forward to meeting you. I understand you have a wonderful disdain for me and my colleagues."

Not sure if this was a challenge, Gwen looked at Nathao for guidance and was shocked as his eyes twinkled. Taking that as permission to speak freely, she turned back to Veron.

"Well, my lord, I'm not sure 'disdain' is the proper word. My introduction to the inner workings of this particular household has been interesting, if not mind-numbing, as occurred on one occasion.

"But, I would expect that you, as the purveyor of justice among these self-styled guides and saviors of the human psyche, would certainly know the fun I've had. And still," she added sweetly, "I maintain an open mind."

"I warned you, Veron," murmured Nathao.

The little god in white waved at him.

"My good King, this is the attitude we need if we are to stay relevant and not become insular. I am so glad you and our friend Errin of Trian make it a point of going outside to find your staff; they bring new blood and energy.

"Courier, please sit here," continued Veron, patting the sofa cushion next to him. "Tell us everything that happened at Bayel's place."

Gwen settled down and was startled at just how small the god in white really was—and how the intense sense of power surrounding him more than made up for the lack of physical stature.

"Where would you like me to begin?"

"When you entered Bayel's temple," said Veron, suddenly very serious.

Gwen recounted the visit, prompted on occasion by Veron for some additional observations and thoughts.

"There is something very wrong there," she added when she finished her report. "This poor man has given his life to his playboy god, and his joy is gone; he's dying from the inside. What does that say about Bayel?"

The Lord of Justice leaned back in the cushions.

"This, together with some other information I have received, suggests our Lord of Joy is reaching a turning point. He has always been a revered, yet somewhat second-level power; I sense a move to change that.

"The question becomes who is behind this, and how do they intend to fuel his rise?"

"As I am learning," said Gwen, also leaning back in the cushions, "power is based on the constituency. If that's so, his power base must be shifting, but that should have taken some time to accomplish, which begs the question: Why didn't anyone in the Pantheon pick up on it?"

"This may have been subtly building for some time, child," chided the god before he sipped from his glass.

"And yet, as I suggested, no one picked up on it? How about the Prometheans, don't they have any data? Growth in numbers, changes in rituals—heck, even use of electricity at temples or increase in incense purchases. There must have been some substantial change somewhere that could have tipped someone off."

Veron chuckled. "Those are all valid points. I can tell you things have changed rather quickly. Bayel's followers have increased in number and there has been a change in rituals. I would have to check on the electricity and incense bills, though."

"How long have you been tracking this? And with whom?" asked Gwen, raising an eyebrow. "And how have his rituals changed?"

The god in white took another sip from his glass.

"You have chosen well with this one, Nathao. Yes, the rituals are crucial."

"Good to know," said Gwen, feeling a slight sense of satisfaction even as she offered a tight, slightly acerbic smile and registered the fact that he had not answered all the questions. "May 'this one' ask how?"

"Courier," murmured Nathao, "take a compliment when it is given."

"Sir," replied his employee, while acknowledging nothing.

Veron reached over to pat Gwen's leg with his little hand.

"Never lose that fearlessness, my dear, and always feel free to express yourself, especially to me." Then his smile faded. "As for the rituals, they are taking a dark turn; I fear there is some blood sacrifice taking place."

"You're kidding," whispered Gwen. "That was outlawed eons ago."

"Yes, it was," said the petite god. "But there are too many signs."

"Can you stop it?" asked the Courier, leaning forward as she tried to ignore a sudden sense of foreboding. "You *are* the Lord of Justice, after all. Get in there and slap him down; quash his leadership and support base."

"That is where we run into a problem," said Veron, taking on a professorial tone. "I cannot interfere with this. Remember, I am the Justiciar of the *gods*, not their followers. I could warn Bayel that this trend is not good, but it is the *human* laws against blood sacrifice that are being broken, and it is *mortals* who must enforce those. I cannot help with that; all I can do is talk to Bayel about transgressing into the world of dreams, and I shall do so."

Gwen paused in thought for a moment and unconsciously tossed back the tendrils of dark hair that had fallen in front of her shoulders.

"After talking to Piale today, may I suggest you be ready for a Bayel you have not known before," she finally warned. "That poor man is hurting, and any god who would treat a loyal follower that way should be ashamed."

"I agree completely," said the little god, looking deeply into her eyes. "But even gods can sometimes be cruel. Remember, for most of us, it is the power that is everything."

"But what about the faith and the trust of the believers? Are they disposable?"

"I cannot govern that; we are what our followers want us to be. You must also remember what I said before—these permutations of Bayel's are relatively abrupt. Changes usually span generations; this is an anomaly."

"An anomaly you cannot stop?"

"No," said the god-in-white very matter-of-factly. "I cannot. I can only advise and warn."

"If you speak with Bayel, I'd like to know what happens," said Gwen.

Veron nodded. "If I decide you need to know, you will."

Nathao then spoke from his chair. "Until then, Courier, go home. I will be in touch."

❋

As the door closed behind Gwen, Veron nodded slowly and deliberately.

"You may have found our weapon, Nathao. She has the attitude, and I sense a crucial inner strength, but there also seems to be something missing that I cannot totally identify."

"She confronted you without flinching. She presented her own questions and challenged you to take action. What would a mortal normally do when facing you, the Lord Justiciar?"

"They would quail and shake and beg pardon for taking my time." The god in white suddenly stopped and raised his now-empty glass. "Bravo, my dear friend, bravo! There is no fear. She is not afraid. Imagine, a mortal who is not afraid, even of death, I hope?"

"Even of death. My brother confirmed that."

"This will short-circuit not only a pompous leech like Bayel who feeds off the emotions of his followers but many others. She is a prize, Nathao, a prize and a very powerful tool."

"We must make sure we do not squander the tool, Veron. We must develop a plan to use it and remove Bayel as a threat. More wine?"

"Indeed."

※❀※

Once in the hallway, Gwen paused and shook her head.

"What the hell have I fallen into?" she mused. "The cast of characters grows more eccentric by the day. And I wonder how and who Veron tracks. I bet he knows more than he lets on."

She was still deep in thought as she began climbing the stairs to her third-floor office and ran into Barnabas and Claire as they were coming down.

"Just the person I wanted to see," said Claire. "I'll pick you up at your house first thing tomorrow morning. It's time to get you in shape."

"Huh?"

"Tomorrow I register you for training sessions at our favorite gym. We all go. Nat's orders."

Gwen looked at her grandfather skeptically. "You train?"

"Well," began Barnabas, glancing at Claire and looking rather awkward. "Some of us train more than others. You, girl, would be smart to make sure you do it a lot. I recommend you use Claire and Jensen as your role models."

"You know you should get to the academy more often," chastised Claire, shaking her finger. "But then, that's between you and your King."

Turning back to Gwen, the female Rider continued, "Also on Nat's orders, I'll set up times for lessons with Armen on the Pantheon and our place in it."

"How was Haliburum?" interrupted her grandfather. "How did the meeting go with Bayel's people?"

Gwen shook her head at the memory of the session and to clear her head of Claire's plans.

"We saw this poor old guy who is supposed to be in charge, but there seems to be a major breakdown in communication between him and Bayel. I just told the King and Lord Veron about the visit, and they agree something is very, very wrong."

"Veron is here? You spoke with him?" asked Claire quietly.

"Yeah. He was comparing notes with the King, I think," said Gwen, turning inward to review the recent conversation. "It's interesting what he can and cannot do, you know? But he plans to talk to Bayel."

Focusing again on the two people with her on the steps, Gwen paused at their startled expressions.

"What? You look like you've seen a ghost or something."

Barnabas raised his hand and said briskly, "It's nothing. We have to go. Be ready when Claire comes for you tomorrow."

"Like you need to tell me that," retorted his granddaughter, trying to cover the fact that she knew she had missed something.

"I'll see you in the morning," said Claire, giving Barnabas a push down the stairs and leaving behind a bewildered Courier.

"You knew it would happen," said Claire as she and Barnabas walked slowly across the courtyard. "It had to, or she wouldn't be able to do what Nat needs her to do and, for that matter, what *we* need her to do."

"It's just harder than I expected. Granted, I was never close to her and I think she made some stupid decisions with her life, but she is still my granddaughter. I feel as if *I* should be the one with all the answers. She's going places I can't."

"That's right. And may I point out again how very few people can fill that job; the King would not have picked her if she didn't have something special. Unfortunately, we both know the chances are very good you will still be here after she's gone."

Barnabas was silent for a moment, but as they reached the other side of the quad, he stopped and turned to his companion.

"She isn't afraid."

Claire looked puzzled. "What do you mean?"

"I mean, she just isn't afraid of anything. She can be startled, cautious, and even anxious, but she is never afraid. I think that's the quality Nat found."

"Oh, that doesn't bode well for us during her tenure. Rushing headlong into a bad situation—"

"No, it isn't like that," interrupted Barnabas. "She's as careful as any of us. It's just that she doesn't seem to experience fear. I saw that in her from the time she was little."

"The gods know there will be plenty of chances to test your theory; let's hope it's a positive talent and not one that puts us in greater danger. Does she know?"

"She recognizes that she doesn't 'get afraid' like other people, but I don't think she sees it as a unique quality. To her it's just the way she handles situations. And, do me a favor, don't help her figure it out. I've seen a few Couriers in my time, and their egos are easily inflated."

"You're still sore about Gunnar, aren't you?" asked the blond Rider in amusement.

"He never gave me or anyone else the time of day. The one exception was you."

"Perhaps I listened to him when he spoke."

"Right."

"I didn't sleep with him."

"Oh, I know that," replied Barnabas, almost apologetically.

"And I still got some lousy assignments while Gunnar was with us. Look at it this way: with Gwen as Courier, you will always get the time of day, and you might even get special treatment from Nat if he feels sorry for you."

Barnabas snorted. "You and I both know the phrase 'special treatment' is not in the King's vocabulary."

"Wait until Gwen learns that too."

14

~

Carmen Piale put his signature on the last paper and with a weary gesture placed it on top of the pile that had grown in the corner of his desk. His administrative assistant would deal with it later. He stretched and, out of habit, settled back in his chair, closed his eyes, and reached for the god who seemed to have severed ties so long ago.

He gently rocked his silver-haired head on the headrest to release the stress in his neck and sighed as he waited and hoped for Bayel.

"My dear servant," rumbled a voice in his head. "You have not abandoned me despite my absence."

His entire body trembling, Piale allowed his feeling of joy to spill into his spoken words.

"How could you ever doubt my devotion to you, lord? Has this been a terrible test of my faith?" He opened his eyes and found the tall, well-dressed bronze god standing in the space on the other side of the room. "Have I done something wrong? Has this been a punishment?"

Bayel slowly shook his head.

"I have been evolving, Carmen, and I fear the transformation is not one you would appreciate. During that growth I did not have the energy to waste sparring with you about petty issues and values."

"Evolving?" echoed Piale suspiciously as he stood and faced his god. "What exactly do you mean?"

"That tone is precisely what I have been trying to avoid," whined Bayel as he toyed with a white ascot and then brushed invisible lint from the sleeve of his dark blue silk shirt. "I do not have to explain myself to you."

"That is true, lord, but in the past, I believe, my advice has tempered other, somewhat radical, intentions and strengthened your standing with your people. I have always made any suggestions out of love."

"I accept your intentions, my Spirit, but they are static, and I have moved beyond them. There are others who offer more progressive, stimulating goals that I have taken up and expanded upon as my own."

Piale shook his head, confused.

"I don't understand. Are you saying my position now belongs to someone else? You wish me to leave?"

"I want you to continue, Carmen. You have the respect of my people, and I need you to bring them together until they understand the new direction we are taking."

"Why would they not understand on their own?"

"It is a quantum leap we are taking in prestige. I intend to challenge my bigger colleagues and move up the Promethean List."

"My lord," began Piale, almost in shock, "why are you driven to do this and how do you—"

"It is enough that you know this is my goal," interrupted Bayel. "I require your support while I reach it. You will continue as my Spirit, and I will continue to speak with you on occasion. But our relationship will change, and you will work with those I have chosen to spearhead the next phase."

The older man was in shock as he listened. He just stared once Bayel finished. The deity pretended to adjust his low-riding, dark-blue pants as he waited for a response; when none came, he looked up and spoke as if Piale had voiced his heartfelt agreement.

"Then it is settled. You will remain in your current position and be my public figurehead, and I will send you the person who will lead my new movement. I trust you will work closely with him and share in our success. We will speak at a future time. Good-bye, Carmen."

15

~

Gwen did not question Claire when she announced they would walk from the chapel in Haliburum to the training session at what she kept calling an academy. The Rider said it would help her learn her way about the city, but Gwen also wanted very much to develop a relationship with the other woman.

Doubts began to dog her when the Rider set a pace through the early-morning crowd that was so brisk conversation was virtually impossible. Gwen concentrated on making mental notes of their route and said little until they turned down a wide alley and merged into a small stream of people headed for the only business there: the Barleycorn Mercenary Academy.

She grabbed her guide's arm and pulled her to the side of the walkway, feeling a touch of nausea.

"Claire, you said Academy, but that sign says Mercenary. Mercenaries fight for a living."

"It also says Academy."

"Oxymoron. Academy and mercenary are not words that go well together."

"Why not learn from the best?" said the Rider, smirking.

"Yeah, well, I'm not ready for this. I have to get into better shape before I can start training here."

"That's the worst excuse I've ever heard. You don't get into shape before you go to a gym; you go to a gym to *get* into shape."

"Where is the word 'gym'...I don't see the word gym. I have flabby arms and my knees creak, and I probably can't do a single sit-up. Claire, any teacher is gonna hate me, *despise* me for being so out of shape."

"No, he won't. He will be pleased to have a student who realizes she needs help to get rid of the flabby arms, creaking knees, and sagging stomach muscles. Right?"

Gwen considered her at-the-moment nemesis. "I didn't say anything was *sagging*."

"Well, stop it; this will be good for you. Don't embarrass me by complaining. This will make you feel better, look better, and do your job better."

Stalling for time, Gwen took a closer look at the people around them and asked about the brown pants and beige shirts with the brown logo of a stylized stalk of grain on the left shoulder.

"They're actual members of the Barleycorn Mercenaries," said Claire.

"More women than I would have expected. Not a lot, but more."

"And that tells you that you will not get short shrift here."

The Courier looked ahead at the glass doors as her competitive nature began to assert itself. "You do this?"

"Yes."

"All right. If you can do this, so can I."

"What *I* do will take you some time to match." The Rider sniffed as she motioned for Gwen to precede her through the entrance.

In the sauna after her evaluation and initial training session, Gwen sighed, leaned back, and closed her eyes.

"I will hurt, Claire. I know I will hurt. This wonderful heat is not going to stop that. That trainer I got, everyone calls him *Master* Holan. *Master*. I don't think that's a good omen for my body. But, tell me about that nice man who did my registration. Daidan was his name? He obviously knew you. You even blushed when he mentioned going for orange blossom tea while I was being tortured. What is orange blossom tea, by the way, I've never heard of it."

When there was no answer, Gwen turned her head toward her partner and opened one eye, secretly smug she may have hit a hot button. "Cat got your tongue?"

Claire did not budge or open her own eyes as she replied, "Orange blossom tea is a specialty of Ao's plantations. Ao, also known as the Old One, is the number one god on the Prometheans' Top 100 List, I might add."

"Right. So this Daidan knows you like this tea? You two have shared hot water before?"

Again, there was a pause, but this time the slim Rider turned her head and gave Gwen a hard, cold look that completely negated the relaxing effects of the sauna's heat.

"If you say one thing to the other Riders about Daidan or the tea, I will make your life with us miserable. Understand?"

Stunned and annoyed at the force of the comments, Gwen held up her hands. "Hey, chill. I can understand wanting to keep an attraction or love interest quiet, but drop the intimidation. There's no need."

Claire said nothing and turned her head back, closing her eyes. After a few minutes of awkward silence, she simply said, "Sorry."

Gwen peered more closely at her companion's profile.

"Not a lot of opportunities for girl talk here with all the guys around? Most of my former coworkers were guys, too, but a lot of the vet techs and the veterinary assistants were women, and we developed our own network. I could use a network here too. Talking helps keep me sane."

The only answer was silence. Disappointed, Gwen tightened her lips, leaned back, and closed her eyes again. She was sweating now from both the heat and the worry that she had badly damaged a relationship she knew she needed.

When Claire finally broke the strained atmosphere, Gwen did not move.

"I'm sorry. Alice was the last woman I could talk with. Before her there was no one. When she died, I was alone again and after her friendship, that was a terrible place to be. I promised myself it would not happen again, and it won't. I don't believe I can be part of any network. I hope you understand."

Surprised at the frankness of the statement and the lack of emotion in its delivery, Gwen decided this was not the time to argue with what she felt was a selfish decision.

"Well, I hope time will change that," she finally said. "I don't relish the prospect of sharing with Marcia."

❋❋

The next day belonged to Armen. Gwen carefully stretched stiff muscles as she and her tutor left the Keep and strode through the dusk across the well-kept lawn into the woods. Not far into the trees, they reached a clearing lit by several lanterns hanging from sturdy branches. His bushy eyebrows spilling over his wire-rimmed glasses, Armen nodded toward some logs and told her to sit down. At the same time, he pulled a thick stack of books out of his knapsack.

"These are for you to take and read later," he said as Gwen frowned at the height of the pile. "I promise you, the more time you spend in your job, the more interesting these books will become."

"I trust your judgment, of course, but there's some mighty small print on these pages," offered the Courier as she flipped through one of the tomes.

Ignoring the observation, Armen jumped right into his lesson.

"First, let me point out that most of the gods we deal with offer the same basic thing to potential followers: the chance to ask for help to make a situation better. You can ask for yourself or for someone else, and in return, you offer attention and worship. It's a simple barter system. Maintain that perspective, and you won't be intimidated."

"OK, lesson one, they're only gods, so don't be intimidated. But, Armen," said Gwen sarcastically, "they can *kill* us."

"Be assured they won't, because it's bad for business," retorted the Rider. "They need worshippers, and if they get a reputation for killing the faithful, their temples will get very empty. They will lose their power base and then fade away and die. You should not be intimidated because they need *us* as much as we need *them*.

"Now, let's review the most popular, and therefore, most powerful gods we usually deal with."

A little annoyed, Gwen raised her hand. "Wait just a second, please."

Armen looked up from his notes in surprise.

"Do you generally just lecture? Do I get to read up in advance? You're zipping along here like I know the topic. I don't."

"We don't have much time, and you have a lot to learn." The Rider frowned.

"Which is why we are having these classes. But can you slow down just a hair? Let me get out a pen. Are these books mine? Can I make notes in them?"

"Yes, of course, the books are yours. Make notes," said Armen, adjusting his glasses. "Now, as I was saying, let's review the most popular and most powerful gods."

"Luke?"

"Actually, no," said Armen, shaking his head and reaching for another book in his backpack. Gwen observed how focused he seemed as he flipped through the pages, as if he shared a special, personal relationship with each and every word and knew where his quarry lived. He found what he wanted and handed the open book to her.

"The King's brother is a special case. You can read a little about it here. He's extremely powerful, but not because of any immediate followers. In fact, he ignores direct entreaties and petitions."

"So, why is he still around? And how is he so powerful?" asked Gwen as she skimmed the material.

"He gets his support, indirectly, through all the other gods in the Pantheon who offer the promise of the Otherworld. Every time one of *their* followers offers prayers for a good afterlife, they are acknowledging Luke's presence, and *that* gives him power. Sooner or later, everyone thinks of what exists beyond this life, so Luke is never forgotten. He may be one of the most important and influential of the gods through no effort on his part.

"Even Demma, one of the Big Three, had to compromise with him and allow her daughter, Persephone, to live with him a few months out of the year."

Gwen smiled. "Having only met Luke, I'm curious to meet Percy. Luke seemed pretty self-controlled and self-absorbed."

"James liked Persephone; said she was cultured."

"Tell me about James."

"No," said Armen firmly, his dark eyes sharp and piercing. "We are here to talk about the gods, their customs, their beliefs, and their idiosyncrasies. If you don't embrace this information and master it, you are of no use to us. You become a liability, and that's something Nathao and we cannot afford."

"Got it," said Gwen, holding up her hands in mock surrender. "I'll hold that question for the King. Speaking of whom, where is he in the standings? Eli says he's a heavy-hitter, but how heavy? And if Luke is so strong, does he top his brother in the Promethean rankings?"

"Nat is a *very* heavy hitter. He is always in the top ten of the Prometheans' ranking, at least until now. I admit I'm a little concerned what this Bayel business could mean for Nat's reputation and strength. If we can show an ability to prevent the God of Joy from invading our territory, that may be enough of a win to balance out the loss of a Rider and Courier. We have about ten months to do it; that's when the next Promethean DRC is scheduled."

"DRC?" asked Gwen, shaking her head.

"Deity Ranking Conference. The Prometheans hold it at their headquarters in Haliburum every two years. I'm sure we already have reservations for at least a few of us to go."

"What about Luke and Nat? Who's more powerful?"

Armen resettled his glasses.

"Read the material. You will find conflicting opinions, especially since the Prometheans rank only those gods with physical places of worship, which Luke does not encourage. For our purposes you should consider them equal in standing.

"But now I want to review the top three names. What do you know about them?"

"Ao is the Primordial Being, Penobba is the Warrior and Demma is the Life Giver and something to do with medicine, I think?"

"Not a bad start. And always remember Demma is family because she is Luke's mother-in-law. There really haven't been any problems since that incident with Persephone, and she and Nat remain on cordial terms."

"Do we have a lot of interaction with her?"

"Another point, Courier—remember that 'we' do not interact. If anyone has business with these entities, it is Nat or you, which is why I said in the beginning there is no reason to be intimidated."

"How many Couriers have you worked with?" asked Gwen, casually leaning forward as she felt a moment of openness in her teacher.

"What?" asked Armen, glancing over his glasses with a confused look.

"How many Couriers have you worked with?"

"That's not relevant."

"Not for you, maybe, but for me, yes—especially if I'm not to be intimidated. It would be nice to understand the job security."

"Five, including you, and you have all the job security you need."

"Five? That seems like a lot. And, yes, I assume there is little danger of being laid off."

"Why does five seem like a lot? And there are no layoffs here."

"How high has the turnover been among the Riders? No, no pink slips, just a check-out time," said Gwen as she cocked her head and held her tutor's gaze.

"This is not productive," said Armen. "You are supposed to be studying. As for turnover among the Riders, that is not the same. There are more of us."

"Uh-uh, the number of you guys is irrelevant. Is the turnover higher among Couriers?"

"And if it is? What are you going to do about it? Let's get back to our review, please."

"Is our tenure shorter than yours?" asked Gwen, speaking deliberately and leaning toward the Rider, the book now closed in her hands.

"I am not a statistician," replied Armen, getting louder and leaning right back in her face as he fidgeted with his glasses. "And you will last a lot longer if you understand the gods you may be dealing with. So shall we return to the material at hand?"

"I only asked so I can understand our relationship a little better." Gwen smiled, sitting back again. "I'm also practicing not being intimidated."

"If we have to stand up to a rival, we will do it from a position of strength. You won't be left out there all alone," said Armen curtly. "Now, shall we discuss the Big Three, plus the Twins? That should be enough for today."

"Actually," said Gwen, becoming serious again to please her teacher, "could we discuss Lord Veron? Having met him, I'm curious about his role in the group and why he is even around."

"Hmm." Armen paused and looked at his companion a little suspiciously. "I heard about your meeting from Claire, but again you've picked someone who doesn't have the traditional support structure of worshippers. He's a favorite of lawyers, and you may see copies of the little white hat he supposedly wears hanging in their offices.

"As the Justiciar of the gods, his actual direct followers are relatively few, but he wields a great deal of power because those followers he *does* have are often very powerful people themselves, and they can sway large portions of the populace. That means they can influence the believers of other gods, so those gods are very careful about listening to what Lord Veron has to say. Is that clear?"

"In a roundabout way, yes. And he does have the hat," said Gwen, leaning back on the log and grimacing as her muscles reminded her of the session at the Academy the day before. "But does he actually *do* anything? He said he's been tracking changes among Bayel's followers, but he can't do anything to stop what a god's *followers* are doing. That may be acceptable, but what stopped him from making *Bayel* aware of what was happening and maybe snap him out of whatever stupor the new worshippers were creating? Make him see what they were doing? And how does he get his information?"

Armen looked at Gwen with a thoughtful expression and then shook his head.

"Those are all good questions, which I honestly would not have expected from you. As for the answers, those you will have to get from Lord Veron himself. And I wouldn't count on that.

"However, I can probably answer any questions you have about Ao, so why don't we start there? Open that book."

✳✲✳

Gwen settled into a comfortable routine that brought a growing sense of confidence. There were sessions with Armen, sessions at the Barleycorn Academy with Master Rymondell Holan, assignments from Nathao, staff meetings, and time for her to do her own research on the Pantheon and its relationship to the human world that fueled its existence.

Overall, she found her world balanced and challenging, with the minor exception of Armen, who she still found to be abrasive.

After an internal debate about Nathao sending dreams to her son and daughter, and remembering Sam's request while he was in rehab, Gwen had asked the Riders to begin coming to the house and visiting the hospital on a regular basis. Becky soon thought nothing of it. She seemed to understand when Gwen's responsibilities kept her away for long hours at a time and especially liked when Eli or Claire showed up because she usually got some one-on-one play or reading time.

Although he initially opposed the idea, Barnabas slowly accepted his granddaughter's decision not to hide the basics of her employment and began to take the Riders with him when he visited Sam at the rehab facility. All were supportive of the boy's progress, but Sam's favorite was Jensen, who regaled him with stories of Vikings and sea battles, and who also gave him additional exercises that strengthened his muscles faster than the usual therapy.

However, there was a limit, and at Gwen's request, none of the Riders used her title in front of the children. As she experienced more of the deferential behavior her position granted her in the outside world, she consciously decided to hide her real title from her children for as long as she could. She encouraged the idea that she was a Rider while never explicitly saying so and steered away from any in-depth conversations with Sam or Becky. Knowing he had lost the overall debate, Barnabas supported the decision with the caveat that she hide the truth from her mother for as long as possible too.

"Sam and Becky are young enough to accept this now and just see you as their mother," he told Gwen. "We'll just pray they still do when they realize how unique your position is. But, your mother will only create a scene."

Gwen did not dispute that, and Karen made it easy. Now that she did not have to supplement any child-care needs she would call once in a while, but visits had dropped to quick mother-daughter meetings over coffee and nothing more. If she knew what Gwen now did for a living, she never admitted it.

Lois and Barry continued to take Becky every other weekend and visit Sam; if they suspected anything about Gwen's new employer, they kept it to themselves. Then, one day when they dropped off Becky after a day together, Lois hinted she understood.

Eli and Barnabas were both in the kitchen when the grandparents arrived; they greeted Barnabas and introduced themselves to Eli, who noted he was a coworker of Gwen's. Pleasantries were exchanged, and when Gwen walked them back to the front door, Lois took her hand.

"I'm glad to know you are well connected with a powerful employer; you could do a lot worse. Please don't cut us out of the picture."

Caught off guard and feeling her emotional façade begin to crumble under the surprise of the kind words, Gwen looked from one in-law to the other, not sure what to say. Then she impulsively pulled them both into a hug, almost overcome with relief.

"After all the times you've been there for me and the kids, how could you think I would ever do that? Obviously I know you follow the King, but now that I know that *you* know that I'm involved with him too, we are so much more closely tied. I'm with him because he saved Sam."

"The King told me a long time ago when I asked what was going on. I respect your decision, my dear, and will pray for your continued safety. Do the children know?"

"That I work for Nathao, yes."

"But not the position?" pressed her mother-in-law shrewdly.

Gwen paused and then took a leap of faith.

"They think I am a Rider."

"But we know you are not."

"That is true. Why didn't he tell me he told you everything?"

Barry just put his arms around his wife. "When Lois asks, no one can say no."

"And I'm glad he did," stated Lois firmly.

"I am too," admitted Gwen. "Now I have someone I can talk to. My mother is useless."

"A mother is never useless."

Her daughter -in-law just snorted.

✺✺

Nan was becoming more important to her too. The more Gwen wore the jacket, the more she came to rely on her not just for a sense of security, but for cues on what people around her were feeling and thinking. The increased time together noticeably improved her ability to understand and interpret shifts in physical pressure and temperature and understand the increasing hints and suggestions that touched her mind.

The maturing emotional connection was making Gwen happier and more confident; she missed Nan when she took off the jacket. She made a conscious effort not to wear her when she was around Sam and Becky and not on the job, even though—thanks to dreams from Nathao—both children understood that the piece of clothing was connected with working for him. But those hours apart from Nan sometimes sparked a longing that was tough to fight.

And, she was feeling more comfortable around the King. Accepting Dreams from him became an efficient routine, although she did notice the discomfort the Riders seemed to feel whenever Nathao mentioned that one was needed. Reflecting on what her grandfather had told her the day she returned with her jacket, she blamed that sense of unease for the slowly increasing distance she began to experience from the Riders, including Barnabas.

Things were more and more routine until the day she arrived in the Step room at the Keep and found Eli and Armen working on a bloodied Claire. Barnabas sat off to the side, cradling his right arm as if in pain.

"Gwen, come hold this and press down," ordered Eli. "The bleeding will stop in a minute."

The Courier quickly obeyed and applied pressure to the thick gauze compress on Claire's thigh. The lanky male Rider then hopped up and moved to Barnabas.

Armen gently pulled blond hair aside and wiped blood from the side of Claire's head. After a close look at the injury the older Rider pronounced that the wound was already healing well.

"What the hell happened?" demanded Gwen, still leaning on the bandage as Nan offered a hint of concern and questions of her own.

"Contrary to what you might think, the King isn't welcomed everywhere," said Armen, still focused on his colleague's scalp. "They were attacked at a mission chapel in Colaranto."

"Huh?"

"Frontier of third-world country," said Claire, sighing. "Like the old days. The Guidant asked for help, so we went to check it out and got jumped."

"How many?" asked Eli as he inspected Barnabas's arm.

"Just a few. We killed several. No one there will mess with the King again."

Gwen checked the wound and was amazed to find the bleeding seemed to have stopped. She tentatively shifted the torn pant material and saw what seemed to be a thin film of skin already forming. Her surprise was evident as she looked up at Claire, and the Rider smiled tightly.

"The jacket; never go out without yours. We also believe the wine Nat has us drink at every meeting has some effect, but no one has asked him directly. Just give it a few minutes, and I'll be fine."

"Your head?"

"Just about done," said Armen, checking the injury again. "Maybe a headache after this."

Gwen turned to Barnabas. "Grandpa?"

"Fine, girl, just a dislocated shoulder."

"And it's back where it should be," observed Eli, sitting back on his heels. "No cuts, just bruises. What did you do? Let Claire take the brunt of the work?"

"They probably thought a woman was an easier target," said Claire. "Barnabas did his share. What did you get? One? I got three."

"My one was bigger."

"Three? You killed three?" breathed Gwen.

"That's not her all-time best," noted Barnabas, testing his arm. "And it's why I like going on assignments with her. I feel safe."

Claire snorted, then moaned and gingerly touched her head.

"You should train more. As predicted by Doctor Armen, the headache is starting. I'm heading to my room."

Gwen and Armen helped her stand just as the door to the room burst open and Jensen rushed in.

After a quick look at his coworkers, he took Gwen's arm.

"The King wants you right away. It needs a Dream. Come now."

❉❉❉

In the office, Gwen stopped short at the sight of the black jacket on the King's desk.

"It is time. I have accepted a new Rider, and I want you to bring him here," said Nathao without any preamble.

"Of course. How do we do this?"

"You will Step to my chapel in Keasbey and claim him there. There may be some sensitivity about his leaving, but I will give you a Dream explaining the basic situation. I suggest you move quickly once you have located him. Are you ready?"

Gwen could not help but smile as she moved to one of the sofas to lie down.

Nathao looked at her and raised his eyebrows. "Is there something humorous?"

"I'm just imagining what could have sparked this 'sensitivity' you mentioned."

"That will be something our new Rider may tell you," said the King, his eyes suddenly sparkling. "I, on the other hand, will only give you tantalizing hints. Now, sleep."

※※

When Gwen woke, Jensen was there again along with Nat, who offered her a glass of the red wine. She sipped it quickly, checked her memories, and then reached into her pocket for a band to tie back her hair.

"I've got it all."

Nat handed her the jacket as she stood.

"Make sure he puts this on right away. Once he is wearing it, their jurisdiction ends."

"Understood. We should be back rather quickly, I think."

"And, Courier, be careful," added the King sternly. "Let Jensen take the lead if there are problems or threats."

"Yes, sir, I remember the part about the authorities. The Guidant there should be able to stall them long enough for us to move."

She paused as Jensen stepped forward.

"Sir, I don't think she will listen to me. What if there is danger, and she doesn't listen?"

The King was silent as Gwen patted her escort on the arm and offered a smile.

"I'll listen, big guy. You know more about this stuff than I do, and you're a lot bigger than I am. Now, let's go get your new brother."

Back in the Step room that bore no residual hints of the earlier scene, Gwen checked the dream one more time, took the picture the King had given her of the Step in Keasbey, opened a Window, and told Jensen to move through first.

The tiny room at the other end was dark and empty; the big Rider insisted the Courier stay behind him while he opened the door to check what might be on the other side. His order was echoed by a pulse of warning from Nan. The door opened easily to an empty, dimly lit hallway, but the pair could hear the sound of people arguing.

They followed the voices down the narrow corridor to the small gathering space outside the main chapel.

Only about half of the lights were on, throwing a patchwork of shadows over the five people present. A plainclothes officer, his shield hung around his neck, was speaking loudly and forcefully to the Guidant, who wore the gray robes of his office.

"Father, I have a warrant for his arrest. You must release him to us."

"I will not," replied the clergyman calmly. "This is a holy place of sanctuary where he is protected."

"I don't want to get technical, but where we are standing is *not* the sanctuary itself. Now, I have the warrant, and I intend to take him with us. Don't make trouble, or I could have you arrested as well."

With that, the officer turned to the tall young man who was to be the next Rider. The Guidant moved to place himself between them, but two uniformed police officers quickly blocked his path.

The resulting confusion gave Gwen an opening. She darted through the shadows and slipped between the officers and the new employee. Jensen matched her step for step.

"Sean Li, welcome to the service of the King," she stated loudly as she held up the coat for the youngest Rider, interrupting the plainclothes detective. She then added in an undertone, "Put it on, boy."

Sean grabbed the garment and began to shove an arm in a sleeve. Gwen turned to face the officers and the Guidant as Jensen took a position next to her, his arms crossed.

"I am the Courier for Nathao, King of Dreams, and I have come to claim a new Rider. As such, he is now beyond your laws, gentlemen, but be sure that the King will see justice done."

Focusing on the Guidant, she tipped her head.

"Thank you, Father. The King is well pleased with your work."

"Go quickly, child" was all he said as he glared at the officers and moved to stand protectively in front of the King's people. "As you can see, gentlemen," he continued, "the boy is now off-limits to you. I am sorry, but your warrant cannot be executed."

While the Guidant spoke, Gwen took firm hold of Sean's arm and forced him to walk quickly with her toward the hall and their escape route. Jensen remained standing in front of the authorities, looking fierce, until the Father spoke to him.

"Rider, go. Take care of the Courier and your new fellow. We shall see you in the chapel soon, I trust."

"You will, Father," rumbled Jensen as he stared down the officers. "And if for some reason we do not find you here, there will be consequences. Do you understand me, all?"

Without waiting to hear the actual response, but very aware of the rising tension, Gwen pushed Sean into a jog, wondering what this innocent-looking young man had done and why Nathao would accept his service.

Once in the Step room, Gwen told her charge to stand beside her and waved her hand to open the Window to the Keep.

"Do you see that other room, Sean?"

"Yeah."

"Good. Now, that place is real, and you will go there in just a moment. You may feel dizzy, but that's normal. Once you get through, just move to the side so we can follow. If you really feel uneasy, just move and sit down."

Just then, Jensen dashed in.

"Go now," he snapped, slamming the door behind him and leaning on it.

The young man looked at the Rider, then back at Gwen, his hazel eyes wide and his face pale.

"All right, then," said Gwen calmly, "let's do it. You first, and we'll be right behind you."

Gwen turned him to face the Window and gave him a gentle push. She watched as the Window went dark and then cleared.

"Nice," murmured Gwen. "He followed directions well. Or, he's fallen flat on his face." Nan's touch in her mind suggested the garment had faith in the new Rider. Gwen chuckled.

Voices began to get louder in the hall.

"Jensen, I'm Stepping; come as soon as you can," said the Courier.

To her pleasant surprise, when she Stepped to the Keep, she found the new Rider standing quite steady on his feet, although he was staring and still very pale. Nan offered one of her *I told you so* mental touches and a hug.

"You all right?" asked the Courier, ignoring the coat. "Can you walk, or would you like to sit for a few minutes?"

"Dude, that was shaky. Could I sit?" he asked quietly.

"Of course," she said, guiding him to one of the white upholstered chairs.

Sean leaned over and put his head in his hands.

"Quite a scene you left behind," observed Gwen, "But, no one can touch you now. You're part of us, and we answer only to the King. Sometimes," she added wryly, "sometimes we answer to each other."

"I'm not afraid, Courier," said the new Rider. "Man, I left everything behind weeks ago. Those guys just weren't supposed to know I was at the chapel. Suggests a big info leak somewhere in the organization, you know?"

With a grunt, Jensen Stepped through and shut the Window.

"You certainly set off a hornets' nest back there, lad," he stated with a tone of respect as he straightened his jacket. "The Guidant had to call the police to deal with the police already there. Are you all right?"

"Yo, yeah, thanks," said Sean, breathing deeply.

"Are you ready to walk?" asked Gwen gently. "It isn't far, and the King wants to see you in his office."

"Now?" asked the new Rider, going pale again.

"Yes. And then, I think, Jensen here, or one of the other Riders, will take you to get settled."

"You won't?"

"I'll be around soon enough. You need to be with the Riders. They know what you need and can do a better job of helping you settle in."

Sean looked at Jensen. "What are the others like, man? The other Riders?"

"Oh, we're just like you," the red-haired man said soothingly. "We don't have police looking for us, at least not anymore, but in the old days—"

"Jensen, this is not the time," admonished Gwen, storing away that tidbit of information. Ignoring Jensen's hurt look, she turned back to Sean. "Like Jensen said, you'll like the Riders. I expect you will have a room near most of them, including Jensen here, he of the glib tongue."

"All right then, let's do this," said the newest addition. Sean took a deep breath, stood, straightened his new jacket, and paused. "By the way, what *is* this? It makes me feel, like, amazing."

"The King and Jensen will explain, but think of it as your new best friend," said Gwen, remembering the injuries her grandfather and Claire had survived.

✳✳

The King dismissed Gwen and ordered Jensen to stay as he accepted his newest employee. Outside the office, the Courier found her grandfather and Eli lounging in the hallway.

"What brings you two here? And, Grandpa, should you be up and about like this?"

"I'm fine, girl, never better. Now tell us about him," said Barnabas as Eli took her arm and guided her down the hall to the stairs and the third floor.

"You ask for information, old man?" she mused. "When the time of day was too difficult to give me just a few weeks ago? I believe I should get something in return, yes?"

"Come, come. This will be old news once we meet him," cajoled Eli.

"And Jensen will tell us if you don't," added her grandfather.

"Not all of it," said the Courier airily.

"Gwen," warned Barnabas brusquely.

"Grandpa," replied his granddaughter in the same tone. "Information for information. I'll even let you choose, how's that?"

The Riders looked at each other, and the taller man shrugged his bony shoulders.

"What are the choices?"

By now, they were climbing the stairs, so Gwen stopped and extricated herself from Eli's hold.

"Choose one: Why doesn't Armen like me, or what's wrong with Claire?"

Both the Riders were silent as they shot startled glances at each other before turning back to her.

"I think we'd better talk privately," suggested her grandfather. "Your office would be fine."

❀❀❀

Gwen sat on the bed and looked at the two Riders, trying not to let her anxiety show.

"Have I done something wrong?"

"Stop it, girl," snapped Barnabas. "Even I accept that you're doing what you must, in the way you would. There is no room for weakness here. It is just that you are our newest addition in a long time, with the exception now of this Rider, and I think you scare some people."

"Too bad," she shot back, hiding her hurt and disappointment. "I'm just trying to do the job that's been handed me."

"*We* know that, but for people like Armen, this life is all they've had for a very long time. He doesn't think you're serious about your responsibilities, and apparently you tease him during your lessons."

"I don't tease him. I ask questions. It's a debate. Didn't he ever hear of Socrates?"

"He doesn't see them as questions; he thinks they're challenges and ridicule."

"What?" Gwen retorted. "Is he so insecure that he can't discuss an issue? Try to look at it from a different viewpoint?"

"He *is* rather set in his ways," said Eli in a conciliatory tone.

"What about you? Are you set in your ways, Eli? You can think, can't you?"

"I haven't been here as long as Armen," noted the Rider. "Perhaps that has something to do with it. I also go out into the world more than he does. He's become rather insular."

"All right, so Armen needs coddling," conceded Gwen. "What about Claire? What's the story there? I know she misses Alice, but does she or does she *not* like me? Were she and Alice lovers?"

"Claire and Alice? No. But Armen and James were," offered Eli matter-of-factly.

Flabbergasted, Gwen stared at the two Riders.

"Armen and James? Why the hell didn't you tell me?" she practically shouted. "Did you ever consider that that might be a reason for his behavior? He probably resents my presence; probably hates me for always reminding him of his loss."

"He has no choice but to get over it," snapped Barnabas, waving his hand in dismissal. "Now, worry about Armen and Claire later. Tell us about this new Rider."

Gwen rolled her eyes in exasperation and then had to laugh at the expectant, almost pleading looks on the Riders' faces.

"Well, he left behind quite a scene," she began.

16

~

Adam Bardhof smoothed the front of his robe and took a deep breath to settle his nerves before knocking on Carmen Piale's office door. He waited but did not hear any invitation to enter. Puzzled, he knocked again, and when there still was no response, he let himself in.

Piale was at his desk, working at his keyboard. Without looking up, he addressed the new arrival.

"I have been told I must work with you; for the love I still feel for Lord Bayel, I will obey. But I do not intend to do so quietly, especially if I disagree with your plots."

Bardhof worked to maintain a pleasant face and not grit his teeth.

"Good day to you, too, Spirit, and 'plots' is a strong word. I hope we are able to accomplish Bayel's will without the need for such harsh remarks or ill feelings."

Piale paused in his typing and turned to face the younger man.

"I will do whatever I feel is in the best interests of Bayel. If we agree on your intent, then there will be no harsh remarks or ill feelings."

"I welcome your experience and insight, Spirit, but in the final tally, it is what Bayel desires that drives my actions."

"Then please enlighten me. I wish to understand what our lord desires that requires the insertion of a level of communication between us that has never existed before."

"You shouldn't think of it as a layer between you, but rather as an opportunity for you to take a step back and relax after your years of service, while still offering your expertise to those picking up the reins of responsibility."

Piale's face turned cold. "Don't try to placate me with platitudes, sir. Whatever you have convinced Bayel to do is obviously not something the mainstream membership or I would approve of. If it were, we would have been working together before this."

Bardhof was silent for a moment as he digested the statement. He felt a growing, albeit begrudging, admiration for this old man who was not about to roll over and let just anyone take control.

"Whether you approve is not the issue, Spirit. I believe Bayel would have included you had he thought you would support the changes. He did not. That having been said, we move forward according to his will. Are you with me on this?"

Piale's blue eyes narrowed for a moment before he nodded curtly.

"I will work for the advancement of Bayel. But, I warn you, if there is any hint that you are using him for your own gains, I will tell him and expose you for what I already suspect you are."

"And that is?"

"A parasite."

Adam schooled his emotions and successfully kept his anger under control and his voice neutral as he returned the Spirit's scorching glare.

"Think what you wish, Carmen, but this is what Bayel commands. We will work together. Now, I want to see your appointment schedule for the next week. We may need to make some changes."

17

The staff meeting was over and the room empty except for Gwen, who remained on her pillow at the King's request. She watched, wary but curious, as Nathao sat in his big chair, his gray jacket subtly shifting hues. Her own jacket offered a brief burst of encouragement before going silent.

"Sam is home and doing well," said the King.

Gwen paused, suspicious.

"You would know, wouldn't you? I assume you're still in touch with him and Becky."

"When necessary. You have not challenged me on that again."

"I don't believe it's an argument I can win, and I don't relish the headache afterward."

"Do you argue with Armen?"

"Armen?" repeated Gwen cautiously as she searched for a common thread in the mild interrogation. "Argue with Armen? I ask questions that he refuses to answer."

"He says he cannot work with you."

"He doesn't try. He won't go beyond the written word in his precious books."

"Do you ask unreasonable questions?"

Gwen shot the King a disgusted look and tossed her hair back in an unconscious movement of defiance.

"I ask what I want to know more about. I'm the one on the diplomatic front line, right? I want to know more to protect you, protect the

Riders, and—forgive me for being foolish—but to protect myself as well. Do the other Riders feel I'm unreasonable?"

It was Nathao's turn to pause. He steepled his fingers in front of him.

"No one has said anything to me."

"Positive or negative?"

"No."

"Screw them," said Gwen, kicking out her legs and leaning back on her elbows.

"Charm them."

"What?"

"Use your unique and considerable personality to charm them into reacting to you. The bonding process with the Riders is often long and difficult; I would not normally intervene, but Veron and I both believe Bayel will threaten again sometime soon. We do not have the luxury of time to cement relationships. Charm them."

※※

Nathao began assigning Gwen to go with one or two Riders to more of the chapels, both large and small, to meet the Guidants and the faithful. She worked hard to use the time to build those individual relationships the King wanted and, just as he had counseled, she turned on the charm, ignoring her colleagues' sideways looks and lapses in conversations.

Barnabas scowled when she tried to sweet-talk him; he still called her "girl" more often than not, but she was delighted when his taciturn expression began to soften just a bit and along with Rakeem, Jensen and Eli, he began to give more weight to her comments. Sean was no problem, and while Claire was taking a little longer to come around, Armen remained cold and even combative, especially during her lessons.

The fact that her well-intentioned efforts met only scorn stung Gwen every time she had to deal with the grizzled Rider, but she vowed to herself that she would make it through his shield of disdain in a respectful, intellectual manner.

That promise did not last very long.

※❂※

Gwen sat on one of the logs under the lanterns, her book open, while Armen lectured. She fought to bring her mind back, but it insisted on drifting away as it toyed with wisps of thought that stretched beyond her teacher's drone. The more she thought, the more annoyed she became at Armen's reluctance to cover current-event topics and the more her patience faded.

For this class, Armen intended to cover some of the gods in the Top Twenty, including The Builder and Errin of Trian. However, as he began to list facts about Trian and the governance for his followers, clergy, and administrators, Gwen's frustration with the Rider's deliberate, step-by-step presentation hit its limit, and she made the conscious decision to cut through the fluff and go for the substantive information she felt was practical and pertinent.

"Armen, you told me during our first session how the people determine the direction their god takes. How long does it take for that change to take hold? And does that god truly understand what's happening if things begin to shift?"

The Rider looked up from his book and frowned.

"This is not the time to discuss that. Today we need to focus on these individuals so you have a solid grounding in their operational structures."

"I agree that I need to understand more of the facts and figures, but the more I think about Bayel, the more I want to understand how people can influence whatever divine character they've chosen.

"How does any shift usually start? How long before it really takes hold? Veron once said it is usually generations. Who has changed the most, and the most quickly, in the last fifty or one hundred years? Is the change driven by new members of the constituency or by those who have been around awhile and might be getting bored? Does technology have a role in this? Is change a threat to the Pantheon?"

Armen scowled at his student. "You need to understand the teachings and the rituals, Gwen. That is what will serve you best when you enter someone else's sanctuary."

"Don't you think they'll tell me what to do?"

"You will embarrass the King if you don't already know."

"But, Armen," she continued as she lazily played with the piece of braided golden silk she used as a bookmark, "don't you think it's more important to understand the 'why' that has sparked changes in a god's behavior?"

The Rider adjusted his glasses, a movement that Gwen now recognized meant he was getting upset, but almost gleefully she continued to explore her current topic, ignoring a warning, almost beseeching thought from her jacket.

"I mean with an understanding of *why*, we can theorize and perhaps anticipate events. You know, we could be *pro*active and *prevent* a situation rather than be *re*active to something that catches us unprepared."

"Gwen, as I have said before, this sort of debate is not productive. You have a lot of basics to learn, and you are not applying yourself."

"I'm not debating, Armen. We've been through the top ten gods, and you yourself said I have a solid understanding of them. This lesson I would like to *think*—and that's with a capital T—not just memorize material. Understanding your enemy is crucial to winning the war, and I believe we will have a war on our hands if we don't understand Bayel now.

"His followers are growing exponentially; I've been checking the Promethean blogs and their Rapid Snapshot Survey numbers. Are you familiar with those surveys? They—"

"Courier," snapped Armen, "we are not here to waste time on talk about blogs and surveys. We are here to study these books! Facts! Do you understand?"

Gwen leaned forward, feeling a shift of power in her favor as the Rider went on the defensive, repeating his old arguments. She sent Nan a mental brush-off as the piece of clothing continued to pulse with concern.

"Armen, have you ever used material beyond the books in front of you? Are you aware of all the great electronic research tools available that could enhance your knowledge and study? You would love them. These surveys—"

"That's it, I've had enough," said the Rider, struggling to stand and gather up his books and papers at the same time. "I will not be challenged by you. You are not concerned about the responsibilities you have to the King, to us, and to everyone else here. You are a liability, and I *cannot* teach you anything, because you simply will *not* learn."

"Or is it that you are afraid of moving beyond your comfort zone?" countered Gwen, still calmly toying with the bookmark. "You're a bright man who doesn't see beyond the past. Armen, this is just a starting point; you know so much, *you* should be writing books. You should be *thinking*."

"And *you* shouldn't even be here," shot back Armen. His arms flew in all directions as he hurriedly and haphazardly stuffed the knapsack. "You are not qualified to be my Courier."

Gwen waited quietly as he finished his work, hefted the knapsack to his shoulder, and spun around to glare at her.

She coolly returned his look and said very clearly, making certain he heard every word, "Armen, I am not *your* Courier; I am the *King's* Courier. Your inability to accept that is a danger to the entire staff. I suggest you consider *that*."

Fidgeting with his glasses again, Armen stared at her. His lips quivered, but nothing came out. Gwen kept an exaggerated, expectant look on her face as she waited for him to say something. After a moment more he hissed, whirled around, and stalked off into the woods toward the Stables.

"You are a silly old man. Brilliant—but silly—old man. And you, Nan, just stop your dithering. It will be all right. This may be what both he and I need." The jacket stopped its twitching and went silent, almost as if sulking. The Courier laughed, very pleased with herself and what she felt was a considerable achievement, and patted a sleeve.

As she picked up her own material, Gwen noticed one of Armen's books still on the ground. She picked it up and, after a pause and thoughts of leaving it right where it was, added it to her own collection.

Walking back to her office, the Courier almost swaggered when she realized the nagging feelings of uncertainty and inferiority that had dogged her since she had first met the Riders were gone, banished by the simple act of standing up to a curmudgeon. She shook her head, chagrined at the unrecognized extent of her former self-doubt. Even the expectation the King would be waiting for her was something to look forward to, not dread. Nan remained conspicuously silent when Gwen mentally reached for her, and the woman laughed.

"You're almost as silly as Armen, you know," she told the jacket. "But, be that as it may, I have crossed a proverbial bridge, thanks to him. I was meant for this."

She had accepted the distasteful routine of the Riders and reported in to Marcia whenever she arrived in the King's wing. This time when she poked her head into the office, the sizeable Administrator only grunted and pointed to the floor above.

"You're expected."

Grinning, she bounded up the stairs, knocked, and opened the engraved wooden door even before she heard the King's permission.

Nathao was in the big chair at the end of the sofas. He did not say a word as she dropped her books on his desk and walked toward him with her hands open and a crooked smile on her face.

"Armen doesn't want to be friends anymore."

"Explain."

"I pushed him. I knew I was doing it, and it was great. Sad for him; great for me. Cathartic, in fact. I finally feel like I belong.

"Why is he so afraid of thinking? He refuses to budge beyond what's printed on the page of a book. I nudged, and he had a meltdown, Nat, right in front of me.

"Dear gods, company included by the way, he of *all* people could do so much with all the material available. He's smart, but he won't think, and that limits him and, by extension, us."

By the time she finished talking, Gwen was perched on one of the sofa arms nearest the imposing, austere King. "I respect him for the facts he knows, but I need more."

"He walked away?"

"Stormed is more like it. I think he realized he can't hide his fear of the bigger world anymore, *and* the fact that his fear is a major weakness."

The shades within Nathao's gray eyes shifted, matching his coat as one corner of his mouth curled up.

"Veron was right. I did choose well."

"Thank you for the vote of confidence, but it doesn't solve this dilemma."

"You are correct about Armen. He *is* afraid of anything new," said Nathao. "He has been here a very long time; I am beginning to fear he has been allowed to stay away from the world too long. However, he is a valuable asset."

"I don't question that," said the Courier, leaning forward to make her point. "I know I can learn facts upon facts from him. But I need someone to help me understand how the facts fit into our reality."

"And that you shall have. You will still spend time with Armen, but you will also have someone with whom you can discuss and question current events."

"That's wonderful," said Gwen, sitting up straight in excitement. "Who is that lucky person?"

"I will arrange for you to meet him. But, as I said, you will continue with Armen as well."

"If I have someone to help me incorporate history and facts with the here and now, I am sure the information I get from Armen will be that much more useful, and the time spent with him will also be that much more tolerable," she added wryly. "Now, what are you going to tell Armen?"

The King folded his hands in his lap, and his angular face remained impassive.

"I am not going to tell Armen, anything. *You* are."

Gwen held Nathao's eyes for a full, long breath, keeping her own face as expressionless as his. Then she grinned again at the thought of facing the disgruntled Rider.

"This shouldn't be allowed to fester because he tends to make more of things than needed or necessary. He's probably hunkered down at the Stables, but I'd rather not have this discussion in front of the others, because it would only embarrass him."

She suddenly remembered Armen's book.

"As soon as he notices it's missing, he'll go back to get it," she told the King. "All his books are precious to him. If I hurry, I'm sure I can catch him in the woods."

Without waiting for approval, she jumped to Nathao's desk and the books strewn across it. Sorting through, she grabbed the one she needed and turned to leave.

"You don't mind if I come back for the others later, do you?"

"No, but there is one other thing. The next chapel you will visit will be Cheo, with Armen. It is the largest of my old-line congregations. Tell him you need to learn about them."

"Yes, sir," said Gwen suspiciously as she stopped and faced her employer. "Because of what happened today?"

"Go" was all he said with a wave of dismissal.

Gwen paused as she thought of more questions, but the King just pointed toward the door.

"Right," she said before sprinting out of the office and down the stairs to the classroom clearing.

※✣※

At the Stables, Eli looked up sharply as Armen stormed in and dropped into an easy chair in the common room.

"I cannot teach her *anything*. She will not listen," he spat through clenched teeth.

The lanky Rider looked across the room at Rakeem and matched his raised eyebrows. Rakeem put down the book he had been reading and Eli sat up, putting a bowl of nuts aside and dusting shells off his lap.

"There is only one 'she' you could be talking about," Rakeem replied, his deep voice easily filling the room. "And it's no secret you don't like her. We just don't understand why. She's making a favorable impression."

"I don't know what favorable impression *you* have received," snapped Armen. "I find her arrogant and not serious about her responsibilities."

"She handled the meeting at Bayel's very well," said Eli, leaning forward, his hands on his thighs and his bony elbows sticking out to the sides. "And she's working very hard to develop and maintain a positive relationship with us, which is something no other Courier has done. I think you should move beyond your relationship with James and accept her."

"My relationship with James has nothing to do with this. And for what it's worth, I have no choice but to accept her."

"Your relationship with James *is* important," pressed Rakeem. "And I agree with Eli. I find her to be a positive influence; someone with a power of her own. James had some of that power; I think maybe you felt it through him, and you miss it now. There's no reason for a battle here."

"Talk to her," added Eli. "And remember, she's come into the job under some tough pressure."

"Pressure is an integral part of the Courier's job. It's there every day," said Armen primly, playing with his glasses. "I saw James face it day in and day out, and he accepted it with dignity."

"And Gunnar?" asked Rakeem, bringing up the name of the Courier before James.

"He accepted it as well. There was no humor. He dealt with it seriously."

"Oh, stop it." The dark Rider snorted. "Are you saying there can't be any laughter? If none of us could laugh or joke or tease, our considerably long tenures here would be miserable."

"Look," snapped Armen, "so far I haven't let my feelings interfere with my responsibilities, but this has become untenable, and I must find a way to deal with it."

"What exactly happened to set you off like this?" asked Eli intently.

"Ja," said Jensen, walking in with Sean right behind him. "What happened here? What did we miss?" The big Rider looked at the three already in the room and paused. "Oh, it must be the Courier. Armen, you don't like her."

Armen offered a loud, exaggerated sigh and opened his arms wide. "No, Jensen, I don't care for her, all right?"

Jensen planted himself in front of the angry, unkempt Rider.

"I like her, and everyone else here likes her. What's your problem? Is it that she's Barnabas's granddaughter? Or is it that she is James's successor? He's dead, my friend. We must move on, and the Courier Nat has chosen is proving herself worthy of our support."

"She is *not* worthy," shouted Armen, slamming his fist on his knee. "She questions and challenges and baits me during our lessons. She does not know what she is up against, and she will not listen. Maybe if you louts paid a little more attention to what she did and said and looked beyond her smiles, you would see that."

"So she challenges," snapped Rakeem. "Isn't that part of what the Courier does? As for baiting, my dear Armen, we all do that to one another on any number of issues."

There was silence for a moment, and then Eli looked at Sean, who had hung back when he arrived with Jensen.

"What do you think about the Courier, Sean?"

The youngest Rider's gazed flicked uncertainly from one person to the next, ending with Armen. "Dude, I think she is incredibly brave."

Armen broke the ensuing silence this time.

"I see I am outnumbered. Perhaps it's time for me to reconsider my position here."

"Stop that," Rakeem said. "Don't even think it."

"Well, I am obviously not seeing what you are, and I fear she will end up harming us. I will have to talk to the King again."

"Again?" observed Eli. "If you've already expressed your dissatisfaction to Nat, why are you here? Why not just go now?"

Armen shook his head vehemently. "No, I'm sure she is there already. I'll wait to be called."

He snatched his knapsack and stomped out of the room as Eli, Rakeem, and Jensen exchanged exasperated looks.

"Sean, my boy, this brotherhood is strong, but sometimes you just want to pummel someone," observed Eli, turning to his young comrade.

"Is he really that upset with the Courier? Why doesn't he just reach out to engage? If he won't stretch to touch, you know, that suggests a problem with the overall structure and calls into question our ability to operate as a cohesive entity. We need transparency, people, and communication. This me-for-me attitude sure doesn't promote a constructive atmosphere or instill confidence and trust."

"Yes, well, there is all that, my boy," agreed Rakeem absently as he waved a hand. "But let's trust Nat and see what happens."

As the tall Rider finished speaking, Armen stalked back into the room, and without saying a word, stormed through the door to the stairs and the stables below.

"See," said Rakeem brightly, but with a concerned look. "There's movement already. I bet he's on his way to the Keep, although I do hope his attitude changes a little before he gets there."

※◈※

Armen was still very angry as he left the stables. He turned, not for the Keep, but for the woods and the logs, where he and Gwen had been sitting.

He muttered under his breath as he stormed through the field, but when he neared the trees, his minimal self-control vanished.

"Damn girl won't listen," he yelled to the leafy canopy. "She'll get us all killed with her lack of focus; feels no responsibility to us; we'll have to clean up her mess...*damn*."

"What 'damn,' Armen?" asked a familiar voice.

The fuming Rider stopped short and swung around to scowl at the woman sitting on the log in the lamplight, holding his book.

"What are you doing here?" he demanded.

Gwen bit her tongue as a litany of caustic responses paraded through her head. After a second of silence, she simply held out the book.

"I thought you might be looking for this. I found it on the ground after you left. You must have dropped it while you were packing. I wanted to make sure you got it."

Armen's eyes narrowed. "Why would you care? It only contains *facts*."

"Facts are important, as you have pointed out to me on more than one occasion. I would like to learn more of them from you, and I promise I will only ask for the book learning."

The Rider continued to stare suspiciously. "What are you plotting? What do you want?"

"Plotting? That's harsh. But what I want from you, Armen, is facts—just facts. They're your strength," said Gwen, watching as he slowly dropped his shoulders and edged a bit closer, almost like a frightened animal. "I very much want to learn what's in your books; now that I understand you truly don't wish to take your thinking beyond what's on the pages, I will respect that boundary.

"I won't go on about how you're wasting your considerable intellect. I won't go on about how you are smarter than just about anyone else here. I won't go on about how your loss of courage to investigate and analyze real-world events could hurt the King and the Riders, not to mention yours truly," she added with a theatrical toss of her long, dark hair back behind her shoulders. "I will simply ask for the facts you know from your books and look elsewhere for knowledge.

"In addition, I will treat you with the utmost respect and camaraderie when we are together. No one needs to know we have an issue. Is that acceptable?"

Armen stood silently for a moment and then stepped forward to take the book that Gwen still held as she sat, almost regally, on the log.

"Everyone knows we have an issue, but what you suggest is acceptable. Did the King tell you to do this?"

"The King is giving me access to tools that will help me develop the facts I learn from you into the information and material we need in the world today."

The Rider chewed his lip for a moment while Gwen remained composed and still, waiting for him to speak. As they faced off, Nan sent a wave of sympathy that centered on Armen, and for the first time, Gwen responded with a thought of sharp annoyance. The jacket seemed startled and then went silent.

"Courier, I regret this relationship has not developed in a more positive manner. Perhaps my expectations were unrealistic. You have very little in common with the people I have worked with in the past and, quite honestly, I do not understand why you were chosen."

"I have to trust the King, but I don't have to agree with his decisions. If he wishes for me to teach you and you wish to learn, I will comply."

"Rider, that's what the King wishes, and it's what I wish. Perhaps someday you may find we have quite a bit in common, and you'll realize the King chose well. I will relish that moment," Gwen added with a wicked grin.

Armen frowned and pointed at the Courier. "That is just the type of behavior that is insolent and dangerous."

"And it's just the type of behavior the King accepted when he offered me employment. I'm truly sorry we're not friends, but we are coworkers, for better or for worse," replied Gwen curtly, suddenly all business again. "We can make it harder on ourselves, or we can make it as pleasant as possible. Shall we meet as usual? The King wishes you to tell me about the old-line congregations."

Armen's frown had not gone away, but he nodded brusquely.

"We will meet as usual and discuss Nathao's old-line chapels. They are quite unlike the moderates at Haliburum. The Courier's role there is very different; it is much more of a *silent* one. I hope you can adjust."

With that, the Rider clasped his book to his chest, sniffed, turned on his heel, and marched away.

"It appears we will get to visit one of those chapels very soon, my friend, and I can only imagine the joy that assignment will give you," observed the Courier. She stretched as she got up from the log. "So, bring it on, Rider; this should be something to keep me on my toes. As for you, Nan," she added, pointedly laying a finger on her right embroidered cuff, "kindly remember with whom you are partnered. Sympathy for an opponent during a face-off is not appreciated."

The garment responded by hanging limply on her frame.

※※

The staff meeting was nearly over and assignments handed out when the King addressed Armen and Jensen.

"Riders, you will escort Gwen to my chapel at Cheo. Father Yial says more and more of the congregants have been asking about the new Courier. It is time she visited."

Rakeem just nodded, but Armen's eyes glittered as he looked at his student.

"What a pleasure that will be, sir. It has been a while since I've visited Cheo, that fine old-line stronghold."

"Yes, Armen, and I trust you to make sure Gwen's first impression with the Father and the people is a positive one," said Nathao. "That includes instruction about the differences between congregations such as Cheo and Haliburum."

"Oh, yes, sir. We've already begun it in our lessons."

"Then I am sure the visit will be a success."

Armen smiled. "Of course, sir."

As the group began leaving, Armen sidled over to Gwen and said sweetly, "Shall we set a date?"

"Whenever you're ready," she said as she matched his feigned smile. "Remember, these special factors apply only in the old-line chapels."

"That's enough for me." The Rider practically danced out of the office.

"Well, you certainly made his day," observed Gwen to the King after the Riders were gone.

"It is protocol you must learn."

"I have no problem with that, and you know it. This should actually be very interesting, even fun, as he will have to do all the talking. I believe I just sit and look good?"

"If I am not sending a message of some sort to the congregation, yes."

"Are you planning some major pronouncement?"

"No, not this time," admitted Nathao. "So go and look good. I should tell you that you are only the second female Courier I have had, so give them something to talk about."

Gwen grinned in disbelief.

"Am I hearing this right? Are you suggesting I play up the fact that I'm a woman? That I do something special with my hair and makeup?"

"Father Yial is not such an old man that he wouldn't appreciate the effort. And..." The King paused, his swirling gray eyes sparkling as he looked down at his employee with a straight face. "You might catch Armen by surprise."

"Oh, now *that* would be worth the effort."

"Talk to Claire. She is one of Cheo's more frequent visitors. Her observations should be very insightful."

❀❀

Two days later, an alarmingly energized Armen and a patient Rakeem met Gwen at the Keep Step for the trip to Cheo. All three wore the black pants and high-collar gray shirts considered formal wear for the Riders and Courier, as well as their black jackets. Nan seemed to enjoy dressing up and had conveyed the sense of bouncing in excitement when Gwen added the thin silver chain that identified her as the Courier. The necklace fell just above her breasts and sparkled with a light of its own; it was an effect she had to admit was eye-catching, especially when paired with a pair of long, thin silver earrings.

While talking to Claire, Gwen had learned many of the people in Cheo were artisans who appreciated fine work and took great care in their personal appearance. Knowing that, she had taken extra time with her makeup and used the dark eyeliner Claire suggested. The Rider explained that both women and men in Cheo used it, especially when they were dressing for something like a public gathering.

Gwen had also pulled the top layer of her hair into a ponytail, and Claire had wrapped about an inch of it with a braided silver tie. The tie had long, unbound threads at its ends, which mingled with the loose bottom layer of dark hair. When the light caught the silver threads, they sparkled and echoed the flashes from the necklace and earrings.

She was pleased with the unexpected combination, and apparently so was Rakeem. The Rider smiled broadly as she entered the room. Armen scowled.

"You look wonderful, Courier," said Rakeem, offering her a slight bow.

Nan responded with a feeling that Gwen could only interpret as a blush.

"Thank you, Rider. The King suggested a little extra attention might go a long way with our old-line brethren. What do you think, Armen?"

"You *should* look good," said Armen brusquely. "That's all you do there—you sit, and people stare at you. Remember: you are silent until spoken to, Courier. Unless the King has a message for the people, you say nothing. Nothing."

"So you've already explained, my teacher. No words, I promise. I do hope there are many people there for you to counsel, because when I am in the sanctuary, I hope to watch you work and learn from a master. In all the chapel visits I've made so far, you've been absent. I've never had the privilege of seeing you work a room. You aren't out of practice, are you?"

"We are never out of practice," said Armen, nearly growling.

"Good to know," said Gwen sweetly, and then, in a professional, no-nonsense tone, she added, "Now, would you please lead the way?"

Without commenting, the older Rider sniffed, adjusted his glasses, and waved his arm to open a Window to Cheo. He was polite enough to let Gwen get a good look and store the scene in her memory before he Stepped through.

"I'll go next, and then you follow," said Rakeem in his melodious voice. "And, may I repeat, you *do* look good."

With that, he left. When the Window cleared, Gwen moved to Cheo.

In the receiving Step room, five figures waited. Instead of the gray robes and tunics worn in most of the King's chapels, these individuals were dressed in the brown hooded robes still used in the old-line communities.

Two men and two women stood behind a tall, broad-shouldered man with brown hair and eyes and a face that was lined and tanned. His arms were crossed, and his hands hidden in the sleeves of his robe.

Walking past Armen and Rakeem, Gwen knelt on one knee before him and bowed her head. As she looked down, she could not help but notice that the feet in the sandals peeking out from under the robe were on the very large side. Quickly pushing away that irreverent fact, she focused her thoughts and said her piece exactly as Armen had directed.

"Father, the King sends his greetings and blessings to you and his people of Cheo."

"Welcome, Courier," replied Yial in a deep voice that seemed to shake the walls. It somehow sounded familiar. "I'm very pleased you have chosen to visit us. I have much to say to you and show you. Please stay by my side during your time here. Now rise."

Without a word, Gwen got up and moved to the side as Yial walked to where Armen and Rakeem waited. Nan suddenly offered a quick, positive pulse that the Courier interpreted as her opinion of Yial.

The Guidant moved with a smooth, almost stealthy grace, and the hands he pulled from within the sleeves of his robe matched the size of the sandaled feet.

"Riders, it's good to see you again. Armen, it's been a long time," said Yial, putting a hand on the older Rider's shoulder and nearly engulfing it.

"Yes, Father, it has," responded Armen with a nod.

"And, Rakeem, is it?" asked the Guidant, turning to the other Rider.

"Yes, sir. May I compliment you on a very good memory, as I have been here only a few times. I believe Eli and Claire usually visit."

"Yes, they do, and we always look forward to those times. Now, a wonderful tea is being prepared for everyone, but first you must go and see the people. They are waiting. My staff will see you to the chapel."

Yial's attendant priests diplomatically ushered out the Riders. Yial turned to Gwen.

"I shouldn't be surprised, or care, but I must say, my dear, you are younger and more attractive than I had expected."

"Well, I'm glad you noticed." Gwen smiled. "The King said you might appreciate a little extra attention to looks, and Claire agreed."

Yial threw back his head and laughed. "Nathao knows what makes an old man's heart race, and Claire is a very perceptive individual. But, you can't be a person who worries about appearances."

"And you can't tell me you're old."

"I'm older at times than I would like to be. My bones protest the mornings after a heavy workout," observed the Guidant as he rubbed his right bicep. "I used to wrestle and lift weights competitively, and while I struggle to maintain some muscle tone, the best days have passed."

"You wrestled professionally?" asked Gwen as things began to come together.

"Certainly did. Have you ever heard of—"

"The Thundering Mountain," exclaimed the Courier, pointing her finger and laughing. "Your voice! I thought it sounded familiar! You're The Thundering Mountain. You were always the good guy in the ring."

"I made sure that was in my contract," said Yial shyly. "It meant I didn't have the most fun, but something told me even a partial history as a villain would come back to haunt me. I'm surprised you would know about me; not too many people do anymore."

"Don't be ridiculous. There are videos everywhere, and certainly T-shirts. Remember, merchandising never dies."

"So true," agreed the Guidant, holding his arms wide. "But now come, I have so much to teach you about Cheo. First, you must show yourself to the faithful. Remember that here you don't speak unless you have a message from the King. So, you shall sit awhile with me and let the Riders mingle with the people. Make sure you smile too," suggested Yial with a grin. "My people appreciate beauty and grace. After the sanctuary I have something to show you on the roof."

Gwen raised her eyebrows. "The roof?"

"What do you know about this area?"

"It's basically an arid region that relies on light manufacturing, although there is an agricultural community that hugs the river at the base of the Lithe Hills to the north. There's also a strong history of pottery, sculpture, and weaving. But, Father," said Gwen, looking around her uncertainly, "forgive me for changing the subject. I'm hearing a hum, and there seems to be a slight vibration. Is this room shaking?"

The Guidant tipped his head back and looked down at his visitor for a moment before answering. "Put your hand on the wall."

Gwen laid her palm on the smooth surface and gasped in awe at the intense tingling that ran up her arm and through her body.

"You are feeling the power of the stone," said Yial when she turned to him in amazement. "The Master Stone that belongs to the King and makes up all his Steps came from Cheo."

"Something else no one told me about," complained Gwen as she put both hands on the wall and felt her jacket stir with excitement in reaction to the new force.

"Perhaps because they don't feel it," chided the former wrestler. "Most people do not. As you see, we have a lot to discuss and discover. But now, come and show yourself to the congregation."

Yial led her to a passageway behind a ceiling-high wooden screen. Through its delicately carved filigree, Gwen could see a raised platform that included what appeared to be a small altar in the center. A lector stood at a podium on the left, reading aloud, while a woman quietly played a dulcimer and another man accompanied her on a small, hand-held drum.

The pair reached the end of the screen and quietly walked around it to the stage area and pillows set right up front. Yial gestured for her to take a seat and settled himself next to her, looking out at the congregation.

Gwen reached for Nan and touched a sense of awe as if the jacket were experiencing something wonderful for the first time. She smiled to herself and gently withdrew her probe to give Nan some time to enjoy the experience.

As with all of Nathao's chapels, Gwen found this one unique and beautiful. The red-brown stone of the Step room continued in the worship space, but instead of the high ceilings common in the other locations she had visited, here it was low, accentuating the room's squareness. Rectangular lights on slender chains supplemented the light from a set of clerestory windows. Rich blue-and-gold area rugs covered the floor, topped by rust-colored pillows with blue-and-gold tassels. The gray that prevailed in other chapels was nonexistent.

Gwen could see the feather symbol for Nathao carved into the wall at the back of the worship space; closer inspection showed the motif echoed in carvings in the wooden railing of the balcony immediately below it. Along each of the side walls were the usual small, darkened niches for personal meditation.

The ceiling appeared painted with intricate figures that the Courier assumed told some story. Unfortunately, she could not get a good look at them without leaning over and twisting her head, something she was not sure would be acceptable under the current circumstances. She made a mental note to ask for a guided tour later.

There was a peace that filled the space, and Gwen settled into it as she watched Rakeem and Armen receive petitioners on opposite sides of the room. Some of the faithful waiting for a moment of counsel wore loose, flowing gowns or robes, while others favored more tailored clothing. But, without exception, the vibrant colors, creative designs, and intricate embroidery raised the garments from a functional piece of clothing to an art form that expressed unique personalities and talent.

Delighting in the scene before her and the music behind, it was several moments before Gwen realized everyone was staring at her. Remembering Yial's suggestion, she smiled and tried to make eye contact with as many people as possible. In return, there would be a nod, a smile, and in a few cases, a tear or two, which surprised and touched her deeply.

She did not realize how intently she was concentrating on the task until the Guidant touched her arm and leaned over.

"Follow me," he whispered.

Back behind the screen, the Guidant was very complimentary. "You were really reaching people."

"Why were some people crying?" asked Gwen as she stretched and stifled a yawn. "That uses up a lot of energy."

"When it's done right, yes. They were crying because they recognize a spirit and talent that connects them directly with the King. You are living proof he cares for them, and that is what keeps them coming back. Now, let's go to the roof. There are stairs over here"—he swept his large hand to the right—"so when you Step through in the future, no one has to see you if you don't want them to."

"You sound like you expect me to stop in on a regular basis."

"Something tells me you will *want* to be here."

At the top of the circular stone staircase, Yial opened a door and moved aside so Gwen could walk out first.

Looking at him coyly, Gwen paused and then stepped out to a sweeping view of the city.

"Wow," she breathed as she walked farther out, taking in the panorama. "This is magnificent."

As she spoke, a strong, tingling sensation, similar to what she experienced when she Stepped, shot up through her legs into her torso, arms, and then her head. She stumbled and sank to her hands and knees as the world around her began to spin. The increased contact with the roof heightened the sensation, and Gwen closed her eyes as she worked to steady herself and figure out what was happening. She was vaguely aware of Nan reaching out to her, but after a few weak pulses, the jacket went silent.

Yial watched anxiously from behind, not interfering. After a moment, the Courier moved slowly but not to stand up, and the Guidant smiled as she stretched out completely.

"I think I have it now" he heard, her voice muffled under her hair. "I just have to let it pass through me, right?"

"That I don't know. In my tenure here, I have known only one other Courier, James, and he never talked to me about this. He would show up on a regular basis and stay for an afternoon; he said he liked to sit and watch the city while he recharged. That's the word he used, 'recharge.' He was very private, though, so I have no idea how he experienced the stones."

"Did he ever mention the hum?"

"No, not to me."

Gwen did not respond for several minutes, and Yial began to get anxious.

"Are you getting lost in this?" he suddenly asked.

"Mmm. No, just give me a little more time to savor this glorious connection," she finally answered. "This is *so* much more than just touching the walls downstairs."

The clergyman tried to be patient, but after a few more minutes of total inaction, he called again. "Courier, is everything all right?"

"It's fine" came the muted reply. "I'm just enjoying, no, I'm *reveling* in the effects of this energy on my muscles and even in my brain. I can *feel* parts of my brain. I can't explain it, but it's as if I'm in touch with myself like I've never been before."

"Are you in control, though? Can you pull yourself away? I don't know if you can overdo this, and I admit I'm getting a little worried. We still need to talk, and there is the reception."

For a moment, there was no answer, but as a very concerned Yial began to move toward Gwen, she stirred and languidly shifted herself back on her heels, still facedown on the roof, her arms stretched overhead. She remained there for a few moments and then rolled up onto her knees and arched her back, her hair cascading behind her.

"Did you know how I would be affected?" she asked quietly without turning to look at the relieved Guidant.

"No," rumbled Yial, mentally thanking his god for his guest's return. "And certainly not to this extent. As I said, James was very private about his time up here."

Gwen sat on her heels for another minute as she evaluated the new strength flowing through her body. The energy brightened her senses and made her muscles tingle, but it also made her hands shake as they rested on her thighs. She opened herself to Nan and was astonished at the powerful, organized entity that responded. The jacket's wistful, sometimes childish response was now a strong, mature element that meshed with her brain and body. It moved through her as a partner, and when she took a deep breath to stand and face Nathao's priest, it faded into the background, content to support and advise.

"Show me your remarkable city, and then let's talk," she said, embracing her newfound balance.

Without a word, Yial extended his left arm and guided the Courier closer to the edge of the roof and its waist-high wall.

The disappointment of leaving her communion with the stones vanished when Gwen took a second look at the city laid out in front of her. The chapel was on a hill, and looking down from their vantage point, the red stone of the buildings surrounding them glowed in the sun, echoing the color of the mountains in the distance.

The streets ran in a formal grid, and Gwen spotted cars, bicycles, camels, horses, and donkeys. Pedestrians appeared to use the sidewalks when convenient but would weave in and out of the slow traffic when they wished, waving their arms and gesturing at drivers.

"I can't hear what's being said down there, but I'm sure it's lively," she observed.

"They *are* a lively people," agreed her partner. "I fell in love with them the first time I came here. Down there it is dry and so very, very busy. However, do you see the gardens on the rooftops around us? The streets and shops are important, but it's up here where the real business is conducted, and it is done among greenery and flowers.

"We don't get much rain, so it's a matter of pride to create the illusion of another world within a rich, vibrant garden using just the morning dew, evening mist, and the rare stray shower. It's a challenge these people thrive on."

"And at which they seem to succeed," noted Gwen, surveying the lush patios. "Why don't you do it here at the chapel?"

Yial pursed his lips. "It isn't easy to maintain plants in this environment, Courier."

"Well, I suggest you try to accomplish what your congregation seems very able to do, because I don't relish getting sunburned when I come to visit. I think I'll be here on a regular basis."

Yial's face brightened. "Wonderful. I believe that is what the King expected. He sent me a dream asking me to help you explore our place as his followers in this world."

"Ah, very nice." The Courier nodded, turning to look at the city again and digest the fact that this man was Nathao's promise of a current-events teacher. "Did he tell you why this arrangement is being made?"

"No," admitted the former wrestler. "He did not."

Gwen was silent as she continued to gaze out over the rooftops. The new warmth and power running through her body made any desire to vent about Armen insignificant; if Nathao had left his Guidant in the dark about the situation, then she decided she would do the same.

"We should set up a time when it is convenient for me to visit, something that fits into your schedule and mine," she finally said, still looking at the streets below.

Yial leaned against the wall to share her view of the city.

"My time is your time. After all, my life is our lord's."

"As is mine," agreed Gwen dryly, looking at the horizon for a moment more before turning to her host and changing the subject. "So, tell me about this tea thing we have on the agenda."

18

~

The underground sanctuary was complete. Tonight Adam Bardhof's plan was to have it properly consecrated. He wiped his damp palms on his khaki pants, adjusted the open collar of his white, oxford-cloth shirt, and finished with a pat-down of the green trim on his open-front white robe. He had practiced the moves for weeks and felt confident in the steps of the ritual; it was his focus that he was worried about. He knew he would have to block out everything around him and remain intent on his goal of raising power for Bayel, but his history of success in that area had been spotty.

At the sound of people's voices, he tried to stop worrying, took a deep breath, and pushed out his chest just a bit.

The First Assistant stationed himself at the base of the maroon-carpeted stairs, greeting members of the inner circle as they made the turn from the enclosed stairwell onto the open landing and the final steps into the worship space. He schooled himself not to smile as more than one gasped at the sight to their right.

The half circle of white sand sparkled under the light from the recessed ceiling fixtures, and the white curved wall behind the expanse echoed the bright flashes with its own embedded glitter.

The dancing light abruptly died inches from the base of a large block of dark stone. The altar sat in the center of the sand, quietly demanding its own attention, absorbing every ray of brightness that dared to approach.

Ralph and Emily were the last ones down the steep stairs; at Adam's nod they arranged their fellow worshippers on the sand facing the stone, backs to the maroon-cushioned bleachers outside the sandy arc.

Tonight the seats were empty. For this special event, all those who belonged to the new movement had been invited to stand within what would become their sacred space.

The God of Joy's voice rolled through the room as he appeared before them dressed in an iridescent green shirt tucked into matching pants. The shirt was open almost to his waist, and several strands of gold and black onyx chains flashed against his chest. The black stones echoed the ominous cold of the altar, and when Bayel raised his hands in benediction, matching onyx rings on both hands continued the theme.

"I am pleased with our progress and I am pleased with our space, but there is more to do. I want Nathao and power," he said without preamble.

"Our next sacrifice should bring you closer to your desire," said Emily, stepping purposefully in front of Adam as the dozen people present watched. "You must make sure to use the power released tonight as effectively as possible. It is only a dog, but it will bring you strength, and then we can move to the ultimate sacrifice to bring down your rival."

"I will use the power you release to me well," replied Bayel in a condescending tone that was not lost on Emily.

The young woman looked at her god, her lips tight, and then quickly softened her face.

"I did not mean to imply that you would not know how to best use the power we will provide you," she continued with a smile and soothing tone. "You are the one I care for and the one I love."

Adam could scarcely contain his glee as he moved to stand next to her while she posed before Bayel, her arms wide and her face lifted to his. For a moment, their god did nothing, but then he walked over and embraced her.

Emily glanced over at Adam with a look of triumph. When he responded with a small, sardonic smile, she frowned and slowly tried to extricate herself from Bayel's hold. Rather than release her, the god tightened his grip.

"Do not be afraid. You are to be mine. The first in this wonderful new space created for me."

Emily glanced at Adam again, and her eyes grew wide as, this time, he smiled.

"He likes strong women, Em. Don't fight it."

As she began to panic and struggle in Bayel's grip, Bardhof nodded to his closest supporters. "Ralph, Ed, take her. Get her ready and up on the altar."

Emily screamed in outrage and struggled wildly as the men took her from Bayel's grip and took off her robe.

"Em," said Adam in a soothing tone, "you've been a major force behind this movement's advance. Now you can be its cornerstone and the first human offering to consecrate this space."

The curly-haired woman spat at Bardhof as she fought their efforts to undress her.

"You bastard," she shrieked. "I kept you going. I found your precious knife. Without me, you would be nothing."

"Bayel," she shouted, twisting to look at the god, who was watching the events with a gleam of anticipation in his eyes. "You are being used."

"No, lovely lady, *you* are being used, to my delight and benefit. That is what you wanted, isn't it?"

"Don't worry, Em," said Adam as they pulled her toward the altar. "The knife is very sharp, and I've been practicing."

19

$\sim$

The developing roof garden at the chapel in Cheo became the scene of many spirited conversations as Gwen and Yial potted plants and devised an irrigation system while debating current events and reviewing facts from Armen's lessons. Occasionally one, two, or more of the other clergy would join them; eventually the garden became the place for discussions and simple contemplation.

Working one hot, overcast afternoon, Gwen stood back from the big, wheeled container where she had just replanted some tall grasses and stretched muscles that were still a little stiff from her session the day before with Master Holan at the Barleycorn Academy. The pause gave her time to look around and appreciate a roof where the dust of the street could be forgotten and a person's spirit refreshed among the abundant greenery and flowers. Wiping her hands on a rag, she acknowledged a sense of accomplishment and, seeing Yial still bent over a raised flowerbed, a growing admiration for both the Guidant's debating and gardening skills.

The moment of introspection was broken as the door to the roof opened and Armen appeared. Surprised that he was Stepping *anywhere*, Gwen waited for him to approach her.

"Courier, the King wants you," said the gray-haired Rider curtly, as his eyes surveyed the plants near her.

"Nice to see you too, Armen. Is it urgent?"

"He just said 'now,' so I would suspect it's an issue of some importance."

Yial joined them with a watering can in his hand.

"How are you, Armen? Did I hear you say the King wants her?"

"Hello, Father, and yes. By the way, I like what you've done to the roof," said the Rider, turning around to take in the entire area. "Very nice."

"It was the Courier's idea," said the priest as he also turned to view the scene. "I think we've done well."

When he learned the plants were Gwen's idea, Armen turned cool again and sniffed. "The King waits, Courier."

"Yes, Armen, I heard you," replied Gwen with a patient sigh. "Let me grab my jacket, and we can go."

✺✺

Gwen bounded up the stairs to Nathao's office and found Eli and Rakeem already standing before the King's desk.

"Sir," she said, joining the Riders and settling her jacket with a shrug.

"Claire and Barnabas are in Haliburum asking my Guidant there to set up another session with Bayel's leadership," began Nathao, his face as stern as Gwen had ever seen. "There has been another Disturbance. Jensen was able to stop it almost as quickly as it began, but not without some injury to himself. I have already alerted Lord Veron.

"Courier, you, Eli, and Rakeem will pay another visit to the God of Joy's people and issue an ultimatum. You will tell Bayel's leadership there will be no more incursions. I have been patient, but now there will be major consequences. I will give you that Dream.

"Gentlemen," continued the King, focusing on the Riders, "this has become a volatile situation. I cannot afford to lose anyone else, and I place no restrictions on your actions.

"Gwen, if there is trouble or you feel threatened in any way, let the Riders do their job. *Listen* to them; they are in charge of your safety. Now, Courier, are you ready?"

The Riders withdrew, and Gwen strode to one of the sofas. She sat down to settle her mind before stretching out to receive the Dream, but

206

before she had the chance to begin, there was a slight *pop* and the little god in white was sitting next to her.

"Lord Veron," she said, a little startled. "What a pleasure."

"Very nice, my dear, but remember I am Justice, and I can sense a mistruth." Her new sofa-mate smiled. "However, it was a nice sentiment."

"But I do mean it." The Courier smiled in return. "I was just a bit surprised. I hope you're here because you have some information to share."

"I do, and it is something you yourself asked for at our last meeting," said the Justiciar. "You should know I did see Bayel, and I warned him about the changes taking place among his constituency. I believe it is important to share his response with you before you go back into his temple."

Gwen frowned slightly. Nan's presence stilled as if also listening.

"When I admonished the Lord of Joy about the behavior of his people, he had the audacity to tell me he did not answer to me, did not *need* to answer to me, and would *crush* me and anyone else who challenged his actions. When I pointed out I had strong suspicions about the legality of the manner in which his followers were conducting their worship, he told me it was not a matter within my domain. He then told me to leave before he decided to follow through on his warning."

"The Bayel of old would never have resorted to threats of violence. He was always out for a good time, not a harmful confrontation," observed Gwen.

"True, and because I like you, I wanted to warn you to expect the same sentiment among his leadership; after all, they feed him. So, be aware."

"Thank you. I wonder if we'll find a new Spirit leading the congregation. I didn't get the impression that Carmen Piale would ever support threats and force; he seemed to be a truly gentle soul. Your information gives new urgency to this meeting."

Veron patted her knee with his little hand.

"As I said, I wanted you to know. My compliments, Nathao," said the god in white, turning to the King. "A good choice."

With that, he was gone.

"Are you ready?" asked the King.

"Yes," said Gwen, lying down. "There's little question Bayel has gone bad. I just wonder how bad."

Nathao sat next to her and put his hands on either side of her head.

"Sleep" was all he said, and Gwen was out.

⚜⚜

When she woke, Nathao was ready with the glass of wine. Eli and Rakeem hovered in the background.

"How do you feel?" asked the King.

Gwen sipped the drink while searching her memory to review the Dream.

"I'm fine, and I have it all," she said, setting the empty glass on a side table. Touching Nan's presence and receiving a wave of support, she stood up. "Gentlemen, let's go."

The King moved to block her way.

She stood her ground and met his eyes, saying nothing.

The tall, austere figure looked at her for a moment, silent. Then he put his hand on her shoulder, causing Nan to warm considerably.

"The Riders are there to protect you. Listen to them."

"Yes, sir. Always," responded Gwen, covering her surprise at the touch and statement with a nod before she led the Riders out of the office.

"So what did you learn?" asked Eli as they walked down the stairs.

"Just as the King said, this could be a bit dicey. Lord Veron literally popped in to say he talked with Bayel, and the session did not go well. In fact, the big one threatened the little one. He warned us to be careful."

"Veron did?" echoed Eli.

"Yes. I hope this doesn't get nasty. I'm not very good at yelling." Gwen glanced at the Riders and caught them exchanging a startled look. "Oh, stop it, guys," she said in exasperation. "Veron is no different than Nat."

"To my knowledge he's never taken an interest in any Rider or Courier," observed Rakeem dryly.

Gwen shrugged. "Maybe it's my winning personality."

"Make sure you use that personality to its fullest at Bayel's," suggested Eli, just as dryly as his companion.

✺❀✺

Piale was waiting for them in the anteroom to his office in Bayel's temple in Haliburum. Gwen was relieved to see his white robe did not sport any of the brightly colored trim that now seemed to be the fashion among most of the people in the building.

"Courier, I am honored you asked for another visit. I was in the process of trying to arrange it myself."

As Gwen accepted his handshake, her jacket tightened ever so slightly, and a brief sense of unease touched her mind.

"Spirit, I am here to tell you that we have a situation that will end with this meeting. Your lord has returned to his wandering ways and trespassed again into the Land of Dreams. This time, we know the incursion was deliberate and the intent was to harm someone. Nathao will not tolerate this, and Lord Veron backs his decision to take whatever action is necessary to stop it immediately."

Gwen thought Piale's face paled before melting into a look of extreme sadness, but he said nothing as he looked down and ushered them into the inner office. Inside was a bald, younger man who wore a robe trimmed in not just bright green but also a brilliant yellow.

As he met Gwen's eyes, he offered a smooth bow.

"Courier, Riders," said Piale softly. "This is First Assistant Adam Bardhof. Adam, this is King Nathao's Courier, Gwen. And these are two of the King's Riders."

Bardhof extended his hand to Gwen. "Welcome. I did not expect the King to have such a lovely representative. How can I help you?"

Gwen accepted his handshake, noting the firm grip and damp palm. Nan offered a subtle feeling of disgust.

"I had planned to speak with the Spirit privately."

"I'm afraid that's not possible," replied the First Assistant as he motioned for Piale to sit down behind his desk.

Gwen cocked her head and raised her eyebrows but said nothing.

"We are undergoing some changes, and what our revered Spirit knows is also known by me. It must be that way, because Lord Bayel has chosen to alter his relationship with the man who has been leading us to this date."

When Gwen looked at him, Piale nodded slowly.

"It is as we discussed before. I heard from Bayel once after our meeting, and he told me of this new arrangement. That is all I have received."

"Spirit Piale is now our administrative leader; Lord Bayel speaks through me," said Bardhof.

"Bayel seems a little confused," suggested Gwen, not keeping the sarcasm out of her voice.

"That's hardly becoming, Courier." The First Assistant rebuked her. "When our god speaks, his will is made known, and we follow. I am sure it is the same for you and your chosen lord. Do you know you have lovely hair?"

"And since you have none, we seem to balance out this microcosm of the world," said Gwen caustically. "I am not here to exchange pleasantries about hair or anything else. I bring an ultimatum from King Nathao."

Her focus shifted from the confident, almost arrogant Bardhof to Piale, who was sitting with his shoulders hunched, staring at the top of his desk. She softened her tone.

"Spirit, with your experience and wisdom, you may be able to offer needed guidance. Will you hear what I have to say?"

Carmen Piale glanced up at his assistant before motioning to some chairs.

"Please sit," he said.

Gwen took the offer, and Rakeem and Eli arranged themselves, still standing, on either side of her.

"The news I have is disturbing, gentlemen. Bayel has again—and I emphasize *again*—trespassed in King Nathao's realm. Moreover, this time there was obvious malice behind the incursion. There will be no more warnings. If Bayel so much as tries to slip a portly *toe* into the King's lands again, he will be destroyed. Instantly annihilated. You will find yourselves sans deity."

When there was no response from Piale or Bardhof, Gwen continued.

"Lord Veron also experienced Bayel's unexplained change in behavior when he warned the Lord of Joy that his transgressions were not to continue. Bayel was threatening and crude to the Lord Justiciar. That is definitely not something we have come to expect from a god who offers happiness.

"Suffice it to say," said Gwen, leaning forward to accentuate her message, "Bayel is not behaving like himself. If there is some insight you would care to share, to help us understand this new behavior, please do. I will bring that information back to the King and Lord Veron for consideration. But, be on notice that Bayel will be exterminated if he crosses into the world of dreams again."

In the ensuing silence, Gwen watched both men for their reactions. She was not surprised when Bardhof spoke first.

"Perhaps it has been the unsettled climate here, Courier, which has resulted in these disturbances."

"You know of this latest transgression?"

"Yes, I know what our lord does."

"And what is driving this poor behavior?"

"He has a need for growth, which is something he has been denied."

"Growth? Spirit, did you know of this need for expansion?" asked Gwen, turning her attention to Piale.

The older man was visibly tense as he stared straight ahead for a moment. He then folded his hands carefully on his desk and looked her in the eyes.

"Child, 'expansion,' as you so rightly put it, is the dream of a new movement within this temple. I knew of the faction seeking to gain power but never dreamt they were moving to dramatically change Bayel."

"How are they trying to change him? Should we discuss the manner of worship?"

Bardhof moved next to Piale and crossed his arms.

"Our worship is our business, Courier, and my patience grows thin. What is it you want?"

Gwen sensed the Riders moving closer to her, and Nan molded herself more closely to her wearer's body.

"I thought I made that clear. Keep Bayel where he belongs and out of King Nathao's territory. If there is *one* more incursion, it will be the last time your god shows up *anywhere,* and that includes in his temples. Is *that* clear enough?"

Piale moved to speak, but Bardhof curtly interrupted.

"Carmen, I will do the speaking for Bayel. Courier, our god will not be denied."

Nan suddenly pulsed and offered a fleeting thought of growing risk.

"Grow up, Adam," said Gwen scornfully. "Your god is very popular. He has always been kind and gentle, giving his faithful solace and strength. What more does he need? Why are you trying to make him something else?"

"He *is* more. He wants to grow."

"And tell me, how you are supporting this growth? Where is he getting the ability to break through property lines and scamper around in a world not his?"

"As I have already made clear, our rites are not for outsiders, and certainly not for Nathao's minions," retorted Bardhof.

"No, because we'd be appalled, wouldn't we? And if the rest of the world were to suspect, what do you think would happen?"

"They would flock to our ranks, grateful for a god who doesn't bow to the backward, ineffectual powers that claim to lead the Pantheon. The Prometheans will take notice and reorder their oh-so-influential rankings. Your Nathao will be gone from the top names and he won't be the only one. We will assimilate or destroy them all, including Demma,

Penobba, and even Ao. Those who do not accept Bayel as their superior will be destroyed, and their followers who refuse our god's offer of love will meet the same fate.

"The slaves who have sold their souls…" Bardhof suddenly stopped and blinked as if coming out of a trance. During his tirade he had leaned across Piale's desk to stare Gwen in the face, but now he self-consciously stood and straightened his robe before crossing his arms again.

Gwen felt Nan move with her as she leaned back in her chair with an insolent half-smile.

"Please continue, sir. Why stop now? Tell us what will happen to those who see your Bayel as the tool he is. The poor boy doesn't even know his own mind, but that's to be expected if his major representatives don't know theirs. Remember, our gods are what we make them. And you are making him into a fool."

Gwen turned to Piale and softened her tone. "Spirit, what do *you* have to say to all this?"

Piale shook his head slowly. "For many years I was in daily contact with Bayel. I knew his mind, his caring, and his strength. Today, there is a wall between us, and I discover that I have been kept in the dark about a great many things. I know nothing of what is happening, although I can suspect. Tell your king and the rest of the Pantheon to beware that the power here is not the Bayel of old."

As he finished, the old man seemed to sink into himself and shut down. In contrast, the First Assistant stood a little straighter, his face unemotional as he looked down at Gwen, his breathing heavy, his face flushed.

"I will inform both King Nathao and Lord Veron of our conversation," said the Courier, rising from her chair, flanked by the Riders as Nan tightened her embrace. "I will also report your suggestion that Bayel intends to continue his forays not only into Nathao's lands but into the realms of others who, at the least, he should respect as his betters.

"And I warn you for the last time that if there is another incident against the King, your god will be crushed."

"Bayel will continue to do whatever he deems most beneficial for his people," replied Bardhof coldly. "And neither your king nor Lord Veron can do anything to stop him."

"That attitude is not beneficial."

"I propose we leave that for Bayel to decide."

"If your god is truly thinking for himself, I have no fear of the outcome," she said. "But I am concerned his people are divided and he is not of sound mind."

She turned to Piale and again softened her tone. "Spirit, I am sorry to learn of your situation, but perhaps it can still be remedied. I will report back now to my King and the Lord Justiciar."

Ignoring the First Assistant, she turned to leave.

"Courier," said Bardhof quietly, "you do not have my permission to leave. I would like to enjoy your personal company for some time yet."

Gwen shot him a look of disdain and tossed back her hair. "Send it in writing. We're going."

"You will stay, Courier—you and the Riders."

"We will not. We came in peace, and while we listened to words of violence, we will leave in peace. There are gods waiting for our report."

"You will stay," repeated Bardhof as Rakeem reached for the door and opened it. "My followers demand it."

In the anteroom stood four men in white robes, all with brightly colored trim. They arranged themselves in a half circle, blocking the door to the hallway.

Nan offered Gwen a surge of supportive confidence and melded tightly to her body.

"*Your* followers demand it, Bardhof?" asked the Courier, turning once more to look at him. "Whom do you serve? Yourself or Bayel? This is ludicrous. Call off your people and let us leave."

"That isn't possible. Bayel commands your presence here. He wants you. I want you."

"When your god wishes to talk civilly, I will be honored to return."

"He requires that you stay *now;* together he and I will determine when you may go," said Bardhof, moving around the desk where Piale had hidden his face in his hands.

While the two talked, Rakeem and Eli moved into the waiting room to face the newcomers.

"Adam, we're leaving."

With that, Gwen turned and walked to join the Riders so all three faced the four men in robes.

"Let us pass," said Gwen, pushing through the line of bodies.

As she did, someone grabbed her right shoulder from behind. Using the moves Master Holan had drilled into her at the academy, Gwen quickly reached up across her chest to grab the offending hand with her left. In a flash, she raised her right arm and, twisting to the right, brought her elbow down, breaking her assailant's arm. As he released his hold and stumbled back, hissing in pain, Gwen sprinted to the door.

In the hallway, Eli was right behind her. She turned and watched as Rakeem sent the last of the robes into the wall with a palm strike to the chin.

"Come on, move!" ordered Eli. "He'll come."

They turned to the left to retrace their steps down the hallway to the reception area, but it was crowded with office workers; most wore robes with the bright trim associated with the new movement.

Together the pair spun around to take the only alternative: the corridor straight ahead that seemed to follow the back of the temple. As they paused, Rakeem jumped out of the mess in the outer office and closed the door firmly. He paused, and Gwen saw him do something to the doorknob before he straightened and pointed down the nearly empty route she and Eli were ready to take.

"Go. I jammed the door; it'll give us a few extra minutes. That hall should get us out. Move it."

"There." Eli pointed. "About halfway down. Looks like steps and a big door."

"Let's just hope the damn thing isn't locked," observed Gwen as someone inside the office discovered the door wouldn't open and began pounding and yelling. A warning thought from Nan prompted her to steal a quick look toward the office wing. She and the Riders were definitely attracting attention, and some of the robe-wearers were heading in their direction.

"Company's coming, guys. Let's get out of here."

The three sprinted toward the hoped-for exit and took the shallow stairs in one leap. The double doors were heavy but swung open as Gwen and Eli each grabbed one and pushed. They slipped into the new room with Rakeem right behind them, pushed the doors closed again, and left their partner to find a lock as they turned to investigate their new situation.

For a moment, disappointment and frustration filled Gwen when all she saw was a large room with racks of robes and shelves of books and paraphernalia, including incense burners and candles. There were a few closed doors that could have been closets, another set of double doors straight ahead, and a large darkened archway in the wall to their left.

Despite impulses from Nan that strongly encouraged fast, decisive movement, Gwen jogged to the dark opening. A stairway led down, but there were no lights. In the dimness, she could make out only a landing below followed by a sharp turn to perhaps more stairs.

"I don't think we want to go *down*," observed Eli, coming up next to her as someone began banging on the now-locked doorway they had just barged through. "Come on. Those doors over there have to be to the main temple."

"Then, go for them, old man," said Rakeem, striding across the space that echoed with the attack on the doors. "They'll be in here in moments. Get Gwen out and go for the main street; I'm right behind you!"

Gwen and Eli jumped toward the second set of doors, pulled them open, and paused for a second. They were on a balcony that overlooked the main floor of the temple. Off the carpeted landing were two staircases, one on the right and one on the left.

"Go, and don't stop until you're outside," ordered the Rider as he pushed her toward the stairs on the left. "I've got your back."

Gwen took the stairs two at a time and plowed her way through the thin crowd of worshippers, aiming for the red exit signs on the wall and, she hoped, the front entrance. The occasional grunt just behind her was proof Eli was keeping up.

There were weak complaints as white robes parted in front of them, but despite some faint calls of "Stop them!," no one interfered with their flight.

Gwen angled her route directly for one of the signs, bounding up the stairs from the sunken sanctuary floor to an archway that led to the temple's outer gathering space and foyer. Once there, she whirled around to find the others. Eli's long strides brought him to her side in a second, but Rakeem was only halfway across the main worship space, and the congregants were coming out of their shock and stupor, converging on the Rider.

"Come on, Gwen," gasped Eli, grabbing her arm. "Get *out*. *You,* of all people, have to get back."

He pulled at her as she strained to find their partner but saw only a pile of robes where he had been.

"Come *on,*" he repeated, yanking on her arm. "I don't want to have to carry you."

Taking one last pleading glance at the temple floor, she gave in to Eli's efforts and Nan's frenetic warnings of imminent peril, dashing with the Rider past the startled attendants staffing the main doors and then down the polished steps into the dusk of the early evening. They ran across the narrow, landscaped front lawn, slipped through the gate in the low fence, and skipped across the wide street to the park on the opposite side.

There, they stepped back into the shadows of the trees, where they caught their breath and watched the activity at the temple. At first, nothing happened, then two men in brightly trimmed robes appeared at the top of the stairs to steer those arriving faithful back down and to the side entrance that Gwen and the Riders had used earlier. As they redirected the traffic, the massive doors behind them swung silently shut; in the growing darkness, the lights lining the walkways and steps began to blink on.

Gwen looked at Eli and was troubled by the hard look on his face.

"What do we do now?" she whispered.

The Rider only shook his head. "We've got to get this back to the King. There's nothing we can do for Rakeem right now. Maybe later, but not now."

"There may not *be* a 'later,'" Gwen snapped.

"I am very aware of that," Eli said calmly but with an edge to his voice. "However, there is nothing you or I can do in there right now, except give them more pawns for whatever game they're playing."

They waited in silence a moment longer while pedestrians passed by, unaware of the two figures standing in the dark under the trees. Then the tall man took Gwen's arm.

"Let's go. We have a report to deliver."

✳✳

Mother Laciane was waiting when they slipped in the side entrance of the chapel. She said nothing at the sight of just two and quickly ushered them to the Step room.

"What the hell happened?" she asked without any preamble.

"The spiritual grapevine is somewhat a-twitter, I gather," said Gwen, not moving to sit even though Laciane had motioned to the other chair in the room as she herself sat down.

"You might say that. Word hit the Promethean network just moments ago that there was an incident at Bayel's and the temple's been closed."

"There was that." Gwen sighed, running her hands through her hair and then tossing it back before rubbing her right sleeve to let Nan know she felt the same urgency to get to Nathao. "They started it, but now they have Rakeem. We learned a lot of disturbing information, Mother, but he may be the one who pays dearly for it."

"What do you mean, they have Rakeem?" asked the Guidant, narrowing her eyes and looking intently at the Courier.

"They're holding him against his will. As I said, we learned a lot of disturbing information, and Rakeem may be in danger. There's a new faction in power, and I have a very strong suspicion its leaders are remaking the God of Joy into a blood god with delusions of grandeur."

Laciane turned a shocked face to Eli, who nodded. "I'm afraid I agree."

"Carmen Piale isn't in charge anymore," continued Gwen. "Bayel's new keepers want more power, and if they have to use force to get it, it seems to be acceptable. Unfortunately, those violent tendencies are showing up in the dear god himself."

Mother Laciane was quiet for a moment and then stood up.

"You two had better report to the King," she said briskly. "I'll see what can be done about the Rider, but I'll tell you now, it may not be much. We can still pray that your suspicions are wrong."

"Whatever you can manage for Rakeem is better than nothing," replied Gwen with a deep breath that did little to ease the tension in her body. "But I don't think I'm wrong about Bayel."

Without another word, she turned, waved her arm to open a Window and Stepped to the King's home base, followed by Eli.

Jensen was waiting for them, sporting some bruises on his face. With a minimum of words, the red-haired Rider ushered them quickly through the Keep to the King's office where Barnabas, Claire, and Sean were also waiting.

"Have a drink; then tell me everything that happened," said the King, pointing to the glasses that sat on the side table.

"Rakeem—" began Gwen, but she stopped as Nathao raised his hand.

"Drink. Get your thoughts in order."

Without any more protest, Gwen accepted a glass from Eli and sank onto her pillow. As they sipped the wine, Nathao told them he had gotten word from Armen, who was out patrolling the area where Disturbances had occurred. All was quiet.

"That would suggest nothing is happening yet, and that's good news for Rakeem," observed Gwen as she held onto her glass, calm despite what she was about to tell everyone.

Without a flicker of emotion, Nathao simply said, "Tell me exactly what happened."

Eli clutched his own glass and leaned back on his sofa, at a right angle to his colleague's position on the pillow, seemingly very glad to let her do the honors.

The Courier detailed their experience, including the threats made by Bardhof to the major members of the Pantheon; at the mention of a possible blood sacrifice, Barnabas and Claire both gasped. Gwen grimly continued to detail their ordeal in the temple, ending quietly with the simple statement, "Rakeem didn't make it out, and I'm afraid it could cost him his life."

Nathao said nothing but looked pensive.

"Are they holding him to draw us back?" asked Jensen. "Maybe they don't think we will stop their incursions here if we are afraid they will harm him."

"Bayel hasn't ever used a death rite before," Barnabas said.

"That was the old Bayel, Grandpa," said Gwen. "The people running the show now would do it. I'm convinced of that. This guy Bardhof is bad."

"I think they would have killed at least *two* of us very quickly if they'd caught us all today," murmured Eli quietly.

Gwen felt his quiet pain and reached up and over to pat his leg. The Rider put his hand on top of hers as they both responded to the need for contact with someone who had shared the perilous experience.

"We should have some time," Claire said. "If I remember correctly, Bayel's workings take a long time to hit their peak, which is then over very quickly."

"Agreed." Nathao nodded. "I will talk to Lord Veron immediately."

"Should we wait for them to make the first move? With all due respect, Veron's efforts haven't really paid off," said Gwen quietly, aware that she was being critical of a powerful god and Nathao's friend.

The King looked at his Courier. "I am not anxious to send you back in there."

"And I certainly have no great desire to see those people again. But is waiting wise?"

Nathao was quiet for a moment, then he leaned back in his chair.

"I will speak with Veron. Barnabas, relieve Armen and let me know the minute anything happens. Gwen, go home; rest. I will be in touch."

The King's tone was definitely that of dismissal. As the group left the office, Barnabas walked over to his granddaughter.

"Girl, be careful."

The office door closed behind them and the other Riders began descending the stairs, but Barnabas hung back a bit, so Gwen did the same.

"What's the matter?"

"I just want to tell you again to be careful," said the older man gruffly. "I think there's going to be more action here than anyone expects, and I'm afraid you'll be in the thick of it."

Pleasantly surprised, Gwen cocked her head. "I believe you yourself told me there could be danger, so here it is. You and Alana are there to take care of Sam and Becky, if I'm away on an assignment."

Barnabas sighed, and his granddaughter held her silence as his usually fierce face crumbled.

"It's the magic. We all feel invincible until something happens. I tried to say this once before, but it didn't come out right. When I took you to Nat the first time, I expected to be paying the bill for Sam myself. I certainly didn't expect him to accept you, and most definitely I didn't expect you to become our Courier.

"It isn't that I didn't think you had something to offer. I just thought the Request could be mine, and you would be free."

Gwen's frustration with her grandfather began to melt just a little at his confession.

"Well, whatever happens, Grandpa, we'll deal with it together. I'm not afraid."

"I know, girl, I know, and that is the crux of this. Nathao also knows you aren't afraid, and I think that's why he took your service instead of extending mine."

"And I'm glad he did," replied Gwen. "This job feels more natural to me every day I'm in it." She patted her left cuff as Nan warmed.

"You are too trusting, girl," said Barnabas urgently. "And that's dangerous. I just hope I'm there when all hell breaks loose, that's all."

"I have confidence in the group," said Gwen. "Didn't *you* once tell me about working together and trusting one another?"

Barnabas glared. "I lied, Courier."

Gwen just snorted in reply.

Without another word, the two headed to the Step room where Barnabas surprised Gwen again, but this time with a quick kiss before he hurriedly Stepped to Armen's location.

"Huh," murmured the Courier. With a perplexed smile, she nodded to the empty space he left behind. "Thanks, Grandpa. I love you too."

20

Adam Bardhof was very, very nervous. He kept taking deep breaths and shaking his arms, hoping that would have a calming effect. But every time he thought of the coming meeting, his heart began to race. Emily's death had been wonderful: clean, quick, and powerful, although he had to admit, it had also been very loud, especially the screaming part. But he had focused and been fully in charge of his movements and intent as he offered her life to Bayel.

His knife work had been top notch, and the energy released had been spectacular. Bayel had absorbed the strength, morphed into his cloud persona, and flowed into King Nathao's lands with the intent to do major damage. Pity that one of Nathao's Riders had been right there when Bayel slipped into the Land of Dreams and had shut him down before he could gather his wits. To Bayel's credit, he had at least inflicted some measureable harm on the Rider and the surrounding area before being forced back home.

That had been the only successful part of the plan. As Adam anticipated, the King had sent his Courier and two Riders back to the temple to protest the incursion. But where he had expected to detain all three and have them available to power Bayel and break Nathao, all they had was one Rider. Admittedly that was something, but it was not what he had promised Bayel, and now he would have to explain what had gone wrong and hope the God of Joy did not decide that the First Assistant should be the next offering.

Taking one more deep breath, Adam nervously smoothed his robe, looked around the big preparation room that was behind the doors to the main temple balcony, and then passed through the dark archway to the steps down to the newly consecrated sanctuary underneath the building.

As he reached the bottom landing, he turned on the lights over the sand but kept them dimmed, hoping a more peaceful atmosphere would work in his favor. Walking down the final few stairs, Bardhof glanced around to make sure he was alone and then moved across the sand to wait near the altar, which now radiated a hunger that suddenly made him anxious enough that he took a few steps back. He did not have to wait long.

"You did not get the one I wanted," rumbled Bayel's voice, even before the god himself appeared.

Adam bowed from the waist.

"You are correct, my lord," he said, standing again to look at the bronze figure dressed in a black jumpsuit with a yellow ascot that clashed with his complexion. Adam noted Bayel's hair seemed a bit disheveled, totally unlike the god, who was always perfectly groomed. "She is proving to be a more worthy adversary than I expected."

"But she has been with Nathao for only a short time—why is she so difficult?"

Adam ignored the faint whine that echoed in the question. "He chooses well. We didn't factor in that she might be this strong, although we should have realized her potential when she was able to reach out and touch you during that visit so many months ago, before Nathao interrupted the contact."

"I hope *I* choose just as well, if not better," murmured Bayel, looking down at his follower with an intensity that echoed the altar's hunger and set the Assistant's heart racing in fear.

"You do, my lord, you do. I trust your judgment, and I pray that you trust mine, because I have a plan."

"Your last one was not totally successful."

"Perhaps not totally, but it gave you the opportunity to test *real* power and truly enjoy the release with Emily. It also gave us the Rider, who will bring the Courier here of her own free will," said Adam, digging deep inside himself for the strength to stay calm, even as Bayel remained silent and continued to stare at him.

"The Rededication Day we're planning would be the perfect time to welcome her here. If we dangle the Rider as bait, she will come, we will take her, and you will accept her as an offering. It would be a double sacrifice that would give you more than enough power to take down the King of Dreams and let everyone else know that you have arrived, so to speak."

Bardhof bowed again, mostly to hide his growing terror and the trembling that was beginning in his lips. He was sure the top of his bald head was sweaty, but he did not dare wipe it dry.

The silence dragged on, and still Adam watched the sand grains at the toes of his bare feet, trying to erase any thought of fear from his mind. He was focusing so hard on staying calm that he jumped and gasped when Bayel grasped his shoulder.

"Relax, Adam. You have taken me farther than anyone else ever has, and I understand why: you want power, and you know I can give it to you. As long as you understand that *I* come first, we will have no trouble shaping this new community.

"However," continued Bayel softly as Adam found the confidence to look at his god again, "if you ever once place yourself and your needs ahead of me, I will crush you publicly and damn you eternally. You are my tool even more than I am yours. Any questions?"

Bardhof tightened his lips and shook his head.

"No, lord, no questions."

21

Gwen tried not to let it show, but her conversation with Barnabas about the dangers that might be ahead sparked several days of mental unrest. She wrestled with the realization that he might be right and her children might be left alone, with no parent at all. The exciting newness of the job and the growing feeling of power had blinded her to the possibility of what she now accepted could be a short tenure.

She dug into the stories and myths surrounding her predecessors, hoping to find something of a pattern in who they were before they joined with Nathao and what happened to them. The information in the available public sources was minimal, and she decided she needed first-hand facts. Thinking about the Riders, she decided Eli or Claire would be the most receptive to questions. She knew Eli was off on an errand for Nathao, so she tracked down Claire.

Gwen had some hope she could get answers. Their relationship had been improving, especially since the Courier now scheduled her training time at Barleycorn so it coincided with Claire's visits, and they could travel there and back together.

But when she tried to ask Claire about the Couriers she had worked with, the Rider scowled.

"You know I can't talk to you about them. You have to ask the King. But," she added, "I will tell you that you are not the first to want to know about those who went before. And the most persistent questioners were those with families."

Gwen was caught unprepared at the hint that Claire understood what she was looking for, and she didn't interrupt as her coworker continued talking.

"Of the Couriers I knew, two had families, and while the concept is important to all of us, it's something we know we may have to give up when we accept service with the King. He supports us where he can, but even he cannot prevent feelings of abandonment and loss."

"What about dreams for family members left behind?"

"Sending a dream is one thing; accepting it is another, as you very well know."

"He's given both my children dreams."

"I know. We *all* know you challenged him on that."

"Yeah, yeah," said Gwen, waving aside what would once have been an awkward moment. "But, Claire, if I'm not around, will he help them then? Or is he only promising support now because I'm a needed tool? Will he drop them once he doesn't need me?"

"Only the King can answer that, and I don't know if he will."

Gwen paused, then abruptly stood up from the table they had been sharing on one of the outside patios. "So, I need to speak with him and make sure he understands his responsibilities."

Claire shook her head in admiration as the other woman walked away, headed, the Rider was sure, for Nathao's office.

"I know of many powerful men who would not do what you are about to, Gwen," she murmured to herself. "Barnabas says you are not afraid, but I doubt the King ever factored in a mother's love."

❊❊

The silence of the King's wing enveloped Gwen as she paused at the base of the stairs to the second floor. She sensed Marcia's presence in the Administrator's office but ignored the usual protocol and began climbing without acknowledging her or receiving any approval to see the King.

At Nathao's door, she knocked politely and waited for permission before entering. The King was at his desk, busy and annoyed.

"We need to talk."

Without another word, Gwen moved to the chair at the side of the desk and settled down, her legs crossed and body relaxed.

"*We*, Courier?" replied Nathao with a chill in his voice.

"Yes, sir, *We*. Admittedly, we're doing this more for *me*, but *we* need to talk."

The King leaned back in his chair, matching her posture, but said nothing.

"I want your word that you'll take care of Sam and Becky if anything happens to me. And I mean take care of them in every way: financially, emotionally, educationally, and whatever else there might be. I want you to reach out to their paternal grandparents, who are already committed constituents of yours, and work with them to support my children as they grow, and into their adult lives. I want it to be their decision to end any communication with you."

"This is very different from the last time we discussed them."

"Yes."

"Have I not provided for their well-being already?"

"Yes, but I want to make sure it continues in the event my services are no longer being utilized."

"Do you expect that to happen?"

"Stop it, Nat," said Gwen calmly but firmly. "I am not here to play word games. This is too important."

"Courier, you barge into my office, sit without permission, and make demands of me. How am I to respond?"

"With an answer and a commitment in the affirmative. The King of Dreams always keeps his promises."

"To his faithful. Are you among the faithful now?"

"What I am transcends your faithful, and you know it. I don't *believe*, I *know*. There's a difference. I know you exist. I know the rest of the Pantheon exists. Faith is for those with doubts.

"But that has nothing to do with Sam and Becky. I want you to agree you will see to their welfare."

Nathao steepled his fingers and looked intently at his employee. Just like their first encounter, what seemed a lifetime ago, Gwen felt his probing and, without reservations, confidently opened her mind.

She knew when he withdrew and watched him as he silently reviewed whatever it was he found.

"You really thought I could abandon Sam and Becky?" he finally said.

"I was concerned you would, yes."

"Let me be very clear about this: I do not abandon those who trust in me. Your children know who I am, and accept that. They do not have to follow me to have my support and protection. They have that through you."

"Even if I am no longer in your employ?"

"Even so."

Gwen allowed herself to smile.

"You find this ridiculous conversation humorous," snapped Nathao.

"You are not as imposing as you once seemed," said the Courier almost gently. "In many ways you are just as human as I am, and for that I love you. Love my kids the same way, and I will be your faithful servant."

"You are my employee forever."

"Yes, sir; yes, I am," replied Gwen with a nod, pleasantly amazed that her attitude seemed to be upsetting the King. "Will you love my son and daughter?"

Nathao glared. "It is not necessary to paint me into a corner, Courier."

"A simple yes, and I will leave this office your humble mendicant."

"You have that. Now leave and remember your role when I call you back."

Gwen stood and bowed to hide what she was sure was an unprofessional glow of pride in wringing the verbal promise out of the King. Once she had her face under control, she straightened and left the office.

⁂

"I don't understand why the King ordered me to come with you," said Armen. "Let's just make sure no one gets left behind this time, shall we, Courier?"

Gwen remained calm at the reference to Rakeem and stared at the paneled elevator door. "Nat's reasons are certainly arcane at times. But how do you know we aren't supposed to leave someone as collateral and that he didn't take my suggestion of a nominee?"

On her left, Clare stifled a laugh.

"Unbecoming, Rider," muttered Armen from where he stood on Gwen's right.

Silence filled the air as the elevator rose to the fifth and top floor of the building that housed the largest law firm in Haliburum: Bailey, Rockman, and Skye.

The doors slid open, and a young man in a pinstripe suit met Nathao's people. He escorted them to a conference room, where Adam Bardhof waited with two companions. All three wore their sleeveless robes with bright trim over white polo shirts and khakis, a wardrobe that contrasted sharply with the black jackets and pants worn by the Courier and the Riders.

"Very stylish, Adam," said Gwen coolly as Nan offered a sense of warning and, for the first time, a hint of disgust. "You must give me the name of your tailor."

"More stylish than black, Courier," replied the First Assistant just as controlled as he shook her hand and held it just a little too long. "You people ought to lighten up."

"Maybe you can give me some reasons to do that today," suggested Gwen, resisting the urge to wipe her hand on her pants when he finally released it. "Where is the Spirit? Carmen Piale? I rather expected him to be here."

Adam nodded as if in agreement. "The Spirit has other things to attend to; he appointed me as his representative and negotiator. Frankly, I think he understands that you and I are more aware of the issues we currently face in the real world and that the chances of an agreement being reached between us are greater than if he were involved."

Gwen frowned a little, but before she could respond, one of the law firm's partners, Angus Bailey, stepped between the two.

"Courier, Mr. Bardhof, I am very pleased you are willing to meet here. May I suggest we three take seats over here and talk? Your friends are welcome to wait outside in the lounge."

The beige walls and monochromatic paintings on the walls of the conference room helped balance the visual weight of the long mahogany table that was the centerpiece of the space. Sprinkled around the room were vases with woody branches sporting pink buds, a hint of the coming spring. Sheer roman shades on the large windows diffused the bright sunlight, reinforcing the benign atmosphere.

Bailey ushered his two guests to the far end of the table while members of his staff guided their entourages to another room.

"It truly is good to see you again, Courier," offered Adam as he took the chair at the end of the table. Gwen took the seat on his left, her back to the windows, while Bailey took the chair on Adam's right.

"Good to see me considering how much fun we had last time?" asked Gwen as she raised an eyebrow and shrugged to let Nan know she had registered the jacket's latest wave of mistrust.

"A misunderstanding. My people would not have hurt you."

"Then where is our Rider?"

Bardhof grimaced. "He is with us, a regrettable result of that misunderstanding."

"And why are you still holding him?"

The First Assistant did not answer for a moment as he looked at Gwen. Then he slid his chair closer and leaned over to stroke the ends of some of her long hair that had fallen in front of her shoulder and onto the table.

"You really have wonderful hair, has anyone told you that? It's shiny and soft."

Pushing aside a feeling of loathing, the Courier calmly reached down and moved his hand to side.

"You mentioned it last time, Adam. Now don't touch, and stay on point. Why are you still holding our Rider?"

"Bayel will tell us when he is to be guided back to you," said the Assistant rather cavalierly as his hand crept back to her hair. He began fondling the ends. "Bayel is a god, you know."

Annoyed and disgusted, Gwen again reached for Bardhof's hand, but this time she also moved closer and took hold of his entire thumb. Slowly and steadily, she began bending it back and to the side, forcing him to bend the arm and pull away.

"This is business, Mr. Bardhof. Pay attention. Speaking of gods, Bayel's fellow deities would like to know why he has been trespassing in places he doesn't belong. Apparently he is now testing himself in places other than the Realm of Dreams; it is not appreciated."

The First Assistant leaned to the side and dropped his shoulder to ease the pain.

Gwen released the hand and felt some tiny satisfaction as Bardhof sighed, rubbed his thumb, and then pulled out a handkerchief to dab away the tiny beads of sweat popping out on his head.

She watched as he wiped away the moisture and noticed his hands shook a little. This, she realized, was someone who could easily jump toward violence or compromise, depending on the level of endorphins in his system at any given time.

"As I explained at our previous meeting, he needs to grow. For him, there will be no limits."

Not wanting to test her theory and possibly push him over the edge, Gwen chose not to make an all-out verbal attack; instead she tried to appear pensive and a little surprised.

"Gods especially need limits, and I'm sure you know that by now. Can you imagine what this world would be like if there weren't restrictions on their behavior? Do you remember your Promethean history classes? Those were abusive and bad times for humans, and the impetus for the laws we have today. It's up to people like us to make sure rules aren't abused, don't you think?"

Bardhof sniffed and regained his composure.

"I'm not a policeman. I am one with Bayel, and I am committed to doing his will. If that means helping him expand his power base, then I will do it."

"Even if the means are messy and illegal?"

"What are you suggesting?" retorted the First Assistant tartly, raising his chin.

"As good citizens we are required to report to the human authorities any suspicions we have of illegal activities. Actions like blood sacrifices. That's murder, Adam, and it's illegal."

Bayel's official shook his head in feigned surprise.

"We have no intention of ever pursuing such a low, venal, plebian enterprise; not at all. But, Courier"—he raised an index finger and pointed it at her—"our lord needs to grow, and he will.

"Now, in the interest of our friendship, I can talk to him and advise that bumping against the Dream King's realm may not be the wisest action. In fact, I would be happy to act as your ambassador unless you would like to come back to the temple and speak to him yourself?"

Nan immediately contracted, and Gwen instinctively rubbed the left cuff in reassurance, feeling the cool smoothness of the raised silver embroidery that marked her as the Courier. As much as she was willing to exchange her life for Rakeem's, she knew this offer would not accomplish that. And, most of all, she knew the King would not approve. Keeping her face impassive, she declined.

"First off, Bayel has not been 'bumping' against the King's lands, Adam; he has been invading and is now pressuring others. Second, you hold one of the King's staff against his will, which is illegal. Third, I would not feel safe in one of Bayel's temples, because I believe he is being manipulated and is developing into something new and dangerous.

"However, that having been said," Gwen continued, lightening the tone of her voice, "I would come to talk if he, first, swore before Lord Veron to not enter the King's lands again, and second, returned the Rider. If those two conditions were to be met, I think the issue of manipulation could be put aside."

"What would there be left to talk about?" asked Bardhof airily as he reached to finger Gwen's hair again.

"Adam, do not touch!" This time, as she reached for his hand, her adversary quickly snatched it from her grasp and placed it on the table in front of him, primly placing his other hand on top.

Frowning intently, the Courier continued. "Bayel's past behavior would still need to be discussed, along with the accusation that he is being supported by an illegal practice."

Bardhof leaned back in his chair and glanced at Angus Bailey before returning his focus to Gwen.

"As I believe I told you before, when you were visiting us with *both* your Riders, the way we worship is none of your business."

Pausing for an exaggerated sigh, the First Assistant shifted his weight forward again and onto his elbows on the table. He leaned closer to Gwen and said softly, "Now, I have offered to bring your requests to my lord, and I have even invited you to come along. I will sweeten the offer with the promise that you will be able to see your Rider. Is that enough to make you happy? Because I *do* want to make you happy, Gwen."

His syrupy tone and the look of greed in Bardhof's eyes underscored the increased danger and hunger suddenly radiating from the man. Gwen kept her face pleasant as Nan pulsed in a protective gesture, and an unspoken sense of alarm flashed though her mind.

"First, a promise of no more invasions is required," she finally said, her voice relaxed and cool. "Will he swear to that before Lord Veron? And return the Rider?"

"I will ask him to speak to Veron, but as for the Rider, I'm afraid that's a no," said the bald Assistant as he abruptly sat back, his eyes once again serene and his voice businesslike. "No more incursions, Courier, but no Rider."

"Why continue to hold him?"

"Perhaps Bayel sees him as insurance."

"That doesn't make sense, Adam. If there won't be any more problems with the trespassing, why do you need the Rider? He came with me to what was supposed to be a cordial meeting with the Spirit; a meeting that you were reluctant to end."

"I think you misinterpreted my intentions. I simply asked you to stay."

"You said we could leave when your followers allowed it. Which brings up the question—does Bayel know how you feel about those faithful you called *your* followers?"

Bardhof waved his hand to suggest the question was a nonissue.

"A phrase only. What's mine is his. Now, how about this: your Rider will remain with us until you decide to come for him?"

"I gave you my two simple requirements for an appearance at your place. You've only partially agreed to one. When Bayel meets with Veron, and when you release the Rider, then I will visit."

"You drive a hard bargain, Courier. I will have to consult with my lord."

"You agreed to stop Bayel's incursions. That would seem to be the hardest goal to achieve," said Gwen.

"When you know Bayel's mind, then you can tell me what is hard and what isn't," said Bardhof condescendingly. "Let me handle him."

"As you say, you should know him best," replied Gwen sarcastically. "But I'd just like to point out, yet again, that there is no reason to stretch out this incident any longer. Maybe things got off track because there has been such little contact between our communities. We can change that and, I agree, it would include a visit from me after our two simple conditions are met."

Bardhof leaned forward, his eyes glittering again; beads of sweat reappeared on his head.

"We're planning a worldwide series of events to rededicate all of Bayel's temples and believers. Your appearance during that would be most welcome. I will happily take the option back to Bayel. I shall suggest that you be welcomed as an honored guest at the temple here in Haliburum and we release your man."

Something did not feel right about the way Adam jumped at the offer and the wording he used, but when Gwen glanced at Angus Bailey, the lawyer nodded.

"All right, then," agreed the Courier, covering her misgivings with a small nod. "How will I know your decision?"

"I will let Mr. Bailey here know. Is that acceptable?"

"Quite." The lawyer nodded.

"I might be able to speed up the process if you were to visit me sooner at the temple," pressed Adam. "We could accomplish a lot together."

"I believe, at this point, it would be best to contact Mr. Bailey," replied Gwen evenly as she held his eyes.

"Then I believe that is all I have to discuss," said the bald man as he quickly stood and extended his hand to the attorney. "Thank you for your hospitality, Mr. Bailey. I will let you know Bayel's decision."

He turned back to Gwen as she rose and took her right hand in both of his, holding it so tightly she could not have pulled away without a struggle.

"I look forward to meeting you under more favorable circumstances and convincing you that I can be a most loyal friend and companion," declared Bardhof before pulling her into an embrace that locked her arms at her sides.

He kissed her on the cheek and stole the moment to brush her hair with his face. Disgusted, Gwen brought up her hands and slowly began pressing up and under his rib cage with her knuckles. She continued until he grunted and released her. When he stood back, his smile was cruel and his eyes glittered.

"Yes, Gwen, I hope to see you at the temple again very soon. Remember, you agreed."

Concerned that any negative reaction on her part could mean dire consequences for Rakeem, Gwen responded with her own hard smile.

"First the vow to Veron, and then Bayel's confirmation that you will release the Rider."

"I will let Mr. Bailey know what is decided," replied Bardhof with a final caress of her arm and a look that had gone from cruel to sly.

With that, he sauntered from the room.

"Oh, I don't like that man." Gwen shuddered as soon as the door closed behind him. "I don't like him at all."

Nan concurred with a wave of concern and doubt.

"I have to admit there is something dark there; something almost unbalanced," concurred Baily, frowning. "But you got him to agree to the most important request."

"He didn't really agree, and he kept changing his wording," corrected Gwen as she slumped back in her chair. "I don't like it."

※※

Gwen was not surprised to find Veron sharing a glass of wine with her employer when she arrived at the King's office to offer her report. The Riders had gone their separate ways, giving her the freedom to talk to Nathao alone.

"It was not really productive, gentlemen. Piale didn't show; it was the new First Assistant, Adam Bardhof. He suggested that Bayel will not trespass again and that he may agree to swear to you, Lord Veron, to stay where he belongs. On the matter of Rakeem, Bardhof agreed to ask Bayel to release him in return for a visit from me during some big rededication event they're planning for all his temples.

"Frankly, I think he lied on all counts, and I don't mind telling you I don't like him. He's evil," she added bluntly.

"Sometimes intuition puts the pieces together faster than intellect," said the little god in white with a high-pitched sigh. "I am here with bad news. I've confirmed with a source that a human blood sacrifice to Bayel *has* taken place."

"Where and when?" Gwen sank onto her usual floor pillow.

"We already confirmed several of the small-animal variety at the temple in Haliburum. But the last one, oh, that one was human."

The Courier shivered at the thought of Rakeem in the hands of the same people and took some small comfort from the protective squeeze offered by her jacket. She looked at Nathao, and he nodded.

"Yes, it coincided with the last Disturbance we had, the one that prompted me to send you and the Riders back to the temple."

"So, was it a high-level test?" asked Gwen thoughtfully. "Or was it planned specifically to push you into sending us back so they could detain us? That would have been quite a coup—three of your people sacrificed to a rival trying to take you down."

"And one of them the Courier," added Veron in his reedy voice. "That would have been a powerful offering, and the King's second loss of a Courier in a rather short period of time.

"The rest of the Pantheon is watching and that could very well have opened you to raids, Nathao."

"Raids?" echoed Gwen. "I thought violence like that was a thing of the past? Although that may be a silly conclusion, since here we are talking about human sacrifice and power. Are you people regressing?"

"If we are regressing, it is because of our constituents," observed the King coolly. "The raids spoken of here are more civilized. My colleagues would begin evangelizing and answering prayers from my followers to gain conversions. That would force me to increase my efforts to support my believers and mean more work for you and the Riders."

"The tactic," added Veron, "would force your King to work from the weaker position of fighting to maintain and not lose constituents, while his competitors have the upper hand in that they face no losses, just gains if they are successful."

"Just who might do that?"

"Anyone with time on his or her hands or the desire to move up the Promethean List," replied the God of Truth.

"What is it about that List that makes it so important?" pressed Gwen. "I would think when you follow someone, you choose the god for what he or she means to you, not for a ranking on a list."

"Then you would think naïvely," countered Veron. "The List is very helpful."

"It keeps certain individuals in their place? And offers employment for hundreds of academics in the League?"

"Courier, this is the not the time to debate that which has contributed to the stability of our world," said Nathao firmly. "We gods have alliances, and I intend to remain where I am. To help ensure that, please continue with the events of your meeting."

"Sir," acknowledged Gwen. "Bardhof did say that if I didn't want to wait for him to send Mr. Bailey an answer on Rakeem, I was welcome to visit him at the temple. Just the thought gives me the chills, but what do we do now? Do we wait for them to kill Rakeem and be ready to deal with the resulting Disturbance here? That won't be the end of it."

"No, it would not be the end of it," agreed the King. "Both Lord Veron and Mother Laciane are working to get more information, and I have asked Errin of Trian to use his network. It might offer information ours will not."

Gwen was silent for a moment as she considered the mention of the lower-ranked god and the facts she had digested in her studies with Armen. Then she nodded in approval.

"That's a great idea. His Speaker talks to animals, and his constituency includes others who can. That's a network that could be priceless."

"I am so glad you agree," said Nathao with a hint of tolerant sarcasm, "because you will meet with his Speaker tomorrow at my chapel in Cheo. Take one of the Riders with you; when you return, come and see me."

✳✷✳

On the third floor, Gwen found her grandfather in his office.

"Grandpa, I need your help. I need you to come to Cheo with me tomorrow," she said, leaning in the open door.

Barnabas turned away from his keyboard and nodded to the other chair in the room.

"Certainly. Why?"

Gwen waved off the offer to sit and remained in the doorway. "I'm meeting with Errin of Trian's Speaker. We need more information if we're going to help Rakeem."

"Errin of Trian?" Barnabas looked puzzled. "Why? His people talk to animals."

"Some of them do, and that's exactly the point. My meeting with Bayel's man didn't go very far, and we need to learn more. Animals go all sorts of places, and no one pays them any attention. So, the Speaker can ask if anyone has been in Bayel's temples and heard or seen anything."

"Hmm," murmured the Rider, obviously not fully convinced. "It sounds plausible, but I don't know."

"Well, we'll find out tomorrow in Cheo. Come by the house in the morning, and we can leave from there."

"Sounds good, Courier," said her grandfather, standing up and moving closer. "But have you thought anymore about how this may be getting dangerous?"

Gwen had been trying to find a new balance in this relationship with her grandfather ever since their conversation outside Nathao's office. Now she put her hand on his arm and summoned all her patience.

"Your concern is appreciated, but don't go overboard. I'm a big girl."

"A big girl in a job that's getting riskier by the moment—or am I the only one who sees that?" The concern in his voice was palpable.

"I'm aware, and so is the King. Don't dwell on it."

"But it was *my* Request that brought you to the King's notice. I should be taking on the responsibility."

"You can't," said Gwen flatly; as Barnabas began to argue again, she quickly raised her hand in his face and snapped. "Just stop. You flatter yourself by thinking you can replace my life with yours. You can't. My decision to accept the job was mine alone. You want to protect me? You'll get that chance tomorrow when you come with me to Cheo."

The Rider faltered for a moment and then, before he could say anything else, they heard footsteps. Gwen glanced down the hall and back at her grandfather.

"That's Claire. As far as I'm concerned, there's nothing more to discuss here. I'll see you in the morning."

With that, she left the doorway to intercept the female Rider.

"Have a minute?"

Claire paused as Barnabas stormed out of his office and down the hall without a word, and then refocused on Gwen.

"Of course."

Gwen outlined her schedule for the next day, and the blond Rider quickly made the connection between Errin's constituency and the King's request for help. She then offered her presence for the trip to Cheo, which Gwen declined.

"Actually, I was hoping you'd stay close to Laciane and let me know right away if she learns something. I've asked my grandfather to come with me."

"He isn't much of a diplomat or bodyguard," warned Claire.

"I know," admitted Gwen. "But I think any action will really come in Haliburum, which is why I would prefer to have you and Eli there, backed up by Jensen. Armen and Sean can be here if the King needs something. That way everyone has at least one buddy, and the talents in each group kind of complement each other."

"Except for you and Barnabas. I don't like that pairing, but it's your call, Courier," said Claire with a disapproving tone. "I'll do my part; just make sure your grandfather does his."

22

He had not expected so much paperwork, and while he told himself this was part of leading a growing organization, Adam was very relieved when Ralph arrived and he could put it all aside. He pulled his friend and supporter to the leather sofa in the office and sighed as he settled down.

"I hate being cooped up in here. I miss the group. What's been going on? Tell me everything."

"Not a lot, really," said Ralph with a shrug. "With Emily gone no one is challenging your authority to speak for Bayel. But they are asking for more details of the rededication plans and want to know what parts they will have in the activities."

"And that's what we will finalize today, you and I. We're agreed the central event for our core members will take place in the new sanctuary."

His number two made a face of frustration.

"Yes, but other than the speeches and tour, what else did you have planned? Some of these people were with us for Emily's sacrifice, and they expect more. They felt the power; *I* felt the power, Adam. A simple toast or 'hurrah' will leave a lot of them disappointed."

"Including you?" suggested Adam slyly.

"As a matter of fact, yes," shot back Ralph. He then relaxed and grinned. "All right, you got me. I know you have something great planned, so share it, my friend!"

The First Assistant laughed. "You, of all people, will appreciate my agenda to celebrate the day. We must talk about Piale's role, and those of a few others that I think will please Bayel and our people. I also think you will agree the plan will make it clear to the rest of the world that we have arrived as a new force."

"What do you plan for Piale? Have you told him?"

"No, I don't think it would be wise to let him in on the details until the last moment. It wouldn't do if one of the guests of honor didn't show up."

Ralph eyed his friend suspiciously and then guffawed as he put it together.

"Brilliant! The faithful servant plays the role to the end of his days. But what else will there be? Is there anything you want me to do? Plans for the festivities in our temples here and in the other cities are on track, so I have the time to back you up. Adam, I want to be the only right-hand man you'll ever need."

Adam felt an unexpected surge of affection for his longtime friend.

"Ralph, we're in this together, and we'll share the success."

23

~

Father Yial was waiting when Barnabas and Gwen Stepped through to Cheo. Knowing Gwen would need a little time to herself when she walked onto the roof, the priest told Barnabas there were some petitioners in the chapel who would appreciate his time.

The Rider glanced at Gwen, who waved him on. "We'll be upstairs when you are done."

"Errin's Speaker is due here shortly," said Yial after Barnabas had gone. "I'll bring him up. Why don't you get settled?"

Gwen thanked him and climbed the stairs, cheerfully anticipating the first few moments with the stone and the energy it offered. Her mind was always clearer and her body refreshed after time here.

The Courier paused outside the door and reveled in the rush of power through her muscles, nerves, and brain. She stretched and could have sworn she heard Nan sigh in delight.

When she felt balanced and grounded, Gwen strolled the area, checking on the various plants that were part of the still-expanding, almost luxurious, roof garden. They were all doing exceptionally well, and she wondered if the stones had anything to do with that. She had a few additional minutes to relax on one of two folded blankets set under several potted orange trees before the door opened and Yial appeared with a large tray and a tall, thin individual.

She rose as they approached and noted how the new man's jeans and brown shirt seemed to hang a little on his skinny frame.

"Gwen, this is Terrill, Speaker for Errin of Trian," began Yial. "Terrill, this is Gwen, Courier for the King of Dreams. Now, I've brought some refreshments; please enjoy them while you talk. I will go back downstairs and wait for the Rider to finish."

"Thank you, Father," said Gwen as Yial knelt down to put the tray next to the blankets before leaving. "Terrill, thank you for coming."

Gwen offered her hand to the brown-haired man with the deep green eyes and nodded to the black squirrel sitting on his shoulder. Nan rippled slightly across her back with a hint of approval, tinged with curiosity.

"I'm surprised we haven't met before," replied the Speaker with a firm handshake while the squirrel chittered.

Gwen chuckled at the noise and folded herself into a seated position again on one of the blankets.

"I haven't been in this job all that long, which could explain why our paths haven't crossed. Please take a chair if you would be more comfortable. Can I pour you some tea? Would your friend like something? I think I see some sesame seeds on those rolls over there."

Terrill smiled and nodded as he joined her at blanket level.

"I would love some, thank you. Kyril here thanks you as well but says he is watching his weight."

"You certainly don't look like you need a diet," said Gwen.

There were a few chitters, and then Terrill laughed. "He says you are too kind."

There was silence while Gwen poured the fragrant tea.

"Ah, orange blossom," she said. "The Father is sparing no expense."

"I recognized the scent as soon as I got near. It's a rare treat," said Terrill as he accepted a cup and then sipped the offering almost reverently.

"Now, Lord Errin gave me a brief explanation of what seems to have been happening, and I'm very concerned to hear of Bayel's new leanings. These animal sacrifices disgust me. What can we do for you?"

"Did Errin tell you that one of our Riders is still being held in Bayel's temple in Haliburum?"

"No."

"He was detained at what was supposed to be a peaceful meeting. Bayel's people never really intended to let us leave. One Rider and I managed to get out," said Gwen, cradling her teacup in her lap with both hands, her blue eyes skipping intently between Terrill and Kyril as she watched for any subtle interaction. "Our efforts to gain our colleague's release haven't been successful.

"We also believe that along with the animal killings, there has been at least one human murder. We fear our Rider may be in danger. We need to know what is being planned so we can stop it.

"Lord Veron is working with the King on this, but we hoped you and Lord Errin might be able to help as well. You have sources that can go places and hear things we cannot. We hoped you might have some of these sources in the temple."

"We can do that." Terrill nodded thoughtfully. "You say Lord Veron is also involved?"

"Yes, and I am sure there are others. Face it, if these illegal practices aren't stopped, Bayel will grow evermore dangerous."

"Why did he choose to take on your King, do you think?"

Gwen shook her head and pushed some wayward strands of hair back over her shoulder.

"I haven't figured that one out, and if the King knows, he hasn't seen fit to share it with me."

"I only ask because, as you know, you and I are unique in our positions. We were chosen specifically because we did *not* follow either Errin or Nathao. I wonder if Bayel sees some weakness in gods who choose outsiders and, if so, whether Errin might be the next target."

"An interesting theory," Gwen said. She did not mention that the Speaker's thought left open the question of why Bayel wouldn't first strike at a god like Errin, with a lower Promethean ranking, before targeting someone stronger like Nathao. "Let's hope we don't find out. More tea?"

"Thank you." Terrill smiled as he held his cup out for a refill. "It will take me a day or two to get someone suitable to Haliburum. There isn't anyone in that city right now with the ability to Speak on the level this will take, and I can't leave here just yet."

The reply was not what Gwen had been hoping to hear. The prospect of a delay annoyed her, and the Speaker's apparent lack of any sense of urgency aggravated that feeling. But before she could frame a polite way to push for faster action, Kyril began chittering and running his paws through Terrill's shoulder-length hair. The Speaker turned his head slowly to look at the squirrel and then extended his arm so the rodent could run down and sit on the blanket. Kyril sat there and continued being very vocal about something.

The squirrel came across as a little bossy, but Gwen hoped he had a better grasp of the situation than his partner. On a hunch, she poured a little tea on a plate to let it cool and waited while her two companions talked.

"That could work, if you're willing," Terrill was saying. "But how do you get there from here?"

Kyril answered, and the Speaker glanced at Gwen.

"I don't know, but we could ask. You do realize there wouldn't be anyone in Haliburum who could talk to you until you got to Errin's temple. When was the last time you were on your own in the city?"

Kyril's response was a sound that Gwen could have sworn was a deprecating comment, but the Speaker just raised his eyebrows and grinned.

"I'm only worried about your safety, you little ingrate."

After a few more minutes of give-and-take, Terrill turned to Gwen, and she handed him his refilled cup. She then put the plate with the cooled tea near Kyril, who chittered once in her direction and began drinking.

"I'll take that as a thank you, and you are welcome. Did you two work something out?" she asked innocently.

"Kyril says he can travel back to Haliburum with you and start to spread the word in the city. I'll contact my Seconds as soon as I get back to the church here, and they can start for Haliburum. By the time they get there, Kyril will have things well in motion."

Relieved and excited, Gwen turned to Kyril, who was sitting back on his haunches.

"You're brilliant. We don't have time to spare, and your help will be very appreciated. I will warn you that the Steps we use to travel can be a little disorienting in the beginning. But I'll be happy to hold you."

Again, there was that deprecating sound, and Terrill laughed.

"He says if he can swing from branch to branch, a little Step won't hurt him."

"We'll see if you're singing the same tune when we get to Haliburum." Gwen grinned.

Kyril chittered and moved closer to her.

"He says he'll ride on your shoulder, if that's all right. He says to let him get up there now, and you can both get comfortable. Just reach out your arm," said Terrill, moving his own as an example.

Gwen mirrored his action, and Kyril scampered up the sleeve of her jacket, which reacted with a slight warming sensation. The squirrel draped himself across her shoulder with his tail around the back of her neck and, as Nan rippled once, he muttered.

"Don't worry," said Gwen, turning her head slightly. "This is a very special coat. King Nathao made it just for me, and it knows me. Now it will know you too."

Another slight ripple ran across her shoulders; this time Kyril did not comment except to cluck once.

"Try standing," said Terrill. "Just go slowly."

Gwen stood in one smooth motion, and Kyril seemed to pat her shoulder in approval.

The Speaker laughed again and shook his head, his brown hair swinging.

"You two-timer. Don't forget where your first home is."

Gwen reached up to pat the squirrel gently. "You are so brave."

"Please," said Terrill with a pained look. "You'll make him unbearable."

"What does he need to eat while he's with us?" asked the Courier as Yial and Barnabas approached.

"Cracked corn, nuts, seeds, fruit, green vegetables, just about anything. Once he delivers the message to his friends, he'll stop back to let you know and then head to Errin's. Right, Kyril?"

The squirrel chittered, and Gwen giggled as his tail jerked, tickling her neck.

"Well, Courier," said Barnabas as he and Yial approached. "Is this a pet?"

"Oh, no, Rider, this is an ally; a very smart and very brave ally. Kyril, this is Barnabas."

The squirrel gave what could have been a tiny sneeze, but the chagrined look on Terrill's face told Gwen it was a lot more than that.

"Kyril has volunteered to come back with us and begin asking around for the information we need. Terrill can't leave here just yet, and his people won't be in Haliburum for a day or two. So, instead of losing time, Kyril will come with us and get things started."

Barnabas looked more closely at the squirrel while Yial stood beside him with his hands in the sleeves of his robe.

"Courier." The priest frowned. "I don't believe we've ever had an animal use a Step before."

"Not so," said Gwen quickly. "Claire told me Alice's guide dog, Saber, did it all the time. In fact, she said he tolerated it better than some of the Riders."

"That's right," agreed Barnabas, still looking dubiously at Kyril. "Saber did just fine. And I suppose if a dog can do it, why not a squirrel?"

Kyril made that sneezing sound again; this time Gwen made eye contact with Terrill, who just shook his head and leaned close to the squirrel.

"Behave yourself, urchin. Courier, if he gets too obnoxious, you can always dump him in a box and return him."

"I don't think that will be a problem, but we should be going. Are you ready?" she asked, looking sideways at her traveling companion.

In response she got a short chitter.

Terrill turned to Yial. "Father, may I see him off?"

"Of course. Follow me, and be careful on the stairs."

In the Step room, Terrill whispered a good-bye to Kyril, tweaked his ear, and moved back as Barnabas waved his arm to open a Window to Haliburum.

The Rider nodded to those in the room and Stepped through. Gwen turned to the Speaker.

"Thank you for your help, Terrill, and I promise to take good care of your friend and our colleague."

Then she turned her head slightly to address the squirrel. "Kyril, welcome to the service of the King. Now hang on, here we go."

With that, she Stepped to Haliburum.

At the other end, Kryil was still on her shoulder, but he was molded to her body and had a death grip on Nan.

The skeptical look on her grandfather's face did not escape Gwen as she praised the squirrel for being so brave. She carefully reached across her chest with her left hand to gently stroke his head.

Kyril grunted and pushed his head against her hand, demanding more attention, which Gwen obligingly provided. Nan backed her up with a burst of warmth right under the squirrel that practically made him purr.

In a minute, the sleek black head was up, and Kyril began to twitch his ears and exercise his voice. Before they reached Laciane's office, the squirrel was crouched on the Courier's shoulder, facing forward and lashing his tail. He was also talking a mile a minute, although his companions had no idea what he was saying.

Gwen enjoyed the stares and looks as she and her companions strode to the Mother's outer office, where Preston looked up and gasped. In one step he was at Gwen's side.

"Wow, a black squirrel. Where did he come from? He's beautiful. Do you know they're really a variant on the gray squirrels?" He paused as Kyril started chittering loudly. "But they are so much smarter and better-looking, aren't they, my friend?"

Kyril seemed mollified by the added comments and stopped yelling. He stretched out to sniff the hand Preston offered and, in a flash, launched himself from Gwen's shoulder to the acolyte's, where he had little trouble finding his equilibrium because Preston barely moved.

Once the squirrel settled, the young man began petting him, murmuring as Kyril quietly responded, and the two then rubbed heads.

Stunned at the turn of events, Gwen just stared at the pair as Laciane came out of her office.

"Preston, can you explain?" asked the Guidant smoothly and calmly at the sight of her aide talking to the squirrel sitting on his shoulder.

"Actually, Mother, he came in with the Courier."

"His name is Kyril." Gwen grinned as she realized one big problem was now unexpectedly solved. "He's going to help us. And this is great, Mother, because I really wasn't sure how we were going to communicate."

"He says he'd like to settle things here and then get on with his work," said Preston, scratching the squirrel's head. "He says there's a lot of territory he needs to cover if we're to get the best information."

"When did you know you could talk to animals?" asked Laciane, folding her hands, her face pleasant but noncommittal.

"I've always been able to, Mother. It runs in the family."

"And it couldn't be a more welcome gift, right?" interrupted Gwen, still grinning as Laciane's face began to take on a more concerned look. "We'll explain more in a minute, but, Kyril, this is Preston. Can you work with him?"

The squirrel sat straight up, his paws folded in front of him, and proceeded to rattle something off.

"I'll take that as a yes," said Gwen when he was done. "Now, let's sit down, because we have a lot to go over."

※※

Barnabas was still shaking his head as he and Gwen Stepped back to the Keep.

"Who would have thought the boy could talk squirrel?"

"Grandpa, it isn't just squirrel—Preston can speak to most animals. I'm curious why he didn't use that and follow Errin, especially if it runs in his family. Wonder if Errin would have chosen him as Speaker if he weren't already sworn to the King."

"He talks to squirrels, girl," repeated her grandfather in exasperation as he opened the door to the hallway. "Squirrels."

His granddaughter gave him a gentle shove.

"Silly. Did you see how happy Kyril seemed to be?"

"Amazing, a happy squirrel," replied Barnabas, cynicism dripping from his comment. "I'm off to the Stables to update the others. You can go tell the King. I'm getting too old for this."

With a gruff noise of derision that reminded Gwen of the rodent they had just left, the Rider disappeared down a side hall to brief his coworkers with what Gwen was sure would be a jaundiced version of the day's events. She crossed the quad for the King's office and a much more accurate telling of the story.

✺◈✺

Over the next few days, there was no word from Bardhof, but things were far from quiet for Nathao's people. Preston was temporarily assigned to Errin's church in Haliburum, and intelligence began coming in from the squirrel's contacts as well as sources tapped by Laciane and Veron. Laciane scored first.

✺◈✺

Gwen was at the breakfast table with the kids at the beginning of what promised to be a hot summer day. Sam had come home a few weeks earlier, and he and Becky planned to spend the day with their cousins in their paternal grandparents' backyard pool. As the siblings finished their cereal, they talked about what to bring. The intense discussion was interrupted by a call from the living room.

"Good morning," said Eli, striding into the kitchen. "I trust you're all well rested?"

253

Gwen tensed, alert to the possibility of new information.

"Good morning. Coffee?"

"The pot's on the counter, right there," said Alana. "Help yourself."

"Eli," observed Sam rather darkly, "almost every time you show up, Mom has another meeting. Is there one today?"

The thin Rider looked at the boy, amused. "And if there is? We do have work to do, you know."

"And, Sam," added Becky in a loud whisper, "she wasn't invited to come with us. This is for the cousins."

Sam scowled and dug into his cereal. "I just wish that sometimes we had advance warning of meetings."

"Well, I hate to say it," said Eli, "but there *is* a meeting, and it may be *very* long."

"Could it be about that trip we were discussing?" suggested Gwen as the kids looked up.

"It just might be," replied Eli nonchalantly, bringing his coffee to the table. "Your mom has an important job, kids, and sometimes there will be travel."

"We've talked about that, remember?" said Gwen, looking at her son and daughter.

There was silence, and then Sam sighed. "I know. I just hate to think you might have to be gone for a while."

"Sam, Alana's here," said Becky, putting her hand on her brother's arm. "Mom will be back as soon as she can."

Gwen's throat tightened at her daughter's surprisingly mature attitude; she was grateful when Alana quickly rose and began picking up dirty dishes.

"Come on, you two, work is work, but you have the chance to play today. Go upstairs and get your things together while I finish cleaning up," said the nanny.

Both children left the kitchen, giving their mother the time she needed to recover her slipping composure.

"Alana, make sure Lois knows what's going on," said Gwen.

"Lois?"

"She knows a lot more than she lets on. And, she knows she may be needed in a big way."

"Understood. Between us the children will be well taken care of. Now concentrate on the job at hand," admonished the nanny, putting the dishes in the dishwasher. Then, without looking at Gwen or Eli, she headed for the bedrooms, saying, "I'll help them get packed."

There was silence for a moment, and Eli raised his cup for another sip of coffee. "Lois?"

"My mother-in-law seems to have the King's confidence. She knows everything."

"Huh. Well, you ready to get to work?"

Gwen gave him a hard look. "Don't ever doubt that, especially when there are outstanding questions about a friend. What's the latest?"

"Nat will give you a Dream; then you go Haliburum. Apparently, Laciane has been able to use her connections to find out what's going on inside Bayel's Temple."

"Go on," prompted Gwen, leaning forward. "What did she learn?"

Eli shrugged. "I'm not privy to that. I assume the King will let you know."

"All right. Finish your coffee and let me say good-bye to my kids."

The Rider said nothing as she left and went upstairs.

❋❋

The atmosphere was considerably lighter a few minutes later when everyone came back down to the kitchen.

"Mom, be careful," said Sam, giving her a kiss, followed by Becky.

"I will, and I'll be home as soon as I can," promised his mother, ushering them off with Alana. "Now you two have fun."

As she heard the front door close, Gwen turned to Eli and raised an eyebrow.

"*You* ready?"

24

~

Ralph and Adam sat on the carpeted risers in the dimly lit underground sanctuary feeling very pleased with themselves. The big event was getting closer, and everything was falling into place.

"Our special guest is doing well?" inquired the First Assistant.

"He's under control and will remain so until his big moment."

"You might want to back off on the drugs soon so he's aware of what's happening when Bayel takes him."

"Don't worry, Adam, it'll be fine."

The two men were silent as they each contemplated the menacing dark altar sitting in the ocean of sparkling sand.

"I wonder how Emily would feel about this," murmured Ralph. "She was the first of what will be a long line of offerings."

"Emily didn't appreciate it then, and she wouldn't appreciate it now." Adam scowled.

"Do you know that some in the inner circle want her to be declared something special? Like a consort of Bayel, or whatever."

The First Assistant rubbed his bald head and grunted.

"No, I didn't know. But that's a ridiculous idea."

"Why would that be so distasteful to you, Adam?" crooned a familiar voice that filled the room and echoed gently off the walls.

The men surged to their feet in shock as Bayel coalesced next to the altar.

"Are you so jealous that you would preclude any honor for your first human offering to me?"

"Of course not, lord. I admit I haven't thought about the possibility that she might be worthy of an honor, but somehow, as a consort for you—well, it just doesn't seem to do you justice."

"Ralph? What do you think?" asked the bronze god, leaning languidly against the altar and toying with the red pocket square in a black suit jacket that appeared a bit worn. Adam noticed his hair continued to get longer and more unkempt every time they met.

Ralph focused on the carpeting at his feet and said nothing.

The man who thought he was in charge suddenly stared at his friend in dismay.

"Ralph, is this consort thing *your* idea?"

There was a pause, and then Bayel answered, stroking the black stone next to him.

"It is, and I like it. It gives us a reason to bring more women to this bed, and some might even be willing partners. I would like to experience that."

Anger and a sense of betrayal filled Adam as his eyes jumped back and forth between his god and the man he had considered his best friend. Slowly, he got his emotions under control and, shrugging, opened his arms to Bayel in a gesture of submission.

"If this is your wish, my lord, we will make it so. I can see the wisdom."

Bayel moved a little closer but remained on the sand.

"It is a brilliant idea. As First Assistant see that Ralph leads the effort to bring it to fruition."

"Of course." Adam bowed.

"And, Ralph, well done. You are most valued."

With that, the room felt empty, and both men knew they were alone.

The awkward silence was broken by Adam.

"You couldn't come to me with the idea?"

"You wouldn't have listened," said Ralph. "You don't want Emily remembered at all, but she was the first, and that's significant. It will help us bring people to our cause, especially women, who will see her as one of Bayel's leaders."

"Leader?" sputtered the First Assistant. "Leader? What have I been doing all these years? She was a roadblock to progress."

"A roadblock to *your* progress in power, Adam. Look, you deserve the titles and the accolades, but think about it: without Emily's constant challenge, you would not have risen this far. She inspired you."

Adam forced himself to appear calm, but his anger was deep.

"I have received inspiration from many people, Ralph, including you. But to believe Emily was a primary force in this journey is ludicrous. She was a bedmate for me and for you. She sewed this colored stuff on our robes. She arranged meals for meetings. She was a woman—nothing more."

"She was all those things and more. She pushed you to be the leader you are. Envy and rivalry are great tools for creating brilliance, *your* brilliance."

There was new silence as Adam digested the strangely couched compliment.

"I thank you for that insight, my friend," he finally allowed. "You are more perceptive than I in these matters. Give me some time to think about this, to understand the wisdom."

Ralph stepped forward and grabbed Adam's hand.

"I'm so glad I can speak about this now. I was afraid you would never accept it."

Adam tolerated the touch and nodded.

"Go now. I need to think."

Ralph grinned and raced up the stairs to the preparation room above them.

Adam watched him go and thought only of betrayal.

25

Gwen raised her hand to knock on the King's office door, but before she could move, it was yanked open from the inside by Marcia. The Administrator stopped and glared.

"Courier, he's been waiting for you," she snapped. "If he's in a foul mood, don't blame me."

Without another word, she stomped toward the stairs, leaving the door open.

Gwen slipped in and, scanning the room, located the King in the big chair he reserved for staff meetings. His face was impassive as she nodded a greeting.

"I came as soon as Eli called, sir."

"Do not listen to Marcia. She gets annoyed when she feels power-less and tends to take it out on others. Lie down; we do not have much time." He indicated one of the sofas. "I will give you my Dream; when you wake, we will talk."

Gwen moved to the sofa and stretched out. The atmosphere in the room was exceedingly tense, which made the sense of confidence and security flowing from Nan a welcome and comforting counterpoint.

"Ready?"

Gwen pulled the pillow higher under her head.

"All right. I'm as relaxed as I'm likely to get."

Nathao put his hands on her head and looked her right in the eyes.

"This is the rough part, child—what you will learn now is what makes being my Courier the hardest job here. This is not something you can share with anyone else, except me. And while the others may try to understand, they can never fully grasp it."

Gwen nodded. "Rather like being a single parent. There isn't anyone who truly knows what you do."

"Sleep," said the King, and Gwen thought she detected a sad note in his voice before she fell into the world of dreams.

What she dreamed was terrible, and when she woke, she felt utterly drained. Before she opened her eyes, she took an extra minute to center her emotions and find the balance she knew she would desperately need. She opened her eyes and sat up, crossing her arms to embrace the intense message of support emanating from Nan. As she took stock of the situation, Nathao appeared at the doors to the balcony.

"How do you feel?"

Gwen could only shake her head. Without another word, the King moved to the decanter of red wine, poured two glasses, and brought them to the sofa. His Courier downed the first in a few gulps and then sipped at the second.

"Thanks," she said, putting the glass on the table. "So, the rededication is when he'll move. That makes sense. And Rakeem has to die?"

"That is not what I said about Rakeem."

"Plain as day, you did."

"We can try to save him, but everything suggests that would be very difficult. The Dream you hold will release him, and since you will have alerted my brother, Luke will be waiting. It will be as quick and as easy as we—and Rakeem—can make it."

"That means a trip across the River. How much time do we have?"

"You can get to Luke's and back before anything has happened. But do not dawdle."

Gwen sighed. "Don't dawdle, so a friend can die quickly. You're right about this being a tough job."

"Step to the Boathouse," said Nathao, ignoring the comment. "After you see my brother, go straight to Haliburum. If Luke has any message for me, send it back from there with one of the Riders."

"And if you have something for me?"

"I will send one of the Riders."

"Right." Gwen stood up and straightened her clothes. "Well, I'm off. For better or worse, I hope to talk to you later."

She began walking to the office door but turned when the King spoke her name.

"Gwen," he said. "Rakeem has been with me for a very long time, and I would miss him."

Gwen paused, unsure what to say, then nodded. "I understand, and I'll do my best."

"And I would miss you too."

The Courier said nothing as her jacket offered a caress that spoke of conviction and commitment. She opened her mouth to say something and stopped because there were no words that fit. Then she smiled a little and tried again.

"I'm not afraid of dying, Nat. I understand that part of your instructions as well, and I appreciate the option. Just remember what you promised me and make sure if I have to choose it that Sam and Becky are well taken care of."

"I promised, and I honor my commitments."

"Then I'll be in touch," Gwen said, echoing Nathao's oft-used phrase, and she left the office.

⌘

The Step to the Boathouse and the trip across the River were uneventful. Dob did not utter a word, but he did raise his head as Gwen told him she shouldn't be gone long before heading through the fog for Luke's stables. Nora talked the entire time she readied Roscoe, which more than made up for Dob's silence, but she was quick and thorough; in minutes Gwen was on the road to Luke's.

She let Roscoe have his head as they moved into the fog.

"Here we go, my friend. We have a chance to help another friend escape some major suffering; let's make sure that happens."

Roscoe said nothing but picked up speed, and eventually the haloed glow of lights ahead began to cut through the fog. Not long after that, Gwen could see a tall stone wall and an archway that led to a cobblestone courtyard, where a man and a boy waited. Light spilled out of a large open door and the windows that ran the length of the yard. Glancing up, she could follow the wall of the structure to a second floor, where windows were also brightly lit, but beyond that the fog took over, and she couldn't tell how much higher it might extend.

She swung down from the horse and told the man and boy she needed to see their king.

"Sorry, ma'am, the king is not in, but the queen is. Shall I send word her brother-in-law's Courier is here?"

Gwen opened her mouth to ask how the man knew who she was, then realized it could hardly be anyone else riding to Death's doorstep.

"Yes, please. It's urgent."

"It always is," muttered the servant as he took Roscoe's reins and handed them to the youth, who led away the horse. "I will let the queen know. Please wait here."

Left alone, Gwen clasped her hands behind her and rocked back and forth, trying to hide her growing impatience. Nan was no help as she seemed to want to investigate the building and...

"Window treatments?" murmured Gwen, almost in disgust. "You want to check the window treatments and decorating?"

The jacket went limp and quiet.

Within minutes, the man reappeared.

"Courier, Her Majesty bids you come right away."

He led her into a simple foyer with a slate floor, burgundy-colored walls, and recessed lighting. Rather than continue through an arched doorway into what looked like a large sitting room with many chairs and sofas, the man guided her to the right through another doorway and up a circular, carpeted ramp that rose several floors. They left it at the third level, where he opened the first door they reached and stood back to let her enter.

"Please make yourself comfortable. The queen will be here in a moment."

"Thank you," she said absently as the door closed behind her.

Nan offered an apologetic hug and warmed slightly as she returned the gesture with a pat on the sleeve. "Well, you got your glimpse, and that better be good enough because we don't have time for the tour."

The coat rippled clumsily in response.

This room was a canvas of rose and cream wall hangings, paintings, lamps, and upholstered furniture. Strolling across the space, Gwen absently dragged her hand across the ornate fabric of a chair back, her mind again focused on her timetable and the message she had hoped to deliver directly to Luke. She neared the open window with the dense, mystifying fog beyond and planted herself, arms crossed, to stare at the atmospheric mass outside. She struggled to see something, anything, but the wall of gray refused to give up any hint of movement or color.

The sound of the door handle intruded on her thoughts, and she turned to face her hostess with a small bow.

"Welcome, Courier, I'm Percy. And it's nice of you to bow, but in private it isn't necessary."

The queen was a small, slight woman. Her dark hair, pulled high on her head, accentuated her fine-boned features while the dark blue of her gown set off her necklace and earrings and picked up accents in her dark eyes.

"Your Majesty, thank you for seeing me."

"I could not do less, could I? Would you care to sit? And please call me Percy. Luke is off on an errand but should not be long. How is my dear brother-in-law, and why has he sent you?"

Gwen declined the offered chair as she outlined the situation.

"We need Luke to be ready to 'guide'—I believe that's the euphemism—to 'guide' Rakeem here as soon as he accepts Nathao's dream. And I assume Rakeem trusts the King enough to give in very quickly," she concluded.

"In other words, an easy death," breathed Persephone.

"And fast," added her guest. "We cannot let the formerly gentle god of pleasure benefit from his suffering."

"I'm concerned about this activism among the gods," said the queen, frowning. "There are many in the Pantheon who could be vulnerable; many who always thought they were untouchable. But, on the other hand, a little bit of fear might be good for some of them."

Gwen shook her head. "I don't understand."

"It's no secret that some of the gods are less than kind; perhaps this will be a wake-up call for them to pay more attention to their own behavior."

"Anyone in particular you might be talking about?" prompted the Courier.

"Yes," responded the queen very matter-of-factly. "But my mother is a discussion for another time."

"Right," exhaled Gwen, a little startled to hear her host critique her own mother, although Demma was known for not tolerating fools. "Your Majesty—"

"Percy," interrupted the queen gently.

"Yes, Percy," her guest acquiesced with a nod and smile. "I'd better be going. If you would let Luke know what's happening, he can do whatever it is he does, and maybe Rakeem won't suffer."

"Is his death already decided?"

Gwen paused. "I think so. Remember, I'm only mortal. I don't decide these things."

"No," said Percy softly as the door opened. "You don't decide, and neither do I."

"And what is it you lovely ladies don't decide?" The King of Death suddenly swept into the room and embraced Percy.

"My beauty," he said, planting a kiss on her lips. "I see you've met my brother's latest acquisition."

"Acquisition? Really, dear, that's degrading."

"Sorry, Gwen," said the Lord of Death, acknowledging the Courier's caustic frown. "Didn't mean it that way. But, you have a message from my brother? Is it Bayel?"

Waving off his apology, Gwen outlined the situation one more time.

"So," murmured Luke, "the God of Joy has made his move. Very well, if he wants a challenge, he will get it. Tell Nat I'll be waiting for his Rider when the moment comes and will welcome him. But, now, is there another dream you hold?"

Gwen looked long and hard at Death and then nodded. "Yes, there is, and I hope I don't have to use it."

"I'll be ready if you do," said Luke quietly but matter-of-factly.

Percy looked back and forth at the pair and then gasped. "No! You've only been in the job a short time. How could he let you die?"

"It isn't his choice; it's the situation."

"Do you have a family?"

The question forced Gwen to reflect on her children and the promise she had won from Nathao to provide for them. There was no anger or sorrow in her review; regret, maybe, that she might not be there for them, but even that was eased by the calmness and clarity of her intentions. Nan bolstered the moment with a wave of acceptance and reassurance that she would not be alone.

"I have a son and daughter. Nat has promised to see to them."

"Could I help?" asked the other woman anxiously.

Pleased at the offer, Gwen nodded. "I'd welcome that. Let Nat know I said so. But now, I'd better be going."

"Then hail and farewell," said the King of Death. "I'll be waiting."

✳❋✳

At the chapel in Haliburum, Gwen sought out Laciane in her office.

"Courier! Come in. Please sit. I think the Riders are all in the chapel waiting for you. They told me you would be here with a plan."

"I am, but first would you tell me what you, Preston, and Kyril have learned?" suggested Gwen. "It can't hurt to hear the facts one more time to make sure nothing has been missed."

"Certainly," said the Mother, taking a deep breath and folding her hands on top of the desk. "This is not easy to talk about, especially with the implications it carries, but there are to be celebrations at all of Bayel's temples starting tonight and continuing for several days.

"Tomorrow is the last full day of spring with the summer solstice at around three-fifteen the following morning. We have it on good authority that there will be special rites of thanksgiving for the inner leadership that will coincide with the celestial event."

"Do you know where?" asked Gwen.

"Here in Haliburum, to be sure, but if you are asking where in the temple or on the grounds..." Laciane shook her head. "I don't know. Piale did once tell me of their plans for an underground sanctuary. Perhaps it's been built, perhaps not, but that would be the perfect place to celebrate illegally and secretly."

"The timing for the solstice could work to our benefit," mused the Courier. "Knowing Bayel's celebrations, most of the revelers should be useless after a full day of food and drink. But *where* is the question."

She reviewed the space she had seen inside the building and kept coming back to the dark doorway in the storage room she, Eli, and Rakeem had quickly searched in their run through Bayel's temple.

The stairs had been carpeted, suggesting they led to something more than a storage area. And if it were the entrance to a sanctuary, access could easily be controlled, leaving the rank and file in the dark about its existence.

"Were you able to learn anything specific about Rakeem?"

"Unfortunately, on that, no. I *am* sorry," said the Guidant sadly.

"No need to apologize," said the younger woman, leaning forward to put her hand on Laciane's. "I'm amazed at what you *did* learn."

"But how will you get into the temple?" asked Laciane. "Because I'm sure that's what you are planning."

"I'll go through it here in the office with everyone who needs to know. Let me get the Riders from the chapel. Where's Preston? I want to include him and Kyril, as well as yourself. Are they here?"

"Yes, they've been waiting. Preston said the squirrel was sure they would be needed."

Laciane went to find her assistant and his companion while Gwen walked to the gathering space and slipped into the sanctuary. From a shadowed corner, she paused to survey the gray, cavernous room and spotted her grandfather and Eli not far away. She stepped out just a little so they could see her and nodded toward the door before leaving the holy space herself.

A few minutes later, Barnabas, Eli, Claire, and Sean appeared in the outer room where the afternoon traffic was a little thin.

"Where are Armen and Jensen?" asked Gwen as they walked back to the Guidant's office.

"Not sure," admitted Claire. "Jensen was still at the Keep the last I saw him. As for Armen, I would guess he's back at the Stables."

"Hmm, well, one of you will have to bring them up to date, then, because I won't be going back there until this over."

"Until what is over?" asked her grandfather, a little too nonchalantly.

"That's what we're going to talk about."

❊❊

In the office, Barnabas was quiet as the group reviewed the plan outlined by the Courier, a fact that did not go unnoticed by his granddaughter even as she answered questions from the others. When everyone seemed as satisfied as they were going to get, he finally spoke.

"You are putting yourself in danger, a lot of danger."

"No more danger than Rakeem faced for me."

"But that was his job, and the situation. You shouldn't do this," said the Rider as he leaned forward and stabbed at the air with a finger. "You will *not* do this, girl. You are not supposed to go into danger like this. We Riders do that."

"We all do it."

The tension in the room climbed as Barnabas plowed on, oblivious to the looks from the others.

"No, we *don't*. Listen to me—*I* will go in. You stay outside. You won't go in there."

"Stop right now," said the Courier slowly. "You're embarrassing yourself and showing us all just how much of a liability you could be. This is exactly why *you* will stay outside."

"Girl," shouted Barnabas sharply as he jumped up from his chair, "*listen* to me."

"*Rider*," snapped Gwen just as sharply, her eyes hard. Her grandfather withered under the tone of cold authority. "*You* listen to *me*. To argue with me means arguing with the King, and you do not *ever* do that. This is the plan, and there are parts of it only I can carry out."

She let her comments sink in before she continued, addressing everyone in the room, her face expressionless and her voice stern.

"I carry three Dreams up here," said the Courier, tapping her head. "The first tells me what the King wants done. The second is for Rakeem, because I cannot let him die as a sacrifice to Bayel. If that happens, there will be chaos, and the King, you, and all his people will be in terrible danger.

"The third Dream is for me, because *I* can't be killed for that bastard god, or something worse than chaos will break loose, and the King could be destroyed. If I have to, I will take this dream and Cross. None of *you* can do that," she stated firmly as she surveyed the group.

When several moments went by and no one spoke, Gwen snapped her glare back to her grandfather, who shrank into his chair.

"I've made the jump, Barnabas. I've become one of those people you once warned me about: someone you just have to tolerate, someone who is a little distant, a little cold. But, maybe now you have a better understanding why. You *will* follow the plan."

When the group remained silent, Gwen nodded curtly.

"All right then. Riders, be here tomorrow night so we can make sure everything is in order. Fill in Jensen, and tell Armen he'll be driving.

"Kyril, Preston, I'll be here tomorrow afternoon for whatever additional information your contacts have gotten to you. Now, I'm going home to set the stage for a little business trip."

Without another word or glance, she left the office, closing the door gently behind her.

Kyril broke the silence as he chittered anxiously from his place next to Preston.

"I don't know, I'll ask," said the young man as he turned to the others, focusing on Barnabas. "Why are you so worried about her? She's the Courier; she knows what she's doing."

"She's an idiot, and it's my fault," said Barnabas in a growl as he rose and stormed out.

The remaining Riders looked at each other for a moment, and then Eli spoke.

"It doesn't go any further than here, please, but in case you didn't know, there is a family connection between them, and Barnabas is probably feeling overprotective."

"I would say so," commented Laciane with arched eyebrows. "It *is* a dangerous plan, but the King approves."

Kyril chittered, and Preston translated, "He says you're all being foolish and shouldn't worry. His people inside the temple will give us enough warning to get there in time. No one will be hurt."

"We aren't the ones who are worried," replied Claire, her face impassive. "But we'll make sure that those who are stop doing it real fast."

❊❊

Barnabas caught up with Gwen in the bedroom of her house where she was packing a suitcase.

"Where is everyone?" he asked from the doorway.

"Alana is picking up the kids from Bill's parents."

The Rider watched from the doorway as his granddaughter tossed a few things haphazardly into the open bag.

"Don't you think you should fold them?"

"Don't you think you should *trust* me?' she spat back, spinning around to face him, her dark hair swinging wide. "What you did back there was totally irresponsible. I've made decisions based on the King's instructions, and you were trying to undermine my authority. Did you ever think that could *kill* people if they start to question any trust they have in me?"

Barnabas waved his arms weakly, his eyes bright with tears. "I'm sorry. It was wrong, but I was scared for you. I *am* scared for you. I'm scared for your kids. I tried to stay emotionally remote, but that's been wrong, and I can't do it; I don't want to do it."

"Stop it," said Gwen, still furious. "I've made sure the kids will be well taken care of if something goes wrong. As for me, do you really think I *want* to die? I'm not crazy about the idea, but I understand the implications if I end up in a corner."

"Then explain it to me," pleaded her grandfather. "If I have to lose you, at least let me understand why."

"Are you that thick? Think it through, old man! If we can't stop Bayel, Nathao will be struggling for his very existence. That means that you and everyone else will be in grave danger, and the kids will have absolutely no one. Bayel has gone very, very bad."

"And?"

"That's it, you dolt! What don't you understand? It's him or us. It's that simple. Now, when I go into that temple, you will stay *outside*. I can't be worrying about if you'll try to play the knight in shining armor and blow everything. Nice to know you're learning to care, but I can't trust you." She threw a shirt into the suitcase in disgust.

Barnabas was silent for a moment and then stepped into the bedroom.

"Can I help you pack? Have you thought of where you're going on this trip? I need to have answers if there is a problem."

"Good thought," said Gwen, tossing her hair back and breathing deeply as the stress level eased. "How about France? Anything can happen in France."

"Fine, but what are you doing in France?" asked Barnabas, refolding the shirt that had been thrown into the suitcase.

"Working with a team for the Dream Trust. Tell the kids it's something the King is doing. I'm with them so I can get first-hand information on environmental advances being made in the renovation of some historic building they plan to turn into a museum. How's that?"

"Huh, Dream Trust." Barnabas snorted. "I forgot that's who you supposedly started to work for."

"It may not be sexy, but it's worked. So, I'll be in France doing environmental work for the foundation."

"Excellent. Now, presents."

"Presents?" asked Gwen, looking up in confusion as she grabbed socks.

"Presents, girl. You have to bring back presents for everyone."

"I'll leave that to you, OK?"

"Oh, be still my heart," said Barnabas as he melodramatically leaned backward and clutched his chest. "She gives me responsibility."

Her anger evaporated, and Gwen offered a tiny, sad smile as she shook her head.

"Don't you understand, you big fool, that you have the greatest responsibility I could give anyone? You're responsible for making sure Sam and Becky don't forget me if something goes wrong."

Her grandfather stopped posing and turned very serious.

"I hope I don't find myself with that job, but if the unthinkable happens, I will follow through to the best of my ability."

"Well, that ability better be damn good," warned his granddaughter. "First, make sure the King follows through on his promises, and then make sure Lois and Barry help you. They know everything and have been wonderfully supportive. Oh, and Luke's wife Percy should be allowed to add her two cents, like she offered."

They both froze as they heard the front door open and new voices enter the house.

"I once promised to watch your back, Courier," said Barnabas, "and as stupidly as I may have acted in the past and today, I'm proud to follow you."

"Well, take that protection and pride and use it to help my kids, Rider," answered Gwen. "They may need you."

With that, she turned and closed the suitcase as Becky came running into the room with her hair still damp from her day in the pool.

✳❈✳

The sky was getting light as Gwen slipped into each child's room to kiss them good-bye. Neither stirred, tired out after the busy day spent swimming with their cousins. Their mother suspected Nathao might be helping the situation too, something she was grateful for this time because it made the parting easier. Even Nan was quiet.

Alana was in her blue bathrobe in the kitchen where the coffee pot was perking furiously, filling the air with its wonderful scent.

"A cup before you go?"

"Yeah, but put it in a travel mug."

"You going to Haliburum?" asked the nanny quietly as she pulled a covered mug from the cabinet.

"Actually, no," said Gwen, just as quietly. "I'm going to Cheo. I find that after being there awhile, I can think better. I'll spend most of the day there."

"And then?" pressed Alana.

Gwen paused, then shook her head. "I wish I could talk about it, but not here, and not now. Maybe grandpa will fill you in later today, but he shouldn't."

"Because I'll worry?"

"Yes."

"Should I worry?"

"No," lied the Courier. "Now, give me that mug of wonderful brew."

There was tapping at the front door, and Gwen glanced at the clock on the oven.

"That's Grandpa. But the kids are sleeping so soundly I don't think we have to go through with the charade of leaving for the airport."

Alana nodded and shuffled off in her slippers to let in Barnabas. The Courier picked up her small blue suitcase and carry-on and followed. At the door, Barnabas was giving the nanny a peck on the cheek.

"Good morning, Grandpa."

"Good morning, girl," he said, surprising her with a kiss as well. "Ready?"

"I think we can do away with the airport thing; the kids are still fast asleep. So, here's the suitcase. Just take it to the car and keep it hidden. I'll head downstairs."

The Rider's eyes began to glisten, and he opened his mouth to speak. Gwen frowned and cut him off.

"Not here, and not now. The plan isn't changing. I'll see you in Haliburum tonight. Good-bye, Grandpa. Good-bye, Alana."

Without another word, she turned and left for the basement, adjusting the shoulder strap of the carry-on and clutching the coffee mug.

"Is it going to be that bad?" whispered Alana. "She said I shouldn't worry."

"I don't know how bad this could be," answered Barnabas. "But I don't think she was entirely honest."

❋❖❋

The sun was clear of the horizon when Gwen got to the roof of the chapel in Cheo. As she walked out and paused to find a balance with the stones, Nan offered her first real touch of the day, but it was only a light brush of affection. Gwen gently rubbed a sleeve while she looked around and then smiled. Under a group of the lush, blooming potted trees, blankets waited. Chuckling to herself, she accepted the invitation and went to lie down, using Nan as a blanket. The half-filled mug of coffee was left on the edge of a planter.

❋❖❋

Hours later, with the overhead sun warming her face through the trees' leaves, Gwen woke to the smell of orange blossom tea. As she stretched, yawned, and opened her eyes, she saw Father Yial sitting nearby, his light brown eyes watching her intently.

275

"Ah, I should have known you would be here."

The big Guidant laughed quietly and began pouring.

"The King sent me a dream that you would need time up here. But he didn't hint at why."

"You'll know soon enough," said Gwen, sitting up and swinging her jacket around to cover her shoulders. "I need to recharge before I go off on an errand for him."

"Hmmm," rumbled Yial, sipping from his cup. "Can I help in some way?"

"You're helping right now. This is wonderful."

"There is soup here as well."

"That's even more wonderful." The Courier smiled, exchanging her teacup for a covered bowl. "Oh, this smells heavenly."

"Miso. There is also some chicken satay over here, and flat bread. I wasn't sure how heavy or light you might want to eat."

"You are precious," exclaimed Gwen as she reached for a spoon. "Why hasn't some lucky woman snared you yet?"

Yial choked on his tea, and his face went red.

"Oh, don't think some haven't tried," he sputtered as he put down his cup and picked up a napkin.

"And?" prompted his guest, gently blowing on her soup while she stirred it.

"Let's just say there's been a lot of trying. And while some were interesting and entertaining, none kept my interest."

Gwen laughed as she continued to stir the soup.

"Their loss," she said as she moved to sip it.

The pair spent the next hour on the roof, talking quietly and sharing the lunch. Then the Courier excused herself to shower and change.

Yial was waiting when she returned to the Step room, refreshed and energized. Gwen reached over and gave him a playful shock.

"Yeah, I'm a little overcharged." She grinned. "But that's good."

"Will you need it?" asked the Guidant quietly.

"I think I'll need every bit of it," she said, suddenly very serious. "It's better if I don't say anything more, but I will tell you that during this night, Nathao will become either stronger than he's ever been, or just a memory. If you're in the chapel at the time of the solstice early tomorrow, you may know the answer."

Yial suddenly reached out and took her arm. "Courier, be careful. I want you back here soon."

Gwen looked at the big man quizzically, and Nan offered a strange observation of surprise and affection.

"We have so much more to talk about." The man blushed. "Much more."

Very sure this was not the time to get involved in any deep discussion, especially if Nan were correct, the Courier gently disengaged herself from Yial's hold.

"My friend, if there is a future for any of us, you will know at the solstice."

Without another word, she waved her arm and Stepped to Haliburum.

26

~

The First Assistant paced his office, trying to control his temper. At the same time, he caustically congratulated himself for what he believed would be an elegant answer to his dilemma.

He wanted Ralph gone from Haliburum, removed from any position where he might challenge Adam's power. He would send the man he now viewed as a rival to Hyoken to lead the rededication rites at the second-largest of Bayel's temples.

As their god had ordered, his one-time friend was preparing the effort to name Emily First Consort to Bayel. Nothing would be done publicly until the new movement had taken power, but upon reviewing the plans, Adam knew they were good and fretted that Ralph's influence would grow accordingly.

Relations between the two men had grown strained since the impromptu meeting with Bayel, and Adam jumped when the knock came at the office door. He was determined not to lose the position and authority he had worked so hard to gain, even if it meant exile for a former trusted lieutenant.

Ralph entered and tentatively bowed as he murmured, "First Assistant."

"Ralph," said Adam, a little too loudly. "Stop—no bowing. It's only me."

The visitor offered a small, nervous smile.

"The last time you said that, you ended up throwing me out of your office. I don't know what to expect anymore."

The First Assistant compressed his lips in chagrin and opened his arms in apology.

"I'm sorry, Ralph. The pressure may be getting to me. You are my closest and most valued friend; I want to make everything right between us."

He almost laughed at the open relief on Ralph's face.

"Adam, I've missed your friendship. Please don't let my feelings about the need for Bayel to have a partner in Emily hurt what we have between us. Even Bayel believes there is value to the idea. It will bring more followers, more women, to him."

"Totally understood, dear friend, totally understood. That is, actually, why I called you here. I have a position of leadership I want you to assume as you continue to orchestrate Emily's recognition."

"Of course," breathed Ralph. "You know I'll support you in whatever way I can."

"I knew I could count on you," said Adam exuberantly. "I want you to lead the rededication ceremonies in Hyoken. You'll have to leave immediately, of course."

Ralph stared as the request sank in.

"You mean I won't share in the activities here?" he asked slowly.

"You will be leading the activities in Hyoken."

"You and I both know those festivities will be a farce and a shadow of what is really happening *here*. *This* is where the power will be raised, and *this* is where I want to be."

"You will not be. You will leave for Hyoken at the end of this conversation. I have notified them that you are coming, and they are to accord you all honors."

"Does Bayel know about this?" asked Ralph with a new menacing tone.

"Don't go there," said Adam as a trickle of sweat ran down the back of his neck. "He is aware and hasn't said no. Take the appointment and revel in it. You will come back when it is time to promote Emily."

Ralph glared. "You will regret this. One day, somehow, you will regret pushing me away because you were jealous. I would have supported you in everything, Adam."

"Prove that and take this assignment. When the time is right, you will return here to a position of greater power. I promise." Adam held his ground, even puffing out his chest a bit, as he spoke. "Now, your transportation is waiting. You will have to hurry to get to the temple in time."

27

Preston and Gwen spent the warm late afternoon and early evening hidden in the park across from Bayel's temple. They watched and listened to the raucous celebration that spilled out of the main building onto the grounds, the sidewalk, and, at one point, the street. It was only then that authorities showed up and pushed the revelers back onto temple property.

The pair sat near a thicket where Kyril was meeting with his contacts. Most of the sessions were with field mice, although one rabbit showed up.

The story from the rabbit had been especially startling. She told them how an entire family living near her in the park had been kidnapped by humans and taken into the temple, never to be seen alive again. Some of their bodies had been discovered in the park later, split down the front but otherwise not mutilated. And that was something she found very strange because, as she pointed out to Kyril, the fur was usually taken by humans, and sometimes the feet and ears.

※※

In the kitchen at the chapel late that night, Gwen, Preston, and Kyril reviewed the latest information one more time as they sat at one of the large tables. As they talked, the Riders began arriving. Barnabas and Claire walked in first, followed by Jensen and Sean and then, a few minutes later, Eli and Armen.

Preston was translating as Kyril outlined the renewed activity taking place in what they were now convinced was the secret sanctuary under the main temple, especially how the human presence bothered the rodents and spiders there.

"It's quite clear they've been giving the place another good cleaning," said Gwen, and the squirrel chittered.

"He says you and I may call it cleaning, but it destroys the homes his contacts have built," translated Preston.

"I totally understand, and they have my sympathy, but it tells us they're getting ready to use it again. You know, maybe you should suggest to your friends that moving somewhere else permanently might be a good idea because, once we stop this movement, I wouldn't be surprised if that place is destroyed."

Kyril began talking again.

"He says a lot have already left. They couldn't stand the smell of blood and the sound of the dying."

"And so we must stop it," said Barnabas. "Let's review this plan again and make sure we all know what we're supposed to do. I don't want anyone messing up."

"Me either," agreed his granddaughter, looking around and taking comfort at the sight of the six black jackets, the young man next to her, and the squirrel lashing his tail as he sat in the middle of the table. She touched the cuff of her own jacket, and Nan signaled she was ready with a burst of warmth and excitement.

Then Gwen gently tapped the stored energy that filled every cell of her body and was rewarded with a controlled charge of power.

"All right. Claire, you first, what are you doing?"

The Courier went around the table, quizzing each person, including Preston and, through him, Kyril. A few minor points were debated and clarified, and then it was midnight.

"There are sandwiches in the refrigerator. Eat something," said Gwen when they were through. "Preston, you especially make sure you put food in that stomach of yours. Gods, you're still growing, and we can't have your stomach growling tonight like it did all afternoon."

The acolyte blushed. "I didn't think you could hear it."

Kyril snorted and muttered something that Preston did not translate.

The group got food. Sean noticed Gwen wasn't eating. He offered to get her something, but she declined, saying, "I've got all the energy I need and then some."

She tapped his hand, giving him a little shock, and when he gasped, her jacket rippled in its expression of laughter.

"I got a little overcharged in Cheo. I'll explain how later, but this is what I need tonight."

Seeing Armen's bushy eyebrows twitch above his glasses as he watched from the other side of Sean, Gwen raised her index finger, reached over to his hand, and gave him a tiny jolt.

"Cheo, Armen. It's a great place."

Stoically, the Rider simply rubbed the spot she had touched and sniffed. "I know."

Before the Courier could say anything else, Mother Laciane glided in to give Preston her blessing and made him blush for the second time that night.

"I'll be here praying," she said authoritatively. "Make sure all of you come back safely and, if it's possible, bring the Rider Rakeem with you."

Then she looked at Gwen and said very deliberately, "Please be careful. It would be difficult for me to offer an honest welcome to a new Courier."

"Thank you," replied Gwen, deeply touched by the comment. "I'll certainly do everything in my power to make sure you won't have to deal with that crisis of conscience."

Mother Laciane paused as if to say something else, but instead she tightened her lips and left the kitchen, her gray robes making a swishing sound in the silence.

Gwen waited a moment and then stood up.

"Here we go. Preston, Kyril, and I are off. You all know what to do. When this is over, we'll celebrate."

❈❈❈

The solstice would occur at three-fifteen in the morning. Two hours before that, Gwen and Preston were back in the park across the avenue from Bayel's temple. This time, they sat under a tree set back about ten yards from the wide sidewalk. Gwen's black jacket blended with the shadows, as did the dark, long-sleeved shirt Preston wore despite the warm evening. Kyril sat on the acolyte's shoulder as they waited for late word from some of the squirrel's contacts.

Yellow light and the dying sounds of the intense day-long partying oozed into the night's darkness through the large front doors of the temple, which were still open.

Unconscious bodies and garbage were strewn across the lawn, but there were still a fair number of robe-wearing celebrants trickling out of the building and stumbling their way down the stairs to the street and, presumably, home.

"They do seem to have had a good time," said Preston quietly. "I don't think they have a clue about their god and his intentions."

"Tonight they don't have to know anything."

"They're fools," scoffed the young man.

Gwen looked at him tolerantly. "They're fools who could kill your King."

"You and I both know that won't happen, Courier," whispered Preston. "Nathao is too strong. We'll prove that tonight, and this guy will be history."

Kyril's tail began lashing, and he jumped off his shoulder perch to dash closer to the sidewalk. The humans watched as he stopped and then came back with a companion, a mouse.

The two stopped about a foot away, and there were several minutes of quiet squeaks. The squirrel approached Preston and began chittering.

"He says there's a lot of activity in the downstairs room and lots of people in robes. There's also the smell of blood, which has them upset."

"Blood already?" mused Gwen, checking her watch and frowning. "It's only one-forty-five. Kyril, would you please ask if the blood smell is from a human and, if so, what they look like?"

Kyril returned to his contact, and there were more quiet squeaks. After a few minutes, he came back and sat straight up, chittering furiously.

"He says the blood was from a man who had trouble walking."

"What color was his skin?" asked Gwen urgently, her stomach getting tight as she began to think they had misread everything and were too late. Nan responded with a hug and slight pulse of concern.

"He says his fur was white and his skin was pale."

"Right," breathed the Courier, vastly relieved that it was not Rakeem but greatly disturbed by the fact that there was apparently more than one human sacrifice on the agenda.

"Just how much power are they planning to raise tonight?" she wondered aloud. "And what will that mean for Nat? And who was the poor bastard? Kyril, ask him if there is anyone else in the room who he thinks might smell like blood soon?"

Kyril raced back and forth a few times because the mouse was too scared to get any closer. By the end of the conversation, Gwen was very sure the dead man was not Rakeem, but who he was and where the Rider might be, she could not determine from the offered information.

"What is it like in the main room of the temple? Are people still standing? Can I get through there unnoticed?"

"He says the people aren't moving," said Preston, listening to Kyril. "He says they smell bad."

They were still pulling out bits and pieces from their source when the mouse suddenly froze and then bolted. A second later, four new shadows appeared, and the squirrel clearly expressed his displeasure that their arrival had scared off his informant.

Eli settled nearest to Gwen, with Barnabas right behind. Jensen and Sean hung back a little and remained standing.

"Claire is ready. She'll alert the authorities at the station house down the block so they get here when the evidence is fresh," said the thin man softly. "Armen has the car and will pull it around so we can move Rakeem as soon as we get him out of there."

287

"Good. You come with me to the main door, we compare notes on what we remember from last time, and then you come back and wait. Kyril's friends will let you know when I get in there and if things start to go haywire.

"I expect you all to show up, police in tow, at three o'clock. The stage should be set with plenty of evidence, and I should make a wonderful eyewitness. Plus we can get Rakeem home."

"Understood. Now, you and I need some party clothes, I think." Eli smiled. "Let me and the others find someone out there who wants to share."

Eli, Jensen, and Sean slipped silently away. Within minutes, they were back with two white, sleeveless robes "borrowed" from a pair of merry-makers weaving their way home. The two would wake up under the trees in the park in a few hours, no doubt wondering how they got there.

"Be careful, girl," whispered Barnabas a little gruffly as he helped Gwen slip one of the long garments over her shoulders and Nan. "Remember we're here."

"Kyril and friends will give Preston the word if something isn't right, and if that happens, you'd better be in there fast. Otherwise, I'll see you at three," she replied quietly before giving him a quick kiss on the cheek.

Eli and Gwen moved quickly across the now almost-empty boulevard. They carefully threaded their way through the human and party-related debris and climbed the wide set of stairs.

Halfway up, Gwen paused to turn and look back. Lit by gas lamps with the trees in full leaf, the street was peaceful; she could hear just a few chirps as the early birds started to prepare for the coming dawn. She remembered the weather forecast was for a sunny, hot day; good weather for the kids to be at their grandparents' pool again. She smiled to herself and then gave into Eli's gentle tug on her sleeve, urging her to move.

The interlopers reached the gathering vestibule, and Gwen understood what the mouse had meant about the smell. She wrinkled her nose at the combination of stale wine, sweat, vomit, and incense that was everywhere and glanced at Eli, who rolled his eyes and screwed his face into a look of disgust.

With a few quick steps, they reached the doors to the main sanctuary and looked down into the huge, domed, salmon-colored room. Oversized, neon-colored banners hung from the high ceiling, and multicolored ribbons several feet wide were twisted around the fat columns that circled the sanctuary. The hazy smoke from the incense gave the already-dimmed lights a slightly diffused glow.

On the carpeted floor of the temple, a few individuals were still engaged in small, intimate, and physical celebrations, but the vast majority lay motionless with their robes askew, sleeping or passed out from all the wine and exertion.

There were stairs leading to balconies and doors all around the huge octagonal temple, but the largest balcony was straight ahead. It was the only one with two staircases.

Gwen turned to Eli, whispering, "That's it, just as the animals said. What do you think?"

Eli nodded as he remembered their run to freedom, which now seemed a lifetime ago. "I agree. What time is it?"

Gwen glanced at her watch. "Only two-ten. I could probably wander over and none of those fools would even notice me, which makes me wonder about the door attendants. Where are they? I expected at least one on duty."

"I wouldn't be surprised if they're among the bodies somewhere. Be careful when you go down there," murmured the Rider, placing his bony hand on her arm. "And remember what Mother Laciane said."

Gwen glanced at him curiously, surprised at the concern in his eyes.

"I, too, would find it hard to offer an honest welcome to a new Courier. Now, go. We'll wait for the mice, or three o'clock."

The Courier touched his hand briefly before she turned to move down the stairs that led to the main floor. There she carefully wended her way between the mounds of people and the single bodies, some moving or groaning, some totally still, making sure not to brush against anyone or do anything that would bring notice to herself.

The tense walk across the floor was successful, and after a slow, deep breath, Gwen began to climb the stairs to the main balcony, staying close to the wall. She glanced toward the outer doors but could not tell if Eli were still there. Reaching out to her jacket, she received a sense of caution and concern, but more importantly, Nan also radiated a constant low-level feed of confidence.

On the balcony, the Courier continued to hug the wall as she slipped closer to the closed double doors at the back of the landing. She carefully and firmly grasped the bronze knob only to feel it suddenly turn on its own as the door was yanked open and someone grabbed her arm. She was violently jerked forward and thrown inside into the arms of a burly young man, who spun her around and pinned her arms behind her as the doors quickly closed, cutting off the hum of the minimal activity in the main room.

As she steadied herself and got her bearings, a chuckle filled the room.

"Little flea. The thorn in my side. Welcome. I rather thought you would come."

Her heart racing, Gwen looked around for the source but only saw three men in the room with her.

"Come in, dearest nuisance, come in. My people will escort you to me. I'm waiting."

"As our lord says, welcome," repeated the man holding her. He released her arms. "This way, please. You are expected."

Gwen paused a few moments to soak up the blasts of strength and confidence being force-fed by Nan and made a concerted effort to appear in control despite her pounding heart. She nodded to herself as her escort indicated their direction. She and Eli had been correct about the entrance to the inner sanctuary; it *was* the door in the wall. Tonight, though, it was much more than just a door. Tonight, torches flanked the entrance and a gold runner covered the stairs.

As they reached the stairs, one of her escorts stopped her and held out his hand.

"We'll take the robe, please."

"I suppose there really isn't any reason to wear it, is there?" Gwen slipped off the white garment.

"And please remove your shoes before entering consecrated space."

Eyeing the plush carpet and runner that covered the steps, Gwen shrugged and reached down to untie her sneakers. She had the chance to glance at the big man's watch when he gestured toward the flight of stairs and thought it showed nearly two twenty-five.

"Lord Bayel now requests your presence. Please watch your step on the way down."

"Right," said Gwen as she began down the stairs, lightly touching the banister, her escort close behind. Below was the landing she had been able to see during her last visit, but this time, there was light from around the ninety-degree turn and the sound of muffled voices. When they reached the landing and turned, Gwen could begin to see the floor of the room below.

The next section of stairs brought her to a small landing in the underground room itself and then two more steps took her to the actual floor.

Ahead, and slightly to her left, were risers covered in the same thick, dark-red carpeting used on the steps and most of the room. About fifty people sat there, all wearing the white robes of Bayel's followers with the neon trim of the new movement.

To her right, about five feet away, a large half-circle of white sand sparkled under recessed lighting. Tiny, clear lights on top of a low berm of red carpeting delineated the two areas.

In that sandy arena, a body lay on top of a large dark rectangle of stone. Gwen felt Nan shudder as she looked at the altar and sent back her own wave of reassurance.

Next to the large block was a smaller stone cube, and Gwen's heart lurched when she saw what appeared to be a black jacket lying on it. Desperately, she rechecked the person sprawled on the platform and breathed a small prayer of thanks when that closer look reaffirmed what her first glance had told her: the body there was not Rakeem. The man was too small and his skin color, though gray now, was too light, just as the mouse had said.

But she knew the man standing near the large, menacing stone altar.

As her escort gently guided Gwen to the right and the sand, she glanced back to the left and was sure she saw a tiny mouse running along the wall. Satisfied that word was going out to her support team, she turned to concentrate on the task at hand and the bald man who was beginning to walk toward her. As she neared the altar, she could also see more details of the motionless person and, sadly, recognized him.

"Welcome, Courier," said Adam Bardhof warmly as he approached. "We've been waiting. Lord Bayel expected you and is pleased by your visit. Let me introduce you."

Turning her to face those watching from the risers, Bardhof raised his arms and his voice.

"Brothers and sisters, this is the Courier for Nathao, Lord of Dreams. See how she stands here before you, just as Bayel promised. He will accept her service as he accepts his right to take control and governance of the King's lands."

Gwen did not say anything as she looked at the long, shiny, silver knife Bardhof was holding aloft and then past him to the body on the dark stone.

"What's going on?" she demanded.

"Bayel has taken a faithful servant unto himself."

As she looked more closely, Gwen could see that Carmen Piale's body had been split open from throat to navel; the grayish-white color of the body suggested he had been drained of blood, but there was no sign of blood anywhere on the stone or in the white sand.

"Don't you think this sacrifice business is going a bit too far?" she finally said, turning to face the bald man.

Bardhof waved over an acolyte standing nearby and gave him the knife.

"Ready this for the next offering."

He placed his hands on Gwen's shoulders and continued speaking loudly, not really to her, but to the rapt audience.

"Piale's sacrifice was an honor. Bayel chose his loyal Spirit to be part of him forever."

"Oh. With the Spirit's approval and acceptance?"

"He served our lord in life, and continues to do the same even after his job here is done," said Bardhof, solemnly lowering his eyes for a moment in what, to Gwen, was clearly feigned respect.

"And the new Spirit?" said Gwen.

"Has been chosen by Bayel, Lord of Life, Delight—"

"And Enigma of Desire. Yes, I know the litany. Let me guess to whom the honor has been offered."

Bardhof just smiled.

"To the victor and all that, huh?"

The new leader shook his head. "This shouldn't be viewed as a battle; the world changes, and so must we. And..." He paused dramatically with his arms outstretched, turning to make sure his audience on the risers was listening. "If you wish, you can help with that change. Bayel will accept your service to him as he conquers Nathao and takes command of the Realm of Dreams."

Gwen raised her eyebrows in surprise. "You're offering me the chance to join your inner circle?"

"Not quite," admitted the Spirit. "But your assistance would be richly rewarded, and Bayel would take you as one of his own."

"What assistance and what rewards?"

"Help us take down Nathao, and you will be one of a special, honored few."

Gwen paused, as if thinking it over, and then shook her head.

"I'm sorry, Adam, but I don't think I could do that. Lord Nathao wouldn't appreciate it. And there is another mitigating factor here," she added, shaking her finger at him didactically. "I really have to think about the afterlife because of the family connection. I mean, you know, the Lord of Death being the King's brother and all that. I'm sure you understand how that could make things a little uncomfortable, to say the least."

"And I'm sure you understand the alternative is to follow the path taken by our esteemed former Spirit," said Bardhof, waving toward Piale.

Ignoring the threat, Gwen looked back at the people sitting on the risers. "Not a big turnout, huh?"

The bald man reached over and gently turned her head to face him. "Are you with us? This is only the beginning; you could be at the start of a great movement with power of your own. You could demand awe and respect."

The Courier held the eye contact for a pause and then announced loudly and clearly, "Awe and respect? Haven't you heard? As King Nathao's Courier, I command awe and respect now."

Bardhof dropped his hand and, a split second later, brought it up to slap her sharply. She staggered with the force of the blow and raised her hand to her face.

The new Spirit motioned to the two big guards. "Take that coat. I want it."

"No," snapped Gwen as one of her escorts gripped her. She struggled, but between the two men, they peeled off Nan and handed the jacket to Bardhof, who stood nearby with a dignified, yet smug smile. Nan's removal severed the important stream of confidence and strength that had been flowing into her system. The Courier scrambled to mentally balance herself and then tap into her anger and stored energy from the stones to fuel her determination. She vented some of her frustration by trying to shake off her guard's hold. Instead, he tightened his grip and pinned her arms behind her.

"I know what it is, and it won't do you any good here," said the Spirit. He accepted the coat and examined it for a moment before tossing it carelessly from one hand to the other. "I have a great interest in these supposed wonders crafted by Nathao."

"I'd appreciate having it back."

"You won't need it," repeated Bardhof as he stopped toying with the jacket and moved closer, staring down at his captive. "I've heard it can save your life. I have another one, you know. Another one that is almost identical. Would you like to see it? It's right over there."

He pinched her jaw between his thumb and index finger and turned her head toward the smaller table next to the altar.

"I saw it on the way in," she mumbled through compressed lips.

"And I'm sure you know the owner." The Spirit smiled. "You asked for his return once."

"A request you never had the courtesy to answer," replied Gwen as he still held her jaw. "I even offered to come here if you let him go."

"Yes, well, things get in the way, and priorities have to be set. You understand, I'm sure," he said, releasing her.

"No, I do not," said Gwen, shaking her head free and unsuccessfully trying to throw her hair back over her shoulder.

"Let me help you with that," offered Adam.

He waved over an acolyte, who took the jacket and then motioned to another for the newly cleansed silver knife.

The Spirit accepted the knife and brandished it high with a theatrical wave before his audience. He then walked slowly and deliberately out of Gwen's field of vision.

Gwen felt her guard move slightly and listened intently to the sound of the sand as it shifted under Bardhof's feet. She knew when he stopped beside her but still flinched when his hand reached over her shoulder and gently pulled her hair back. She fought a shudder as he paused to rub his hand against her cheek and then her neck.

"In fact, let me offer a solution to the problem," he whispered in her ear. "This knife is very sharp. It is *so* sharp the recipient doesn't feel its touch until everything is over."

Gwen did not answer as he continued to gather her hair and gently pulled it taut. She stared straight ahead, her face impassive, as the man holding her tightened his grip.

"Remember, Adam," she said quietly, "don't touch."

"Ha," he said just as quietly and then, leaning again next to her ear, he breathed, "I'm not touching, I'm taking."

She felt a slight tug and then a weight was gone.

"A very sharp knife," repeated Bardhof, walking in front of the Courier with the long, dark hair he had sliced off, holding it high for all to see. "A memento."

Gwen said nothing as a wave of applause ran through the audience. She smiled sweetly at the new Spirit as he held his trophy in front of her.

"You're welcome to it, Adam, especially it if it makes you feel more adequate."

Without a word, his own face impassive, Bardhof stepped closer and set the blade of the silver knife against her left cheek. Deliberately he drew the edge down, leaving a thin line that slowly began to bleed.

Gwen hissed and closed her eyes for a moment as the pain set in.

"Nice, Adam," she said when she could look at him again. "That's real self-control, but it won't help you grow hair—or balls."

"Nice comeback, Gwen, real intellectual," retorted the Spirit, leaning close enough for her to see the damp spots on his white oxford shirt and smell his sweat. "But we are running out of time."

With that, he turned, swept his arms in the air while still holding the knife and the dark hair, and proclaimed, "Bayel is ready and calls for what should be his."

An acolyte reclaimed the knife while Bardhof walked to the smaller dark cube and carefully set the hair he had cut from Gwen next to the two jackets. Beyond him, two men in sleeveless robes cleared the altar of Piale's body. They carried it a short distance away, respectfully laid it out on the sand, and arranged the former Spirit's hands on his chest before covering him with a gold cloth.

The Courier's guard eased his crushing grip on her arms, which allowed her to lift a hand to brush away the blood dripping down her cheek. She wiped her hand on her pants and tentatively shook her head, getting a feel for her new, shorter hairstyle. When she looked again for Bardhof, he was standing in front of the congregation, his feet wide, his arms high, and the top of his head glistening in the lights.

"Brothers and sisters, we approach a major ceremony in the growth of our chosen lord. This is a new world, and Bayel is ready to take what shall be his. Richard, bring in our offering!"

Gwen groaned as a stumbling Rakeem entered the sandy area from a door camouflaged in the sparkling wall. He was gaunt and bare-chested, and appeared disoriented as two men guided him before the bleachers and toward the altar.

Realizing this might be her only chance to deliver Nathao's Dream, the Courier shook off her guard and began walking to meet the Rider.

When the big man grabbed her arm, she glared and snapped, "Don't touch me."

Bardhof laughed and waved him back. "Bayel is compassionate. Let her speak to him one last time in this world."

Gwen turned her thoughts inward and isolated the Dream from Nathao while she crossed the sand to stand before the Rider. For some reason, the warm sand under her socks felt comforting and bolstered a feeling of control.

Rakeem was expressionless as he looked at her, but she smiled confidently and, moving close to him, reached up and put her hands on either side of his head.

"My dear friend," she said softly, "I am the Courier, and I have his Dream for you. Take it quickly. He waits."

With that, she poured Nathao's gift into Rakeem's mind. She would swear later that she saw a flash of gratitude in his dark eyes before they closed and he slumped to the ground.

The brief moment of calm exploded into chaos. Exclamations and screams erupted from the audience, and someone violently thrust Gwen, face first, into the crushing arms of a large, robed man. Her new handler spun her around, pulled her right arm up behind her, and slapped his well-muscled left arm across her throat, crushing her head and shoulders into his chest. She pawed weakly at his arm with her left hand.

"One move and I break it," he said.

Careful not to give him any reason to follow through, Gwen froze and moved only her eyes as she watched Bardhof kneel next to Rakeem, furiously poking and prodding the Rider's neck.

"There's still a pulse—get him to the altar! And get *her* next to it." He growled deeply, a look of pure hatred on his face. "We will have a sacrifice that will please Bayel very much."

The acolytes dragged Rakeem's body to the ominous dark stone and wrestled it on top while the man gripping Gwen dragged her behind. He shifted his grip to her arms and pulled them back. Bardhof stalked to the side table, grabbed a cloth soaked with something from a silver bowl, and stormed over to stand in front of her.

The sweating man jerked his head at an acolyte, who hurriedly jumped in front of the Courier and grabbed each side of her shirt collar. In two motions, he ripped it open and yanked the sides apart, baring her torso.

The Spirit moved in and, using the cloth, slathered Gwen's chest and neck with oil that smelled strongly of patchouli.

"Consider yourself consecrated," he spat. "And prepare to become one with Bayel."

He grabbed the silver knife being offered by an assistant and paused, glaring thoughtfully at her unprotected chest for just a moment. Gwen braced herself for the knife and began to concentrate on isolating Nathao's Dream for her, but Bardhof frowned and then spun around to stalk his way to the stone where Rakeem's body lay with several men holding his arms and legs.

Intoning something Gwen could not understand, Bardhof raised the knife above his head and lifted his face toward the sparkling ceiling before plunging the knife into the Rider's chest.

Gwen gasped as blood began to well up as the Spirit dragged the knife down Rakeem's motionless body. As the blood appeared, it almost instantaneously disappeared and a crystal cloud began to coalesce, hovering over the body, slowly encompassing Bardhof and the other robed figures around the altar.

"No," she said as her frustration and anger began to grow. "No, that can't be. He took the Dream. This can't be working; he should be dead."

The robed crowd on the risers left their seats and began prostrating themselves along the boundary of the sand pit, praising Bayel and encouraging him to take up the new life being offered and use it.

The cloud became more opaque as it grew in size and luminescence. Almost frantic, Gwen strained to see through the brightening veil that enveloped those around Rakeem. Instinctively, she tried to move closer, but her guard shifted his grip. In a smooth, lightning-fast move, he slipped his hold to her right forearm and again yanked it up behind her while slapping his left arm across her throat. He twisted her arm behind her so fiercely she thought it was going to break and, forced to deal with the pain and concentrate on breathing, she lost track of everything else that was happening.

When her burly warden finally eased his hold, Gwen coughed to fill her lungs and focus beyond the pain to the events at the altar. Bardhof was still standing with his hands in the air, his head thrown back in ecstasy, but Bayel's shimmering cloud seemed to be thinning. Wisps began to break off.

Her hopes soared as more of the cloud began to shred and melt away, and the Spirit's stance of power and ecstasy collapsed into one of entreaty as he began begging Bayel to stay strong and remain. The worshippers on the carpeted floor also began crying out, echoing their leader's urgent petition.

Abruptly Bardhof raised his arms again and yelled, "My lord, we have another sacrifice for you. One more powerful and even closer to those gods you wish to overwhelm. Stay, my lord, and drink!"

With that, he turned to Gwen and thundered, "You, Courier, will turn this around for me."

"Don't do this, Adam, it's a losing battle," said Gwen as she was shoved toward the Spirit. "You'll regret this, Adam—this is murder."

She watched him advance and began calming her mind again to isolate and accept Nathao's Dream for her.

"Oh, no, Gwen, there is no regret, and if it's murder, so be it," replied the Spirit through clenched teeth, as he raised the shining knife. "You die for the betterment of my Lord Bayel. And believe me, it will hurt."

With that he brought the knife down toward Gwen's chest, but she managed to squirm and shift just enough that it pierced her below her right shoulder, slicing down into the junction of nerves near the joint.

At first she was surprised at the lack of sensation as the razor-sharp blade went in, but the sense of cold that followed its path was replaced by an explosion of pain as Bardhof pulled it out, making her gasp as her arm went numb and useless. She screamed as the pain washed through the rest of her body.

Once again, the enraged Spirit raised the knife, but again she twisted even as her guard yanked her right arm higher, forcing her to arch in pain and offer her neck and chest as exposed, clear targets.

This time the knife hit her collarbone and slid to the right center, slicing through the pectoral muscles and deeper into her chest.

"Little nuisance," echoed Bayel's whispered, dismembered voice. "If I die, so do you."

"Gods don't die, fool." The Courier gasped. "You go into retirement. Take a rest. Find some decent worshippers."

Suddenly she was released and slipped to the sand; not only was her right arm not responding, but neither was the rest of her body. Then there were other sounds, lots of shouting and someone touching her gently.

"Funny, never thought it'd be like this. Focus, girl, take the Dream. Bayel can't get credit for your death," Gwen thought, very tired as she mustered the strength to give into Nathao's gift.

Her efforts were abruptly derailed by a commanding voice that cut through the pain fogging her consciousness.

No, Courier! Do not take the dream, you are not about to die.

Nat? she asked wordlessly.

It's Luke, Gwen. Nat is very busy. But, do not take the Dream and do not sleep, not yet. It is not clear at my brother's end, and you could be caught in the purge of Bayel's residue. Stay awake until I tell you it is all right. Do you understand me? Stay awake, Gwen!

"But, Luke, I'm so tired and so cold," she murmured.

Then another voice was calling to her as a gentle touch became firmer and more insistent.

"Gwen, we're here. You're safe, it's over. Stay with me, Gwen!"

"Grandpa?" she whispered, then groaned and nearly blacked out from the pain as someone rolled her over. She thought she heard a voice shouting: "Eli, get the coats *now*! They're over there. By the gods, there's so much blood. Get them over here!" But she wasn't really sure.

❋❋

Bayel clutched at the meager power released by the dying Rider. The death had been too fast and the fear that enhanced his absorption of a dissipating life force had been minimal.

Frustrated and growing angry, he sought an equilibrium in the energy he had left from Piale's screaming demise and conserved his waning strength to wait for the next offering; one he was sure would provide the force he needed to explode through Nathao's kingdom and destroy it. He was almost giddy with anticipation as he primed his mind to receive it.

A small tendril of energy touched him, carrying the faint hint of a new death. Bayel tasted the dying and laughed because it was the Courier. He reveled in the thought of her disgust and loathing when he took everything from her, but most of all, he giggled at the thought of her dread. Tapping his energy reserve, the god reached to feed on the released life and the fear he desperately needed.

He latched onto the power and choked in disbelief, and then alarm, when he found next to nothing and no taste of fear at all. Frantically, he began sucking in whatever life force he could find, knowing his own existence was in jeopardy.

Despicable, Bayel. You are despicable.

The statement echoed through his amorphous being, shaking it like jelly.

You are done. You will become nothing. You dared to threaten me, and now you will know how worthless and pathetic your existence has been. You have wasted my time and cost me several valued servants. You will now pay the price: annihilation.

"Nathao," said Bayel, "*you* are the useless one. I am about to wipe away any trace of you. Your people have fed me, and it is your Courier's

301

life force and fear that will move me to a level of power from which I will crush you."

Before you rejoice in victory, check your victim. My Courier lives, and she is not afraid. She does not know fear. There is nothing to sustain you. For your transgressions the Pantheon agrees I am due revenge, and I choose your death. I also choose the death of your Spirit, and I will finish him after you are destroyed so you do not benefit from the release of his feeble essence.

Bayel grabbed for the thread of death he had felt earlier and began to curse when, this time, he found nothing. His resources fading, the God of Joy fought to gather what he had left.

"Nathao, you cannot ruin this moment. You are the dead one. I will crash into your world and rip the shadows apart. I will shine my light into the corners of your realm and take your people as my own. You are finished," he spat.

In a final defiant effort, he forced what was left of his being into Nathao's realm, intent on causing damage. But his surge across the boundary cost the god too much of his dwindling resources, and he felt himself beginning to dissipate. With nothing left to power his existence, he struggled against impending oblivion.

There is no fear or death to feed you, Bayel. Die. And as you die and fade, be very aware that you will never be worshipped again. You will be forgotten.

"Bastard," croaked the fading god as his voice began to crack. "I am not done here, and you can be sure I will come for you."

"No, you will not be coming for anyone ever again," said Nathao without emotion as the last vestige of the God of Joy wafted into nonexistence.

✖✖

"Grandpa," whispered Gwen. She began to shiver despite the fact that Nan, who was now wrapped firmly around her upper body, was pumping warmth and healing into her partner. There was also a second jacket shoved against her chest that offered a sense of strength she hadn't felt before. "Luke says I can't sleep yet."

"Whatever he says, listen to him, girl," said Barnabas near her ear. "Listen to him. If he says *stay*, then you *stay* with me. We'll stop the bleeding; we're not too late. You've got the jackets, yours and Rakeem's both, to protect you and help. Don't sleep."

A few more minutes, Gwen. Luke was once again in her head. *Bayel is being taken down right now. Come on, Courier, concentrate. Stay there just a few more moments.*

"But I'm so cold and tired."

Stop whining. My brother doesn't choose losers.

Just a few more moments and then you can sleep.

Gwen began tasting something metallic and found herself starting to choke even as someone rolled her on her side so she could cough up something and breathe again.

'Blood,' she thought. 'Must be bad. Maybe I'll sleep just a little.'

This time Eli's voice cut through the growing darkness.

"Gwen, you did great. We've got these bastards. The authorities are here, and there's plenty of proof of seriously illegal activities. The dreams of this group have been crushed for good.

"Can you hear me? Barnabas says the bleeding is under control, and real soon we'll get you someplace comfortable where you can tell us everything that happened."

Gwen was hearing but not understanding all the talk as she struggled just to stay conscious and fight the shivering that began to rack her body again.

Suddenly Luke was back in her mind. *Nat's done with Bayel. It's clear. Sleep. Well done, Courier, well done.*

Rakeem? asked Gwen wordlessly.

He's earned his rest and is welcome here. Be content knowing he's grateful to you for helping him Cross, and that you will see him again in time. Now, sleep.

"Luke says I can sleep," whispered Gwen to her grandfather, even as she slipped into oblivion.

"Rest then. I'll take care of you," he said in her ear.

❊❊

While Barnabas, Eli, and Jensen worked with Gwen, Claire watched the authorities gather up the people and the evidence of the illegal rite. Backed by Sean and Preston, she made sure the officers knew the Riders and Courier were beyond their jurisdiction and were not to be bothered, no matter how bad the situation appeared.

A few of Bayel's followers were crying, but most of the white-robed group sat stony-faced. With Bardhof's body on the sand on one side of the altar, Piale's on the other, and Rakeem still on the stone, most in the group knew they were facing serious criminal charges.

❊❊

As Gwen fell into unconsciousness, Eli turned to Jensen.

"We have to get her back to the chapel. Can you carry her to the car?"

Without a word, the big redhead slipped his arms gently under the Courier. "Make sure the coats are secure, Barnabas, before I move her."

The senior Rider was already working on that. After a moment of tucking in things here and there, he nodded, and in one smooth movement, Jensen lifted Gwen and turned to cross the sand. Before he could move, there was a *pop,* and a small man in white, wearing a broad-brimmed hat, appeared in front of him.

"Give her to me," he demanded in a thin, reedy voice.

"No," barked Jensen. "Get out of my vay; this is urgent."

"Rider, she won't live unless you give her to me. I can stabilize her. Now, *give* her to me, you lout!" commanded the little man.

Confused, Jensen looked to his colleagues for guidance, and Eli jumped to his side.

"Do it, man. Give her to Lord Veron."

304

The little god quickly accepted the body, unfazed by the weight and size, and disappeared.

Stunned silence filled the underground room as the Riders and Bayel's people tried to digest what they had just seen.

Claire broke the hush and addressed her coworkers.

"If Veron has her, there isn't anything more you can do here. Preston and I will stay a little longer. You lot, go."

✳✳

Mother Laciane was waiting in the chapel's Step room.

"I have instructions for you from Lord Veron," she said calmly.

"Veron was here too?" echoed Eli as he narrowed his eyes.

"Yes, and he said you are to stay here, Eli, and wait for a doctor from Demma. You will take the doctor back to the Keep. The Courier will be there. The rest of you are to return to the King immediately."

"Gwen's at the Keep?" asked Sean, already moving toward the Step.

"He made it sound like she *will* be there, but isn't yet," replied Laciane. "However, you are to go back now."

"We're off then," said the youngest Rider brusquely. Without looking back at the others, he quickly waved his arm to open a Window and Stepped through, followed by Jensen and Armen.

Barnabas hung back. "Did Veron say anything else about the Courier?" he asked hopefully.

Laciane shook her head. "I'm sorry, no."

"This is testing my faith, old friend," said Barnabas, looking at Eli.

His fellow Rider smiled sympathetically and grasped his arm.

"It will be all right. If Veron and Demma are involved, it will be all right. Go. I'll be there soon."

After Barnabas disappeared, Laciane moved to one of the two blue-and-white chairs in the room and sat down with a sigh.

"Now, tell me what the blazing fires happened. From the talk of a doctor, I assume the Courier was injured. How badly? What about the Rider? And, by the way, where is my assistant?"

"You should be very proud of Preston, Mother." Eli grinned. "That young man saw and did a lot tonight, and he didn't flinch. He's still helping Claire with the authorities. But, before I tell you what happened, please explain about Lord Veron."

Laciane tilted her head, and her expression became thoughtful.

"It was very strange. I was waiting here as planned, praying that everything was going as it should, when Lord Veron just popped in. He told me he would make sure the Courier was taken to safety, but he needed my help to make sure you, and you specifically, were here to take one of Demma's physicians to the King's. Everyone else was to report back immediately." Here Laciane paused and shrugged. "And that's all he said before he kissed my hand and disappeared."

Eli almost began laughing as he ran his fingers through his gray hair and shook his head.

"By the gods, Laciane, I think the Lord Justiciar took Gwen to make sure she didn't die."

"Die?" The Guidant covered her mouth in shock.

The Rider paused and then took his companion's hand as he sat down in the chair next to her.

"I can tell you that it *was* bad, and may still be bad. We were able to stop Bayel, but at what may become a very great loss. Rakeem is dead, and Gwen is seriously hurt.

"If she dies as well, it will be a huge blow to Nathao's numbers and Promethean ranking. It could leave him vulnerable to every god checking out opportunities to move in and make points with our constituency. We—and I mean you and the other brothers and sisters, as well as those of us in the King's direct service—could be in a difficult position."

Laciane waved off the warning. "I'm not worried and, as for Rakeem, we'll meet again in time, as we are taught. But tell me, what happened to Carmen Piale?"

"I'm sorry, he's dead. Killed for Bayel."

"That assistant of his?"

"Apparently he had become the new Spirit, but he's dead now too."

"Well," said Laciane primly, "there is some justice in that."

Eli smiled and nodded. "Did Veron give you any idea how long I might have to wait for this doctor?"

"Actually, no, so why don't we wait in my office? I have a nice bottle of wine there. I'll tell the novice on night duty to let us know when our guest arrives."

Eli sighed. "That sounds like a wonderful idea."

28

The major celebrations had concluded late in the evening at the temple in Hyoken, and most of the congregants had gone home. Ralph remained awake, watching the few who were left still enjoying themselves, but more than that he was waiting for some sign that the events in Haliburum had concluded. The time of the Solstice neared, and he felt a slight shudder run through the sanctuary, something only he seemed to notice. Knowing the planned schedule, he assumed it reflected the first of the offerings and gritted his teeth in frustration.

"I should be there," he muttered. "I backed that bastard from the beginning; without me he wouldn't be anything more than a second-level bureaucrat in Bayel's temple. When this is over, I'll make sure Emily's ascendancy eclipses anything that has happened before."

For a moment, he was silent, then a sly smile began to creep across his face.

"Wouldn't it be interesting if I could orchestrate her climb in power to the point where she rivaled Bayel. That would give me an edge over the son of a bitch who exiled me here *and* the god who let him do it."

Ralph became so consumed with designing the road to his new goal that he lost track of time. When a tiny, weak tremor rippled through the temple, he sat up and checked his watch. It was close enough to the expected time that it could have been one of the culminating sacrifices, but he was very puzzled; he had expected a major eruption of power based on the results of other killings. He waited, and when nothing more happened, he frowned. The frown slowly turned into a smile and then a hearty laugh.

"Dear Adam, did you miscalculate something, as usual? Are there pieces to be picked up and fixed? Oh, Bayel, you poor, misled fool. I think it's time Emily began to prepare for her appearance, with my help, of course."

29

King Nathao and Marcia were waiting for the Riders in the Keep's Step room.

"Is Gwen here?" asked Sean immediately when he appeared.

"She will be," answered Nathao.

"Then she's alive?" asked Barnabas anxiously.

"She is alive and being cared for. But there is a great deal of work to do to make sure my lands are secure. Armen, you will come with me. The rest of you will get assignments from Marcia on sectors that need to be checked for any possible residue of Bayel."

As the King turned to leave, Barnabas jumped forward.

"Sir! I'd rather stay here."

Nathao looked at him and in an almost-gentle tone said, "No, Barnabas, you need to be out doing something. I will let you know when there is news." Then he brushed past the Rider without another look.

Armen hurried to open the door for the King and hustled to match his pace in the hallway. Nothing was said between the two as the busy crowds parted to let them through. The atmosphere was quiet and intense without the usual conversations and greetings. Once they reached Nathao's office, the King waved Armen toward his desk and a small pitcher of red liquid.

Armen glanced at it and then looked back, his bushy eyebrows raised.

"It is just wine now," said Nathao, "but Demma's doctor is bringing a powder we will mix with it, and it will be given to the Courier. I want you to help because it is a difficult substance for human bodies to metabolize, and she may need to be restrained. This is a variation on a substance that was used at one time by some of the lesser gods to increase their strength and charisma."

"I've read about that," said Armen tentatively as he searched his memory. "Obviously it's still around and being used?"

"Used? I do not believe so, but why lose knowledge simply because it is not being used? We will give some of it to the Courier to improve her chances of recovery."

"Improve her chances? What's the problem?" pressed Armen, surprised by the alarm he began to feel. "You said she was alive."

"And she is. I did not say she would live."

"You inferred that."

"I made a statement," replied Nathao sitting behind his desk. "Now, take this to Gwen's office. Lord Veron should be there with her shortly. Follow his instructions and those of the doctor."

"Yes, sir," said Armen as he picked up the vial and examined it closely. "Nat, will this really work?"

"If the dosage is correct, we believe it should."

The Rider winced and looked somewhat accusingly at the King. "You aren't sure of the dosage?"

"It is up to the doctor to determine what should work. Would you rather we did nothing? Of course, that could mean a new Courier, one you might approve of," said Nathao calmly.

Armen knew his face was getting red, and he dropped his gaze.

"This one grows on you with time," he said brusquely before nodding curtly and leaving the office.

�✖

The Rider knocked tentatively on the closed door of the Courier's office and heard a muffled, high-pitched voice tell him to enter.

Inside, the closed window shutters blocked even the faint twilight. In the dimness, he could make out a figure under the covers on the bed to his right. It appeared to be the person he expected, but there was something different: the hair seemed to sparkle faintly. Startled, Armen looked at the very small person who actually glowed as he sat perched on a chair at the foot of the bed.

The Rider paused and then bowed in recognition.

"No hat, my lord?"

Veron laughed softly in his reedy voice.

"Well met, Armen. You are the scholar here, correct?"

"The Courier might argue that point. What happened to her? She looks different. What happened to her hair?"

"Things change, Scholar. Her hair is not long anymore and, after traveling in my world, it is no longer dark. One must be willing to adapt to new developments if one is to remain useful."

Armen looked closely at the little god, suspicious about how much he knew of his troubled relationship with Gwen. "Are you suggesting something, my lord?"

"Nothing you are not already aware of," said Veron airily. "But come, sit, let's talk as we wait for our good doctor to arrive."

"How is the Courier? What has been done? Does she have her jacket?" asked the Rider as he pulled up a chair and put the wine on the desk.

"She is stable. Time in my world completed as much healing as she is currently able to tolerate. Those fantastic coats your King made for her and the Rider you lost were critical; without those she wouldn't have left the temple alive. Under the blanket, she is wrapped by them both."

"And what is planned now?" urged Armen as he glanced at the motionless, white-haired form in the bed, trying to ignore an unexpected tightness in his chest.

"We believe an additional boost to her system will improve her chances for a full recovery."

"The King didn't seem as optimistic just a few minutes ago," countered the Rider.

"He does not have the latest information," said Veron, waving off Armen's concern. "The Courier will live; we just want to make sure it is a complete and speedy recovery."

"Do you need to prove something to some people?" inquired Armen coyly.

"Most certainly." The little god giggled. "Is there any other reason to work so hard to keep her alive?"

Armen frowned and then jumped slightly at a soft knock on the door.

Eli poked in his head.

"I have the doctor with me," he said quietly without entering the room. "Is it all right for her to come in?"

"Yes," answered Armen, rising and waving the new guest into the small room. "Doctor, the wine is on the desk."

"Thank you," said the small, plump woman easing her way past him.

Armen moved to let Eli in as well, but the tall Rider shook his head. "The King wants me back down there. Is she all right?"

"Apparently she will be," answered Armen, more abruptly than he had intended. In an effort to soften his tone, he added, "But we can talk later."

He closed the door and turned to the doctor, who was opening the shutters. As the room brightened just a bit, the plump little woman transformed into a tall, regal figure.

Veron smiled from his place at the foot of the bed.

"I knew you wouldn't send just any doctor, my dear. It's so good to see you."

"You silly little man," replied the woman, bending over to give him a kiss on the cheek. "We've never done this, so I should be the one to oversee it, don't you think?"

Armen suddenly realized who the doctor was and bowed low.

"Thank you, Rider, but now I need your help," said Demma briskly. "Nathao said that of his people, you would be the least impressed by our presence and therefore the most useful. Now, please, wake the Courier. Gently."

"Of course, Lady. And then, the mixture?"

"I want to see how alert she is first—"

"Alert enough to smile." Veron tittered. "Courier, I saw that!"

A small sigh that could have been a tiny laugh escaped Gwen as she whispered, "I'm so glad you're here, Armen."

The Rider fought to keep his face impassive as he turned to the woman in the bed.

"You didn't follow the plan. You were supposed to come back unhurt," he said flatly.

"We got most of the results we wanted. How are the others?"

"They're well."

"Courier," said Demma, putting one hand on Gwen's forehead and the other on the side of her neck. "Breathe deeply for me."

※※

Gwen closed her eyes and tried to comply but stopped and grimaced. "Sorry, Lady, everything in my chest seems so tight and tender."

"That's fine, my dear. It's actually better than the last time. A few more minutes, and we will give you some medicine."

"I don't remember a last time," murmured Gwen.

"You won't," stated the goddess matter-of-factly. "But let me review what we will be doing. I will give you two drops of a liquid at five-minute intervals. There will be five doses, and there may be some discomfort, which is why your Rider is here."

"Armen is going to comfort me?" rasped Gwen with a wan smile as she opened her eyes again.

"He is here to hold you down so you don't hurt yourself."

Armen blandly returned Gwen's look of surprise before she turned to the goddess and croaked, "What exactly is this medicine?"

"This is a mixture some of our minor colleagues would have taken in the ancient past to enhance their bodies," explained Demma, as if teaching a student. "We believe that in this dosage it will enable you to heal very quickly."

"Very, *very* quickly," added Veron. "That is why there may be some discomfort. And, we should add, we don't know what the long-term effects might be."

※❋※

Gwen glimpsed a fleeting look of concern on Armen's face before he caught her eyeing him and his face once more became expressionless. She reached for Nan and was rewarded with a gentle hug. There was another wave of support from a newer presence, which she knew she had felt since the temple but couldn't quite place.

Looking back at the goddess, she whispered, "Well, if there is a chance this will work, let's do it. Let me try that breath again, Lady."

Demma moved forward to place her hands on the Courier, and Gwen took a few small breaths before trying for a larger one.

"That was better. I could feel it," she murmured.

"Yes, I think we can move forward. Veron, come next to me. Rider, go to the foot of the bed and be ready to hold her legs."

Demma turned to the desk and pulled a tiny container from the black bag she had placed there. Mixing its contents into the wine, she took a dropper, drew some of the liquid into it, and held it up to the limited light from the window. After examining it for a moment, she returned to the bedside and paused.

"Just one more thing: once we start this, we cannot stop. You will die if we do. The reaction will be mild at first but will become stronger and, I believe, should peak with the third or fourth dose. Are you ready?"

Armen's face remained impassive as Gwen looked at him one last time, although she noted he was fidgeting with his glasses again.

Shifting her glance to Veron and then Demma, the Courier nodded and whispered, "Lady, let's do it."

She opened her mouth, and two drops of the medicine hit her tongue. For a moment, there was nothing. Then her lungs started getting tight, and a stinging sensation began to grow at the places where the knife had penetrated her neck, shoulder, and chest.

Remembering the meditation breathing Master Holan had been having her practice; Gwen tried to focus on her inhales and exhales to deal with the uncomfortable sensations. In the background, she felt Nan and that other presence supporting her efforts to breathe.

Demma placed her hands on her patient's forehead and neck to monitor her body's reaction.

After a few minutes, the effects eased, and Gwen began breathing normally.

"Courier?" asked the goddess quietly. "How are you?"

"It's fine; I'm fine," whispered Gwen, her eyes closed. "I can deal with it. How much time?"

Veron piped up. "Two minutes."

Gwen began to breathe deeply and opened her mind to the energy being pushed by her jacket and what she now recognized as another of Nat's creations.

"One minute."

The Courier felt Armen take hold of her ankles.

"Thirty seconds."

"Ready when you are," murmured Gwen. She opened her mouth.

Two more two drops hit her tongue, and again the tightness and burning raced throughout Gwen's body. The discomfort was the most intense inside her chest, where the knife had damaged tissue and organs. She found herself squirming as she tried to ease the pain and pressure, and absently she felt Armen's grip move up her legs to just above her knees. She also sensed Demma leaning over her and then felt the goddess take hold of her upper arms.

As the effects began easing for the second time, Gwen immediately began the deep breathing. When she felt she was in some control, she warned the others, including Nan and her new friend, "The next one will be worse, so be ready. After that, dear goddess, I pray we're home free?"

"That or the next dose, child. Be strong."

"Thirty seconds," said Veron quietly.

"I'm ready."

Gwen opened her mouth and felt the drops hit her tongue before they rolled back into her mouth and throat. In the seconds before the pain hit, the Courier saw Veron quickly take the dropper from the goddess and, as she closed her eyes, Gwen felt Demma grab her upper arms even as Armen tightened his hold on her legs.

This time, the burning feeling exploded in her body, and Gwen arched in pain as she gasped for breath. As her body tried to thrash, Armen and Demma struggled to keep her from hurting herself. Gwen felt as if every nerve pathway was on fire; her muscles screamed and threatened to rip as they strained to break free of their restraints.

Armen would only admit it to Gwen much later, but these minutes, when he glimpsed the agony on her face as he fought her body's efforts to throw itself off the bed, were among the worst in his life as a Rider. But only "among the worst," because, he reminded her, she hadn't followed the plan that night at Bayel's and come back unhurt.

The third episode began to ease and, as Gwen came back to herself, she could sense that a difference *was* being made in her body.

"Two more doses, Courier," she heard Demma say. "Although I believe the worst should be over."

Nan and the other presence offered a cool, peaceful river of energy that negated most of the lingering pain.

"Yes, I can feel it," whispered Gwen, trying to control her breathing again.

Nevertheless, it seemed all too soon when Veron warned, "Thirty seconds to go."

Pulling from all the energy sources available, including her own deep and growing personal sense of strength, Gwen opened her mouth again.

The tightness and the deep burning pain hit one more time, but the intensity was not quite so bad, and even less so with the final round of drops.

Then the medicine was gone, and Gwen murmured a "thank you" before falling into a deep sleep in Nan's embrace and that of the mysterious second entity.

�֎❀�֎

In the King's office one floor below Gwen's office, Eli paused and sipped his wine.

"The squirrel's contact got to us as soon as it sensed something was going wrong. We went right in, but for some reason Bayel's leadership had moved a little earlier than we expected.

"Claire got the authorities there on time, but like I said, Bayel's people had already acted. I must tell you that Laciane's aide, Preston, was invaluable. He didn't flinch at anything, and he and Kyril willingly stayed behind to help Claire."

The lanky Rider paused again and shifted in his chair as he glanced down at the glass in his hands. Without looking up, he addressed the King.

"You obviously were aware of Lord Veron's decision to take Gwen from us."

"Lord Veron did indeed move with my knowledge and with the knowledge of every other god on the Promethean's Top Ten list. We all agreed his intercession was necessary."

"Why was anyone's approval necessary?" asked Eli carefully.

"I tell you this because you should understand how important your actions have been, and I include the actions of all of you," said the King, leaning further back and steepling his fingers. "If Bayel had succeeded and continued to gain strength using murder, not only would *I* have been in very deep jeopardy, but so would my fellows. No one could be sure he or she would not be the next target.

"We may not often work together, but in this situation it was the best option. The Courier living is more important to *all* of us than the Courier dying. Her survival sends a strong message to anyone else who thinks they can destroy us and take our power."

Eli was silent as he reviewed the King's answer; he sipped his wine while slowly framing his thoughts.

"Earlier, as I began to think about what could happen to you—and to us—if Gwen died, I thought the biggest threat would come from the others in the Top Ten. I didn't consider that you might all have similar worries about the smaller fish in the pond. To know that everyone else is just as concerned is rather comforting. It suggests they won't do anything radical to change the status quo."

"We are all very aware of what a shift in the power balance could do," replied Nathao. "We like what we have."

"Even the competition created by the Promethean List?"

"A move one notch higher or lower will not ruin us."

"And dare I suggest that if Gwen makes it through this, you might actually see a move one notch higher?" Eli smiled.

"Let us not draw attention to ourselves, Rider. We have suffered losses in this battle. But there is a time for coordination and a time for competition."

30

Ralph wasted no time on sleep and returned immediately to Haliburum. He reentered the office wing midday after the night of the thwarted attack on Nathao, ready to accept the acclamations and accolades of a conquering hero. Instead, the former friend of the former First Assistant found himself shunned; his only greeting was averted eyes and what he perceived to be a sense of embarrassment.

Setting his jaw, the man who would be the new leader of this forlorn flock straightened his back and marched through the thin crowd in the office corridor to a point between the reception area and Piale's old office.

There he stopped, opened his arms, and stated loudly, "People, people, what is the problem here? We have an organization to revive, a god to reinvigorate, and his consort to acknowledge. Come, come, my friends, gather with me and let us celebrate a new purpose."

Slowly the remaining supporters of the defunct, disgraced god gathered around him. Ralph smiled warmly.

"All is not lost; be brave. We have our lord's consort to help us weather this storm. We shall raise her flag, honor her name, and bring new life to our movement. Who is with me?"

For a moment, there was no response; then a young man stepped forward and raised his hand.

"I'm here, sir. I remember you from before. I'm here for you."

"Good," crooned Ralph. "And your name?"

"Lawrence."

"Well done, Lawrence. Who else is ready for a challenge and a victory?"

In quick succession, hands and voices were raised.

"My children, we have a lot of work ahead of us," announced Ralph, lifting his chin imperiously. "And Bayel's consort, Emily, will give us direction and power."

"Yes, but will she give us Nathao's Courier? The one who brought down Bayel?"

The new Spirit regarded Lawrence closely, wary of the passion in the younger man's voice.

"We will put that on the agenda, son. I understand your desire for revenge, but we must move beyond the catastrophe engineered by the now-deceased First Assistant if we are to regain respect and influence. However, I promise you that we will put that on the agenda."

31

~

She felt at peace, wrapped in a cocoon of healing warmth. A slight movement and reassuring sense of support confirmed the presence of Nan
and the additional being she now knew was Savon, Rakeem's jacket. It
also underscored the fact that she was still weak and hurting.

After a pause to let the pain diminish, Gwen opened her eyes. The
window shutters were wide open and the room's lamps lit, making it
easy to see the small crowd around her bed.

"Well, where have you been?" she whispered.

Seated next to the bed, Barnabas reached for her hand, his eyes suspiciously bright. "We haven't been gallivanting, like you, in gods-know-
what universe, girl. We've been cleaning up the mess you left behind
and waiting for you to get well."

"I'm here now. How're the kids? How long have I been out?"

Barnabas reached for a handkerchief and began wiping his eyes.

"Claire," wheezed Gwen.

The blond Rider was not crying, but her face was pale as she knelt
down next to Barnabas and put her hand on Gwen's arm.

"I was really scared, too. I didn't want another Alice."

"And that isn't going to happen," said the patient. "I'm healing. But
how are my kids? How long have I been away, and what happened to
that bastard Bardhof?"

Barnabas cleared his throat and managed to speak a few words
before wiping his eyes again. "Sam and Becky are fine. They miss you."

"You've been sleeping awhile, Courier. And Bardhof is dead," said Sean from the foot of the bed. "But, hey, Bayel is gone, and there are lots of people facing murder charges."

"Rakeem?"

"Honored," rumbled Nat, stepping into her field of vision.

"He was brave. He saved my life once, and now so did his jacket, his partner in life. He shared his name," whispered Gwen as she closed her eyes and pictured her friend's face in his final moments. Nan echoed her feelings of sadness, which were matched by a sense of pride radiated by the second coat.

"You may speak the name, now that Rakeem has Crossed," said the King.

"Savon."

"And when you are well, you will take Savon to Luke, who will reunite him with our Rider."

"And we will see him again in time," added Eli, a statement echoed quietly by everyone there. "Now, how are you?"

The Courier opened her eyes again and saw the scrawny Rider next to the bed with Jensen towering behind him.

"I still hurt," she admitted. "But every minute it gets better. Right, Armen? They said it would be fast."

Armen was next to Sean at the end of the bed. He nodded stiffly. "So they said."

When Gwen noticed the other Riders looking oddly at Armen, she frowned. "Armen, didn't you tell them who you met?"

There was a pause as Armen reached to adjust his glasses. "No, not exactly."

"Well, then allow me. Lady and gentlemen, you are in the presence of a celebrity. Armen here worked side-by-side with Veron and Demma themselves to make me healthy. I believe Demma even said he had a gift for healing."

"She did not," snapped Armen as his bushy eyebrows came together in a frown.

"You're right, but it adds to the story's mystique," said Gwen, letting her eyes drift shut for a moment.

A warm hand covered her forehead, and a slow stream of rich energy flowed from her head down the length of her body, sparking an extra warmth and a slight pain inside her chest, where the knife wounds were still healing.

When she reopened her eyes, Nathao removed his hand.

"You must teach me how to do that. It makes a wonderful difference. Here, Grandpa, help me sit up. What else has happened that I should know about?"

There was an awkward silence as Gwen leaned back against the wall with her grandfather's help. She scanned the faces near her and then settled on the King, who remained stone-faced. When he said nothing, she turned to Claire.

"What? What is it?"

The Rider sighed and then told Eli to take the mirror down from the wall.

"Men," she said, holding it where Gwen could see. "Sometimes they're afraid to tell a woman anything. But, there have been some changes, Gwen."

The Courier studied the stranger looking back at her. The face was familiar, with the high cheekbones she remembered and the laugh lines and nose she knew, but the sparkling white hair and eyebrows were a shock, and the eyes were the lightest, iciest blue she had ever seen.

She lifted her hand and traced the well-defined red line that ran down her left cheek where Bardhof had used his knife, and she realized other changes could have been a lot worse.

"The changes to your hair and eyes are a function of the time spent with Lord Veron," said the King. "You were dying. He took you to his space to save you. Now, I must leave, but I suggest you spend some time in Cheo. You will heal faster there."

There was silence as the King left. Gwen continued to consider the image in the mirror.

"Dying?" prompted Sean from the end of the bed. "Yo, you were dying?"

"Yes, I do remember feeling that," said Gwen, still examining her new look. "I was getting ready to take the King's Dream. I must thank Veron the next time I see him."

After a few more seconds spent deep in thought, the Courier shook herself out of her reverie and addressed the Riders. "But it all worked out, and Nat is right. I need to get to Cheo."

"Cheo?" asked Armen suspiciously.

"You might think I would hate the old-line chapels, right, Armen? Places where I have little or no say in things? But I'm beginning to think the teachings got a little messed up somewhere in the past. I don't think the original teaching was that the Courier isn't *allowed* to speak; I think it's that the Courier doesn't *want* to speak because there is an energy there that sparks so much activity at other levels and demands your attention. Nat's right; that's where I can heal the fastest. And I should go there as soon as possible."

"You need a haircut," observed Armen. "Or you will scare them at the chapel."

Gwen looked balefully at the Rider. "And I suppose you have a hairdresser in mind?"

"As a matter of fact, I do. Tiffany."

"Tiffany. You get your hair cut by someone named Tiffany?"

"It isn't as if we have a large talent pool here to choose from," noted Claire. "But she *is* good."

After a shower and a visit from Tiffany, Claire told Gwen that Armen was going to help get her to the Step and Cheo.

"Armen? I'm shocked."

"Hey, he *asked* to help. I think that night with Bayel changed our Armen's attitude."

"Oh, I just had to nearly get killed to win his respect?" Gwen said with a touch of sarcasm.

"It helped." Claire shrugged. "The entire episode has sparked a new interest in the outside world. He's living again."

The Step to Cheo was tougher than Gwen expected, but Father Yial was waiting, and the former wrestler moved quickly to catch her as she stumbled through. He carried her up the stairs to the roof, where blankets waited in the lush, starlit roof garden.

"Thank you," she whispered as he set her down. Two women in brown robes moved in to help.

The Guidant stepped back and pulled Claire and Armen with him.

"She will be well taken care of. A few hours here will make a big difference. I'll have people watching all night; you are both welcome to stay in guest rooms if you'd like. I can have someone let you know the minute she wakes."

The Riders exchanged glances and then shook their heads.

"Thank you, but we should get back. Someone will be here early tomorrow."

"As you wish." Yial nodded. "But before you go, please tell me what happened to her hair."

❈❈

Gwen slept deeply through the night and most of the day. After a shower, then a meal with Yial, Armen and Claire arrived to escort her back to her house, where Barnabas was waiting.

"Like the haircut, girl. You've got some wavy, curly action going on," observed her grandfather as she Stepped through into the basement.

"Tiffany does have a gift," agreed his granddaughter, soaking up the confidence radiating from Nan as she steadied herself. "Are the kids ready?"

"Alana has them in the kitchen. I'm supposedly bringing you home from the airport, remember."

Excited and anxious to see her children again, Gwen turned quickly for the stairs, and Barnabas reached to help.

"I'm fine, Grandpa," said Gwen, waving him off. "Really, I'm fine. Claire, Eli—give us a few minutes and then come on up."

The early evening summer sun filled the living room as she entered and took a deep breath of the familiar smell of "Home" before calling out, "Hey, where is everyone?"

"Mommy! Mommy! Mommy!" Becky raced out of the kitchen and launched herself into her mother's arms.

"I'm back, baby; I missed you. How are you and your brother?"

"I'm fine, Mom," exclaimed Sam from the kitchen door. "I missed you too! But what happened to your hair?" He stared in shock. "And your eyes are different. Is that a cut on your face? What happened?"

"Oh, honey, come here; give me lots of hugs, and I'll tell you all about my adventure," said Gwen, offering her son an open arm. "You don't know how much I missed you both."

"Gwen, you forgot the presents you brought back from your trip," said Barnabas, coming in behind her.

"Oh, right, the presents," echoed his granddaughter, remembering how he had said he would take care of that detail the afternoon they had argued in her bedroom.

"I'll get the luggage," he responded with a wave. "You said they were in there."

Alana walked out of the kitchen, grinning and drying her hands on her apron. Gwen registered the quick look of surprise that flashed across her face before the nanny was close enough for a hug and a whisper of "Welcome back. You were missed."

The crowd got a little bigger with the arrival of Claire and Armen, and then the doorbell rang, and Lois and Barry joined the group. Alana offered a dinner invitation to everyone.

"We're having salmon, and I planned for several people."

"You got them to eat salmon?" asked Gwen in surprise.

"Oh, Mom, it's so good the way Alana makes it on the grill," said Becky. "It's rich, yet flaky and full of taste."

Gwen looked dubiously at Alana. "How many cooking shows have you been watching?"

"It piques their curiosity about foods." The nanny blushed. "Plus your grandfather likes those shows."

Barnabas took that moment to walk back in with a big bag.

"It took me a while to find this in the suitcase, my dear. You packed very carefully."

"I'm so glad you did find it," replied Gwen, trying to cover her own intense curiosity. "I hope everyone likes what I got them."

❄❄

During dinner, under questioning from Becky and Sam, Gwen explained there had been an accident in a building she was exploring.

"We didn't know there were old canisters of some sort of gas stored in a sealed room, or that they had rusted and leaked. We broke the seal and walked right into the stuff.

"Our eyes started to burn, and it got hard to breathe. The air from outside rushed in and created a fog, so it took a few minutes for us to find our way out again and, in that time, the gas turned our hair white. One of the men with me had a brown beard that's now all white too.

"My eyes weren't hurt, but it seems their color is changing a little. I hope you can get used to it, because the company doctor doesn't think there is anything we can do to change them back."

"No one else has a mom with hair like that. Some are a bad white or gray, but yours sparkles. I like it," said Becky. "I like your eyes, too. My friends will all be surprised."

Sam did not speak immediately. He just looked at Gwen, obviously thinking hard. No one spoke, waiting for him to express those thoughts.

"What about that cut on your face?"

"As we were trying to find our way out, we knocked over some things, and one cut me pretty deeply. Took a couple of stitches, but the scar should fade with time."

The boy was silent again as if weighing her comments.

329

"You're my mother, and I don't care what you look like," he finally said as he looked intently at Gwen. "But I want to know more."

"That's fair," she replied. "We'll talk about it all later."

※※

It was Sam's bedtime when he brought up the issue again. Gwen sat on his bed, and the teenager perched himself a few feet away on the edge of the mattress.

"Was it as bad as the blogs say?" he asked.

For a moment, Gwen said nothing, but then she raised an eyebrow. "First, what might have been so bad, and who told you about any blogs?"

Sam clucked and shook his head. "Mom, your so-called trip. No one told me specifically about any blogs, but the Promethean website isn't secret. So tell me, was it bad? You were obviously hurt. Is that why your hair and eyes are different?"

Gwen sighed and reached for her son, grateful that he allowed her to pull him close.

"I will give you honest answers where I can because you deserve them, but please don't share this with anyone else. That includes your sister and great-grandfather; he already knows all that he needs to know.

"Yes, it was bad. Yes, I was hurt. And yes, that's why my hair and eyes are different, and I have this lovely new haircut. But, as you can see, I'm fine now. What else do the blogs say?"

"That some people died, and one was a King's Rider. Isn't that what you and Pop-Pop are? That's why I was scared. The King's Courier was also hurt very badly. The blog said the injuries were so bad the Courier almost died."

"Oh, Sam, you've learned too much." Gwen sighed, hoping that when he got older, he would understand why she wasn't going to share everything now.

"Mom, I'm not stupid, you know. The King says you're working for him, and I can put facts together."

"I have never, ever thought you were stupid, Sam. But this is too much for someone your age to deal with, no matter how smart."

"No, it isn't. Remember Ricky Steggs? His father was killed working for Penobba, the Warrior. Ricky says lots of people come to his house now and help his mom. So, who died, and is the Courier OK?"

Gwen paused for a moment and then simply said, "The Courier is fine, healing very nicely. And it was Rakeem who gave his life to stop a god who had gone bad and wanted to destroy the King."

"Bayel?"

"Yes, Bayel. Was that in the blog?"

"Yes. How did Rakeem die?"

Again, Gwen paused and then just shook her head. "I don't know; I wasn't there. It's enough to say that a threat to the King is gone for good, and Rakeem is a hero."

"Will there be a funeral like Dad's?" asked the boy intently.

"No," said Gwen gently. "He asked for something different, and the King honored that request. He Crossed the River of the Dead. But we will meet again in time."

"Why would he want that? And isn't that what the King's people say about dying?"

"It *is* what they say, and Nathao's people believe Crossing the River is the way to a better place."

"Wow," murmured the boy, and Gwen could see his mind was racing. "Can anyone ask for that?"

"I honestly don't know."

"I guess what I mean is, are *you* going to do that?" asked Sam, clearly trying to be cool and factual about the possibility but at the same time, not able to completely cover the quaver in his voice.

Gwen sat up straight and put her hands on her son's shoulders.

"Sam, I do not intend to die for a long time, and right now crossing any river is the furthest thing from my mind. I have you and your sister to take care of, not to mention your great-grandfather. I am not going anywhere," she said, emphasizing each of the final five words.

The boy's mouth twisted for a moment as he obviously toyed with a thought. Then, suddenly he leaned forward and gave her a quick, strong hug.

"I know I'm the reason you're a Rider, and I'm sorry."

"There's no reason to be sorry," said Gwen firmly. "The King helped us, and I would do it again in a heartbeat. Plus, don't tell anyone," she added with a guilty smile, "but I kinda like it. This is what I was meant to do."

32

~

The police questioning was over for the time being, but Ralph knew the investigation itself would last a long time.

Many people had mentioned his name, and he was cooperative as he met with the officers and detectives. He pointed out that he had been reassigned before the incident; he blamed that change in responsibilities on his reluctance to agree with the leadership on what he insisted he believed was only a proposed idea.

When asked why he had not reported the possibility of a blood sacrifice, which the authorities pointed out was illegal, the new leader of the temple shrugged, admitted he was embarrassed, and then wondered aloud whether anyone would have believed such an outrageous story. He also nervously told the officers that ever since he had been caught in an affair with the former leader's wife, he had not exactly been on good terms with the people in power.

The playacting seemed to meet the needs of the police, who thanked him for his time and said they might be back with additional questions. Ralph assured them he was happy to be of help and would make himself available whenever necessary.

Now, the new Spirit was reviewing the bank statements of the organization. He was pleasantly impressed with the numbers.

"This will go a long way toward rebuilding our name and member base," he said, looking across the table at the new comptroller. The man had been the assistant to the old chief financial officer who now sat in a jail cell, and Ralph had only a passing acquaintance with him.

"We have generous congregations, and we've always been diversified in our investments," replied Henry DiMeglio, leaning back in his chair. "It is my vowed obligation to use our resources to further the teachings of Bayel." He paused. "Or whatever is left of them, I suppose. I'm hearing rumors about a change in direction."

Ralph offered a knowing smile.

"Do you have any thoughts on where we should go from here, Henry? I'd like to hear them. Quite frankly, the people I worked with before are mostly gone and the ones who are left—well, let's just say there are reasons why many of them were never included in the big plans."

The accountant pursed his lips. "Were you included?"

Ralph barked out a loud laugh and slammed the table with his hand.

"That's precisely the kind of incisive questioning I appreciate. Someday I'll tell you the whole story, but not here and not now. It's enough that you remember that *you* were not included and that we can change that now."

Henry nodded, leaned forward, and extended his hand.

"I am your humble servant, Spirit. And my first suggestion is to change your title—that one brings back too many negative memories."

Epilogue

V eron sat in the big chair, relaxed and holding a snifter of his favorite brandy.

"What time did we get the story online, Charles?"

"Within minutes of your communique, sir. The news organizations were clamoring for interviews, and the feedback from subscribers nearly took down our comment site. The Promethean League looked very good."

"Excellent. We must maintain that edge; that is what sets us apart."

"Yes, sir, and may I say how honored I am to be included as a decision maker in this empire you have built. I know the other facilitators feel the same respect and gratitude. When we first became academic researchers, none of us expected to gain this kind of access to knowledge."

"And that is what you have, Charles, access to the latest knowledge with the caveat you cannot tell anyone your source. In the centuries since I established the League, with your far-in-the-past predecessors, never once has there been a leak about my association with you. I would not want that to change."

"For academics there is no reward greater than information, and you provide us with the most intriguing and insightful. We would be foolish to destroy that relationship. The number of applicants for research grants and staff positions has never been higher, and our reputation for accuracy and unbiased analysis is pristine. This is our heaven."

"Remember that, my chief facilitator, and I will make you even more powerful. By the way, what was the feedback on Nathao's Courier?"

"Incredible." Charles laughed, saluting his boss with his own snifter. "She's a media darling, and she plays to the coverage as long as no one oversteps bounds. The unwritten rule continues: when she's working—that means wearing that remarkable coat—she's accessible. One reporter apparently tried to intercept her at a non-business situation, food shopping I believe, and she humiliated him in front of everyone there by accusing him very loudly of being a stalker. The store manager called the police, and the said reporter spent some time at the station explaining himself. We have also sanctioned him for a year: no credentials for our events."

"Well done, Charles. If we must enforce simple manners among the rabble, we will. We must protect the Courier. She promises to play a big role in our future."

Made in the USA
Lexington, KY
11 October 2014